Dylan
&
Raven

Willow Winters &
Lauren Landish
Wall street journal & usa today bestselling authors

You know the saying, the enemy of my enemy is my friend?
Well, the enemy of my ex is my rebound.
And he f*cks better than that bastard who cheated on me.

They're both rich and powerful and have a debt to settle in the wealthy circles of NYC.
Then there's me... the naive girl trying to make it in this city, pissed off and seemingly a willing pawn.

It was supposed to be one night to get over one man by getting under another.
Then one thing led to another, and it all spiraled out of control.
It was never supposed to go this far.

I was never supposed to fall for him.
And he was never supposed to risk it all for me.

IT'S
JUST
BUSINESS

PROLOGUE

DYLAN

My heart races as I jolt up from a dead sleep. I'm breathless with a lingering cold sweat as I take in my surroundings. Outside, the sky rumbles with thunder and lightning. The bright light cracks across the sky, and a moment later, as my pulse steadies, the grumble of the pitch-black night sky is barely heard in the distance.

It's not the thunder that's woken me, though. I know that much.

It's something much more terrifying in its destructive power. Worse, it's inside me.

I swallow thickly, checking my bedside clock. The bed groans slightly as she stirs in her sleep, and all at once, it comes back to me.

Raven.

My eyes settle on the gorgeous rise of her nude hip lying

in my bed. If it were any other night, the sight of her bare back, lightly tanned skin, and gorgeous black hair cascading over the pillow would have me hard as a rock in seconds, ready to wake her and take her and hear her moan my name again and again. It's the most addictive sound I've ever heard.

This time, there's nothing but guilt, though.

That's what this pained tightness in my chest must be. Guilt over what I've done, and what it'll cost her. Even if she doesn't know it yet, she'll hate me when she finds out what I've done.

If only I could keep it a secret. If only I could take it back. But it was the only way out for us both.

If I were a better man, I'd tell her and let her leave, let her prepare herself for the storm that's coming.

But I'm not that good.

I can't let her go. She's everything I've ever wanted, and with each encounter, I feel both damned and blessed.

After all, it was supposed to be just business. Nothing more than that. I thought I could resist her, keep her tucked securely into the cold, scarred landscape of my heart so that when the time was right, I could do what's needed. But somewhere along the way, we became something more. What I feel is deeper and stronger than I thought myself capable of. And though I've done what I set out to do, all I truly want is her. I want all of her. But it's already too late.

With guilt sinking into my chest, I settle down into the sheets, and her soft body molds to mine as if she's meant to be here. Hell, tonight's the first time she hasn't slipped out of my house before the early hours. Once the sun rises and she finds out what I've done, it very well may be the last time.

I want nothing more than to dream of her and wake up with her in my arms so I can wake her up with my tongue, bringing her to the trembling edge of orgasm and having the first words on her lips be my name.

Her phone buzzes, and she stirs. Her phone goes off a third time, this time making an audible *ping* sound, but before she can wake up, I reach over to the other side of the bed and pick it up to silence the phone.

As I turn the screen over, the little 'bubble' stays up, and I see *his* name. Her fucking ex. The prick who set all of this into motion. "Dylan?"

She's turned over with sleep in her eyes. I put her phone back and tuck a lock of hair behind her ear. "It's okay, darling," I whisper, lying down next to her as if everything is alright, feeling her warm skin against mine. "Nothing that can't wait until tomorrow."

"Oh," she murmurs, nestling into my arms. "I should go."

"Stay the night," I whisper, holding her close. Before she can protest, I kiss the curve of her neck, my desire for her making my cock stir.

A simper slips across her lips as she murmurs, "that's why you want me to stay," her gaze dropping below the sheets.

My heart pounds, and I wish I could tell her. But selfishness quiets my tongue. This might be my last chance, so I need to have as much of her now as I can before everything falls apart and I lose her forever.

Does that make me as evil as some have suggested I am? Perhaps. But if I were purely evil, I wouldn't be capable of remorse, would I? So there may be more to me than even I think myself capable of.

That thought is too heavy for tonight, when our time together is short, so I focus on the here and now as I gather Raven closer to my chest and press a kiss to her forehead. "Sleep, darling."

All I want is to go back and start over. If I'd known I would fall for her, I never would have set us up to be destroyed.

CHAPTER 1

RAVEN

6 MONTHS PRIOR

Standing in front of the full-length mirror in my apartment, I carefully check my reflection as I get ready for the meeting at Lionfish. My skin is flawless, my eyes faintly lined, and my lashes are curled and coated with dark mascara. Most importantly, my lipstick is lined with my favorite shade of red, the one that gives me an immediate confidence boost. I'm going to need it. Polished, but not overdone, is exactly what I was going for, and I've achieved it.

I glance at the clock. There are still two hours left to tick away before the meeting at the upscale restaurant, which gives me enough time to finish getting ready, have a moment of panic, reset myself and my armor of practiced poise, and then take the subway to the restaurant. Perfect.

It's 'just' a lunch meeting, but the truth is, it could change my life. Which is why, with each passing second, I have to work harder to pretend I'm not growing more and more nervous.

The morning sunlight streams through the window, casting a soft glow over my tiny bedroom. Well, it technically doesn't qualify as a bedroom, but it's where I sleep in the too-small apartment I share with my roommate and bestie, Maggie. We've done what we can, but it's nothing special—too bland due to the clauses in our rental contract, and too expensive to do anything about it, anyway.

I take a deep breath, trying to calm my nerves by staring into my eyes in the mirror instead of focusing on the paint on my bedroom walls because that isn't going to help. What is going to help is nailing this meeting, because if it works out, I'll be able to afford a place that can't be mistaken for a closet.

I can't be anything short of perfect at this business lunch.

I head to the closet I share with Maggie, staring at the array of clothes hanging before me. If there's one area that I don't need to splurge on, it's clothes. My closet goes all the way back to my high school days. I'd gotten a summer job as a receptionist, and with my first paycheck, I bought myself a layered silk blouse that made me feel unstoppable. Back then, it'd taken so little for me to stand tall and proud, but that naivete has been tested through the years. Still, the blouse makes me smile wistfully.

I run my fingers over the different fabrics and colors, each piece holding a memory or an emotion. There's the jade green

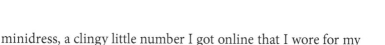

minidress, a clingy little number I got online that I wore for my twenty-first birthday celebration, and again on my twenty-fifth. Both good memories. *Absolutely not appropriate.*

There's the black and white skirt and suit combo that I wore for my grandmother's funeral. A tough memory that I don't know I'll ever be able to let go of. Gramma was a sweet lady who might not have had much, but she always had a lot of love and an infinite amount of patience with her rambunctious granddaughter. I still miss her, and I promised her that I'd wear this suit when I 'make it'.

But that's not today… *yet.*

My eyes land on a sleek black knee-length dress, its silhouette simple yet elegant. It was a gift from Evan, my boyfriend, a few months ago. At the time, things between the two of us had started to get a bit rocky because I'd been busy and stressed about landing a job after my internship. He'd bought the dress, saying it was a show of faith in my skills. I'd read it as a show of faith in our future too.

It's all going to work out, sooner rather than later, and starting with today. First, and most importantly, get the job. Second, get the guy. Third, happily ever after.

I snag the dress off the hanger, feeling like it'll bring me good luck, and hold it against my body. It's perfect against my curves. It really is one of the finest dresses I've ever seen, let alone owned, and when I'm in it, I feel invincible. Evan has wealth I can only imagine, so of course, the most expensive dresses in here are from him.

As I stare in the mirror, considering my reflection, all I can think is that even though the dress is expensive, it isn't memorable. And today requires making a statement.

Reluctantly, I put it back. Indecision doesn't typically follow me around every corner. I know who I am, what I'm capable of, and have perfected the art of putting on an armor to disguise my ho-hum upbringing, lack of an Ivy League education, and barely established upper-crust contacts. But today will make or break me. This is the opportunity of my lifetime, and I've never felt as much pressure as I do in this moment.

The hangers slip across the metal rod as I search through every single dress I have and then scope out Maggie's clothes, too. Thankfully, she doesn't mind sharing, and we're not too far off size-wise, but her style is significantly more fashion-forward than my conservative wear.

Maggie and I met freshman year of college when we were assigned roommates. Despite our differences—who'd think a fashion marketing major and an economics major would be friends?—we became thick as thieves. We later chose to remain roommates, even after graduation, when she generously invited me to continue our arrangement. I pay a pro-rated amount that's significantly less than what she and her supportive parents pay, but she still helps clean the bathroom every week, the same way I do.

Finally, I spot the perfect ensemble—a deep emerald-green blouse, paired with a tailored black pencil skirt. Not mine, unfortunately, but Maggie won't mind sharing.

The green and black go perfectly with my long, black hair, giving me a professional and eye-catching look that's entirely badass future executive.

I'll look like not only do I belong there, but my presence is what's been missing.

I quickly change into the outfit, feeling a surge of confidence as I smooth out the fabric over my thighs.

Checking out my backside, I smile. *This is the one.* I can *feel* it. "Next time we go out," I tell my reflection, "remind me that Maggie's drinks are on us."

I'm just deciding on what purse to pair it with when my phone goes off. I glance, grinning as I see it's a pair of group chat texts, one from Maggie and the other from our mutual friend, Ami.

You got this!

Yasssssss! You don't need luck, you're that damn good!

It's both inspirational and eye-rolling, but they serve their purpose in making me smile. At that same moment, I see that Evan hasn't messaged me yet, but we talked last night, where I wished him good luck before a business dinner of his own. Later, I asked how it went, but he didn't respond.

He's probably busy this morning, I tell myself as I take a steadying breath. I make a mental note to check in with him after the interview. He'll want to know how it goes, and I want to hear about his dinner. I'm sure it went well for him. Failure isn't something he's familiar with. After all, he grew up in the Wall Street life.

With my outfit and makeup complete, I give myself one last

look in the mirror, taking in the sophisticated image I've created. The nervousness still lingers, but I've hidden it away so deeply that it's not visible. I won't let something as flighty as butterflies hold me back.

Fake it 'til you make it.

It's probably not the best piece of cliché advice, but it's worked in the past so I'm not messing with it.

I left a small town to come to the big city for school, made the most of that opportunity, and have worked damned hard to make a name for myself. I've hustled, doing side jobs to keep the bills paid while working an unpaid internship. I joined the right social groups and showed up at all the right events. I've outworked every other twenty-seven-year-old from London to Los Angeles and in the space between. I've got the education, the work experience, and the instincts to be more than just a paper pusher.

My goal? The stock market.

I've built my own portfolio doing day trading, and it's a badge of honor that I've shoved in the face of every trading house that talks to me. I've outperformed not just the market, but the flagship funds and managers at all of the big firms for eight quarters straight. I'm ready to handle more. I'm ready to *be* more.

I'm ready to be the girl on the other end of the line when the head of some big wig association calls saying they need more money on their investments and asks how they can get an extra two percent.

And that's a high bar to get over. A lot of it is all about who you know. I've done my own socializing and networking, making contacts and cultivating relationships, even though I could have short-circuited the process through Evan. He's the kind of man who was born with not a silver spoon, but a platinum one in his mouth. He could pull strings and get me in front of the right people in a heartbeat.

But I don't want him to. If I want to be taken seriously, I have to do this on my own... even if I fail. "The first step to success is failure," I quote aloud. And I have done that. I've been on countless interviews already. I need this one to go differently, be better, and start my actual career.

Today's interview is everything.

I smooth my skirt down one more time. "Failure is not an option. Today, we succeed."

I nod at myself in the mirror, needlessly practicing the professional, friendly, closed lip smile I've perfected. I grab my black leather work tote, the small clutch I'll hide inside, and my keys before heading to the restaurant. As I get off the subway, surrounded by the hustle of the city, and walk the two blocks I still need to go, I repeat a self-confidence mantra in my mind. *I'm strong, I'm capable, and I can handle anything that comes my way.*

I'm even starting to believe it as I stop in front of the door to Lionfish, one of those restaurants known by everyone in the Financial District. The owner caters to the most elite clientele in the city, and it's known for ruthless business being bartered across these elegant tables.

For a woman like me, Lionfish is the place to make my

career. As I step into the upscale restaurant, my heart pounds, and though this time it's with excitement, not nerves, I still don't let it show on my face. I need to appear calm, cool, and collected, no matter what.

The dim lighting casts a warm glow over the polished wooden floors and elegant, ivory tablecloths. Crystal chandeliers shimmer above, reflecting off the fine glassware that adorns each table. The murmur of hushed conversations and the clinking of silverware on gilt edged china fills the air, creating a symphony of sophistication.

As I follow the maitre d' through the dining room and take the offered seat at the reserved table, nerves try to bubble up again, but I squash them by glancing around the room, looking for people I may know or want to know.

My peace is shattered when I see Evan, his confident stride drawing my attention as much as his good looks. I do a double-take, not fully believing my eyes at first.

What's he doing here?

My boyfriend of almost two years should not be here. Not in this restaurant, not now, mere moments before my important interview, and not when he didn't so much as text me good luck this morning. He approaches the table, and I stand to greet him automatically. "Evan?"

His persuasive charm shines through as he acknowledges me with the smile that once disarmed me completely. "Raven, you look beautiful," he says, making my heart flutter despite my growing concerns.

I can't help but smile. He's being sweet. It's unexpected, but an appreciated gesture, regardless. One quick kiss, and I expect him to head out.

He looks down at me, his eyes raking me up and down. My heart races as I glance around the room. "Evan, thank you for coming, but…"

I start, trying to politely tell him to shoo, but he interrupts me, clearing his throat a little too loudly. I can feel eyes around the room finding us.

I've only got a few minutes before the interview, right here at this table, and Evan's not supposed to be here. I don't want to 'succeed' because of being seen with him. If that's what he's thinking, it's not at all appropriate or necessary, which we've discussed.

"We're breaking up."

I blink, sure I must've heard his clipped statement wrong. "Excuse me?" I don't know how any words even escape given how frozen my entire body feels. Instantly, my fingertips go numb and my heart beats a single thud. *Breaking up?*

"I didn't want to do this over a text message, and I knew you'd be here, so this seemed efficient. We're done." His voice is completely void of any emotion, his face set in stone, though there's a hungry glint in his eyes that confuses me.

My legs turn to Jell-O as I grip the edge of the table and then slowly take a seat so I don't collapse. I stare at him in disbelief, feeling the anger and hurt rise within me. Both emotions compete for equal measure.

Is he serious? Breaking up?

"Evan, what do you mean?" I hold my hands together in my lap to hide their trembling. "I know it's been a little chaotic with…" I attempt to go over the last weeks, maybe a couple of months in my head, as I've had to finish off every project for the internship.

"It's been over for months, Raven. Let's be honest with one another."

Anger over takes the pain, and as my throat dries out, I can't find the words to express what I'm thinking.

Months? *Months*??? We've been fucking and telling each other we love one another for months, so how the hell was it over? I can feel the fury starting to bubble up, looking for an outlet and seeing only one in front of me.

Evan leans forward, not getting closer to me but rather, not letting the tables around us hear him. "Don't cause a scene, Raven," he warns.

I swallow down the rage and the instant response, realizing he's right. I'm in the middle of Lionfish, the most important restaurant in the district, and in only seconds, I will have to perform for the most important interview of my life.

A fact Evan knows very fucking well.

It's a struggle, but I get myself under control, forcing my face to something akin to neutrality and my tone to a harsh whisper. "Of all the times to do this, you choose now? Why would—"

He cuts me off, unapologetic and looking robotic. If anything, he sounds like he's the one who's been offended. "Don't be melodramatic. I mean, this lasted longer than we thought it would, didn't it?"

Evan looks at me expectantly, like he thinks I'm going to agree with him. And when I look into his eyes, that glint is growing. And that's when I recognize it. It's excitement, shockingly similar to the look he gets when he's gotten one over on his opponent at the negotiation table.

Is that what this is to him?

I search his face, looking for some sign that I'm wrong, but find none. He's not heartbroken over this. In fact, it's as if he's done this at the worst possible time for maximum devastation. I never knew he could be so cruel.

Didn't you?

Okay, but in business is one thing. In matters of the heart, quite another, and I thought Evan and I had something. I thought we were going to *be* something.

"Excuse me?" It seems to be a mantra now, but it's all I can think to say without causing a scene. Though I'm wondering if perhaps he does want me to do or say something inappropriate, something that would sabotage my interview.

"We had some fun. You got your foot in the door into this world, and we enjoyed some sport fucking. But we both knew this wasn't going anywhere. We're not… compatible." He actually scrunches his face as though that's ridiculous.

Damn, that one's painful. Devastation barely graces the emotions that swarm inside me.

So that's all he wanted out of this?

He's the one who said he wanted to think about us moving in together. He's the one who put a label on us first. What the hell does he even mean? My mind races with every thought and every little moment that convinced me he was the one.

He shifts, and something comes to mind. There were always a few lines I wouldn't cross, and a few... "It's Elise, isn't it?" I guess aloud, and the bastard smirks.

A cold wave washes over me, and the realization hits me like a ton of bricks. His 'executive assistant', Elise, is gorgeous and flirty, and I've known for a while that she's had a crush on Evan. He told me I had nothing to worry about and that things were strictly professional with her. But now he's just demeaned our two-year relationship down to 'sport fucking'.

His audacity takes my breath away, but I dig deep into my soul, finding the strength to hold it together. I put the pain and confusion into a box, setting it on a high shelf in the back corner of my heart, to deal with it later. I have one priority today... the interview. The rest? It can wait.

It'll *have* to wait.

"Fine," I reply, folding my hands on top of my white cloth napkin and looking him straight in the eye with the most neutral expression I can muster. "We're done. You delivered your message. Now you can go. I wish you and Elise the best."

Evan's eyes widen with surprise, like he expected me to react more than I am. If only he could see me on the inside. "Raven—"

"Get. Out," I repeat, my voice turning acidic. "Now."

Evan looks like he wants to protest, but when the lady at the table a few feet away gasps at my words, he dips his chin sharply and turns.

My causing a scene is one thing. Him? Unconscionable.

Instead, he leaves, his handmade Italian wingtips clicking on the tile of the restaurant. I don't watch him go. I've got work to do and not enough time to prepare. I take a long, steadying breath and look at my watch.

Two minutes.

I've got two minutes to get my shit together, and I don't have a second to waste.

I'll fall apart later.

CHAPTER 2

DYLAN

One of the benefits of being a silent partner in Lionfish is having my own private table. It's in the corner of the luxurious bar, a table that's slightly cloaked in shadow and allows me the chance to observe the social world of finance without having to be seen. Wealth certainly has its perks in this city.

I chose to invest in Lionfish because of its location. Within walking distance of my penthouse and my office, it's one of the most exclusive spots in the Financial District. I'm often here late into the night, watching those who are celebrating and those who are commiserating. I wouldn't call it insider trading, but seeing a certain fund manager sit at the bar and down shot after shot of bottom-shelf whiskey one night led to my putting in a massive short call on his biggest client the next day… and netted me thirty million dollars.

Checking my phone, I see a message from my executive assistant, telling me I've got a meeting at two o'clock after this interview is finished.

Like I'd forget, but that's her job, and she does it well. Every detail of my day is scheduled, including arriving early to review Raven Hill's resume and refresh myself on the details.

It ticks all the boxes. Then again, every resume that reaches my desk ticks all the right boxes, has all the right qualifications.

What I want to know is if Raven will be a good fit for my company in motivation, morale, achievement, and longevity. Can she really handle the bullshit of the day to day and the demanding hours and clientele? The clientele, especially. It takes thick skin to succeed here. Many think they have what it takes... and to be blunt, they don't. Plain and simple, they can't handle the pressure, nor the abuse and greed that come with it. And secondarily, can she work in those questionable conditions while creating a revenue stream worthy of the Sharpe name?

Successful interviewees must possess both sides of the coin—toughness and shrewdness.

I want hard chargers, yes. But not those who will literally do anything for a buck. They are all too frequent, and with my reputation, they think they'll find a common ground with me. But while I might be seen as somewhat of a Machiavellian asshole, and that admittedly isn't too far off the mark, I'm definitely better than some of the players in this game.

Cold, calculating, all business? That's who I am, who I've had to become to succeed. And though I play dirty, I ensure my clients' names stay pristine.

And of course, my team is nothing but professional.

Taking another swig, I prepare to move to my reserved table when I hear a familiar voice. Evan Faulkner is a longtime colleague and friend turned enemy turned rival. At one point, I would have considered him one of my closest confidants. He was someone to lean on when I first got started. Someone who went out of his way to make me feel like I belonged. Someone I shouldn't have trusted. But even that was a lesson in itself, and fuck, did I learn from it.

I don't mind a cutthroat shark. After all, this is business. But Evan exists on an entirely different level of deceit and disgust. Despite his family's generational wealth, he's one of the 'anything for a buck' types and would throw his grandmother out of her home if there were profit in it. I hate him for what he's done and what he represents. And that's barely the start of his assholery.

I watch Evan approach a table, *my* fucking table, right as a beautiful woman sits down. *Raven Hill.* Anger rises as I watch what I think is him poaching a potential new hire, only to see something entirely different develop.

She included her social media links in her resume submission, as is required, so I've seen what Raven looks like, but the camera doesn't do her justice. She's beautiful, stunning in a way that draws attention without her seemingly being aware of it. Her surprise at seeing Evan is gone in a flash, replaced with a warm smile. Despite being a keen observer of others, I don't need any special skills to deduce that they know each other...

intimately.

I narrow my eyes, compiling what I've seen of Miss Hill's resume and online persona into a more complete image with what's in front of me. She's too good for him. He's wealthy and charming in a cobra's kiss type of way, but surely, she sees through that?

If not, this interview might be over before it begins.

Still looking from my hidden table, I can't help but feel drawn to her. Curiosity isn't something I'm accustomed to feeling, but it's there now, at the back of my consciousness.

I sit back, sipping the finger of my personal stock of Glenfiddich they keep at the bar, and watch while I consider my options. Every possibility runs through my mind.

The most obvious answer is that she's a plant, spying on my firm for Evan. But if that's the case, he knows better than to be seen with her, so I dismiss that outright. Evan's evil, but he's not stupid.

So what the fuck is he doing with her, and more importantly, what's he doing with her right now, only minutes before our meeting?

If they're as close as it initially looked, there isn't a shot in hell of her joining my firm. I can't trust Evan to not try and use any relationship with Raven to either one-up me or hamstring me. I would do the same thing if I had a valuable resource in his inner circle, so he wouldn't give that a moment's hesitation.

I'm thinking of further alternatives when everything changes.

Evan says something, and I can see Raven blink in shock.

While she hides it well, her eyes flash with outrage. It's as if someone just slapped her in the face. Probably Evan, by the way those emerald eyes are burning right now.

I'm surprised by my own reaction to watching their exchange play out because I feel pulled to intervene, perhaps even to help her, which is an odd sensation, given I'm far from a white knight. Instead, I absently swirl the whiskey as intrigue settles in.

While I'm no expert at reading lips, Raven's mouth is in clear view, and I can read one of the words she says. *Elise.* Elise Draeger is Evan's assistant and has been seen with him at a handful of meetings. It's always seemed professional, but perhaps not?

The picture becomes sharply clear in a flash. Raven's reaction going from warm to icy, her stunned expression, and the anger building beneath her serene guise at the mention of another woman.

Evan truly is an idiot. What makes it worse is that he chose now, in Lionfish, to break up with Raven. He has to know the importance of this meeting, and to choose now...

I shouldn't be surprised, but I am. He really is a callous asshole.

It's only a matter of seconds before he's gone.

I watch closely, waiting to see what she does. Will she leave, or stay? Can she put together a sentence after that humiliating experience? The answers to those questions will tell me more about Raven Hill than the piece of paper in front of me.

Her stern expression slowly fades into professionalism, but the haunted look in her eyes doesn't change. When she takes a sip of water, her hand trembles, but she doesn't spill a drop. Perhaps she's made of sturdier stuff than Evan thought. Maybe that was the problem?

As I swallow the last of the whiskey, I genuinely feel sorry for the young woman. Or maybe not sorry. This feels like kinship, which would make sense considering Evan fucked me over too. No one was there to help me at the time, but perhaps I could help Miss Hill?

And in turn, help myself to a bit of cold revenge.

The little spark of an idea invites an asymmetrical grin to play at my lips. A mere instant later, the plan is fully plotted out in my mind—a way to use the information I've gleaned before our meeting and maximize the resource I've been gifted in the beautiful and surprising Miss Raven Hill.

There's a reason Evan's one of the best at making enemies in this industry. And you know what they say, the enemy of my enemy is… well, I'd take Raven as more than just my friend.

Standing up, I approach the table, a minute late but still close to our appointment. "Raven Hill? Good afternoon, I'm Dylan Sharpe."

She looks up, and I'm struck by how unusual her green eyes are. Now I'm sure of it. Evan's a dumb fuck. How could any man who has a woman this gorgeous with him be tempted by anyone else?

"Mr. Sharpe," Raven says, and while there's tension in her voice, it's nothing that couldn't be explained by simple nerves over this meeting. In fact, if I hadn't just observed her break-up with Evan, I'd have written off the tension as exactly that.

I'm impressed by her strength and resilience and have to remind myself that though a small mercy is kind, I need to be careful here. My assumptions are most likely correct, but there's still a chance this whole display is one of Evan's machinations.

She stands to greet me, stretching out her hand. I expect her skin to be cold, or maybe clammy, after the emotional upheaval, but it's simply warm in mine as we shake professionally. Her touch, though… is like fire. My heart races, and heat surges through me as I release her and unbutton my jacket.

"May I sit?" I ask wryly, and Raven blinks and smiles while tucking a loose strand behind her ear. Her smile is even more enchanting, and as I take my seat, I can feel myself falling under her spell. "Tell me about yourself. Not what I can read on your resume, but tell me about you." I should mean professionally. I absolutely mean personally… intimately.

Thankfully, she has her wits about her and keeps us on track, seeming unaware of my visceral response to her. "I'm interested in your firm because I can fill a role for you in a way no other candidate can. I have an uncanny ability to find extra percentage points of profit in the market news and—"

"Wait," I interrupt, rudely holding up a hand to test her reaction. "I know all that. I read your resume, compared your personal portfolio info to mine and my colleagues'. I know your professional qualifications, and I've heard a thousand people tell me that they're bloodhounds when it comes to sniffing out profit." Her expression doesn't fall at the chastisement. In fact, she leans in, nodding slightly, as if she's hanging on every word I say. "They all tell me that they're the next star of the stock market. I said, tell me about *you*. Why do you want to bust your ass so hard for a position at my firm?"

"This is my passion," Raven confides, continuing when I don't shut her down, "It's not an interest or a job that pays well. It's honestly not even about the money. The dollars kind of become meaningless when you focus on the percentages up or down, the points here, the gains there. It's not a game, and I certainly don't treat it as such when I'm handling people's livelihoods, but it's the power of beating… myself. It's what I obsess over, what I look at before bed and the first thing I check when I wake up. I love the industry, the fight of it, the grueling gives and takes. I'm prepared for all of it. In fact, I can't wait, which is why I've already been doing so much for my own portfolio."

Her eyes read an intensity that I've seen before. In several of my own employees. Her answer is spot-on to what I usually look for. Someone who loves the process as much as the result. Not to mention, she did a great job of answering my question and guiding me right back to her strengths. She'd be adept with client conversations, I bet.

We're momentarily interrupted by a waiter who refills her water and takes our orders of coffee, mine black, and hers with both cream and sugar.

"I'm glad you understand that it's not a game," I warn. "The stakes with your own investments are quite different from those at firms like mine. You cannot avoid falls, and those drops can be devastating when you're dealing with hundreds of millions."

Raven nods. "I'm more than aware." Her voice is strident, her words low and passionate, and I can't help but feel drawn to her.

Professionally speaking. But this is more than that, too. The sparkle in her eyes, the flush in her cheeks that's more than her makeup, those soft, pillowy lips that would feel perfect wrapped around...

"I see," I reply, clearing my throat. I tap my thumb on the table, considering how much to tell her as the coffees are set down on the table and the waiter leaves.

"I have a confession for you, Miss Hill. I was here," —I gesture to the corner— "just over there before our meeting. I was watching you." She swallows thickly, no doubt knowing where this is going. To her credit, she doesn't rush to explain... or lie, as many would. "I feel that finding the right fit, person-wise, is more than paper achievements. Unfortunately, that also means I have to know what happened between you and Evan Faulkner. You two are a thing? *Were* a thing?"

"Correct," she answers, her voice tight. "Were," Raven says coldly but doesn't offer more.

A beat passes while I wait to see what she does, but she stays steady, simply returning my gaze. That's when I know it's time to test her further.

"I'm surprised you didn't try and name drop him on your way up the interview ladder."

"I want to earn my position on my own merits," Raven says

matter-of-factly.

"I could know nothing about you and tell you that you're much better off, professionally and personally, without him."

Her gaze slips for a moment, down to the table, and I wonder what she's thinking. It's not too hard to guess that she's coming to the conclusion that this position is lost to her. It should be. If I could contain my desire to fuck over that prick, I would more than likely send her away, simply because of the connection. However, I am a prick myself.

And not one to throw away opportunities such as this.

"He's a fucking idiot," I tell her evenly, watching closely for her reaction. Raven lifts narrowed eyes back to mine, and then one brow arches mere millimeters as she considers my words, seemingly unsure what to think. "He and I have history."

There's more to that story. So much more. But now is not the time, nor the place, to explain. Besides, Raven doesn't need the background to help with the plan I'm considering her for.

"I see," she says, prepared for the polite dismissal she should be receiving.

Instead, I cut her off. "I have an idea." That gets her attention quickly, reigniting the fire of hope in her eyes. Oh, she still has some fight in her. That's good, she'll need it. "Are you aware of the Faulkner Estate event this upcoming Friday?" I speak barely above a murmur.

"Of course," she says, and her expression softens. It's the first glimpse through her façade to a different—and deeper—side of her. "I had hoped to go with Evan. Guess that won't matter now," she scoffs.

"Why don't you come with me instead?" I suggest, leaning back in the chair. I'm already celebrating the events unveiling themselves in my head and my well-deserved triumph over Evan as I dangle a tantalizing carrot in front of her. "I have a friend who might be able to use you in his firm."

Raven considers me, her gaze searching my face. I can clearly see the pain and sadness in her eyes as she understands the unsaid truth. She can't work for me. Not after a relationship with Evan Faulkner. As beautiful as she is, I'm not that rash. Or stupid.

"I don't have the job at Sharpe." It's not a question, but rather a blunt statement of the facts as she sees them. "So, why are you asking me to the fundraiser?"

Clever girl. She knows that her brains are not all she brings to the table. The question is… is she willing to use her beauty as a door-opener so that her brilliant mind has a chance to shine?

I hesitate. The truth is, after talking with her, I think she's someone who could fit in with my firm. But all of this between her and Evan is something I can't overlook. "No," I agree coldly, "but coming with me will help you make connections you couldn't make otherwise. Your resume's good. Better than good. You'll be a good fit somewhere, but not with my firm."

I stare into her eyes, feeling more alive than I have in ages. I'm on the cusp of a revenge I should've had long ago but was too young and too green to enact at the time. That's no longer the case, and Raven's appearance today is an opportunity I couldn't have scripted to be more perfect.

I was barely even considering going to the Faulkner event Friday night. These fundraisers are mostly a chance for rich men and their trophy wives to pat each other on the backs under the guise of do-gooding, which is something I neither want nor need.

In truth, along with all the ass-kissing, there's a fair amount of networking. Not something I worry about, but Raven? It's a rare invitation to the big table. If she wants it.

If she turns me down, it's not going to hurt me in the slightest. Really, it's her own demise.

She nods tersely, not quite trusting me. "What's in it for you?" she asks, obviously recognizing that my invitation comes with an ulterior motive. "Is that all? Just attending the event?"

Many women would make that sound like a proposition of their own, offering much more than an evening with them on my arm at the slightest promise of something in return. Raven does no such thing. She's clarifying that she's not interested in that sort of arrangement without spelling it out.

She rises another notch in my estimation.

"If that's what you prefer," I reply with a gentlemanly nod, despite not being one, and giving her the appearance of being in charge though we both know that's not the case. "As for me, I will get to attend a function with a beautiful, intelligent woman at my side. One who was recently involved with someone I would enjoy knocking off his pedestal." I measure the way her eyes flare at my blunt statement and offer a victoriously feral smile. "Is your answer yes, then?"

"I'll think about it and let you know by tomorrow," she answers. "Email?"

"No," I reply, reaching into my pocket and taking out my phone. She takes out her own, and within seconds, I have her contact information, and she has mine.

There's no way in fucking hell I'm giving her a business card. Though I'm playing it cool, I want this too much.

Revenge? Raven? Perhaps both? Surprisingly, that feels most accurate.

Standing up, she picks up her purse and outstretches her hand. "I'll call you. Thank you for your time, Mr. Sharpe."

"Dylan," I correct as we shake. She blinks twice, her lashes fluttering as if she's shocked at the concept of using my actual name.

With that, she leaves me questioning everything I've just said and done. The only thing I know for sure is... *fuck Evan Faulkner.*

CHAPTER 3

RAVEN

That's it. I'm done.

Done with men. Done with today. Just done.

It took all of a single minute walking as quickly as I could down the crowded street before the tears started falling. I didn't even try to stop them. I cried for the wasted time with Evan, the unexpected and public heartbreak, and the loss of the future I thought I had on lock with him. I cried for bombing my important meeting, losing any chance at the job with Sharpe, and for the interview turning into a request for a semi-date situation. Thankfully, the tears stopped before I made it to the subway, replaced with anger that's carried me the rest of the way home.

"Fuck it all!" I growl as I unlock my front door, struggling with the key like it wants to let me down too. Down the hall, Mr. Anderson, our neighbor who seems to spend all of his time in the combination of sweatpants and a bathrobe regardless of the time of day, the time of year, or what he might be doing, shoots me a judgmental glance. "What?" I bite back, not interested in his opinion of me at this moment.

"Nothin," Mr. Anderson says, even though the scowl of moral high ground is still firmly in place. "Just—"

"In this city, the word 'fuck' is heard more often than 'thank you', and I've had a rough day, so can you give me some grace?" Finally getting my door open, I step inside, and before he can answer, I slam it closed behind me. The sound is as final as my chances with Sharpe.

Laughter and chatter in the living room stops instantly, all eyes landing on me and my loud entrance. Maggie and her best friend-slash-sorority sister, Ami, are sitting at opposite ends of the couch, wine glasses in hand. They both work remote jobs, based around deadlines rather than hours, but it's unexpected for them to be here mid-afternoon. It's like they were waiting on me, ready to toast my new job the moment I walked through the door. Too bad that's definitely not happening now.

"Whoa, whoa, whoa," Maggie says, holding a hand up dramatically. "What happened?"

I can't even begin to process how to explain what happened, so I start by hanging up my bag and slipping my heels off as I mumble to myself.

How could I have been so blind? How could Evan break up with me so... easily? So cruelly? And to twist the knife even deeper, he's been cheating on me for who knows how long with

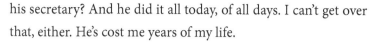

his secretary? And he did it all today, of all days. I can't get over that, either. He's cost me years of my life.

Because instead of getting the job I would be perfect at, I'm offered a fucking date instead. Bullshit!

I wish I were dreaming. I wish this were all a nightmare I could wake up from. I pinch my arm, but no luck. Maggie and Ami both look at me like I'm crazy.

"Raven?" Maggie says, her voice gentled in concern.

"You okay?" Ami asks. "You look like you've been crying."

Ami's tall frame and straight blonde hair are at complete odds with Maggie's perfectly curled reddish brown, but both look back at me with matching widened eyes and worry.

"I… I…" I start, but before I can form a full sentence, Maggie's right there, hugging me.

"Shh, come on, whatever it is, you'll be okay," she says, her chin digging into the top of my head. I'm not short by any means, but she's model-tall so she can tuck me up under her chin in a motherly way I didn't know I needed right now. "Come here. The couch has a spot with your name on it."

I nod. "Okay… yeah," I whisper, and I can see Maggie and Ami exchange looks. Without a word, Ami pours me a glass of her white wine, bringing it over and handing it to me before sitting on the floor so I have room on the couch. "Thanks."

"We were ready to celebrate, but we can commiserate too," Maggie says, sitting down next to me. "What happened?"

I take a deep breath, and a sip of wine. It helps, but I set the glass back on the coffee table to tell them everything. "Well, I got to Lionfish with about five or six minutes to spare, and got seated just fine when… Evan showed up."

"Evan?" Ami asks, her eyes narrowing. Her tone turns harsh. "What the hell was he doing there? He knew how important that meeting was to do on your own…"

"He was there to… he was there to break up with me," I tell them, waiting for the tears to fall. But for some reason, they don't. I mean, I still feel like I've been socked in the gut, but I don't feel like crying. I'm more angry than anything else. "He's been cheating on me with his secretary."

"That fucker," Maggie hisses quietly. "I knew he could be an asshole sometimes, but… shit. I didn't know about Elise, Raven. Swear to God."

Maggie and Ami are from families that do well, but nothing like Evan's family, who reign from the tippy-top of the hierarchy. Still, those circles can be interwoven, especially when you take into account that New York City is smaller than people think, and you typically don't need six degrees of Kevin Bacon to find a connection with anyone.

"I know," I say, reassuring her. She's a good friend, and if she'd had any clue about Evan, she would've told me right away. "Anyway, after Evan breaking up with me exactly five minutes before my interview, I had to pull myself together. I still felt like a total mess when Mr. Sharpe walked over and introduced himself. It… didn't go well. He saw everything."

Ami chimes in, "What the hell does getting broken up with have to do with stocks?" Her tone is full of indignation on my behalf. "It's about how fucking hard you've worked."

Maggie agrees, and I take a deep breath. Instead of trying to explain more, I pick up the glass of wine and take a small sip, but Maggie upends it, making me gulp down the rest. "Good, now breathe," she coaches helpfully.

"It's going to be all right," Ami says, trying to sound hopeful, but we both know the financial district eats hard cores for breakfast and flosses their teeth with the bones of the dead.

"So," Maggie asks, "he didn't offer you the job, or do you just think that the interview didn't go well?"

"No. I don't have the job, but..." Something confusing stirs inside of me as I remember his offer.

Ami lifts an eyebrow. "But?"

"He said he saw what happened between me and Evan, and apparently, those two have history. He asked for details, and I was honest with him. Mr. Sharpe called Evan a fucking idiot." A smile steals across my face, and then an unexpected chuckle escapes at the memory. Maggie and Ami snort out laughs of surprise as well. "I wasn't in the mood to object, obviously. But he said that I wouldn't be a good fit in his firm. He didn't give a reason, but I got the feeling that it was because of Evan, so I guess I can thank that asshole for that, too."

"I officially hate that guy," Ami declares. She's likely planning a smear effort on-par with a political attack campaign, something she's entirely capable of spearheading.

Maggie holds up her hand in solidarity. "Me too." She'd design, print, and distribute the *Evan Sucks* pins at every club in a five-block radius if I asked her to.

"Well… maybe there's something else," I reply. "Even though he didn't hire me, he said he might have an *opportunity* for me." As wary about the sound of that as I was, my friends raise their brows skeptically.

"I don't know if I like the sound of that," Maggie warns.

"This Friday is the Faulkner fundraising event, and he offered to take me as his plus-one."

"He asked you on a date?" Ami asks, horrified. "Are you serious?"

She's offended on my behalf, and while I'm grateful she has my back, and despite my thoughts initially being along the same line, I'm not sure I have another option right now.

"It's not a date," I protest a little too vehemently. "He basically said he'll introduce me to a colleague of his, someone who might have a position for me. It's networking. And a little bit of poking the bear on Dylan's behalf, I think? He said something about knocking Evan off his pedestal." I shrug, not exactly sure what he meant but pretty on-board with some pedestal crashing myself.

"Uh-huh," Maggie says, smirking. "And the fact that Dylan Sharpe is sexy as hell doesn't have anything to do with it?"

As part of my interview preparation, I learned everything I could about Dylan Sharpe and his firm. That may or may not have included showing Maggie some pictures I found of him online. To say he's attractive is like saying the sun's a little warm. More important to me, though, is his mind, and the man is whip-smart and a prime example of the trajectory I'd like to follow myself, working up from the ground floor to create an empire. An evening picking his brain and watching him work is a wish come true.

"Not really," I reply, my voice surprisingly steady. "Though the idea of showing up to Evan's fundraiser with a man who's hotter and maybe even richer sounds... intriguing."

"When you put it that way..." Ami says with a smirk. "Break out the petty confetti! I'm Team Raven!"

Maggie seems less sure but agrees reluctantly. "Team Raven, all the way." But after taking a sip of her wine, she warns, "Be careful, though, okay? Play it smart and do what's best for you, and not anyone else. I get the whole 'get over one guy by getting under another' vibe, but these aren't guys from Tinder that you're rebound fucking. You're playing with the big dogs, and either of them, or both of them, could tank your career before it even starts."

She's right, obviously. And while I'm not as experienced in chess-level maneuvers as Evan or Mr. Sharpe—no, *Dylan*—are, I'm not completely without skills. I can attend the fundraiser, press palms to make the connections I need, show Evan that he didn't break me, and leave with my head held high.

"*Or*," Ami drawls out dramatically, "you leave Evan in your dust, make Dylan Sharpe fall in love with you, and get that big corner office in the sky."

I shake my head. "That's not happening. I haven't even fully committed to going to the fundraiser yet. I told Dylan I'd let him know by tomorrow so I didn't sound desperate."

"You're going," Maggie declares, seemingly reversing her previous doubts. "What other choice do you have?"

None. I have no other options, no more interviews scheduled, and only a couple of resumes I haven't heard back on yet. I wouldn't let that stop me, but a little shortcut to a possible opening at another firm is a gift I can't refuse. Even if it comes with complications, like going to my ex's family fundraiser on the arm of the man whose company I desperately wanted to work for.

"I'm going," I agree. "I'll let him know tomorrow."

CHAPTER 4

DYLAN

Leaning back in my chair, I take a moment and ponder my office. There are floor to ceiling windows, an Italian leather sofa against one wall that allows me a view out of said windows, and a commanding desk that sweeps around in a forty-five-degree angle in order to give me multiple work areas. I could easily run my empire from one end and fuck at the other and that would be just fine. No need to throw anything off the surface or disturb a single sheet of paper. I've yet to enjoy that feature. Truthfully, I've never considered it until this moment, and I'm not entirely sure what brought the idea to mind now. *You know*, my subconscious whispers slyly.

More than anything, my office drips of new wealth, because that's exactly what I have and what I am.

There's no pedigree, no photos of well-known families. No

photos at all, in fact. There are no antique bookcases with texts and expensive books. It's rather spacious, and as my assistant put it, 'coldly masculine but obviously expensive'. Does that describe me or my office? Probably both, which is exactly the way I like it.

The hints of my work are on my desk, the trio of monitors that can, at any time, feed me information from all the markets across the world.

But as I loosen my tie, I'm not focused on the feeds. I'm focused on the text message I got five minutes ago on my phone from Raven. *I'm in. What time should I be ready on Friday? I assume you'll pick me up?*

Her pluckiness makes me smile. She's accepting my offer, while at the same time having enough confidence in herself and her feminine charm to expect that I would go to her place instead of making her come to me.

It's good. I like that about her.

I'm just about to message her back and tell her to give me her home address when my phone rings. The screen reads *Austin Rogers*, and the timing of his call would seem like a sign if I believed in that sort of thing.

In a world where ninety percent of people range from 'flaming asshole' to 'minor-league irritant,' Austin's the rarity.

He's a no-bullshit person. And that makes him one of my only friends.

I answer it. "Austin."

"Dylan, what's shaking, man?" Austin greets me, sounding pleased with himself. "How's the world's best money maker?"

"And why are you interested in my money maker?" I reply, smirking at the old, silly joke we've repeated dozens of times.

"Because it pays for my vacation house," Austin answers with a laugh, completing the script. "But seriously, how's life going? Are you going to the Faulkner Fuckfest on Friday?"

He assumes he knows the answer, and normally, he'd be right. But not this time. "Actually, I am. In fact, I'm bringing someone."

"You?" Austin says in utter shock. "Why? And when did that happen?"

"What do you mean, why?" I ask, and Austin's knowing hum on the other side reminds me that he knows my history. I haven't had a significant other in a few years. I've been too focused on work, and it's been hard to trust anyone after what happened with Olivia.

"Just surprised is all," Austin says and then pesters for more information.

"Well, it's not exactly what you're thinking," I admit, acknowledging that he makes it sound like I'm bringing a date whom I'm on the verge of pledging my undying fealty to, which is not the case. "It's more of a networking situation. Her name's Raven Hill, and I interviewed her a few days ago for an open position. She's not a fit for me." The thought trails off because in all honesty, she would have been a great candidate. "But I know that Ollie will be there. I want to introduce them."

"Hmm… Raven Hill?" he echoes, trying to place the name's familiarity. "As in, Evan Faulkner's girl?"

Anger simmers inside me at the thought of someone like

Raven, beautiful and smart, being with that fucking snake. I didn't consider others would even realize her history. I really have been keeping my nose to the grindstone and staying out of people's personal lives a bit too much recently, it seems. "You know her?" I ask with all trace of humor gone.

"I know *of* her," Austin replies. "She's a hustler, does some day trading on her own to build her own portfolio... absolute stunner, too. But it sounds like you know that already."

My hand clenches on my desk, my knuckles turning white, and I crack them as I steady myself. "I know all of that, and more," I concede. I wouldn't typically share intel with anyone, but Austin is different. And this situation is unique. I could use his insight to see if there might be an angle I'm missing or gossip I'm unaware of. "I had an interview scheduled with her earlier this week. Five minutes before, Faulkner strolls into Lionfish, drops a 'break up' bomb on her, and then smirks when she called him out on cheating with his assistant."

He clucks his tongue. "In the middle of Lionfish?" Austin repeats, sighing a humorless huff. "The fucking balls on that bastard."

Austin recognizes that of everything Evan did that day, the most surprising was that he dared to enter my sanctum. For all his standing in the finance industry, Lionfish is not a place he goes, nor is welcome.

"Agreed." I shove the memory down and focus on the event. On having her on my arm... on what could happen between the two of us. On watching that cocky smirk fall from Evan's face when he sees me with Raven. "Anyway... she'll be with me."

"It sounds like there's more to it than just trying to get her a spot with Ollie," Austin surmises as if reading my mind.

I stop myself from answering harshly, reminding myself that he's being cautious and looking out for me. My thoughts go back to the fact that I've known Austin for over a decade. We met at one of the innumerable socialization events that go on around the Financial District. I was trying to make my way in the world, a little too naive, a little too eager, when I spotted Austin standing out among the sea of suits and ties.

He was like me, hungry and not yet firmly established. His demeanor was relaxed, yet confident, and he commanded attention without trying. I envied him, if I'm honest. I had to hide every insecurity. I had to mimic a wealthy class I was very aware I wasn't a part of.

Most of the men at that event weren't like us. They didn't need to network because they were born into the network. They didn't need to hustle because their daddy or their uncle or whoever already owned a firm.

Austin wasn't like that. I could see that he was different in the same way I was, but rather than try to forcefully fit in with the others the way I was prone to do, he made them want to be his friend. There was a rawness to him, a street-smart edge that was impossible to miss, and his charisma created a vortex that pulled everyone to him. We struck up a conversation, and I quickly discovered that Austin was a self-made man who had clawed his way to the top through sheer intelligence and willpower alone.

I wasn't the only one who envied him. But for me, it was his couldn't-give-a-fuck attitude. For them, it was the ease of money.

In this world, there's never enough in a bank account, never enough in the market.

Finances aside, over the years, I've found that I respect Austin more than I do most people.

"Can I tell you something?" I ask Austin, cutting him off from whatever the fuck he was saying and addressing his previous question about this being about more than introducing Raven and Ollie.

"You know you can," Austin says, "but I can already guess, given what I know of her. And you. You wanted to bend her over the table and get back at him?"

"Crude, but… fairly accurate." Sighing, I admit, "She is a good candidate, and I'm attracted to her, genuinely. The fact that she was wronged by Evan is tempting extra icing on the cake, though."

It's a big confession, one I wouldn't make to anyone but Austin, who knows my backstory as well as I know his.

"To do what with?" he hedges. When I don't answer, he puts himself in my shoes, likely coming up with some variation of my exact plan, and advises, "Be careful, Dylan. Evan might be a douche, but he's a Faulkner. He's powerful. We move in the same circles, and you don't want to ruffle feathers you can't afford to soothe."

I scoff. Does he think I don't know who the Faulkners are? I'm more aware than most of exactly what they're capable of. "I know, but I can't let Evan get away with what he did." It dawns on me that it's not the first time I've said that aloud, but he has gotten away with it for all these years. There wasn't a damn thing I could do. Maybe now, there is.

Austin pauses for a moment. "I get it. But you've already won, Dylan. You're successful, and Evan is on the decline. He's skating by on his family name, and by the time he's ready to pass the torch, there won't be a torch to pass. Just a burned-out matchstick. Don't do anything to jeopardize that. Don't get in his way of screwing himself over. Just sit back and watch, enjoy the show. There's no need to throw kerosene on things now."

"But it could be fun," I reply, tapping my thumb rhythmically on the desk as I think through my plan again. If a street scrapper like Austin is saying this is a fight I don't want to mess with, then he's probably right, and taking Raven with me is a dangerous proposition. But deep in my gut, I want to see more of Raven. I want to show her that I wasn't just bullshitting when I said that Evan is a dumbass who made a bad decision, and she can move on from his cruelty, succeeding despite him, not because of him. And I want to see Evan's grin fall when he realizes that of all possible people, Raven is with me, even if only for the night.

And maybe, just maybe, I want to feel what Austin so bluntly stated—Raven Hill's legs wrapped around my waist while she moans my name.

It's admittedly convoluted, revenge and attraction melting into one potent Molotov cocktail, but I've never been one to play things safe. With risk comes reward. Without risk, you have nothing. I will simply need to monitor and adjust throughout the evening accordingly, ensuring maximum impact for Raven's benefit, Evan's destruction, and my enjoyment of both.

"I already made the invitation, but I'll keep that in mind," I tell Austin. "In the meantime, I've got half a dozen meetings on my schedule and three politicians to pay off before the end of the day," I joke, "So if you'll excuse me."

He laughs and tells me he'll see me at the event before letting me go.

I hang up, knowing that what I'm about to do might not be the smartest thing in the world. I should be focused on work the way I always am.

Instead, I pick up my phone again, texting a reply to Raven before I change my mind. *I'll pick you up at 6. Send me your address.*

Austin's warning resonates with me, though. I'm not sure what to make of Raven or my instant and powerful fascination with her. She's somehow gotten under my skin in the most intoxicating way possible, and a feeling like that to a man like me… is dangerous.

CHAPTER 5

RAVEN

"You know," I tell Maggie as I set my hairbrush aside, "This could be a huge mistake." Decisions based on emotion are typically not the best, and I'd be a fool to ignore how emotional I am.

For three days, I've buried myself in work, resumes, and applications from sunup to sundown, focusing on my increasingly desperate job search, only to barely keep from crying myself to sleep at night. The blindside of this breakup and the betrayal of his cheating have been worse on me than I'm trying to show. The amount of concealer I need under my eyes is a testament to that.

"I keep thinking about how Evan is going to be there and how I hope he regrets it all when he sees me." I tilt my head, running my hands through my hair. "But it's a business event, and I've already missed one opportunity because of him. I don't want to burn the whole house of cards down over one Joker." I turn to face her fully, ignoring the turmoil rolling around in the pit of my stomach as I look her dead in the eyes. "I shouldn't be going to spite him. I don't want to make a mistake I can't take back."

"You'd better not be talking about backing out tonight," Maggie says from her perch on the bed. "Dylan's picking you up in forty-five minutes. If you back out now, you'd better be bleeding from some major body part." When I don't automatically agree, she adds, "Blowing him off would be the worst mistake of all."

Shit. I try to tell myself it's no big deal. Just business. Focus on the logical and the fact that networking at this level really is a golden ticket I won't get a second chance at grabbing.

I head for the closet, feeling sick to my stomach, and she follows me.

"I know. It's just…" I reply as I take a dress out and hold it up for Maggie's inspection. She shakes her head, and I put it back. "I don't want this to be like my internship."

I'd been desperate then too, needing something I could put on my resume to show I worked in a legit firm. That I've spent the past year as a low-level business researcher at a small firm hasn't helped as much as I'd hoped, ironically, because of Evan's name, which is why I didn't want to use it to help me find a more permanent job placement. "Do you think Evan helped me with that to keep me pigeon-holed? Or to, you know, keep me out of his hair?"

"I didn't think so at the time. You two seemed to be doing pretty well then. But now?" She shrugs. "Yeah, I wouldn't put anything past him."

"The red one." I go back two dresses and have another look at the scarlet red number while Maggie continues her pep talk. "Regardless of how you got that internship, you've done a great job and you'll get a stellar reference from it. And maybe Dylan Sharpe and this event tonight can help you land something new. Worst case scenario, you'll know you tried everything when you fill out an application at Starbucks. And being a barista would give you more time to work on your day trading portfolio."

I gawk. She's got it all figured out. I mean, it sucks as far as a plan goes. But at least she's got one for my life. I certainly don't. Not anymore, when everything I've been working for seems to have vanished into smoke.

Maggie stands, bringing the black dress I was considering with her and holding it up in front of me. When she moves, I hold the red dress in its place and she nods.

I look in the mirror, contemplating the red dress. "You're sure?"

"It's more confident. Says you're a sexy bitch... which you are, but also confident and coming to shake things up. Which you're going to do in more ways than one."

She's right. Or at least I can fake that she is and make it so.

I do a little twirl with my finger so she turns around, and Maggie obliges, focusing on her phone so she can't see as I undress. Picking up the red dress, I shrug off my bathrobe and hang it back up.

"Hey, forgot to mention," Maggie says as I pick out my sexiest, most confidence boosting lingerie, "your mom called while you were in the shower."

As if my stomach couldn't sink any lower.

Mom's been worried about my job hunt too. Not because she doesn't have faith in me, but because she knows how much I want this. If there were a way for Dianne Hill to make my dream job appear, she'd do it in a heartbeat.

"What'd she say?" I ask, fastening my bra and turning it around. It's strapless, so it's a little tight around the chest, but it makes the girls look perky as hell.

If Maggie didn't have an amazing mom of her own, my mom would've adopted her years ago. Since that's not happening, they've instead become friends, and often, Maggie will have spoken with my mom as recently as I have. Plus, Mom basically becomes besties with people everywhere she goes. She knows all about the lady at the bank whose dog is having cataract surgery, and the man at the post office who is definitely going to win the sweepstakes this time, and on and on. She'll tell you her business, listen to yours, share her snacks, and be your biggest cheerleader. And that's all before you reach the checkout cashier at the grocery store. She's pretty great.

"Well, she seemed to think your interview went well... and that you're still with Evan?"

I wince, knowing I should have told Mom the truth but trusting that Maggie covered for me. "Uhh... sorry about that. Mom's been really excited about this interview. She thinks I'm going to be a millionaire by next year or something. I just didn't want to disappoint her, so I sort of sent her a text saying the interviews are still going on but I'm hopeful."

"And Evan?" she questions, and I swallow thickly.

I pick up the rest of my lingerie, which are undoubtedly lacy and a little butt-flossy. "I didn't lie, I just didn't tell her." I reluctantly admit, "I wasn't ready."

I expect Maggie to be disappointed, but she nods in understanding.

"Hose or no hose?" I ask, considering my legs and the dress. "Black, maybe?"

"I gotcha," she says, digging in her dresser drawer and coming out a moment later with a garter belt and some stockings. "Here. You'll be erecting tent poles in these." She's doing her best to keep me distracted and make me laugh so I don't call the whole thing off, and her silly joke does the trick.

With a bittersweet smile, I take the garter belt, which is black silk that almost perfectly matches my black bra and panty set, and hold it up to my waist. "Thanks."

"Under the panties if you're DTF, over the panties if you're a good girl," Maggie quips, pouting when I pull the belt on over my panties. "Hmph."

"I'm going to network, not have sex," I comment before pausing and running the straps under my panties. "But I might have to pee," I concede.

"Party pooper," Maggie teases as she sits back down on her bed cross-legged. "Mama Hill also asked if she could start planning a visit. I told her to put a hold on it, because with you hopefully starting a new job soon, your schedule might be iffy. Good?"

I nod, unzipping the red dress and slipping it on. "Thank you so much," I tell her, appreciating her temporarily diverting my mom more than she could know. "Zip up? And remind me that I need to grab the train and head home for a visit soon."

"That's good, Mama nearly talked my ear off telling me the latest and greatest," Maggie says as she zips up the dress. "Damn, that looks good on you."

"Thanks," I reply, checking that I can still breathe with the zipper done. "Fill me in. I can use the distraction."

"Well, let's see. Your dad's bowling team is apparently screwed, something about how their top hooker pulled his calf?" She looks at me like she doesn't know what those words mean.

"A guy on the team who puts a lot of curve in his throws," I explain, picking out some lip gloss to go with the dress while holding back a grin. If I'm going to go red, I'm going to go really red, and fire engine red lip gloss is the way to go.

"Your little brother's nerding out with his community improvement project," Maggie says, talking about my brother Mark. He's a senior in high school and is trying to do community work to improve his college chances. "He's building computers, which apparently has something to do with rooting through the trash?" I shrug, not knowing on that one. "Your mom said he worked a deal with the garbage pickup guys and some of the schools. According to your mom, he's got half a dozen done, and he's going to donate them to a local charity to give to kids who don't have one. He's hoping to complete one computer a week between now and when he graduates, maybe more if he starts getting decently good stuff that isn't too fucked up. My words, not your mom's."

I laugh lightly, trying to imagine Diane Hill uttering the words 'fucked up' and coming up short.

I pull out the best and sexiest stilettos I own—black, five-inch, red-bottomed 'So Kate' Louboutins. They were a gift to myself the first time I had a four-figure day. Even so, I hadn't eaten for two days in my guilt over the cost. Tonight, I'm glad I have them.

"What do you think?" I ask Maggie, who gives me a full once-over.

"Okay… hair's good, makeup's good, dress is hot as hell… You're good to go. Knock 'em dead."

"I will," I promise her. "I'm dressed to grab attention tonight, so everyone can see that I'm fine—better than fine!—without Evan and ready to tackle my next big undertaking. For their firm, because I'm not leaving this fundraiser without a job offer tonight. It's going to happen," I say as if I can manifest it.

"That's the spirit," Maggie assures me. "And one other thing. Pertaining to Mr. Sharpe?"

"Yeah?" I turn to face her, grateful for whatever advice she has.

Maggie chews on her lip, suddenly hesitant to speak. But finally, she says, "Just be careful. Be smart. But also, spending time with him is a big opportunity, so don't be too risk-averse. You gotta go big or go home, or something like that." She takes a deep breath as though she's going to continue her rambling of cliched idioms, but she stops herself and nods. "Yeah, that's it." She smiles as though she imparted the wisdom of the ages despite basically giving the same insight a stack of fortune cookies would.

I shake my head, laughing off her nerves so they don't become my own. If I'm honest with myself, I've already thought tonight through dozens of times, with hundreds of scenarios. My primary mission hasn't changed—get the job. It just has a little asterisk beside it that if the chance arises to rub Evan's nose in my greatness a little bit, that a small side step is an acceptable detour, as long as I quickly get back on track to my objective.

CHAPTER 6

DYLAN

"Mr. Sharpe, we may be delayed a minute or two," my driver, Vince, says from up front. Dressed all in black, he's a classic chauffeur, minus the cap. "Looks like there's a traffic accident up ahead."

I crane my neck, looking through the currently lowered black-tinted separation window in the Mercedes and see a sea of cherry red brake lights, and just beyond that, the swirling blue light of a police car.

"We'll get there in time, Mr. Sharpe," he adds, and my gaze finds his in the rearview mirror.

Vince is a quiet man, older and gentleman-like. He's worked for me for over three years now and mostly keeps to himself. Which I appreciate.

Which means when he says something, he's got a reason.

I nod, finding his assurance out of character, and vaguely wonder what he thinks of my decision to bring a date tonight. In the time I've known him, I've never felt compelled to do so. I only attend what I must or what benefits me to do so. Plus-ones aren't necessary. In fact, they're usually a danger—highlighting weakness, serving as potential targets, and hindering the business at hand.

Unless the plus-one is the business.

His gaze shifts back to the street, and I let the conversation die. I don't really need to respond, and I don't plan to. Vince is my employee because he's got the class and refinement of a chauffeur, with the pathfinding and driving skills of an experienced taxi driver. The man can practically sniff out the fastest route from anywhere in the city, and I've never missed an appointment because of him.

As it should be.

My suit is pressed, black as midnight and sharper than a razor. The champagne that's chilling to my left is equally high end, ten-year-old Louis Roederer Brut. I picked it out because it reminds me of Raven. To the uneducated masses, they might overlook it because it's not a trending name like vintage Dom Perignon. But they'd be missing out in doing so.

In much the same way, I would be a fool to ignore the potential Miss Hill possesses. But I'd be an even bigger fool to bring her into my employ. Especially given how my dick reacts to the mere thought of her.

All week, while the markets opened and closed, projections

were presented, and people have volleyed for my attention, I've thought of nothing but tonight. I've plotted and planned, being more thorough than I had a chance to be during my lunch with Raven. In every scenario, one truth reigns.

Business should remain business. There's no need to muddy the waters with silly, transient things like lust when clean, strategic, logic provides the best return on investment.

So I will be a man of my word and introduce Raven to the right people. I will not hold her down the way Evan Faulkner clearly did, sabotaging her career.

And though I wouldn't mind holding her down in another way, I won't do that either. She is a risk I shouldn't take.

Which means my intention tonight must be singular—burn what's left of the ashes between myself and Evan.

I'm playing out the evening in my mind as the city passes by outside the window. Lost in possibilities, I'm surprised when Vince alerts me to the fact that we've arrived at our destination. Raven's apartment. The neighborhood itself is up and coming. I'm certain it's not cheap, as nothing in the city is, but it's not at all what I'm accustomed to these days.

Buzzing the apartment, I'm surprised when the door lock simply clicks open without any verification that I should be permitted entrance. I glance back at Vince, who moves as if to escort me into the building. I hold up a staying hand, and he stills. I'm fine and don't need protection from whatever potentially lurks inside. He chuckles but hides it with a sharp clearing of his throat.

Beyond the door, I find my first annoyance. A complete lack of an elevator. Raven's text said she lives in apartment 4C, which means I have several flights of stairs ahead of me.

Moments later, I take a deep breath to steady myself as I reach the top and look up and down Raven's hallway. The building's old enough to still try and carpet their hallways, although I suspect by the worn-down appearance that this generation of rugs will be the last before a more budget-friendly option is employed. The hallway lights are LED bulbs in shatterproof glass globes, and the walls are painted a very economical off-white.

Down the hallway, a door opens and a man with a round belly like he's got a basketball stuffed under his bathrobe shuffles to a garbage chute, dumping his trash inside before turning and giving me a once-over. "How you doin'?"

"Just fine, thanks," I reply, knocking on Raven's door. I ignore the man, not inviting further conversation, and focus all my attention on the painted black door before me. I hear high heels approach, and then the door opens to reveal Raven.

My heart beats in a way that multiple flights of stairs can't hold a candle to as I take her in. Her red dress is absolutely stunning, hugging her lush curves in all the right places and highlighting her assets in a way her professional attire at our interview did not. Her hair falls in a straight sheet down her back, her green eyes look feline with sharp black liner, and her lips shine with gloss. The total effect is one of elegant seductiveness.

My dick twitches in my slacks, arguing with our current plan of business only.

She's fucking gorgeous. I thought my memory might've been playing tricks on me, or that my eagerness to get back at Evan had made Raven seem more attractive that she was in reality. The truth is, my memory didn't serve her justice in the least.

Words escape me a touch too long as I'm lost in the vision before me. "Too much?" she asks, and her voice brings me back to her gorgeous gaze.

"Miss Hill, you look…" I clear my throat, steadying myself.

"Please, Raven," she speaks as I hesitate.

"Raven," I correct myself, "you look absolutely beautiful." Behind the door, I hear a hushed squeal. I arch a brow, guessing at the noise. "Roommate?"

An auburn head and blue eyes sneak around the edge of the door to look at me, and the woman gives a short wave. "Hi." She appears to be around the same age as Raven, who's several years younger than I am.

Raven doesn't offer an introduction, so I follow her lead and simply say, "Hello." Looking back at Raven, I ask, "Are you ready?"

"Yes. See you when I get home, Maggie," Raven says, a hint of warmth coming to her voice. They're obviously more than just roommates. They're friends as well.

The two exchange a look I'm not quick enough to discern, and then Raven smiles warmly as she steps into the hallway with me, closing the door behind her. For the first time, I'm alone with Raven. Even in these less than five-star environments, with industrial grade overhead lighting and plain walls that seem to make everything a little dingy, she looks gorgeous. "Thank you for accepting my invitation."

"You're welcome," she says, turning to her left. When I don't follow, she glances over her shoulder, never breaking her stride. "You took the stairs, didn't you?"

"I did," I answer in confusion, and Raven gives a shy yet devilish smile that's contagious even though I don't know what's causing my lips to unconsciously rise.

"There's a cargo lift down the hall," she says, tucking a strand of her hair behind her ear. It's perfectly straight and stunning how it drapes over her shoulders. My fingers itch to push the locks from her neck and expose the bare skin beneath.

In the hallway, her quiet confidence comes to the fore again, and despite the nerves that must be ripping through her, she doesn't allow them to show at all. In fact, she's comfortably leading me as if it's the most natural thing in the world, and to my own surprise, I follow her quite willingly. She's a warm contrast to my cold reserve.

"Normally, I take the stairs too, but I'm not daring it in these heels."

Her tone is almost self-deprecating, as if she's not certain of her skills despite her sure-footed, even strides. The effect of the off-hand comment is quite different, though. It drags my eyes down to her gorgeous legs, where her calf emerges from the red hem of her dress, which drapes to the floor but is cut dramatically in the front and along her left leg.

I have to resist the urge to end tonight's plans early by pinning her against the wall and slipping between her legs right now.

Fuck.

"The elevator is fine," I finally declare, forcing my mind to not imagine what she tastes like and wonder if she feels the same tension I do. I hold onto my professionalism with every bit of grit and determination I possess after seeing her into the small, enclosed space, clasping one hand over my wrist in front of me, standing tall with my shoulders straight and my eyes on the door.

The ride down the elevator is quiet, mainly because the elevator itself is, as Raven said, a cargo style elevator that's too noisy and open for any sort of actual conversation.

We reach the street level, and Raven stops just shy of the car. I can feel tension rise in her as she sees Vince. Turning to look at her, I ask, "Is there a problem?"

"No, I just… never mind," she says, climbing in as I hold the car door open for her.

Vince waits until I'm seated before smoothly pulling away and raising the privacy screen to allow Raven and me a chance to speak privately before the event.

"Champagne?" I offer, and Raven's façade of calm cracks ever so slightly.

Is it being alone with me? The alcohol? Or more likely, a show of nerves about tonight's undertaking? I do wonder if that's more about Evan or the professional opportunities I've promised her.

"Thank you," she finally responds, and I carefully pour her a flute of champagne. She takes a sip and lets out a breath. "Thank you. This is good."

"You're welcome," I reply, pleased that she seems to be shaking off her moment of reservations. "Have you applied anywhere else?" I question, thinking that her potential job prospects may be a good place to begin conversationally to ease us into the deeper discussion we should have before our arrival at the fundraiser.

"Practically everywhere," she admits. "Initially, I applied to as many places as I could, hoping for interviews to hone my skills, so that when I had the chance at my top-choice firms, I was ready to wow." She flashes a wry smile as if we both know how that worked out. "Now, I'm back to a 'beggars can't be choosers' situation. If I can get my foot in the door somewhere, I know I can impress. I just need the chance."

A part of me balks at the idea of passing Raven on to another firm, despite that being the carrot I dangled to get her to come tonight. *Raven Hill is mine*, a voice roars in my head. But that's not the case. She is a means to an end, as I am for her. Nothing more and nothing less.

Which we should address.

"I see." I take a sip of my own champagne and decide to be blunt. "Let's discuss tonight. Who do you know in the Financial District, besides the obvious? Is there anyone in particular you'd like to meet?"

Raven takes another sip of champagne and thinks before answering. "I trust your judgment of my resume and your contacts. I'm open to whoever you feel might have a role for me and appreciate any and all introductions. I've met some people during my internship and recent interviews, but by no means everyone. And to be frank, though Evan talked shop, that only let me know people's reputations. He never went so far as to introduce me to those who might be in a position to hire me."

"Reputations," I repeat. "Their public or private ones?"

"Most of them," she says, sounding amused, "both."

"Ah," I reply, turned on by the sparkle in her eyes. I shouldn't ask, but I'm curious about both what Evan has said and how Raven feels about it, so I venture, "And what sort of reputation do I have?"

"That depends," she says, turning the full impact of those twinkling green eyes on me. "Some people say you're ambitious, principled, and that your work ethic is only outweighed by your brilliance."

"Some?"

"Others say you can be… brutal, even ruthless. I've also heard you described as a menace." She holds my gaze as she says it, as if studying my reaction.

The way she says that last word sends a thrill through my body, straight to my balls. She makes it sound like… a compliment. To me, it is. I've worked too hard to amass wealth and power to be seen as anything less than the ultimate threat.

"I feel like I should thank you," I say lightly.

Her lips purse as if she's hiding a smile. "Why are you doing this, Mr. Sharpe?" she asks suddenly. "You said there's history with you and Evan so you can't bring me into your firm—which, to be clear, would not be an issue on my side." She pauses, one brow arched as if giving me an opportunity to correct her. I drop my chin in a silent answer, and undeterred, she continues, "But there must be more than merely parading me around like a show pony to irritate him."

I consider how best to answer her. Some degree of truth seems prudent, but I'm not prone to showing all my cards just yet.

"I'm an asshole who holds a particular grudge for Evan Faulkner. The hatred I feel for him is likely my only vice," I admit with a sigh. "Long ago, he crossed a line that should never be crossed, and he did it with ease, taking joy in my pain. For that, I will happily watch him suffer and enjoy making him look like a fool, and feel like one too." I pin her with a cold look, ensuring she sees the depth of my depravity. "Raven, I invited you tonight because I want to see Evan Faulkner's cocky fucking smile fall at the sight of you on my arm. That moment." I hold my fingers up, as if I can pluck that precious second and hold it in my hand.

"So, this isn't about me?"

I'm careful with what I say next. "Yes and no. No, if he hadn't done that to you right before our interview, I would not have made the offer I did and we would not be here now. Then again, if you weren't his jilted ex, our lunch interview likely would have gone very differently." I almost tell her I would have hired her without a second thought, but I resist. "Yes, it is about you because I've spent a good amount of time since we met wondering first, how Evan got a woman as intelligent and beautiful as you to fall for his shit, and second, why he'd fuck that up. Especially at that time, in my restaurant, by throwing a meaningless affair in your face. It was needlessly sadistic, even for him."

She winces slightly when I mention Evan's indiscretion, and for a moment, I regret being so blunt. She swallows thickly before murmuring, "I've been wondering the same thing."

Her eyes glimmer with pain but also anger, and I nod approvingly, glad to see it. "Good. Remember that anger and use it. Tonight, you will be on my arm, and I promise you, that will sting Evan like salt on an open wound."

She lifts her chin, stubbornly jutting it forward as she resets her armor.

"You will be the talk of the event, so be prepared." Her eyes widen slightly, as though she hadn't considered that. "Raven, you'll be walking in with me, a man who rarely attends these things, and never with a guest. Everyone there will know who you are within moments of our arrival, and they'll know about your recent relationship with Evan. Not to mention, your beauty could incite wars." I scan her face reverently before chuckling under my breath at the irony. "In fact, it very well might." More seriously, I conclude, "Like me, everyone there will have their eyes on you."

She breathes in deeply and then stills, as if holding her breath.

"I'll make the introductions," I tell her, reminding her of the carrot in case the honesty of what we're walking in to has scared her. "But the charming, the arranging of interviews and meetings? That will be all on your merits, Raven."

She nods, and I'm pleased to see her rising to the challenge. She clears her throat, her eyes sharp and absorbing everything. She's in learning mode, which is smart for her. "How do you anticipate tonight's events?"

"Well, other than a relatively long-winded welcome speech by one of the Faulkners, most likely Jerome Faulkner since he likes to style himself the head of the family, you can expect a passionate yet relatively empty speech by… well, I'm not honestly sure," I tell her. "Each year, the Faulkners pick some charity to donate the money to, and they'll have someone connected with the charity speak. They'll spout a five-minute or so-long plea for donations, everyone will clap, and the rest of the evening is pretty much your standard cocktail party. Drinks, hors d'oeuvres, an area set aside for dancing, and the rest is all schmoozing."

"So, mingle, be sociable and relatable, and allow the conversion to flow."

She gets it. "Exactly. Any other questions?"

"One," she says slowly, as though still formulating the question in her mind. "What happens after? I mean, I'll get interviews, and hopefully, a job. But what about you and Evan? And you and me?" Her gaze drops as if she knows that sounds oddly intimate for what we're doing. This isn't a date, after all. It's revenge via teamwork.

"And you and Evan?" I add, nearly choking on the idea, so I swallow it down with the remainder of my champagne. "There won't be a big moment that fixes what Evan's done to either of us. This is a win of symbolic increments. After tonight, my hope is that we walk out with an ounce of satisfaction at seeing Evan fall—publicly, personally, and professionally."

"An ounce?" she echoes in disappointment. She lifts fiery eyes to mine. "I wish there were a way to hurt him more, *really* hurt him, for what he's done."

She's not talking about killing him or anything that diabolical. I might've dreamed about it a time or two, but Raven doesn't seem the type to find even imaginary joy in that. Still, as she stares into my eyes, the tension between us grows, and there is only one clear and obvious way to hurt Evan the way she's insinuating. I'm a little surprised at the suggestion, but I'm certainly not averse to the idea.

"Perhaps we could discuss something further," I suggest darkly, not sure how far she wants to take this. But I watch, transfixed, as a pretty blush races up her chest to color her cheeks.

She is a beautiful woman, and I'm a bastard of a man. There would be a delightful irony in fucking Raven hard cnough to rattle any memories of Evan loose from her mind and rewrite myself onto her psyche.

We come to a sudden but smooth stop, and there's a knock on the car's door a moment before it opens. There are a few muted flashes from photographers outside, and Raven glances back at me, holding my gaze for a long moment. Not because she needs me, but rather because she's with me.

"Ready, Dylan?" she asks, a polite, polished, perfect smile settling on her face.

"Ready, Raven."

The greeter offers a hand to help her out of the car, and I watch as the round curve of her ass moves in front of me. Fuck, I'm going to need to adjust my dick just to walk this ridiculous red carpet.

This is going to be an eventful evening. I can't wait.

CHAPTER 7

RAVEN

The Faulkner Building is a landmark here in the city. It used to be the third tallest skyscraper in the Financial District, and was built at the height of the family's power and influence. At one time, the name 'Faulkner' was whispered in the same category as Ford, or Rockefeller, or Morgan.

Not that the Faulkners aren't still influential, but the family's not at the same echelon of beyond-the-law levels of influence as they used to be. In fact, I didn't know any of the family history when I first met Evan. He was simply an attractive man who charmed me with his confidence, charisma, and intelligence.

And though those things could also be said about the man stepping onto the red carpet at my side tonight, Evan and Dylan could not be more different. Most importantly, Dylan is upfront with his intentions. All of them—his plan to use me to get back at Evan, and his plan to get underneath, behind, or on top of me. He's being polite about it, but I could see his eyes roaming to my legs when I would shift them in my seat. And when he wasn't looking there, his gaze was a mix of cold-hearted brutality and fiercely tamped down desire. Dylan is a man of hardness and raw emotion.

Days ago, I would've put him off. Now, his attraction to me, as well as his willingness to involve me in what seems to be a long-deserved revenge plot, both give me an extra jolt of confidence as a flash goes off in my face.

"Everything alright?" Dylan asks under his breath, and it brings me back to the moment. He offers me a hand, and I nod, taking it and wrapping my arm through his. His warmth is at odds with the chill air of fall.

He looks completely unbothered by all of this—me, our conversation, the car ride, the photographers. But to me, the entire ride from my apartment to here felt almost surreal, like a blend of luxury and style but with all of the matter-of-factness of taking the SATs. While nakedly vulnerable. Not physically, but mentally. Because Dylan seems to know everything, see everything.

I never felt *seen* when I was with Evan. My heart twists, and I hate it. Tonight is not for my weak little heart. It's for vengeance.

"Is it always like this?" I murmur to Dylan, who nods slightly and gives a cold smile to the photographers. Taking the cue from him, I smile as well, although I hope my smile for the paparazzi is a bit warmer. It serves both of our goals if I look like

I'm enjoying myself.

I am enjoying myself, I remind my racing heart as anxiousness stirs in the pit of my stomach. I push aside thoughts of Evan, revenge, and even Dylan, trying to focus on the professional reasons I'm here.

"You're going to do fine. Relax," Dylan comments as we pass through the high arched doorway.

His bicep flexes, holding me to him, as we get into the elevator, and I notice he's not letting me go. It's comforting, almost, like I can lean on him a moment while I get a grip on my bearings. "Any last-minute advice?" My head goes light for a moment as we rush higher into the sky.

"Be yourself," he says. "You're charming and smart and would be an asset to any firm, so use every advantage you've got to make an impression."

I nod as if that's ground-breaking advice. It does help slightly, though.

The heart of the event is the ballroom of the Continental Hotel, which takes up fifteen floors of the Faulkner Building. Getting off the elevator on the top floor of the hotel, we walk down the hallway toward the 'Grand Ballroom'.

"Tell me something about yourself," I demand quickly, pulling him to a stop. "I know people will make assumptions, but it'd be nice to have at least one personal fact about you to deflect them with."

Dylan looks down at me, considering his answer. "I built a model aircraft carrier in my office."

"You built a what?" I ask, surprised at the randomness.

"Complete with an air wing. Hand built, hand painted, and thirty-six inches long," he says as if merely stating facts. I can only guess how much time and effort he put into it, and simply because... what? He wanted to?

"So you like model aircrafts?"

"I admire the history behind aircraft development, but that particular project was... meditative."

"Healing?" I guess.

"Something like that," he states but doesn't offer more.

We go through the entrance line, Dylan handing over his engraved invitation, and I let out a huff of a silent laugh. Dylan looks over. "What?"

"Thought you didn't come to these?"

He shrugs, unbothered by his small exaggeration. "Rarely, not never."

He starts to say something else, but a man catches his eye and begins walking intently toward us. "The man approaching is named Tyler. He's a business associate." Dylan's quick with the information, uttering it under his breath before turning to the man.

"Dylan, how's it going?" Tyler asks, offering his hand. They shake, much more enthusiastically than I sense Dylan would prefer. I also notice Dylan's hand going around my waist, his fingers resting just outside my low back as if ready to pull me tight at a moment's notice. "I scouted out the food. They've got bacon wrapped shrimp that's gonna go fast." He says it as though he's sharing valuable information.

"Tyler," Dylan says evenly. "Good to know."

"And who is your beautiful companion?" Tyler continues on, as if on one long monologue. "Tyler Hunt," he says, introducing himself before Dylan has a chance to make the introductions.

I take his offered hand, adding a warm smile. Dylan's hand tightens slightly on my waist, and though I take it as a warning to stick close to him, it also feels surprisingly intimate. "Raven Hill," I answer more breathily than I intended. I clear my throat delicately and allow Dylan to do the talking.

To me, he explains, "Tyler's a senior account manager at First National. He and I have done a number of deals together."

"It's wonderful to meet you," I tell Tyler. I'm more than aware of First National. This man has no idea who I am, but I hope one day, he will.

At Dylan's silent encouragement, I practice how I'm going to approach the night with Tyler. For the rest of our conversation, I try to find the balance between chatting up Tyler, meeting him as a strong and intelligent equal, while at the same time staying with Dylan.

It's hard not to want to cling to him. Not only because this room is full of people who are intimidating as hell, but also because Dylan is... magnetic. Even though he says little, I'm constantly aware of his presence, and when he does say something, his words carry weight.

"Raven is currently looking for a position deserving of her skills," Dylan confides, and Tyler's lips lift into a smile.

"I see. She doesn't work in your firm?" His brow furrows in surprise as he looks from Dylan to me, and back.

"I'm considering all offers at the moment, Mr. Hunt," I reply coyly.

He lets out a short laugh. "I might know someone who's moving up the chain, leaving a gap in our trading arm." He reaches into his jacket pocket and pulls out a business card. "Here. Give me a call on Monday. We can talk details."

The two of them chat a moment longer as I slip the card into my clutch, ignoring my racing heart and the overwhelming pride flowing through me.

I did it. I'm doing it. This is going to work.

After he leaves, Dylan gives me a look. "Easy enough?" he questions.

"Very," I agree, although my heart is still pounding as I take in the expansive room and sea of suits and ties who suddenly seem all-too-real with the potential to hire me. "I need to think of these like job interviews, mixed with a bit of speed dating."

Dylan's arm tightens again on my waist, and I feel a fresh thrill go through me. "Not speed dating."

"Not like that," I concede easily. My heart twists at the site of a navy-blue blazer I thought I recognized. It's not him, though. Before I can think twice, I ask, "Have you seen Evan?"

"Not yet, but when I do, I won't tell you," Dylan says as he leads me across the room. It's an odd sense of relief and irritation at his admission. "I want you to appear natural. Just you being your lovely self." The compliment is delivered with a fair amount of charm before he goes cold, adding, "I'll handle him. Just follow my lead."

"Like a dance," I tease.

"Something like that."

He looks at me, his eyes focusing on my right eye, then left, then falling to my lips. While his gaze is there, I watch an unexpected smile bloom across his lips and feel like I've done something right, though all I'm doing right now is standing here. I guess that's following his lead. Reaching up, he brushes a lock of hair behind my ear, the move reminiscent of my own habit, except his fingers teasing against my skin make my body flush.

He seems completely unfazed even though the touch nearly makes me come undone.

He takes my hand, guiding me through the crowd, and we continue mingling. As the night goes on, I find myself grateful again and again to Dylan, while simultaneously becoming more and more attracted to him.

Every person we talk to is connected. With each conversation, I highlight my skills and talents beyond what my resume might contain. I even steer some of the conversations, and as we make our way around the room, I get a glimpse of the world that Dylan Sharpe lives in.

One of wealth and power, and that revolves around whom you know.

And all the while, he's completely at ease, giving me opportunities to shine, including me in discussions, and never leaving my side for something or someone more important.

The truth is, even with Dylan's reassurances, several conversations that have all flowed easily, and all the acting that I can muster, I've spent the past hour feeling unprepared and out of place among these wealthy and powerful people. I've been to a number of events, but none like this. It's top-tier invitation-only, and Evan always told me it was best not to come.

It's not hard to deny that I'm out of place. In the last conversation, the guy mentioned his new car… his sixth. And it's a McLaren, simply because he wanted to complete his 'Formula 1 Set' consisting of a Mercedes, a Ferrari, a Honda, an Aston-Martin, a Renault, and now, a McLaren. "God help me in a couple of years. I'll have to rent a whole garage."

Never mind the rent for a single parking spot in his neighborhood costs more than my half of the rent for my apartment. Now I'm trying to regain my mental composure, and having Dylan's arm helps. It's like he sees through all the fakeness and pretentiousness, reminding me that this is *just a game.* But at the same time, he understands how seriously I need to play this game to get to where I want to be.

As a tray of champagne is passed by us and we both decline, Dylan turns toward me and says, "After Faulkner's speech, we'll go talk to Ollie. He's almost always notoriously late, and he'll be able to listen after that speech is out of the way. In the meantime, relax. You've chatted with half a dozen senior partners and they've all loved you. Trust me, you're making all the right impressions."

I swallow, grateful for the pep talk. Comfortable with him, I lift his arm to take a peek at his watch. Nearly two hours have already slipped by. I glance around the floor again and answer him. "I hope so. And our other goal?"

It seems only fair to put a bit of effort toward that mission as well, especially considering how much he's helped me already.

Dylan catches my hand in his own, lifting my knuckles to his lips to brush a kiss against them unbidden. "You are the talk of the event so far. You have been noticed, and while I doubt he'll approach, I've kept my ears open. Just keep being yourself." His smile has a hint of a chill, but it doesn't intimidate me any longer.

I've actually come up with a trick. It's quite similar to the 'picture them in their underwear' method of dealing with nerves, but it's more along the lines of 'picture them with magnifying glasses on that make their eyes look comically enlarged while they glue tiny pieces of plastic to other tiny pieces of plastic'. It seems Dylan's little fact about himself and the model aircraft has helped me more than he probably guessed and has made him delightfully endearing, though I certainly won't tell him that. I suspect it'd mess with his self-perception as a ruthless asshole.

The clinking of glasses and murmur of conversations fill my ear, and the crowd quiets as a man comes up to a podium at the front of the room. "Good evening," he says, and I can hear the money in his voice. There's a certain tone to it, a cadence and pitch that I'm familiar with.

This is the Faulkner Dylan was telling me about. Jerome Faulkner is, I believe, Evan's grandfather or granduncle. I'm not sure which, never wanting to seem like I was cozying up to the family name, ironically enough. Either way, I haven't met the man before, but there's something in the way he talks, a certain pitch to his voice, that reminds me of Evan. It makes my throat go dry.

I must swallow audibly because Dylan offers to get me a water from the bar. Part of me wants to go with him, cling to his side as though he's my security blanket, but I can do this. I can stand here in a room full of sharks and listen to a speech for a few minutes until he gets back. So, I wave him off, promising to stay right here until he returns and flashing a smile I hope reads as serene.

As soon as I'm alone, anxiety sets in. I fight it off, but it builds with an unexpected fervor, and I glance around me, not searching for Dylan, but Evan. I feel vulnerable, which means this would likely be the moment he strikes. It's what men like him do. And though a few people return polite smiles when we meet eyes, I don't see any incoming threats.

Once the senior Faulkner has finished his speech, he thanks everyone for their attendance before passing the podium over to tonight's guest of honor, the chairman of Healing Through Business, a charity that promotes building up local economies after wars or natural disasters. It at least sounds like a worthy cause, although I've never heard of it before.

Suddenly, I feel a strong arm wrap around my waist. It's a relatively unfamiliar yet immediately comforting feeling. But I've been holding this arm all night, and I turn my head to see Dylan giving me a warm look. My chest tightens with a flash of something I felt back in the car before it's gone as quickly as it came.

"Everything is going as it should," he whispers in my ear, sending shivers down my spine. To anyone around us, it must seem intimate, and in a way, it is, even though he's merely coaching me through the evening the same as he's done all night.

"Thank you," I say for what feels like the millionth time this evening. Still, it will never be enough. I'm going to forever be grateful to him, not only for this chance but for his presence. Because in the mere moment he's been back at my side, my pulse has settled, my breathing steadied, and my nerves have all but dissipated. I look up to find his eyes on me, a spark there that resonates deep in my core. He holds my gaze, and heat rushes through my veins. I know exactly what he's thinking.

Sex.

It permeates the room around us, not in a vulgar, in your face way, but it's there, nonetheless. It's in the power, the money, even in the way everyone is dressed. They politely touch each other, a hand on an arm or an arm wrapped around each other, but it's there in the glances if you pay attention.

But of all the people I've met so far at this party, Dylan's the most powerful, the most sexual. He's merely polite to almost everyone but me, and I know he's only more to me because he sees me as a means to an end, but the line between revenge and pleasure is getting murkier every time his hand grazes along my spine. Perhaps they are one and the same, though.

"Too bad Evan doesn't work in this building," I murmur as I sip the water he's returned with, and Dylan lifts an eyebrow. "He definitely took her on his desk. It'd only be fair to do the same."

Dylan's grin is sharklike, and he nods in approval of my callous suggestion. "I'm sure I can think of something appropriate, if you'd like."

His grin is infectious as we teasingly test the waters and each other's limits, which does nothing to help settle the growing tension between us. If anything, it heats the air around and between us a few more degrees.

After a long moment where we simply look into one another's eyes—me, imagining what Dylan would be like as a lover, and him, likely plotting and scheming how to use me for maximum impact—he glances away. Before I follow his lead of returning my attention to the speaker, I note the slight tilt of a smile at the corner of his lips.

I work to keep myself occupied mentally as the guest of honor continues his speech. It goes a lot longer than it should, but I don't think I'm the only one who feels that way. There's a few people shifting around as he drones on, and as the speech finally comes to an end, the room erupts in applause that sounds more grateful for the chairman getting off the stage than anything else.

A flash of light catches my attention. A photographer snaps photos of the event. As I smile for another photo, I catch my first sight of Evan this evening. He's with his mother and father, and on his arm is Elise… but Evan's not looking at her. If anything, he's staring this way. My stomach drops, and a rush of cold slips down my spine. Every emotion swarms me, but I keep my expression still, using the skills I've practiced for years to fit in to the tiny corner of this world I've clawed my way into.

I pretend like I didn't see him. I might be embarrassed by the way he treated me a few days ago, but I'm for damn sure not going to let anyone see that. Instead, I turn in to Dylan.

"He's at your eleven o'clock. He brought *her*," I tell him, placing my hand on his chest. I can feel the warmth of his skin through his shirt. It's not enough to help with the shock of seeing not only Evan, but Elise at his side with his parents smiling at her welcomingly.

Dylan must see what I'm talking about because I feel a rumble in his chest. He captures my upper arms in his large hands and dips down to quietly say, "It could mean nothing. Many people bring assistants with them to take discrete notes throughout the event." I look up at him through my lashes, hopeful it means that and not what I automatically assumed—that Evan is hard launching his relationship with Elise. But Dylan concedes, "It could also mean more. You okay?"

I force myself to nod. "Just unexpected. I was prepared for *him*, not *them*."

"You've got this," he says encouragingly.

I trust that he's right, turning back to the podium and taking a drink of my water. When a waiter passes by, I set the now empty glass on his tray. All the while, I can feel both Dylan and Evan's eyes on me.

Up front, another Faulkner is speaking, really giving the hard push for everyone to show generous support of tonight's featured charity. When he wraps up, the room breaks out in muted applause. After it dies down, Dylan gives my hand a gentle squeeze and points with his eyes across the room. "There's Ollie." It's a name I recognize from a list Dylan rattled off earlier of important contacts I should meet.

I nod, confident in my skills and ready for this because I'm on Dylan's arm. *I've got this*, I remind myself as we cross the room to approach a balding man in his upper fifties. He's surreptitiously sneaking what looks like one of the event's single bite meatballs into his mouth.

"Ollie, you know Wendy's going to be upset with you for that," Dylan says, mock menacingly, and the man legitimately blushes as he licks his lips. Dylan breaks into a polite smile and offers a hand. "Your secret's safe with me, though. For now," he teasingly warns. "How have you been?"

"Dylan, it's been too long," Ollie replies, shaking hands enthusiastically.

This is a completely different introduction than all the others tonight. Dylan and Ollie sound like actual friends.

"You're right. About what, thirty pounds lighter or so?" Dylan compliments him, and Ollie puffs his chest out a little.

"Doctor said I had to work on my blood pressure. Apparently, red meat and scotch aren't good for me," he sighs wistfully despite having just eaten a meatball that likely isn't on his doctor's nutrition plan. "I tried to tell him it's not the food, but the stress. Unfortunately for me, it seems he was right because it's working. Blood pressure's down several points now, which means Wendy's got the chef feeding me chicken every damn day."

"Good for you," Dylan says. "How is your lovely wife? She here?"

I watch the two of them chatting, and just as I begin to feel as if I'm intruding, Dylan's thumb slips down the small of my back and then his hand is on my hip. He squeezes ever so slightly, telling me to be patient, and I lean into his soothing touch, smiling politely as they talk.

"She's just fine, visiting our new granddaughter in Seattle," Ollie says proudly. "I'd have gone, but with the quarterly meeting next week, I had to stick around. I promised I'd go over the holidays, though."

"About that. I may have the best opportunity you'll get this year to get away for a long winter break," Dylan says, getting to business as he indicates to me. "Ollie, I'd like to introduce you to Raven Hill. She recently interviewed with me, so you know she's smart, ambitious, and skilled, but I think she might actually fit better with you at your firm."

"Oh, really?" Ollie says, turning interested eyes to me. Dylan's introduction clearly shows how well he knows Ollie, and how much forethought he gave this introduction.

"Dylan mentioned you have a position at your firm for a fund manager, and I expressed my interest."

"I do, in fact," Ollie says as Dylan quietly excuses himself to get drinks. "I'm looking for someone who can do the research and make the calls on trades, letting me focus on the big picture operations of the firm. While leaving the office at five might not be in my immediate future, I would like to see the sunset from

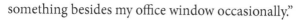

something besides my office window occasionally."

"I see. That's exactly what I want to do."

"See the sunset from an office window?" he asks comically, and with my laugh, the conversation moves easily. It's obvious that he's passionate about business but wanting to slow down. I could see myself very easily working for him and filling a spot that could give him an opportunity to spend more time with family.

After several minutes of talking, Dylan reappears as if he senses our impromptu interview is drawing to a close. He bids Ollie goodbye, sending his regard to Wendy, and we continue working around the room.

I feel accomplished. This is what I'm meant to be doing and where I'm meant to do it. I've met so many people tonight, those in positions of power, not only in the stock markets, but in the world. I've done my best to make a good impression and engage in polite small talk, all the while trying to hide the fact that at times, I'm still shaking with nerves. I could see the measuring look in peoples' eyes, but even the ones who were clearly just networking or meeting me because I was with Dylan were at least respectful of my skills and my talents.

How did I go this long without this? Sure, part of it was my own stubbornness about wanting to 'do it myself'. But as I think back, I realize that something, or more accurately, someone else, was holding me back too.

Evan. He told me more than once that events like this weren't worth it and he only attended because of his father. And after I mentioned doing things on my own, he latched on to that idea, making it seem like attending as his girlfriend would mark me as a gold-digging ladder jumper. Just thinking his name brings back that twist in my stomach.

As if thinking of him summoned the devil himself, I look up from a tray of champagne, picking up my third glass of the night, to find his sharp gaze piercing mine. Before I can turn, he calls out my name loud enough for everyone around us to hear.

I wish I didn't look up. I wish I walked off as though I didn't hear him. Instead, I plaster on a fake smile, one that hopefully reads as 'fancy seeing you here' and not 'I hate you with the flames of a thousand suns'. I don't go to him. I'm not that stupid. I know exactly how that would appear to those around us. But rather, I hold my ground and allow him to walk over to me.

Where's Dylan? My heart races with apprehension and a flash of annoyance pricks at my skin. The one time he excuses himself for the restroom, Evan finds me.

He was waiting for this moment, I realize.

"Raven," he says with a shark's smile before leaning in as though he's going to kiss my cheek. Instead, he whispers, "They would all line up to fuck you, but not a single one of them would hire you."

He stands tall, leaving me stunned and wondering if he really just said that. His cruelty is vicious, hitting my weak spot with deadly accuracy, blasting it to smithereens and leaving a gaping hole in my confidence.

"After all, that's what Sharpe is doing, right?" he murmurs, raising his brow sharply at the accusation. And then, he acts as if he's just seen a friend, leaving me alone.

I'm left breathless, frozen in place, with my smile crumbling at the edges.

Is that all he sees me as? All he used me for? All that time, was it truly nothing more than sex? Was I that blind?

I thought I had prepared to see him tonight. I was wrong. A fatal mistake on my part, it seems, because our little tete-a-tete has garnered attention from those around us, and they're watching me fall apart with barely disguised hunger, as if my embarrassment is reality-TV fodder for their enjoyment. Even those I had thought respectful and polite are now whispering to one another, their laughter-filled eyes fastened on me as if I'm a living, breathing car crash they can't look away from.

Get it together, Raven!

Clearing my throat, I force my smile to return by sheer willpower, meet eyes with three people around me, and take a measured sip of my champagne. I'm doing everything I can to shut it all down—the shock, the horror, the feeling of not belonging.

I keep to myself on the edge of the ballroom, wishing Dylan would come back so we can leave. I've done what I wanted, meeting Ollie and the others, though I have serious doubts it'll do any good after Evan's comment. Secondarily, irritating Evan seems to be a lost cause. He wasn't upset. He was amused by my appearance on Dylan's arm. As if it proves what he thought all along—that I'm willing to do anything to make it.

"Fuck that," I whisper, finishing off my champagne a bit too quickly. "And fuck him."

"I do hope you're using that in a positive way if you're talking about me," Dylan says, reappearing at my side. His warm hand finds its way to the small of my back again, and he gives me a flirtatious smirk.

He has no idea. I debate on telling him. But I also wonder if what Evan said is true. Dylan didn't hire me, and while he's been gentlemanly, there's been a growing tension between us. Is he simply biding his time before he makes a move? Am I destined to be nothing more than a plaything for those in power, no matter how hard I work?

The idea startles me more than it should. Perhaps I'm more naïve than I would've thought because I truly felt that my experience and dedication would matter, that my skills and instincts would mean something.

I stare into Dylan's eyes, feeling my foundation crumble beneath me but too lost to find new footholds. There's concern sparkling in his gaze, a question of what's changed, but when I lick my lips to speak, his attention drops to my mouth and that's when I know.

He wants to fuck me.

Hell, I want to fuck him too.

Does that make it wrong? It definitely doesn't make it right. But I'm not sure I care. This whole night suddenly feels like a waste, so maybe I should get something out of it.

Something for me. Evan can burn in hell. Dylan can too, for all I care right now. But I still have one play to make. A Hail Mary that'll let the desire burning between us overflow into something tangible. An orgasm, hopefully.

A job?

The tiny voice of disappointment whimpers in the back of my mind, and I tell it to shut up. I'm not sleeping my way to the top, but am I willing to possibly sleep my way through the front door?

"Where can we go?" I whisper.

CHAPTER 8

DYLAN

Something happened while I was gone. I don't know what, and I should definitely ask, but when Raven looks at me with desire in her eyes, my trademark logic and judgment take a backseat to lust.

Leading Raven through the crowded ballroom, I can't ignore the burning little ember of her hand in mine. She doesn't ask where we're going, trusting that I know where we can be alone. And I do.

I've been waiting all fucking night for this, and the feel of her hand in mine only fuels me to get her to a private room faster. On the elevator, I nearly jam the button for the tenth floor. She doesn't say a word, but her chest rises and falls with heated anticipation, and I have to grit my teeth to stop from taking her right here.

The chime dings our arrival on the requested floor and the elevator doors open. The sound of her heels on the tile as we walk down the deserted hallway sends sparks through me, and by the time we get to an empty conference room, I'm as hard as a rock and in desperate need of this woman. Her green eyes darken as she steps past me and allows me to quietly close the door behind us. It doesn't lock, but no one followed us here and I'm certain there will be enough privacy for what we need right now. So long as she's quiet.

The conference room is dominated by a long table that's at just the right height for what we have in mind, and there's a small amount of ambient light from the moon shining through the blinds and the tiny, dim LEDs around the perimeter of the room that make the fire in her eyes plain to see.

My pulse quickens, and I'm eager, far too eager to finally have her how I've wanted from the moment I first saw her. She has bewitched me with not only her beauty, but her poise and intelligence.

I close the distance between us, and she meets me halfway, confidently pushing my jacket back. *My needy girl.* I let it fall from my shoulders, tossing it to the table behind me in favor of touching her.

Without a word, she leans in. Her kiss is breathtaking, her lips warm and inviting, and the pressure of her soft, yielding curves beneath my palms stokes the fire inside me to a blazing inferno.

A gentle moan passes over her lips into the heated air between us, and I want to do anything to elicit that sound again and again. I chase it to her mouth, then along her jawline to the sensitive spot beneath her ear. She tilts her head, allowing me further access, but I slip my fingers to her chin, angling her even more. I want all of her, want to claim every inch and mark her with my touch. She braces herself with her palms on my chest, letting me overwhelm us both with growing need.

I return to her mouth, kissing her deeply. She tastes of champagne, and it only adds to the intoxicating hold she has on me. I want more, now.

Not breaking our kiss, I lead her to the table until she's caught between myself and the hardwood. With one hand gripping her hip to keep her where I want her, the other reaches up her neck to the nape of her hair, gathering a fistful and tugging gently.

As her back bows and I work my way down her neck and across her collarbone with open mouthed kisses, she moans yet again, this time with my name slipping through her lips, which are already swollen from our passion.

She's gorgeous and eager and everything I need right now. Best of all, she gives it back just as much. She's not shy, knowing what she wants.

As we kiss, Raven's hands move down my back, tugging my shirt out of my pants and deftly working at the buttons as I push her dress up higher, my fingers finding first, the silken softness of her stockings, and then, the warm, smooth skin of her thigh above them. I nip at her neck at the same time I grip her ass firmly beneath her dress, and she gasps for me.

I can feel myself losing control, my body taking over as the passion between us rises into an all-consuming fire. Finally, I pull back, my chest heaving as Raven looks at me. The moment is heavy with intensity.

I know what I want.

And looking into Raven's emerald eyes, I know what she wants.

"Say it." It's my one demand.

"Fuck me, Dylan," she whispers hotly, her breasts already trembling with shaky breath. "Please."

I don't know what changed for her. I'm not sure I care. I never claimed to be a good man, and while I'm utterly gone for Raven in this moment, deep in my psyche, there's a tiny hint of triumph that my plan is coming to fruition so perfectly.

Fuck Evan Faulkner.

Reaching for my neck, I loosen my tie before finishing the work of undoing the buttons on my shirt as Raven reaches behind her. She pulls the zipper on her dress down, the sound filling the room, and then the fabric falls at her ankles.

"Fuck me," I utter reverently.

I knew that she would be remarkable, but as my gaze roams her body in the dim light… she's perfect. Her curves are cradled in sexy satin lingerie, her full breasts lifted temptingly in her strapless bra, the flare of her hip highlighted by the hug of her garter belt, and the V at her core barely covered in panties that make my cock strain against the fabric of my pants.

"You knew what you were doing when you chose this," I comment in a murmur as I let my fingers slip along the edge of her bra, barely teasing at her skin. A blush sweeps across her chest and flushes up her cheeks as she only nods in response.

Without another word, I pull my shirt off before lifting Raven onto the long table, her legs parting to make space for me to stand between her thighs. She more than meets me, her touch sending tingles through my skin as I stroke her body, memorizing every curve as we continue to kiss. Cupping her ass, I squeeze hard, and she moans, liking the rough caress. I pull her against me sharply, pressing my hardened cock in my pants against her satin covered mound, and her soft, whimpering moan tells me that this is just the beginning of what promises to be a much-needed release for us both.

I kiss down her neck, leaving open-mouth kisses down her silky soft skin until I reach the tops of her breasts. With a smirk, I catch the top fabric with my teeth and tug it down, freeing her breast down to her hardened nipple, which begs for my lips and teeth.

"*Yes,*" Raven hisses as I suck hard on her breast. Once again, her back arches, and I fucking love it. The bold purity of her responsiveness is addictive.

This might be a revenge fuck. For me, and for her. I'm under no illusion that it's anything but that. But maybe even because it's a one-time thing, I feel compelled to ensure that we both enjoy every damn minute of it.

I want to touch, taste, and feel every inch of her body all at once. I've got five senses, and every single one of them wants to be overwhelmed by the woman before me.

I let myself be guided by her hands, her voice, and in the

way she squirms, presenting her body to me, begging for the release that I can bring her, but I take my time, drawing out her pleasure.

I'm rough with purpose, listening and paying attention to her every hitched breath and needy moan. When her soft cries go from pleasure to a gasp on the edge of pain, I pull back, soothing the abused nipple with gentle kisses and long licks, sucking and licking and bringing her to the edge of her release each and every time.

"Please," she moans. "I need you."

Finally, I guide her to lie back, her hair fanning out beneath her in a dark halo. I slip her panties down her legs and over the heels she's still wearing. I run my palms up her thighs, spreading them wide and humming deeply as I feel her soft lips part for my fingertips.

"So fucking wet for me," I groan and love how her bottom lip drops open on a sigh of relief as I strum her clit. She's at my mercy and so fucking close.

I watch, almost amused as Raven writhes, her hips lifting to meet my touch. Her nipples are red and raw from my mouth, and I'm pretty sure there will be a mark on her right breast tomorrow. The idea of leaving that reminder of our passion excites me.

She says my name again, pleading with me for more, and that's my undoing.

I give in to her, slipping my fingers over her clit faster and watching with anticipation as her head falls back and her thighs tremble. "Good girl," I murmur, although I'm not sure she even hears me over her heavy breathing and soft cries of pleasure.

I pause a moment to reach into my pocket at the last moment. Pulling out the condom, I rush to undo my belt, drop my slacks, and free my cock. I rip open the packet and prepare myself quickly, not wanting to hold back any further.

Just as the high of her release seems to dim, I pull her to the edge of the table and slam inside her in a swift, brutal stroke.

I still inside her, buried to the hilt, and give her time to adjust. *She's fucking heaven.*

Her pussy is soft, warm, wet, tight… everything I could imagine. Her body tightens as her back arches on the table, and I take the moment to pluck her nipple once more. She wraps her legs around my waist, pulling me deeper, and I have to grab her hips, my fingers digging into her flesh to hold myself back from selfishly taking her before she's ready.

When her body relaxes, I give her exactly what she wants. What we both want.

I fuck her deeply until my hips smack into her upturned ass and the backs of her thighs, thrusting in and out of her rough and recklessly.

Raven gives it back to me, though, locking her ankles behind my back and pulling me in, crying out in deep, lustful moans as I fuck her mercilessly. Her body shakes with every stroke, and time loses all meaning.

All that exists is her black hair, spread out on the table, her flushed skin beneath my palms, and her full breasts which jostle with every stroke. My pulse roars in my ears as I use my grip on her waist to pull her onto my cock, pounding her harder and making her back arch up off the table until she comes on my cock, her mouth dropping open in a gorgeous 'O' that should be etched in artwork. It's so perfect that I unconsciously memorize it for my own later enjoyment.

As soon as her wave passes, I thrust hard again, chasing my own climax. My strokes are brutal and dominating as she gives me strangled cries of pleasure. I should cover her mouth so no one hears us. It'd be the smart thing to do, but I'm barely in control as I ravage her body, feeling her throb and tighten around me, and a primal part of me wants everyone to hear her shouting my name.

Pulling out, I step back and turn her over on the table, not giving her a chance to put her feet on the ground before I slam my cock balls deep into her once again.

Unbidden, I fist a handful of her dark hair at the nape of her neck, pulling her tight to me. "Like this, darling?" I growl as I fuck her deep and hard. "This is what you want?"

"Yes! More! Harder!" she begs, and I give it to her, pumping in and out so forcefully that her ass quickly turns pink from my hips smacking against her flesh. In seconds, we're both on the cusp, and with a groan buried deep in my chest, I plunge over the edge, coming deep and hard. Raven's there with me, and together, we ride the crest together, falling apart in the intense wave of our release.

When it passes, I pull back reluctantly. Slowly, she pushes away from the table, and both of us look silently at the streaks of sweat and sex that mar the surface. We should probably wipe that evidence away, but I won't. I rather like that they're there, proof of what just happened.

The moment is over, but it was everything I wanted it to be and more.

The sight of her is etched into my memory forever. Fucking gorgeous. Her hair is tousled from my hands and from writhing on the table, her lips are plump from my kisses with no trace of her lipstick remaining, and her skin is flushed. And I was right, her nipple is still reddened and stiff, a memory for her as well.

She murmurs a sound I can't place as she covers herself and then looks away to find her dress.

It's at my feet, so I grab it for her. I don't miss that she doesn't look me in the eyes as she takes it from me.

Awkwardness spreads between us, and I wish we were in my office… or penthouse. Anywhere but here.

I step away to the credenza at the side of the room, disposing of the condom in the trash there before pulling my slacks back up. I pick up a few napkins for us to clean up, and when I turn back around, she's silently righted her bra and is holding her panties. I take those from her with a dark look, slipping them into my pocket, and hand her the napkins.

Still catching my breath, I debate on what to tell her as she avoids my gaze. How fucking good she was. How beautiful she looks. But then it dawns on me, from the forlorn expression on her face, that her thoughts are either of regret or of Evan.

It *was* a revenge fuck, after all. We both knew that, so I'm not hurt by her second thoughts. But I wasn't expecting it to be... as amazing as it was. Clearing my throat, I swallow thickly and wait for her to be ready enough to leave.

Finally, her eyes meet mine, and she blushes as a smirk turns her lips up.

It soothes me in a way that's unexpected. There's a moment, a flicker of time, where the easiness of earlier returns, and I'm thankful it's still there beneath the awkwardness.

She plucks a tissue from the table and wets it on the tip of her tongue before wiping my lips and cheek. "Red's not your color." Her hushed tone does something to me. The sweetness in the gesture. *Fuck, I want her again.*

"I do prefer the color on you," I admit. "It matches your blush." I capture her hand and kiss her fingertips. I don't know why. Our 'arrangement' has been concluded. But I don't want to let go. Her hand stills, and for a moment, both of us freeze.

"We should go," she whispers, her gaze flicking to the door behind me, and I nod.

This was supposed to be a business arrangement. It was supposed to be a fun physical activity, a 'revenge fuck' for Raven and me to both get back at Evan for the wrongdoing he committed against us. But as we leave the conference room behind us, I keep her hand in mine as I lead the way down the hall to the elevator.

I'm about to push the call button when the elevator dings and the doors open before us. Bronson Faulkner emerges with a couple of his cronies, clearly ready for a nightcap. He's the younger of the Faulkner brothers and more importantly, he's Evan's father.

"So I—" Bronson says before the entire group stops, staring. In the silence, Bronson's eyes go to me, then to the clearly still-disheveled Raven, and to our hands, which are clasped together.

I stare back boldly, daring him to say a single word. Bronson finally gives me a short nod that I return before he leads his buddies away, leaving Raven and me in the empty hallway. "Holy... *fuck*," Raven whispers, her face going pale. "Was that...?"

"Yes," I reply, letting go of her hand to push her into the elevator.

That certainly wasn't a good look. I don't care for myself. I can handle any consequences Bronson or Evan dish out. But Raven? I calculate the number of contacts she made tonight who simply won't return her call once word gets around that I fucked her in the conference room at the charity event. A relationship of sorts is one thing, public sex inside Faulkner's own kingdom quite another.

And word will definitely spread. Evan will make sure of that because it paints both Raven and me in a poor light, and he would take delight in that for sure.

My body turns tense, and I hope she doesn't know. For her sake, I give her a semblance of a smile and kiss her knuckles once more.

Downstairs, the event has wrapped up and people are milling about the hotel lobby, waiting for their chauffeurs and cars to come to the front, and Raven excuses herself to the restroom.

While I wait for her, Ollie, of all people, emerges from down the hallway, looking surprised to see me.

"Dylan," Ollie says, extending a hand again. "Where's your guest, Raven, was it?"

"Touching up her makeup," I reply. "The restroom is always crowded as everyone heads out."

"How true," Ollie agrees.

"Care for a drink with us?" I offer him, hoping to keep Raven a bit longer tonight and possibly undo any damage caused.

"No, no… I think I've had enough for one night, and my driver's waiting for me," Ollie says, pointing toward the door.

"Next time, then."

Ollie claps me on the shoulder, making his exit, and I turn to search the hall where the restroom is for Raven. But I don't see her. How long is that line?

Finally, my phone pings.

Decided to take a cab home. Safer that way. Thank you for tonight.

I stare at the message, more hurt than I should be. She took a cab and left?

Frustration and disappointment course through me as I go to the valet, who calls for my car to come around. "Did you see a young lady in red come by here?"

"Yes sir," the valet says. "She grabbed a taxi just a few minutes ago."

Fuck.

Vince arrives, and I climb into my backseat, telling him, "Home, please."

Thankfully, he doesn't ask any questions even though I catch him watching in the rearview with the questions obviously there. As we pull away into late night traffic, I stare at her text, not understanding how this woman is making me feel like this. Like I just fucked up and lost her.

CHAPTER 9

RAVEN

Still thankful that the coat check room attendant doesn't ask any questions nearly forty minutes later, I unlock my apartment door. Stepping inside, I let out a sigh of relief although I'm still unsettled from the shitstorm that happened.

I'll admit I freaked out. I've never been one for casual sex, and as much as I wish I could just shut out all thoughts of him, Evan's still on my mind. Judging me. Hating me. And belittling me for his own amusement. There are also thoughts of screaming at him all the vile shit he deserves… but still. I wish I didn't care about him at all.

Realization that what he said was right—Dylan didn't hire me, but was all too willing to fuck me—hit hard once my orgasm faded. And what had seemed like a sexy risk of being caught doing something naughty where we shouldn't had suddenly been an ugly reality when I saw the shrewd judgment in Bronson's eyes and the amused smirks on his cohorts' faces. The charity and the funds they raised were definitely not the talk of their nightcap. I was. And not in a flattering light.

He's probably telling Evan what a bullet he dodged with me right now. As far as he's concerned, I've been confirmed as the social climber, gold digger, and disposable arm candy they likely thought I was.

And word will surely spread. Evan will make certain of that. The finance world is smaller than a dime.

It feels like the entire night was not only a waste, but the active destruction of everything I've worked for.

"Hey, babe," Maggie says as I slip off my heels and jacket, still not quite able to process everything right. As I bend over, my thighs clench and I feel him… again. I have to hide my expression before turning back around to face her.

She sits upright and cross-legged on the couch, looking quite comfy in her sleepy time shorts and cutoff T-shirt that make her look like a homebody single guy's wet dream. Her tablet is on her lap, where I see she's been doing some binge watching.

"How did it go?" She's smiling, looking hopeful that all my problems were solved in the last few hours since I walked out the door.

Unfortunately, it's quite the opposite.

"It was… a mess," I finally reply when I can sum it up in one word, letting out a shaky breath as my emotions threaten to fully bubble up. Her face falls, concern appearing in her eyes.

I hold up a finger. "Let me get comfy first. Unzip me?" I undid it on my own when my only desperate thought was of sex with Dylan. Now, I don't have the strength to pull the contortionist act it takes.

Maggie unzips me, and I head to my bedroom, changing into some flannel matching pants and button-down pajamas before going back out to find her brewing tea. "Figure if you're going to spill it, I should offer it," she explains as I settle onto the couch. "Sugar?"

"Please," I reply as my mind wanders back to the events of the night.

I find myself staring at my hands as those unsettling feelings resurface. I can't stop thinking about the way Dylan held my hand as he led me to the conference room. It felt like it was supposed to happen. Like it wasn't at all a forbidden romp that could end my career. Like whatever was happening between me and Dylan wasn't exactly what Evan had assumed.

But it was.

I can feel the regret slowly consume me as I sit there on the sofa.

It's all my fault. I was the one who practically begged him to take me somewhere, anywhere. I was the one who shushed the voice in my head saying this was exactly what I *shouldn't* do. I was the one who answered all too quickly when Dylan told me to 'say it.'

"So, did you get to meet people?" Maggie asks me, shaking me out of my reverie, but before I can answer, my phone buzzes.

Nervously, I pick it up, half-expecting it to be Evan gloating or an automated message that says, 'don't call us, we'll call you' or some professional version of that from one of the people I did talk to tonight.

But it's not. It's Dylan.

I would have taken you home.

Heat flows over my body as I stare at my phone, ignoring Maggie's gaze that's boring into me. I hit *Reply*, but then my thumbs pause. I don't know how to respond.

He gave me everything I wanted and needed, pleasure and satisfaction. But I've never traded sex to get ahead, and it definitely feels like that's what I did tonight. I'm disappointed in myself and unsure what Dylan thinks of me and about what we did.

I wish I could go back to the moment Dylan walked up to me after Evan spewed his toxicity into my mind. I wish I would've told him what Evan said and let him reassure me that it was completely off-base. We could've finished the night with a little more networking, a polite drive home, and a hint of acknowledgement of the sexual tension between us.

That would've been infinitely better than this.

Fuck, my head is a mess, and I shove my phone away before snatching it right back up. I glance up for just one second, and Maggie's wide eyes are matched with an arched brow as she stares at me from our tiny kitchenette.

Finally, I simply text back, *Thank you for tonight,* and shove my phone under the couch cushion so I don't say more. Maggie's eyes seemingly haven't left me, and I realize she's still waiting for me to answer. "I did meet people. I got some interviews, and some good leads… I hope." I sound bitter even to my own ears.

I sink back into the sofa and pull my knees into my chest. My phone buzzes again, but I make no move to grab it.

"You hope?" Maggie asks with her tone prying. She stalks into the room, no doubt wondering what the hell is going on before handing me my tea. I accept the warm mug with both hands, needing every bit of comfort. Without asking, she's put milk in it, just how I like it at night.

"I fucked up," I admit, letting the overwhelming feeling take over. I can't believe I actually slept with him… and that I got caught doing it. *And that it was that good.* What a foolish thing to do. I can't help thinking how dumb it is, how I have probably just ruined my career.

Maggie gives me a worried look, her eyebrow lifting yet again. I'm going to give this poor girl premature wrinkles on her forehead. "What do you mean?"

Before I can answer, my phone buzzes again, and this time, Maggie points toward its cushion hideout, silently telling me to deal with that. I pull it out, reading the message.

Come to dinner next weekend. Just business.

Just business.

As if it could ever be just business now. What we did… I swallow thickly and shove it down. One of the best pieces of advice I was given by a college professor was to meet every offer with a response, never a closed door. And as much as I don't want to admit it, Dylan opened so many doors for me tonight.

If even one of them stays open, I'm still on better footing than I was yesterday.

I read his text again.

It's too tempting of an offer, and I have to give Dylan credit for one thing. He hasn't lied to me. He told me exactly why he wanted me to come with him tonight, even when it made him look bad. And when we discussed doing more to exact our revenge on Evan, he was direct and clear about it and what we'd be doing. So if Dylan says something, he means it.

Besides, I'm not sure I can afford to slam any potential doors closed at this point.

Okay. Send details, I'll meet you there.

As if he was waiting for my answer, he quickly replies, *I will. I enjoyed tonight, Raven. I'm glad you were there.*

Me too. Goodnight, Dylan.

As I hit *Send* and the words turn into a bubble marked *Read* on the screen, I second-guess telling him good night. It feels like something more. Like an offer that will end with my heart shattered.

"Raven," Maggie says, literally snapping me back to our tiny living room with her right hand. *Snap, snap.* "What do you mean, you fucked up?"

"I mean, I shouldn't have gotten involved with Dylan," I reply, taking a sip of my tea. "I'm playing with fire."

"Involved?" Maggie asks, lifting an eyebrow. "Explain."

"I… might have slept with him tonight," I admit. "Uhm, not slept with, but you get my point." I'm definitely not telling her the details about exactly *where* Dylan and I had sex. I'll let Maggie assume that it happened at his place, or in the car afterward, or whatever her heart desires.

I expect Maggie to be shocked, but instead, she smiles happily. "Good for you," she exclaims matter-of-factly, lifting her own tea cup to clink mugs with me although I keep mine still. "What's wrong with that?"

I blink, knowing damn well my best friend is playing down the fact that I *am* playing with fire.

"You know exactly why."

"Well, no one else knows," she says, and I meet her with a side eye.

"They might."

"And so what if they do?" she says as if it's a non-issue. "First off, Evan cheated on *you*. Second, you two went how long since you last had sex? I mean seriously, I think Ami's been getting more action than you recently, and you know how much of a goody two-shoes she can be."

None of that can erase the look of those men's faces at the elevator from my memory. Men in the industry. Men who talk. And if what Evan told me is what he's telling everyone else...

She must see the doubt on my face because she adds, "It's no biggie, Raven. You got yours, he got some, you both get back at Evan. Win-win-win, yeah? And the whole industry and everyone in it is basically trading partners like it's a square dance. It's the way of the rich."

I think I nod, but mostly, my brain is whirling like a tornado.

Could Maggie be right? Could I have overreacted to being spotted post-sex because Evan's words were in the back of my mind?

"Maybe," I say, not sure but feeling a tiny seed of hope that maybe it's not as bad as I feared. "I just… I've never had sex on a first time out with someone before, let alone had sex with someone who could be my boss or help me get hired," I finally reply, and Maggie waves me off. "No, I'm serious."

"So am I, that this *isn't* serious," Maggie stresses. "Look, having a fling with Dylan isn't a problem. You've more than earned some free dick, and as long as it stays that way, casual fun between you two, then you're cool. One time, hit it, quit it, and don't let what Evan 'Eh' Faulkner thinks of you and your potential dictate your future."

"Eh?" I ask, and Maggie nods, grinning. "Where'd you get that from?"

"From that one night, about eight months or so ago, when you let him stay over?" Maggie says, and I remember. She'd said she was staying over at her parents' place, but her mother's stomach flu had canceled plans at the last minute. I hadn't known, and Maggie had been cool about it, sleeping on the couch and not saying anything negative as I had Evan over. That he stayed at my place at all had been a big deal because he hated even coming to my neighborhood to pick me up for dates, absolutely refused to sleep in my tiny bed, and made rude jokes about Maggie and me 'slumming it' together. I definitely remember that we had sex that weekend, because it was the first time we had sex at my place instead of his.

"Wait, you heard us having sex?" I ask, and Maggie nods. "Mags!"

"What? That's what he sounded like when he was fucking. Eh, eh, eh, eh!" Maggie exclaims, dropping her voice half an octave into an eerie imitation of Evan in the sack. "That was the most cringe-worthy ninety seconds of my life, by the way."

I tilt my head, knowing what she meant. It had been a pretty quick, and unsatisfying, encounter. Though that wasn't unusual.

Damn, what did I see in Evan?

He was everything you want to be, I admit to myself. Not personally. I can see that he's kind of a shit human being now that I have some distance from him and his occasional charm, but professionally, he's successful and powerful. It might be due to his family, but he still does the actual work and I always found that exciting.

"Now, I've got a series drama I want to finish before bed. You mind if I wrap it up?"

After a moment of staring in awe at my sweet friend whom I don't know whether I deserve, I nod gratefully. I let Maggie go back to her tablet while I finish my cup and go to bed, where I lie in the dark, hoping for sleep.

Tonight has been a roller coaster of emotions. Up, down, twisty corkscrew gravitational pulls that make you feel sick? Yep, all of them... repeatedly.

Which only makes me more scared of what might happen next.

CHAPTER 10

DYLAN

"Mr. Sharpe?"

I look up from my screens at the sound of a faint knock along with my name and see my assistant, Tamara, in the doorway. Glancing at the clock on the wall next to where she's standing, I realize I've been focusing on these projects a bit too much this morning. Over the last week, I've put off far too much while focusing on thoughts of beautiful curves and lush lips that should not be haunting me as they are.

"They're here?" I question, although it's more of a statement, closing the three thick folders in front of me and minimizing several tabs on the screen.

She nods and politely responds, "Mr. Miller and his daughter are in conference room A." Tamara is damn good at her job. She worked for several corporations for twenty years before coming to work for me. She's professional and a minimalist, never saying more than she has to.

"Thank you," I reply, standing up, grabbing my suit coat, and slipping it on as I walk down the hallway. She walks beside me, handing me several folders for the meeting. Our main conference room overlooks the Financial District, a view I find the pair admiring as I open the large glass door and join them, leaving my assistant behind.

Inside, Geno Miller and his daughter, Denise, are waiting for me. When we first started discussing this deal, I was taken aback by Geno's insistence on his daughter being brought in on everything. But it only took me one meeting to understand why.

He's looking to cash out and wants to pass something along to his only child. It's worked out for me as well, as Denise is eager to step up and move out of her role as the Chief Operations Officer of Miller Technological Minerals.

She wants the big chair. Whether or not she's prepared for that is another story.

"Geno, Denise, thank you for coming," I greet them, offering a hand as I cross the room. We shake hands, Geno first, Denise second. "How was your flight from Nevada?"

"Smooth as could be," Denise says, looking around the conference room she's been in a number of times. She's dressed the part in a sharp suit, but she's young, and to hand over such a large asset to someone so green could very well be a mistake.

"I'm glad," I reply, unbuttoning the jacket I've just buttoned in the hall to have a seat and motion to the two chairs. The table's shaped subtly, myself on one side, the Millers on the other, but the slight curve of the table gives me the 'head' compared to them. It's faint, but I've become very familiar with what the firm calls the 'Conference Room A Effect.'

"Dylan, I do have to ask, why fly us all the way out here just for a sit down?" Geno asks. "We could have handled it in Nevada. After all, that's where our factory is."

And that's exactly why I didn't want to meet you there. You're too confident and casual on your own terrain. You'd probably insist on finishing the deal with a couple rounds of poker or a ribeye.

Not that I'm averse to either, and have certainly done business over both, but I want Geno and Denise to feel the weight of this agreement, and it becomes very real in a cold conference room in the middle of the city.

"Perhaps, but I wanted you to have a sense of what this deal offers you," I reply. "The advantages here are enormous."

"I thought the deal was done, Dad," Denise says. "We've been over this again and again. What is there still to debate?"

Geno purses his lips as his shoulders stiffen slightly at her tone. "I'm concerned that there's something missing." His gaze moves from her to me. I don't miss the tapping of his shoe against the floor.

"Geno, I understand," I reply, not letting my frustration show. "Truth is, if I had more time, I'd be happy to run through things with you until we're both sporting long beards. But time is running short."

Geno, who wears a bit of a frost-trimmed beard, tilts his

head. "Oh?"

"A couple of my sources have revealed that relations with one of your factories might thaw soon," I tell him.

"Why's that?"

"They're going under," I tell him blankly.

Denise sits up in her chair and leans forward. "How soon?" she questions.

"There are a lot of balls in the air," I tell her, careful not to discuss matters brought to me by NDAs. Either they'll trust me or they won't. "But if we can sign this here, today, *now*, I can get the company guaranteed contracts with the two largest US based companies who can replace anything that's lost."

Geno licks his lips, his eyes going slightly hazy. In his mind, he sees it. He's been down this road before. But there's still something missing. He wants it all. He wants to cash out, but he also wants to be the man who gets the credit for it all as well, saving a company and earning his wage as CEO.

And probably that big ol' honkin' ribeye too.

"What you're proposing is just such a huge… risk," Geno says, and I chuckle. Intentionally.

"And here I was thinking you know as well as I do that without risk, there's no reward," I comment, slyly calling Geno to the floor. "Geno, you're holding two kings, and the flop's shown a third. Sign this deal, and the only thing that's going to show on the river is that fourth damn king. Now—"

My private phone rings, and I stop, frustrated with myself. If an associate of mine were to *ever* leave their phone on in a meeting and it made the slightest noise, it would be the last meeting they went to.

Yet here I am, making the same mistake. And I know damn well why. I'm distracted by Raven. It can't be denied as I think of her again while turning the ringer silent. Wondering if it was her. Hoping that it is and that she understands.

"My apologies," I offer, resisting the urge to check to see whether or not it's her. I clear my throat and put the phone face down on the table.

"Dylan?" Denise asks, slightly concerned. "Is there a problem?"

"No," I answer, but I notice the quick flick of Denise's eyes to her father. They're worried the disruption has something to do with them. I decide to use the opportunity to apply gentle pressure to get this deal done. And also maybe to give in to the temptation to see if it was actually Raven calling me. "No, but I should check this," I tell them, standing up. "Geno, I'm telling you, sign the contract as it is. No more negotiating. It's in everyone's best interest. I'll give you a few minutes to think about it."

I leave the conference room and go down the hallway to the executive washroom. Only six people in the firm have the electronic tag to get through this door, so I'm able to be alone as I look and see what it is.

The call was from a blocked number, and they left no voicemail. But they did send a text from the same blocked number.

Did you make her suck you off? She's good, right? You're welcome for training her. No hard feelings about the pity fuck, but why the fuck did you bring a no-name climber like her to the event? She's nothing but a slut with good holes. Don't worry, I dealt with it. Like I always do.

Rage instantly consumes me. With heat lingering on the back of my neck, it takes everything in me not to throw the fucking phone. I glance up at the mirror before reading it one more time, adrenaline surging through my veins.

The number might be blocked, but I've been down this road before and know exactly who it's from. That son of a bitch has the balls to send me this?

He makes it sound like we're old buddies talking smack about a woman who's passed around the friend group like a party favor. He's reminding me that he had Raven first. He's putting her down, likely the way he did when they were together, either aloud or in his mind.

He's working an angle to get back at me, I realize.

He's playing the same game I am.

After all, I took Raven to the event to get under Evan's skin and was expecting a counterpunch, especially after his father saw us looking like the aftermath of a porn film. It seems my plan to irritate Evan by shoving Raven under his nose worked... maybe a bit too well. Especially if he's still ruminating on it days later to the point of resorting to frat boy name-calling and veiled threats.

So if my plan worked, why do I feel like shit?

I think back to Friday. I enjoyed spending time with Raven, which is not to be overlooked because fun at a dry charity event is nearly an impossibility, and she was able to meet some heavy hitters. I hope those connections hold steady in the wake of whatever rumors might be swirling as word spread of our actions, but that's out of my control for the moment. And the sex was phenomenal. Her responsiveness, her complete surrender to pleasure, and her beautiful body have permeated my dreams all week.

But then there was the after—when we were spotted, when she wouldn't meet my eyes, when she left.

She did respond to my invitation for dinner, though, I remind myself. That's a good sign.

Unease churns in my stomach. It was my game, and I set up all the pieces on the board, but I feel like I might be the one getting played. By Raven? I don't think so. By Evan? Perhaps. By my own weakness for Raven? Unwilling to admit the hold she has on me, I don't answer myself, not even in my mind.

I glance at the words on my phone once again, reading and then deleting them. I don't want that ugliness on my device where someone else might see it.

I stare at my reflection in the mirror, composing myself. A wounded part of me from the past is elated that Evan knows exactly what Raven and I did, and there's a sick sense of triumph in knowing that it pissed him off. The more mature part of me worries about the 'dealt with it' part of his message. As much as I hate to admit it, he does hold some sway in the district with his family's power. Does he mean that? Or is he referring to something he did Friday? Maybe something that had Raven riled up and ready to hop on my dick with a sudden urgency she hadn't shown all evening.

Fuck. I should've asked what happened when I stepped away. But I was too desperate for her. Regret churns in my stomach. Not for fucking her, but for not considering why she might want to fuck me. I narrow my eyes, staring into my own hard gaze as I mentally chastise myself.

Quickly, I text Raven.

Still on for dinner?

A moment later, her reply begins. *I'm looking forward to it.*

Me too. I want you to know, I don't regret a single minute of what happened.

I hit *Send* before I can doubt my words, because there's more honesty to them than I normally show. Raven's silent for a long time, and I wonder if I've been too forward when she replies, *Me too... mostly. I wish I'd accepted your ride home.*

It makes me smile. *That won't be a problem this time, Miss Hill.*

Her reply is much faster this time. *Then I'm eagerly waiting for the details, Mr. Sharpe. See you at dinner.*

I sigh in relief, slipping my phone into my pocket. Head clear of the lovely distraction of Raven, I mentally return to the other thing I need to deal with.

I go back to the conference room, where Geno and Denise are in deep discussion. "I trust you've had enough time to consider my proposal and are ready to sign," I comment, coming back around the table to push the contract their way.

"My father has one request," Denise says when Geno hems and haws for a moment. "A namesake."

"Namesake?" I ask, and Denise nods. "How so?"

"The minerals we mine," she says, "the copper, the silver, the lithium and palladium, goes into the technology that keeps the world running. We're quite proud of the fact that the copper for the wires that bring electricity throughout our home state are mined in our mines."

"You should be."

"But nobody remembers where the damned wires come from," Geno says hotly. "I'm not saying I want a college named after me or a town or some shit. But as an old man, I'd like *something* with my name on it."

He's old school, thinks his legacy is written in his last name. The truth is, legacy is in what you possess and who you share it with, like his mine and his daughter. The way Denise grits her teeth, looking at me like 'I know, I tried to explain it to him', lets me know that she is better suited than I first thought to be the future company leader.

I nod, confident in my ability to make anything happen. "How about a Miller Hall of Mining at Nevada State? Their campus goals of sustainability go hand in hand with the technology that Miller minerals will provide. Or perhaps the Miller Technological Mineralogy Scholarship?" I offer. "A handful of full-ride scholarships a year, in your name?"

Geno looks at me like I'm insane. "How? That's not in the budget."

"It helps when you own the bank, Geno," I reply. Opening the folder on the table, I turn it around. "So, how about we get this thing handled?"

The two share a look. It's everything they could ever want, and when Geno reaches for his coat pocket, I know I've won. Five minutes later, we're all professional smiles, shaking hands and clapping shoulders as brand-new joint business partners. Including Denise, who'll serve as the incoming CEO of Miller Technological Minerals when Geno's ready to step back.

After a bit of casual conversations, the meeting is adjourned. All the while, my mind is elsewhere. I open the door to escort them on their way, already thinking of the next meeting and the other projects that require my attention. Tamara is at the end of the hall, and I know she'll see them out. "I'll be in touch."

Paperwork firmly in hand, I head back to the office. A few moments later, Tamara appears in my doorway, ready to do her part to wrap up the meeting.

"Tamara, get this to legal," I tell her, handing her the folder. "Miller signed the letter of intent. I want the rest of the contract signed, sealed, and delivered by next Thursday."

"Yes, Mr. Sharpe," Tamara says as she accepts the contracts.

"And get me Richard Benson," I add. "I want full financial projections on what it would take to get a college building built in Henderson, Nevada."

"Planning on a Sharpe School of Business, sir?" Tamara asks wryly, and I smirk.

"No," I reply. "Geno Miller wants to leave his mark on the world."

"Wouldn't we all, sir," Tamara says with a touch of humor, slipping her thinned rimmed glasses on. "I'll run this over to legal before heading to lunch, if you don't mind?"

"Perfect," I assure her. "Thank you."

She closes my office door as she leaves, and the moment I'm alone, work falls away and my thoughts are once again consumed with one thing and one thing only...

Raven Hill.

CHAPTER 11

RAVEN

The clock keeps ticking. Somehow, it's both too fast and not fast enough. There are only a few days remaining until my Saturday night date with Dylan Sharpe. I swallow down the nerves like I've been doing since he messaged me. Just the idea of seeing him again has me twisted up in knots all week, and I can't get away from him in my thoughts. I've dreamed of seeing him again every single night.

All the other nerves, though, are for something else entirely. I can't shake them off. I've made follow-up calls, sent emails, and even had a meeting with one of the people I met Friday night, but each time, the connections have been complete dead ends, and I'm starting to feel like the common denominator is me.

But I'm not giving up. Not yet. Not ever.

I check my phone again as I sit in the conference room

waiting for my next meeting to begin. Dylan told me that this was one of the 'small fish' interviews, but I think that had more to do with the fact that Michael Styles doesn't strike me as friends with Dylan. They're too similar in personalities, two rival companies.

With a steadying inhale, I look up at the sound of smacking oxfords echoing from the hall to my right. The door opens, and Mr. Styles comes in, his tall, commanding presence filling the space. "Miss Hill. Have you been waiting long?"

"No, thank you," I reply, offering a hand as I stand from the chair I was designated by his assistant. We shake, and he sits at the head of the table. He's in his early forties, with a haircut that's clearly touched up by a stylist every other week, a tailored suit that's less than six months old, and a well-done shave. He's the sort of man who takes care of himself. His skin's got the well-hydrated glow of an expensive skin cream, and his hand was baby soft in mine, probably from a recent manicure. "Thank you for seeing me so quickly."

"Well, when you make an impression like you did the other night, I knew that you wouldn't be on the market for long," he says. He smiles, but something about it feels off. "By the way, I talked with our HR department. You put in an application with our firm a year ago?"

"Yes," I reply, reaching into my bag and taking out my updated resume. "I was in business school at the time and was looking for an internship."

"But you weren't interviewed," Michael notes, taking my updated resume from me. "Would you like to make a guess as to why?"

"I know that a firm like this gets dozens, if not hundreds, of applications for every internship spot available. And while I was a top-notch student, with a 4.0 GPA and an impressive senior project portfolio..." I pause, letting those highlights sink in. "When you don't have a prestigious name or a prestigious university name on your application, you're banging on the door from the sidewalk. I assumed you received more applications with Yale or the Wharton School on them than you had opportunities."

Michael hums, neither confirming nor denying my assumption as he gives my resume a cursory glance. "And you didn't reach out here again why?"

The truth is that I've heard the rumors about this firm— their freshman interns and new hires are predominantly three things—white, male, and wealthy, so I focused my efforts on other firms who might be a better fit for me. That's not what I tell Michael, of course. "I wasn't aware you had a position available," I reply. "But I think if you look at my portfolio numbers, you'll see that I more than fit in on your team."

Michael flips to my portfolio, lifting an eyebrow. "The dollar amounts are on the smaller side, but your margins are impressive. Better than some of my current managers, if I'm being honest."

He absolutely just intentionally called me poor, but I'm taking the compliment on my margins because I worked hard for them and have the instincts to make them even better.

"The dollar amounts are low because I didn't have a lot to

work with as an intern," I explain. "You know the old lyric, trying to make a dollar out of fifteen cents?"

"I recall that back from my college days," Michael says, and I feel a bit surprised that he gets the reference.

"I can make a dollar out of my fifteen cents. After our talk the other night, you know I can take ten grand and turn it into a hundred k, and take a hundred k and turn it into a million. That's what I bring to your firm."

"And of course, you'd take your percentage," Michael says with a nod as he meets my gaze, but there's respect in his comment. He knows how this works. The money-makers should make some money of their own.

"If I'm going to make this firm tens of millions of dollars a year, I think it's fair that I can at least afford my own apartment in the city." It's not exactly a compensation package negotiation, but we're both testing our expectations without spelling out 'I want X percentage' or 'I'm offering Y salary.' I add a small smile with the comment, and thankfully, it lands how I hoped it would.

Michael laughs. "I don't know, with the way residential real estate's been going around town, I heard a rumor that the Yankees are having their rookies double up on apartment rent in order to save some cash."

Reading between the lines, he means don't get your hopes too high.

"True, but the commercial market's seen better days," I point out. "A sharp person with the right connections could possibly look at rezoning and turning commercial space into residential space." My return volley lets him know that I'm all too aware that he has the funds to pay so don't lowball me.

"With the right connections," Michael agrees, glancing down at my resume again and then looking back at me as if searching my expression for something. "Such as Dylan Sharpe?"

I tilt my head, acting as if this is an innocent question even though I hear the change in his tone loud and clear. "From what I know of Mr. Sharpe's firm, he's not deeply involved in that particular industry. Actually, many of his investments are located outside the city. What about this firm, though? The opportunity could be lucrative."

"Opportunities are like fresh fruit, though," Michael says. "Jump in too early, and you've got something sour that you've got to wait on. But you buy too late, and you've got a sticky, spoiled mess on your hands."

"It's a good thing this opportunity is being presented at the perfect time, then. Neither sour, nor a mess," I say firmly. "Simply good, money-making investments."

I'm doing my best to keep this meeting on track, without ruining my chances, but I'm getting the feeling Michael is meeting with me, not to hire me, but rather so he can garner favor with Dylan. Like this is a 'favor' he's doing for him.

"You did make quite the impression at the Faulkner event," he surmises.

His eyes skate down my upper body to my hands resting on the table before returning to my face. It happens so fast that if I'd have blinked, I would've missed it. But I didn't. And I know exactly what he's referring to. Bronson Faulkner seeing Dylan and me at the elevator. It has to be.

"Excuse me?"

This is worse than I feared. I'm not here as a 'favor'. I think I'm here so Michael can get a firsthand look at the car crash that's drawn Dylan's attention.

Michael clears his throat. "One's reputation could reflect back on the firm, you understand?"

It's only the sheer force of my determination that keeps me sitting here because I do need this job.

"Reputations are subjective. I prefer to deal in facts. And the facts are, I produce results." I straighten my shoulders and harden my voice. "Look at my resume, and if you want, I'll pull up my accounts so you can see my margins are accurate. I'm not looking to have my name on the door, Michael. Not yet. I'm looking for a desk, a computer, and maybe a cubicle. That doesn't reflect on anyone."

Michael frowns, the deep parentheses lines around his mouth highlighting the downturn of his thin lips. "I see. Well, I'll need to have a few conversations. We'll be in touch."

I keep my smile steady and nod even though turmoil rolls in the pit of my stomach.

We'll be in touch. I've heard those same words too many times this week, delivered in the same way, to not know the meaning. Don't call us, because we're not calling you.

I've blown it. Again.

With the last shred of my self-control, I stand up as he does, shaking his hand politely. But he doesn't look me in the eyes, and his handshake is nowhere near as firm as it was in the beginning. And instead of handing me off to an assistant, he walks me out himself. As we do, I can see the assistants and secretaries glancing at me. A few of them have little smirks, and twice, I see someone bend down to whisper into someone else's ear.

Are they all talking about me?

Have they heard about the fundraising event?

Am I now branded a harlot in the Financial District?

Did I make a mistake the other night?

And maybe most importantly, am I still making a mistake with Dylan?

Michael walks me to the elevator, waiting for the doors to open before saying anything. "It was nice to meet you, Miss Hill. Word of advice? When you're investing everything you have against those merely playing quarter slots, you will always lose. Be careful, Miss Hill." He offers me a tight-lipped smile, seeming significantly less predatory and maybe more… fatherly for a moment.

The doors close, and I can feel the eyes of the other two people on the elevator looking at me. I face directly forward, seeing the warped reflection of my face in the slightly shiny steel doors.

All the while, my heart hammers and my palms turn clammy. I hate everything about all of this. I've never felt so inferior and helpless.

I thought that event was going to be the beginning of something amazing. Connections, contacts, and opportunities, all right in the palm of my hand.

But now, walking out of the building and onto the street, I feel like I've made the biggest mistake of my life. The skyscrapers around me, once staid, solid monuments to the industry that I want to get into, now tower over me like domineering, judgmental figures.

You're not good enough.

You were never good enough.

The only way someone like you gets into an office here is on their knees.

I swallow, realizing I'm almost on the verge of tears. Blinking, I wipe at my eyes and for an instant consider taking a taxi back to my apartment. But I don't have a job yet, and the difference between a taxi ride and the subway is a day's worth of food.

Taking a deep, steadying breath, I turn and walk toward the station I'll need to take me back home. As I walk, I force my chin to stay up and to look like I'm not fleeing from the Financial District.

Getting off the subway, I pause before going home, stopping at the little corner market that I've gotten to know very well over the past few years. Mrs. Hyunh, the owner, is behind the register when I enter, old-fashioned music playing on the radio she keeps under the counter.

"Oh, Raven!" she greets me, waving a wrinkled hand. "You're here early."

"Just a job interview today, Mrs. Hyunh," I tell her, heading toward the back of the store where I know she keeps the Cup

Noodles that are one of my go-to comfort foods. Just before grabbing my favorite, Chili Lime Shrimp, my phone buzzes.

For a stupid moment, hope that it's a job offer rises in my chest, and then disappointment hits me freshly when I realize it's not.

It's Dylan.

Which is a good thing. A great thing. Probably the only thing that could bring the slightest hint of a smile to my face right now.

Do you have a preference for dinner?

My throat tightens as Michael's words flash in my mind. I have truly invested everything and am losing at every turn. No more interviews, no scheduled meetings, no calls to return. So, should I tell Dylan that I can't go out with him?

Dylan, I don't think we should… I start to text before quickly hitting *Delete*.

If I do that, it will have all been for nothing.

And I did truly have fun with Dylan at the event. At least until I freaked out, but he was understanding about that.

Instead I text back, *I am open to whatever you'd prefer. I hope your day is going well. I want to thank you for helping me. Even if it's not in the cards, I appreciate your help.*

Dylan lives up to his last name, and a moment later texts back, *Did something happen?*

I assume he means more than basically being accused of having a reputation for using men by sleeping with them. But I went into things thinking my eyes were open and won't blame him for my actions, however ill-advised they might've been.

No. I just wanted to make sure you knew I was grateful. Regardless of what happens.

Almost as soon as I send the message, his reply comes back as if he was texting even while I was typing. *Let's do dinner tonight instead.*

I can't. Plans.

I can, of course. But I need to get my head straight and do some self-analysis on what happened at the event, and how I feel about it and Dylan. Plus, I have big plans tonight. I'm going to eat Cup Noodles in my pajamas and complain to Maggie about my week. I've earned it after the day I've had.

Okay, Saturday still?

I think for a moment, but ultimately send back, *Yes, Saturday.*

I grab my Cup Noodles. Taking them back up to Mrs. Hyunh, at least I know I've made one good decision today.

CHAPTER 12

DYLAN

I despise working on the weekends.

The stock markets run from Monday to Friday. And while there may be a lot to pack into those days, the entire system is predicated on the simple fact that on Saturdays and Sundays, not too damn much happens.

Sure, there's social power to be gathered, traded on, and banked away. But that's not the same, and if I want to participate, fine. Or if I want to take Saturday morning off and laze on the couch, I can. Not that I ever do something like that. If I'm sitting down, I'm reading, learning, and researching.

Obsessive? Yes, I've never claimed otherwise.

But I have a new obsession—Raven Hill, who's taken a considerable portion of my mental focus this week, so I'm making up for lost time by spending the day in the office.

Glancing up from the computer to the ticking clock, I know I'm simply counting down hours. My shirt is unbuttoned at the neck with my suit jacket draped over the back of my chair. My tapping foot keeps track of the seconds, and it's all far too aggravating.

She gets to me. This woman has some kind of hold over me that I can't ignore.

It's not about Raven's looks. I've come to that conclusion easily enough. As beautiful as she is, and as sensual an aura as she puts off, I haven't been merely distracted by thoughts of how intensely we fucked on that conference room table.

I think it's about the risk.

And out of shared fucking hatred of Evan Faulkner.

But if that's all it was, I'd be thinking of Evan, and I'm definitely not thinking about that asshole. I can't stop thinking about her. What she's thinking about it all. Where she'll be going. What she's doing. So many questions about a woman I should never have slept with.

Every time I consider this evenings' goals, I'm left with conflicting images in my mind. On one hand, there's Raven, the professional businesswoman. Full of potential, and with the skills to make any firm that lands her millions of dollars in her first year. She's the sort of talent that could be signing billion dollar deals by her thirtieth birthday. If her career isn't derailed by Faulkner and his wrath and the bullshit social circles that exist in this business.

On the other hand, I also see Raven in that weak moment,

her eyes large and pleading, her lips swollen from our kiss, and her body needing me and no one else. I hear her sighing my name, coming on my cock, and squeezing me just right. The memory alone makes my cock twitch with need.

It's… disconcerting.

Finally, just after lunch, I give in to the urge I've had all day. Not to jerk off at the memory of her beneath me on that table, but rather to text Raven.

I'll pick you up at 6:30.

I will meet you there, she texts back.

Hesitating, I temper my response. It feels like when she left me at the fundraiser. I can sense her doubts in the few words and don't want to push too hard, too fast.

So I concede, restraining myself. *Okay. 7PM, A Taste of Bangkok.*

It's one of the best Thai restaurants in the state and notoriously difficult to get a reservation for.

Raven sends back a simple *Thank you.*

With that taken care of, I go back to work. Mostly, I decide to use these few hours to figure out how to use my power and influence to check on Faulkner and his bullshit. He hasn't called or sent any more texts, but I know he's up to something. It's his way.

I start with a bit of online snooping. It's amazing what people post these days. You can find out more about a person, a company, and possible situations from their Instagrams than their business websites. Mix that with some society page gossip and pictures and you have a good idea of who's having private dinners with whom.

But I need more, so I send a message to Austin, trusting that he'll keep my inquiry between us.

What's the latest on Faulkner?

While I wait, I try to focus on the stacks of work on my desk. But when my phone pings, I virtually lunge for it before the sound finishes to see what he answers.

Did you fuck Raven at the Faulkner thing? You really know how to blow shit up, huh? Word is, she's getting the polite decline everywhere, courtesy of Evan himself.

Fuck. That's exactly what I was afraid of.

He messaged me. Said he 'dealt with it'. Guess that's what he meant.

I don't answer his question about whether Raven and I had sex. By the sound of it, he already knows the answer.

Now what?

That's the question, isn't it? I set this whole thing into motion, and now, I unexpectedly care about the collateral damage I've caused. I'm having dinner with her tonight.

It's an answer that's more than the sum of its parts. With the few words, Austin now knows that Raven is more than a revenge fuck. He can tell that she means something to me. What that is, I'm not entirely sure just yet.

He sends back a GIF of Coyote trying to light an entire bundle of dynamite on fire with his last match. It feels fairly accurate to what I'm doing.

I don't get any more work done. I spend the next couple of hours sitting and ruminating on ways this can play out. In the end, I know my next move.

I arrive to the restaurant ten minutes early, my driver catching a lucky break in traffic, and take a seat at the intimately-lit table. And once again, I'm lost in thoughts of her and why the hell I can't stop thinking about her.

The sound of heels clicking across the parquet tile floor brings me out of my reverie as a waitress walks up to my table, her smile bright and welcoming. "Would you like something to drink while you wait, sir?" she asks, her pen poised over her notepad.

"Bourbon, neat."

The waitress says something, but I don't hear a damn word, because at that moment, I see her. Raven.

The form-fitting black dress hugs her curves in the most tempting of ways, her hair cascading down her back in shiny waves to match with the rest of her outfit. She strides toward me, carrying herself with an air of confidence as a soft smile plays at her glossy lips.

I stand to greet her, desperately wanting to wrap my arms around her, needing to kiss her, and seriously considering pushing her back to the closest surface to slam balls-deep into her. I settle for pulling her chair out for her.

"Raven, you look beautiful," I say quietly.

Her smile grows, but as her green eyes meet mine, I see something that makes me question how this night will go.

She's nervous. It's the same look that I saw before the fundraiser, where she's attempting to be cool, calm, and collected. But she's clearly feeling what I'm feeling, uncertainty, and is only holding things together through guts and brains.

As she takes her seat, she thanks me and then turns her attention to the waitress.

"Would you like a moment or do you know what you'd like to drink?"

"A glass of the Calafuria Rose," Raven answers quickly after scanning the menu.

As soon as the waitress walks away, I look at Raven and, in an attempt to quiet her nerves, offer her what I should have when I first met her.

"Are you ready to come work for me?" I question, loving the slight shock in her widening eyes. "The position's yours."

I expect Raven to be grateful. Relieved, almost. This is the only way I can imagine correcting the situation I've thrust her into.

I use people. It's a way of life at my professional level. I play chess with lives, using people as pawns. You fuck with me, I crush your company. I've broken reputations when it was warranted, and I've elevated others when it served me. But never have I put someone at risk the way I have Raven, and this odd feeling in my chest is uncomfortable.

Is it guilt?

That seems most likely. In this particular chess game, I've sacrificed her to save the king—myself. It was somewhat unintentional, but the fallout is the same, regardless.

But I can save her. Fix this. She only needs to say 'yes'.

Instead, Raven folds her hands in her lap, giving me a look that would make a professional poker player nod in admiration. Only her eyes betray her emotions. "I'm not sure that would be a good idea, Dylan."

"No?" I ask, surprised myself. She's turning me down?

It's a splash of ice-cold water in my face. But at the same time, it's intriguing, and I find myself wanting her more. She has to know what's happening. She's not that fucking naive.

The more I stare at her across the table, the more I want her to give in and trust me. Take the position and let me fix this.

I guess it is true, you chase what you can't get. I just need this to be a very short chase. My reputation is also on the line.

"You're struggling," I tell her bluntly. "If I'm getting the whispers, then you're getting it worse. Am I wrong?"

Raven swallows, and I see her bottom lip tremble. She murmurs her response, "No."

"Tell me about what you've been through since the event," I instruct her. "How many interviews have you been to?"

"Just three," she admits. "Mr. Styles was the last. It wasn't productive."

I nod, not letting my anger show. Michael Styles wishes his firm were in my position. Hell, the way the man cheats on his wife with both his mistress and his wife's friend on the side, he probably wishes that he were in my position with Raven the other night as well.

"Only three?" I question, hating the way anger brews inside me. She nods, and I swirl the glass of bourbon, hating this.

My intention was to help her and show Evan he was nothing, and that he couldn't fuck her over like he's done so many other times. Instead, he's winning. All because I couldn't keep my dick in my pants for the few minutes it would've taken to get an actual room at the hotel.

"And the others?"

"Two flat out cancellations, and Ollie's delayed our meeting until next week," she says. Of course Ollie did. That's unrelated to Evan's machinations, but Raven doesn't know that. I could tell her that Ollie took a quick flight out to check an investment in Wyoming and ease her mind, but instead, I keep quiet, letting her think that I'm her only option.

Does it make me an asshole? No. It makes me a shrewd businessman. And that's what this is. In this moment, this is just business between the two of us, me hiring a new prospect.

"So accept my offer," I tell her. "At my firm, no one is going to say a goddamn thing. And if you can produce as well as your resume says and as well as you talked at the party, then in five years, nobody's going to give a shit about a rumor."

Raven shifts around, clearly uncomfortable. "It's not just that. Dylan, what we did that night was… fun," Raven explains, heat coloring her high cheekbones. She looks away for a moment, and I bite my tongue, preventing myself from teasing her for the word 'fun' to describe what happened between us. "It was everything that I needed at that moment… but it was not a good decision for my career, and I can't imagine working for you would…"

She struggles to express herself, letting out a frustrated sigh.

"I imagine you have concerns about working for me further hurting your reputation?" I surmise.

"Correct," she answers with a grateful nod that I understand as her wine is delivered quietly by the waitress. She accepts it and immediately takes a gulp.

"Raven, I'm not saying there haven't been consequences to what happened. Admittedly, more for you than me. But consider this. What am I getting out of making this offer to you? What advantage does it give me? Because that's the bottom line in this business."

"You're not a charity, so don't treat me like a charity case," Raven hisses, anger showing for the first time, and I'm glad. I want her this way, not feeling sorry for herself but trying to figure out her best path forward. It's a tough lesson in the Financial District, but in some ways, it's a good thing she's getting it so early in her career. "And I know what you want. You want a second go around… in a different location."

I don't bother refuting her comment. Because I would love to put my face between her legs and have more than one go around. I haven't fucked her out of my system yet… obviously.

"I think I could have that without offering you a job, Raven," I tell her bluntly, and her mouth drops open in offense. Before she can tell me to fuck off, I say, "I think I could because you can't deny that you came harder than you ever have in your life when we were fucking on that table. You can't deny that as pissed off as you might feel right now, there's another part of you that's wondering what it would be like to go back to my place and let me explore your body in all the ways you deserve, and in all the ways Evan never would. Tell me when I say something untrue."

Raven attempts to say something but swallows whatever she was going to say down. Her restraint is both infuriating and admirable.

"You've been thinking about me all week," I venture. "Not what I could offer your career, but what I made you feel, and greedily, you want it again. And again. And again." I say it as though promising orgasms, sex, repeated rounds of anything and everything she could possibly dream of, and her breath hitches.

She squares her shoulders. "Then why are you offering me the position?"

Smart girl. I basically just told her I want to fuck her as much as humanly possible, which isn't the best start of a professional, business-only relationship. It's not the worst start either, but still...

"Because one thing hasn't changed," I tell her. "You're one of the largest unrecognized talents I've seen in years." She narrows her eyes, measuring my complimentary words against any signs that I might be lying. "Do you actually think I'd risk my firm for sex? Do you think me that corrupt, or yourself that cheap?"

Raven licks her lips and takes a deep breath. "No."

"Then recognize yourself. And recognize that regardless of any attraction we might have for each other, your dream job was working at my firm," I tell her. "That's undeniable."

Raven leans forward, cradling her chin with her fingers. "You promise me this isn't just because you want to fuck again?"

I can see her considering it—the position and the fucking. But the job is winning out... for now.

"This job offer is just business," I assure her. "Raven, as a woman, you are… tempting. But if you choose, I can keep my hands to myself. Just say the word."

Raven laughs, a beautiful sound that's only slightly tinged by bitterness over her situation. I could listen to it for hours, even if she's laughing at me. "You're leaving the choice in my hands? Dylan, I suspect you don't give anyone a choice in anything, ever. Not in business, not in life."

I can't explain why the comment cuts me as deep as it does. "You think I'm that manipulative?"

She doesn't hesitate to answer. "I think you're that controlled."

I allow the observation to soothe over whatever the hell it is that I'm feeling because the last thing I've felt lately is controlled. I've felt preoccupied, distracted, manic, even desperate. But she doesn't need to know that. It puts too much power in her hands, power I'm not ready to let her know she holds over me.

As I consider my response, she seems to realize that she's wounded me and says, "I don't think you're manipulative, Dylan. But if we're in the same building day in and day out …"

She doesn't finish, and she doesn't have to. I know exactly what she's saying.

I keep the conversation on point. "I think just business means a starting salary that's in the six figures, with a performance package that'll get you where you want to be in life faster than anyone else."

Her eyes catch mine, and I know she's mine. At least professionally-speaking.

"Just business?" she nearly whispers, sounding hopeful.

I nod, needing her to take the job. If she does, she'll be able to create the portfolio that will transcend any rumors about the beginning of her career. She'll be able to build her reputation to the point that her abilities will be undeniable. It might take four or five years, but eventually, the industry will see her for her talents.

But if she goes out there, still trying to find a place with these landmine interviews, Evan will be able to blow up her career permanently. He has the name and the power to do so, and that's the last thing I want. I'd have won the night's battle, and he'll have won the fucking war.

And having Raven close by could have its advantages beyond the purely physical ones that have haunted my mind, my dreams, and my body.

The fact is, at the event, she made a number of great points during various conversations. She has insight on some of the social trends that are shaping the business world today and could provide a fresh perspective that a lot of the silver spoon set in the Financial District would never see. In a world and industry where trends run like schools of fish, being able to get a different point of view can be the difference between being average and being exceptional.

Raven studies the wine in her glass, running the tip of her perfectly manicured finger around the rim before stroking up and down the stem of the glass in a way that has me hard as a fucking rock. I readjust in my seat, ignoring the voice screaming in the back of my head that there is no fucking way I could see this woman day in and day out and not want to bend her over my desk. Her lips twitch. She knows what she's doing.

She's testing me, more than likely thinking the same thoughts.

"I'll make you a counteroffer," she finally says, forcing me to tear my eyes away from her stroking fingers and back to her face. "If we can get through dinner with everything being entirely professional, not a single mention of appearance, attraction, or sex… I'll accept your offer."

"Just dinner?" I clarify, and she nods. I lean back, smirking as I pick up my bourbon and take a sip, as though seriously contemplating her offer. "I'm almost insulted. Do you think I'm some dick-driven asshole who is unable to think of anything other than what's under your dress?"

Raven chuckles weakly and picks up her wine glass. Before saying anything, she takes a sip that almost seems like she's kissing the rim of her glass. Underneath the table, my cock twitches in my pants. But hard or not, my expression remains slightly impassive.

"And what is under my dress?" she virtually purrs.

"You're breaking your counteroffer mighty early, darling." I love how she smiles at the nickname and blushes, looking down as she tucks a lock of hair behind her ear.

She looks me dead in the eyes, a smoldering want reflecting in her gorgeous gaze as she whispers, "You haven't accepted it yet."

"Agreed," I tell her, leaning forward. "I think that under your dress, you're wearing lingerie that some part of you wants to be seen in. I think that since you've sat down, even as upset and conflicted as you've been, you're feeling a warmth building between your legs. And I think that every time you glance down, you're remembering what I have under the table, and that desire gets just a bit more maddening."

Raven's breath catches. "That's why this is a bad idea."

I force my voice to steady, my face to go neutral, leaving no trace of the words I spoke mere moments ago. By all appearances, I am the powerhouse at the head of my own conference table leading a hard-fought contract negotiation. "Miss Hill, I accept your counteroffer starting now. Just business, nothing more, nothing less. I'm certain you will be an asset at my firm and that you are smart enough to agree."

I hold my hand out over the table, waiting for her to shake on it.

She hesitates, and there's a moment where I think she might actually turn me down, but eventually, she smiles as she shakes my hand.

Over her wine and my bourbon, followed by a light, tasty Thai meal, we discuss business.

We discuss recent trends in various markets and deals I made because of those trends. Raven tells me how she would have acted in each situation, and more importantly, asks what and why I did what I did on these deals. Once again, I'm left impressed by what Raven's been able to do in such a short amount of experience, and more importantly, without the advantage of being born to money and bred to understand how the market works.

After a wonderful dessert of khao mao tod, a fried coconut

and banana fritter type thing that's absolutely the perfect end to our meal, I hand the waitress my credit card. "I really should do Thai food more often," I tell Raven.

"There's a Thai noodle place near my apartment, nowhere near the atmosphere as this," she says, glancing around the restaurant, "but they've got a dozen desserts that are worth the trip."

When the waitress brings back my card, Raven thanks me for dinner.

I reach into my pocket, pulling out my phone and tapping for a moment. "Your car is out front."

Her brow furrows. "What?"

"I called a car for you. I promised you that I would be professional tonight. And while my original plan was to drive you home, calling you a car is the better, more professional option."

I can see that she appreciates the gesture. Even if she sees right through it.

The truth is, there were plenty of elements of tonight that have been more like a date than a business meeting. Even though we've been focused on everything but the attraction we feel for each other and have talked numbers and business strategies, this still feels to me like a date.

When the driver messages, I walk Raven out front, opening the door for her. "You never answered my question."

Raven pauses, looking at me curiously. "Your question?"

"I believe we have met the terms of your counteroffer, so do you accept the position at my firm?"

"Just business?" she clarifies again.

I give her a thin-lipped smile. "That is the agreement."

She smiles in a way that soothes every nerve in me and steps closer to me than is professionally-acceptable. Even the small concession of our agreed-upon boundaries has my cock straining.

As if she knows exactly what she's doing to me, she says, "Yes, I accept. See you Monday morning, Mr. Sharpe. Thank you for a wonderful evening."

I'm frozen in place as she climbs into the car and it pulls away. I watch the red taillights turn the corner, swallowing.

There's no fucking way I'm going to be able to keep it just business between us.

CHAPTER 13

RAVEN

My heart hammers, excitement and fear course through my veins, and my nerves tingle as I step into the Baxter building, the skyscraper that houses Dylan's hedge fund. Any other time I've visited buildings like this before, it's always been for interviews. And it's always the same—sign in at the front desk, take a seat in the lobby, and get the side eye from everyone as if they can sense I don't belong. Or at least, that's what my mind tells me they're thinking.

This time, there's more than a little something different about being surrounded by the polished floors, pristine glass walls, and sleek chrome accents. This time, I know that it's going to become my building, and as I approach the modern reception area, I'm impressed by every little detail, from the architecture to the decor.

"Hi there, you can sign in here." A petite woman with an upbeat tone and wide smile cuts through my thoughts from her seat behind the large desk that spans at least ten feet.

"Hi. I'm Raven Hill. I'm starting at Sharpe Fund Management," I tell her. I didn't realize how incredible it would feel to say that out loud. I have to resist the urge to pump my fist and do a little happy dance after scribbling my name down. "First day."

"Welcome," the young woman says, giving me my temporary badge for the elevator as she points across the lobby to it. "They should get you an official employee badge today, so just drop this one off on the way out."

"Thank you very much." I answer her smile with one of my own and then nod. "I will do that."

Swallowing down my nerves, I focus on only the positives and not my clammy hands and racing heart.

I'm starting my new job. This is the moment I've worked for.

I clip the badge to the waistband of the skirt I obsessed over last night when I was getting ready. I needed something conservative, professional, and that says 'trust me with your money.' And after way too long, I finally decided on a knee-length black pencil skirt. A classic. I stuck with the theme, choosing a tailored button-down blouse that's a baby's breath of blue above white, and black high heels. A tasteful watch, stud earrings, and my leather bag complete my outfit.

I even woke up a super-grumpy Maggie at dark-thirty this morning to confirm that I look perfect. I'm walking into the lion's den, but I'm certainly not going to give them ammunition by showing up in something less than beyond reproach.

The elevator up to the forty-second floor is whisper quiet, with no music and barely even the hum of the elevator's mechanics audible inside the large, well-lit car. It makes the cargo elevator at my apartment look like a death trap… which it honestly might be, if I remember when the last inspection sticker was dated.

Taking a deep breath as the numbers tick upward, I steady myself. This is an unparalleled opportunity for me, and I can't afford to ruin it. I know there's more to Dylan's offer than just business, or a healthy amount of greed. I know that he wants me, and honestly, he was right on Saturday night. I want him too. I was still hot and bothered when I got back to my apartment, and I was only able to get myself to sleep with the help of my vibrator.

It doesn't matter. I'm going to prove myself. *Stay focused on the mission, Raven.*

All of the confidence I manage to delude myself into thinking I have is lost the moment I think about everyone else I'll meet on the forty-second floor. If America runs on Dunkin, offices run on gossip, and the idea that everyone is going to accept me based on my performance is pretty much a fairy tale.

I'm sure that people at the firm will know I was on Dylan's arm at the Faulkner charity event, and some have probably heard that Dylan and I fucked. My stomach dropping has nothing to do with the speed of the elevator's rise.

But I'm going to prove myself, starting with them.

I repeat the mantra to myself, letting my fears move into the background, replaced by steely determination and excitement about the chance I get today. When the elevator doors open, revealing a spacious and bustling office with employees moving about without even sparing a newcomer a glance, I'm awestruck.

I'm here.

One deep breath in, and I force my giddy grin to morph into a professional smile as I approach the receptionist's desk.

"Hi, Raven Hill," I greet the receptionist, and a few minutes later, I'm introduced to Juliana Reed, the head of Human Resources. "Thank you for helping me this morning."

"Actually, I won't be doing much," Juliana says, leading me past a line of desks.

The furniture is all high-end and expensive, with sleek but comfortable looking leather chairs, dark wood desks, and massive computer monitors. The walls are adorned with various awards and accolades, along with photos of Dylan and other high-profile figures.

Juliana is tall and thin, with long pin-straight, dark hair. "I've got a state comptroller inspection today, and the SEC will be stopping by later this week. So you'll be doing most of your onboarding yourself." She talks while walking and hardly looks my way as she leads me to what's apparently my space. "Don't worry, I'll get you logged on and set up, though."

It's essentially a cubicle, but my reaction is as though it's a corner office on the top floor. At least inside, where I'm basically doing backflips. Outside, I smile politely at Juliana as I scan the small area. The desk is L-shaped, clearly designed to be functional and make the most of the space, with a pair of computer screens on top of it. There's a large, comfortable looking 'executive' style office chair pushed beneath the desk, but looking around, I don't see anything else. "Where's the computer?"

"You'd be amazed at how small a work computer can be nowadays," Juliana says, tapping a box not much larger than my fist underneath the monitor in the corner. "This'll handle everything you need. Try out your chair."

The leather chair might as well be a throne as far as I'm concerned.

"Okay, here's your username, but you need to pick out your password," Juliana says, taking a wireless keyboard out of the desk drawer and sliding it over to me. I put in my chosen password, and Juliana takes the keyboard back. "There's a wireless mouse in here too, but this keyboard's got a trackpad in it if it breaks."

Juliana points to my larger computer screen.

"All of what you need to know will be here. Just follow along with the website I'm pulling up. It's an internal one that doesn't connect outside the firm," she says as she clicks on the screen, and I watch carefully, not wanting to miss a thing. "Once you complete onboarding, you'll get wider permissions."

She looks at me expectantly, making sure I'm following along with her rapid-fire pace, and I nod.

"Good. Next, lockers."

Juliana walks away, and I rush to follow her over to the wall opposite my cubicle. She taps on an inlaid door, where a card scanner is set into the panel.

"Every cubicle and office has one of these," she explains, handing me an employee badge with my name already printed on it. "You can keep your purse, snacks, or whatever in it and it's secure. Although if you want to bring your own lunch, there's a fridge down the hall. You hold your card up to the scanner, wait for the chimes, and it unlocks." I do as she instructs and hear the lock disengage. "Your card won't work on any door but your own," she says, gesturing toward the other lockers on the wall, "but the head of Security, me, and Mr. Sharpe have all-access to any locker, at any time."

I nod, but she doesn't notice because she looks at the smartwatch on her wrist, reading a message. "Shoot, the inspector's early." She glances back at me. "You good? I showed you your locker, work on your onboarding, and the bathroom is down the hall to the left, which will be covered in the Unit One building introduction. Yeah?" she looks at me hopefully.

I smile, thinking I'm going to like Juliana. She's busy, but no-nonsense. "I'm good. I'll check in with the receptionist if I have any problems."

She walks away at a fast clip, and I realize I'm an actual employee of Sharpe Fund Management.

Internally, I squeal in delighted excitement. Once more, I hold my card up to the scanner, wait for the chimes and the lock to disengage, and then open it, expecting it to be empty.

I'm surprised when I see a small white box on the upper shelf, right above the bar that's meant for a coat or my bag. *Open me.*

My heart does that racing, pounding thing again… and I

look to my left and right as if someone may be watching. And though there are people at their own desks, and in their cubicles and offices, everyone is heads-down, working. Curiously, I take the box out of my locker and return to my desk. As soon as I flip open the top, I have to smile.

The note on the underside of the lid reads,

A little congratulations. I'm looking forward to working with you.—*Dylan*

It's a single, fancy chocolate. A truffle, maybe? I wonder if he does this for every new employee. I could see that, considering how much attention he seems to have paid to everything, from comfort to security. But deep down, I know he doesn't do this for everyone. He did it for me.

I'm not sure how I feel about that. It feels almost as though he's testing the waters with me already. *Or maybe it's an olive branch*, I tell myself.

With a smile firmly in place, I put the box of chocolate and my bag on the desk—no, not *the* desk—on *my* desk and get to work, letting the excitement outweigh everything else.

I quickly put the rest of my personal things away. I didn't bring much, just a tiny little potted plant that's in a coffee mug, which fits perfectly next to one of my monitors. A simple notepad, and set of skinny black luxe pens. And that's it for the moment. The rest of my desk I'm keeping bare. I don't want to settle in until I've earned it.

And I get to work.

"Knock, knock."

I look up, and I can't help the heat that rises from the tips of my toes all the way up to my cheeks when I see Dylan standing in the doorway of my cubicle, his wide shoulders filling most of the open space.

He really is devilishly handsome. His suit is on point, as I expect, a well-fitting gray that makes him look approachable but still powerful. His patterned blue tie is knotted perfectly at the neck, and it definitely gives him sexy boss vibes. Swallowing down the emotions brewing, and the desire that's instantly ignited by his presence, I greet him professionally but warmly.

"Good morning, Mr. Sharpe."

"Miss Hill, how are things going this morning?"

"Very well," I answer, feeling like there's more to the question than there should be. "I met Juliana, who walked me through onboarding, which is what I've been working on. If I maintain my pace, I should be finished in about thirty minutes. I thought I could check in on the Chicago commodities market? Unless there's something else?"

Business only. Nothing weird or personal or intimate happening here.

Other than the CEO of the company stopping by my desk on my first day. And the tension cracking between us as he grins at my desperate attempt to give a concise report of the last two hours of my morning. And my heart racing when he offers me an asymmetrical smile.

"That's fine," Dylan says. "Tell you what, do some starter trading for me and we'll see how you do. What do you say we start you with… a million dollars?"

I gawk, nearly choking on my tongue. "Mr. Sharpe, I know that this firm controls a lot and it's numbers on a screen, but… are you sure?"

Dylan stares at me, his eyes warm but hard.

This is a challenge, a test.

"I am. That nervousness shows me you understand the weight of your responsibilities. Too many new hires come into the business thinking that they're just doing a big boy version of fantasy stock market trading. To them, it's like playing online poker for free, or fantasy football."

"This isn't a nickel ante game, though," I point out, and Dylan nods.

I understand, and that's part of the test. On one hand, this is just like playing around on the fantasy markets. The goal is to get 'points'. And I need to relax in order to make the most points. On the other hand, these points are real dollars. There are consequences for fucking around. This million dollars could mean multiple people's life savings. I could help them retire early or put them into an early grave with losses.

This is the exact reason I want to be in this business. I want to make a meaningful difference for people who put their hard-earned dollars in my hands. One steadying breath in, and I wipe my palms on my skirt.

"Okay, I'll do my best," I tell him.

Dylan steps back, giving me an evaluating look. "Good. I expect nothing less. How about you stop by my office at the end of the day, then? Say, six o'clock. I would like an update on your gains and losses."

His professional tone never changes. If anyone overheard him, they wouldn't think an inappropriate thing about it. But I see the fire in his eyes and can see the smirk pulling at his lips. And I definitely don't miss the way his gaze scans my face, lingering on my lips when I lick them, suddenly feeling very dry in some places and very wet in others.

Six o'clock will likely be after most people have left, but it could still be seen as a professional meeting. But I don't think it will be.

My heart rampages in my chest, and it has nothing to do with the million dollars he's letting me play with. I don't know if I'll be able to resist him if he wants more. I don't know if I want to resist him.

"Yes, sir. Six o'clock. I'll have the figures for you," I agree. "Thank you," I say, touching the corner of the box of chocolate, so he knows I'm thanking him for the opportunity, the trust, as well as the gift.

"Till then," Dylan says before leaving me to get back to work.

I finish up my onboarding, and as soon as I do, my system reboots. When it comes up this time, I've got a full, real-time connection to multiple markets, and under my unique account identifier, I see the figure. $1,000,000.

A million dollars.

It's madness. It's too much. It's everything I've ever dreamed of. Swallowing thickly, I pull up the Chicago commodities market and get to work. Luckily, I've kept my finger on the pulse of the market even when it was just 'fantasy stock trading', and I have some personal investments already in place, but this is different in more than mere scale.

Clicking through options, I look for what I want—stable for most, but some risks. Not too risky, though. I've never liked to gamble, really, which some might consider odd, given what I want to do. But this isn't gambling if you know what you're doing, or it shouldn't be. It should be about using research, experience, and knowledge more than your gut instincts or hopeful hunches.

And though I work hard, my gaze keeps flicking to the clock… counting down the hours until I'm in Mr. Sharpe's office.

CHAPTER 14

DYLAN

"If you don't mind, I'm going to head home," Juliana says as she closes the cover on her tablet. She's one of the few members of the firm who've been around since day one of this business. She was the second person I ever hired, and unlike the first, I'm grateful I hired her when I did.

She lets out a heavy breath as she swings her purse over her shoulder. Her phone in hand has her attention for a moment before she says, "My daughter's got a science fair to prepare for, and that means I have a science fair to prepare for." A huff of a laugh leaves me as I nod in acknowledgement.

I like Juliana. She's a mother who's done a good job of juggling career and family success. She knows how to balance, and part of that is not settling. "Of course. How is she doing, anyway? She's a junior now?"

"And already getting letters from schools trying to recruit

her," Juliana says with more than a hint of pride. My smile widens for her, and I wave her off.

"I'll see you tomorrow. You can tell me about the rest of the state comptroller visit in the morning."

I've already dismissed her in my mind, returning my attention to the deal I was working on before she came in. It's a complex venture, one I haven't decided on investing in yet, mostly because what they're creating sounds like science fiction. I mean, computer networks built along plant-based highways, information passed along DNA strands? Paper thin computers that can outperform modern high-end laptops yet be rolled up into a tube and powered by the equivalent of a solar cell phone charger? That's game changing advancements right there. It's wildly outlandish, but also, if even one of their projects comes to fruition, the return on investment will be in the trillions.

"Sounds good," Juliana says, and I glance up at her tone. She cuts her eyes to the door.

"Tamara's gone for the day. Say what you want to," I tell her, leaning back in my chair.

"Your new acquisition," she says with an arched brow. "I have a feeling she'll do well here."

"Did you check up on her?" I ask. "You were busy with the inspector, no?"

She gives me a wry look. She's known around the office as 'Sharpe's Razor' for a reason. She has little to no time nor inclination for bullshit or niceties. Straight to the point, getting things done is how Juliana manages everything in her purview.

"We both know she comes with baggage," Juliana says bluntly, acknowledging that she's aware of the rumors. "She did well, though. When I went downstairs, the markets had just closed and she was picking the other traders' brains, wanting to know how they do things the 'Sharpe Way'. She seems eager to fit in, learn, and make you a lot of money. Don't fuck it up for her, Dylan."

"Noted," I say stiffly. Juliana is calling me to the carpet as a friend, and as the head of my HR department, which is what I pay her to be, so I can't be too upset.

Having said her piece, she leaves, ranting about science project hypotheses and results charting.

Over the next hour, I find myself checking the clock more often than not, unable to get Raven off my mind and certainly not understanding the nuances of DNA splicing in the report I'm trying to read.

Finally, at exactly six o'clock, there's a knock on my door, and I'm surprised by the intense sense of relief I feel. I think there was a part of me that worried she wouldn't come.

"Come in," I call out, and when the door opens, I'm spellbound. She's utterly captivating. Raven comes in, closing the door behind her, and takes a seat in the chair across from me. Instantly, I'm hard. Fuck.

With my hands clasped together, I put them on the desk and ignore every impulse that begs me to sit her on my desk, push that conservative skirt up her thighs, spread her legs, and get my fill. Clearing my throat, I ask, "So, how was your first day?"

"I feel like I ran the gamut today," Raven jokes, letting out a held breath but managing a smile. "Restarting my computer after completing my firm onboarding, pulling up the trading software, and seeing that one and six zeroes freaked me out a bit at first, I'll admit."

"Is that why you only spent a quarter of it on soy futures?" I ask, and Raven lifts an eyebrow. "I was keeping tabs on you, just in case." Rather than seem offended, she relaxes slightly. As if my oversight could keep her from making any major missteps. "I can check on any of the traders or trading at my discretion. I simply kept yours up on a background screen today." I gesture to one of my monitors.

The truth is, I rarely check on the individual traders or their trades. It's like worrying about a single rain drop while swimming in the ocean. But I watched Raven today, interested to see what she did and trying to figure how her mind works.

"Then did you see that I put the funds out the way I did to create an integrated investment system, the pieces interlocking with each other?"

I lean back in my seat, rocking slightly. "I did. I like the way you think."

Her eyes light up with the compliment. Fucking hell, she's even more gorgeous when she smiles. I swear, this woman put a fucking spell on me.

"And your plan is to use what's not the minimum maintenance to shift the engine each rotation," I conclude, and Raven nods. "A very gestalt idea. Most traders would just juice the engine."

"If you're looking for a quarterly bump, sure," Raven says. "But this system will create wealth for a generation. With a bit more tweaking, and applying this idea to other cycles, multiple generations. Already, I've made more profit than I got paid in the past twelve months."

I turn, pulling up Raven's account and seeing the figures. "You were underpaid."

"Maybe, but this is just the start. I'll get better, I know it."

"I'm sure you will too," I reply.

That's it. She's given me the report of her figures for the day, and I should let her go.

But I can't. I won't. Not yet.

Thinking quickly, I glance at my monitor, seeing the report I was trying to make heads or tails of for the last hour. "I'd like your take on this," I tell her, waving her around to my side of the desk. "It's a deal I'm considering with Dexstrom."

She gets up, her hips swaying as she comes to stand beside me. Her eyes are wary, like she can read the duality of my intentions. Sure, any help I can get with this gibberish would be appreciated, but getting Raven closer to me is what I want.

She's so close I can feel her warmth. I can smell her perfume. The tension crackles, and I ignore it. Just like I ignore my cock.

"Bleeding edge tech," she says, leaning over to look at my screen more closely as she starts to look through the slide show I've watched a half-dozen times. I don't know if she realizes it, but it puts her right breast within mere inches of my forearm. Glancing at my other monitor, she sees the numbers. "Seventeen million… not a lot, in your eyes?"

"No," I reply, my voice slightly raspy. Professional? All I want to do is turn my hand, tease her breast, and ravish her body like it deserves. "What more do you see?"

Raven pushes in closer. "You mind?" she asks, gesturing toward the mouse.

I back up, giving her space and trying to prevent an issue as she reaches across me, taking control of the tiny arrow on the screen.

And though she's driving me insane, Raven doesn't seem to notice. She's intently focused, peering at my monitors, her head only moving when she switches from one to the other. Worse, with her completely distracted, I let my eyes trace down her body… the nape of her neck, her shoulder, her hip, the length of her leg. With barely a tug, I could bring her skirt up and bury my face in paradise, my tongue stroking her pussy until she screams my name.

Business, Dylan. It's just business.

"From a strictly business perspective, the short term outlooks are break even at best," she says, pointing at the screen, and I force my gaze to follow where she's indicating even though I have the whole thing nearly memorized at this point. "Their P&L looks atrocious in that regard. But on the other hand…"

"Yes?" I whisper, my voice catching as I have to physically restrain myself from reaching out and touching her. "Raven."

She stops and looks from the computer to me, and it's more than obvious from her change in expression that she knows exactly what I've been thinking. Her shoulders square as she stands up straighter, but she doesn't move away from me. She's still so close.

"I have a confession to make," she says, not nearly as confidently as she just was, but she pins me with her green eyes, unafraid of me, at least. "I was worried all day about whether I could actually work here."

"Why?" I ask, and Raven licks her lips. My tone is more stern when she doesn't immediately answer. "Why, Miss Hill?" I use her last name intentionally, putting space between us even if it's only verbally.

"Today has been amazing. It's everything I hoped it would be. But…" She trails off, glancing off to the side, and I lift my brows expectantly, bidding her to go on. "I spent too much time thinking about you." Her eyes return to mine, temptation stirring in them.

"And what did you think about me?" I demand, needing the answer more than I need air.

She doesn't answer. Well, not with words. But she tenses her thighs together, nearly scissoring them as she searches for relief. Just like that, I know I'm going to fuck her tonight. I'm going to fuck her like she wants me to… like I want to.

The temperature in the room rises. Or maybe it's only the heat building in my body. Either way, I'm on fire for her, and I haven't laid a hand on her yet.

"Raven," I say sternly, "Understand that this has nothing to do with your work. You did a great job today and can continue to do so. Even if you walk out that door right now."

She glances at the closed door, not moving. I scoot back from my desk, creating room so she can stand in front of me.

"Here?" she whispers. "I think poor location choice was our downfall last time." Rather than the horror I know she felt then and probably still feels about the aftermath, she sounds unsure at best.

With the push of a button, the door locks remotely, the sound filling the room. "Worst case scenario, I have a private exit that can take us to the parking garage. It's a long way down, but it can be done. And everyone leaves by six-fifteen at the latest, other than me and the custodial crew."

I'm trying to allay her fears. I'm also trying to distract her as I pull her between my spread thighs by her hips.

Raven's eyes stay on me as I knead the rich swells of her ass, rub my hands down her legs, and tease the hem of her skirt higher. She moans softly, her breath catching as I find the zipper and undo it. With each tooth, her skirt relaxes slightly until it falls down her thighs to puddle at her feet.

"I have a confession too," I tell her as I inhale her scent. "I spent all day the same way, wanting you more with each passing moment."

I squeeze her ass, running my hand along the curve and down the edge of her panties to between her legs. Her mound is hot and her panties damp in the center. A tiny shudder works its way through her at the barest touch. Fucking hell, she's intoxicating.

"Wanting me for what?" she whimpers as my fingers begin massaging her.

It seems there is still one concern I haven't addressed.

"Raven, I don't do this," I tell her, emphasizing my words with circular strokes over her clit through the thin, soaked lace. "I'm not seeing anyone else. I'm not fucking anyone else. I don't give a shit if everyone knows about us." She gasps, and I don't think it's about what my fingers are doing. "Or we can keep this between us for your sake. You work, you make money, you make me money. And we fuck. We help each other relax at the end of the day. You want that, darling?"

Her legs part, seemingly unconsciously, and I grin, knowing her answer before she does. "Dylan."

I look up to find her cheeks flushed, her mouth already open as she pants slightly, her eyes glassy. She doesn't say anything else, but there's a Shakespeare's monologue worth of hopes, dreams, promises, and threats in her green gaze.

I dip my chin, in agreement with it all. "Turn around." I guide her to spin in place and lean over the desk, giving me her ass, and when she arches sharply, her pussy.

I pull her panties to the side, feeling like I'm in fucking heaven. Office fantasies come to life, and wishes are fulfilled. Slipping a finger into Raven's tight pussy, we both gasp as her warm tightness envelops my finger and I stroke her inner walls. I know I hit that sensitive spot the moment she covers her mouth with her hand and tries to stifle her moans.

Fuck, I love playing with her, toying with her like she was made for my enjoyment. I lean back, enjoying the view and needing to prolong it.

"Keep telling me about your analysis," I tell Raven as I withdraw my finger. With my other hand, I undo my belt and pants, my cock springing straight up as I do. "Have a seat. Tell me all you can see."

Raven looks at my cock, swallowing her nervousness, and I realize… this time, there's no condom.

Fuck.

"I'm on birth control," she says before I can say anything. "It's alright if… you're alright with…"

I nod once and stroke my cock, eager to be in her again.

Raven smiles and backs into me, sinking onto my stiff cock as she sits down in my lap. We both moan thickly as I enter her.

Pleasure is instant, and so is the desire to fuck her over the desk, but I resist, drawing out our pleasure.

Turning her head, she kisses me, and in her kiss, I know that the risks are worth it. Our tongues massage against one another, enjoying the warmth and intimacy. I play with her clit, adding to the intensity as Raven lifts herself up and down on my cock. *Fuck, she's too fucking good.*

I reach around her waist, pulling her back to me and lifting her legs off the ground. She plants her feet on the edge of my desk as I caress her body, kissing her neck and thrusting slowly in and out of her.

Fucking heaven. Every stroke is deep, and each feels better than the last as I push the high of falling further and further. She throws her head back, and I kiss her neck, nipping the lobe of her ear and then kissing her in that sensitive spot just below.

"So, should I close the deal, darling?" I ask teasingly as I undo her blouse, stroking her breasts through her bra. "Seventeen million?"

I don't give a shit about the deal right now, but I like this naughty mix of business and pleasure. But only with her. My Raven.

"Do it," Raven gasps, and I speed up, thrusting deeper into her. She grips the arms of my chair as she steadies us. Between her feet on my desk, the rocking of my chair, and my own hips, we're tumbling back and forth in desire, letting our passions guide us. "It's worth the risk."

God, is she. I can feel my balls tighten, her walls gripping me. "Raven... fuck," I grunt, and she cries out softly, slamming down on my cock as she leads me into ecstasy. Her fluttering, clenching walls trigger me, and I explode, grunting as we find our release together.

She hisses, "*Yes...*"

Fuck, yes.

I'm all too aware as we come down from the high that this is a dangerous game we're playing. My breathing is still heavy as I glance at the clock. It's late, but not too late.

We could stay a bit longer. Go again.

Fuck... I'm already thinking about the next time.

She has some kind of fucking hold on me. And all I know is that I want more.

CHAPTER 15

RAVEN

Walking up the last half flight of stairs, I note how badly my thighs ache, and it's not from the effort of climbing the very familiar stairs.

It's from giving in to the temptation that is *him*.

The warm butterflies stir inside me as I reach the top stair and almost sway drunkenly. I lay a hand on the wall, steadying myself and taking a deep breath. If I am drunk, it's on one thing—sex with Dylan.

God damn, can Dylan do things to my body. In addition to the feeling between my legs, my skin still tingles where he touched me, and my throat still aches from the cry I held back at the end in deference to our location. He might've reassured me about the lock, elevator, and potential audience, but I'm no fool. I learned that lesson the first time. Well, mostly.

Dylan Sharpe shook me from the tips of my toes to the roots of my hair, from my brain to my pussy to my soul. And I get to do it all again tomorrow.

Unable to stop smiling, I get my door open and half stumble inside, where I hear a hoot and a cheer from Ami. "Hell yeah, the gang's all here!"

I wince, having forgotten about tonight's plans. I'm quick to correct my expression and give an excited tone when I say, "It's your birthday!"

Not officially. Actually, Ami's birthday isn't for a few more weeks, and there's going to be an official party then. But Ami's a believer in celebrating not just birthdays, but birth months. In her mind, the anniversary of your appearance on this planet is something that should be celebrated on an epically large scale. Which means at least five, if not more times this month, we're going to be celebrating the blonde ambition that is Ami.

Some of the celebrations are probably going to be small, like her saying our after-work hang-out tonight is in her honor when we do this fairly regularly. Others are going to be larger, with various friends and groups, and of course, the main event itself is going to deliver on the celebration.

"Oof, we were thinking karaoke, but you don't look like you're up for cocktails n' crooning," Ami says, walking over with a tall glass that looks suspiciously like a mojito, her favorite, and looking at me closely. She's definitely pregaming. "Everything go okay today? He didn't jerk you around on all of this, did he?" Her voice hardens in that protective way that makes me love her, and I have to smile.

"Oh, my God, he didn't fire you on your first day, did he?" Maggie asks, getting up and joining in on the worry parade. I must really, really, look a mess, and at that realization, my smile widens to a full-blown grin.

"I'm okay," I assure them, toeing my heels off and hanging my bag by the door. Running my hand through my hair to try and smooth away the freshly-fucked look to my tresses, I add, making sure my tone is light, "I promise. Just tired, that's all."

Both of them stare at me, Maggie in leather leggings and a crop top sweater I doubt I could pull off and Ami in flared jeans and a sexy hot pink blouse. I look down at myself and realize this is not going to cut it tonight. The heels can stay. The rest needs to be changed.

"Good tired or bad tired?" Maggie asks and then heads to the kitchen, pouring me a glass of wine. My savior. "Come on, sit down and share while you gird your loins with some good stuff."

"I don't think I… okay," I reply as Ami pushes me toward the couch, not taking no for an answer. I guess since I'm putting a damper on her birth month celebration tonight, I've got to do what she says. My mind races with exactly what I should tell them. My instinct is to divulge every single freaking detail because they're my best friends. But I'm not entirely sure that's wise. I've had enough judgy looks in the last week to last me a lifetime, and I don't want to add their frowning faces to the lineup.

Maggie comes over with one of the big glasses, filled with far too much wine for the shape, and sits down next to me. The sofa shifts, and I worry for that wine, but somehow, it doesn't spill.

"Take a drink and spill."

I take a deep sip of the wine, once again appreciating Maggie's background. She grew up with a lot more refinement and education where it comes to taste, and that carries over to her pick of *il vino*. It's a good wine, probably a lot more expensive than the cheap corner store stuff I normally pick out, and as I take another pull of the wine, I'm thankful for it and mostly for her and our friendship.

"Work today was smooth," I start off, trying to organize my thoughts and twirling my glass between my fingers. The wine sloshes, not spilling out but making waves that help me focus. "They had me do a bunch of HR related stuff at first."

Maggie rolls her hand at the wrist. "Get to the good stuff. Did you see him?"

I'm about to say something, though I'm not sure what, when Ami screeches, "Wait. Hold that thought. If we're not going out, I'm still going to celebrate me and my awesomeness. And I know a place that makes this mac n' cheese that you will swear is better than sex. Best of all, they deliver."

"Are you sure?" I ask her quickly, the apology clear in my tone, leaning closer. "I can rally," I tell them, and they both shake their heads.

"Gossip is better, and I'm a bit tired too," Maggie confesses quietly. Ami's focused on her phone, desperate for mac n' cheese, and doesn't hear our shared groan of relief at not having to summon energy for the club tonight.

"Aaaand... done," Ami cheers, doing a little dance. "Dinner

will be here in forty." Looking back at Maggie and me, she says, "Where were we? Oh, yeah, did you see him?"

I smile into my wine, which is answer enough, apparently, because in unison, they both say, "Ooh!"

I can feel a blush heating my cheeks. "He came by my desk this morning to check in. Make sure I was getting settled, you know."

Ami takes a sip of her mojito, smiling around the straw. "Of course he did."

I should give what I'm about to say next a little build-up, a bit of warning, but I don't. "And he dropped a million dollars in my lap for me to trade with," I say, acting like it's no big deal.

Maggie, who's taking a sip of wine, chokes slightly. "He what?"

"For me to invest. To make money with," I clarify. "It's not like I could go to Tiffany's with it or something."

"And did you make money?" Ami asks.

"Well, yeah," I say with a touch of pride. "I mean, it takes time and all, but yeah.. And then… he called me to his office to go over my numbers and…"

Maggie and Ami both look at me eagerly, their eyebrows climbing as they see me squirm some at the comment. "He called you in his office?" Maggie's tone is comical. "Is this going where I think it's going?"

"Sort of?" I reply before attempting to hold back a grin and failing. Maybe it's the wine, or maybe I'm just still flushed with post-sex hormones. I don't know, but I know Ami and Mags won't blab about things. "At the end of the day, I went to his office to talk about my trade performance. He said I did a great job." I slowly recall everything and how it all happened. "Then he had me look at a deal he's working on."

Maggie looks at Ami and throws up quotation marks like 'deal' as she nods knowingly.

I shift as memories of what Dylan and I did in his office come to the forefront of my mind. I can still feel the ache between my thighs, and my heart does that flip thing I wish it would stop doing. "I guess the important part was that one thing led to another and…"

"In his office?" Maggie balks. She's giving me that judgy look I was worried about.

Ami kicks out at Maggie. "Quit ruining it for her. This is amazing. Like a fairy tale."

Maggie tilts her head, looking at Ami. "What fairytales are you reading? I think you mean porn. She's fucking her boss in his office, after hours. Not exactly Cinderella."

Ouch. That hurts.

The jolt must show on my face because Maggie changes her expression really quickly and seems to understand where I'm coming from. "Sorry, girl. I didn't mean it like that," she says quickly, attempting to backtrack. "Look, I know I told you it was no big deal, but that was when it was a one-off and you weren't working there. Just… be careful, okay?"

I feel like everyone keeps telling me that. Like I don't see the red flags myself even though they're nearly on fire and waving around like a pyrotechnic show.

But I also feel what I feel, and I know what Dylan said.

I meet Maggie's eyes, understanding that she's doing her best to look out for me and be a good friend. "I hear you. Really, I do. But we talked."

"Before or after?" Ami asks with a grin. At least she's on my side, wanting sordid details more than conversational ones.

"Both," I say, fighting back a grin to match Ami's. "He told me that it had nothing to do with my work. That we can keep them separate. And he said that no one has to know unless I want them to. He's not hiding me, like Evan was." That causes a little unexpected twinge in my gut because that's exactly what Evan did. Shaking my head, I add, "He's not sleeping with anyone else or seeing anyone else. Just me."

That means more to me than he realizes. It should be an automatic, but as I've recently learned, it's most definitely not.

Maggie and Ami have been listening closely as I tell them everything, so now I hold my hands out. "Okay, hit me with it. Have I completely fucked my life up? Am I a disaster waiting to happen?"

They silently meet eyes, making me wait for what feels like an eternity but is probably less than two seconds.

Maggie sighs. "I don't think so, but I will not be held responsible if it all blows up. I'm hereby releasing you to the wilds of your own decisions."

Ami laughs, ticking off on her fingers. "All I'm hearing is Hottie McMoneybags has it bad for you. You love your new job. And your boss said you're great at it. So, congratulations!"

As if dinner is agreement with her, the buzzer goes off. "I've got it," Ami shouts, hopping up to let the delivery person in the door downstairs and then the apartment door.

She comes back a moment later and passes out cardboard containers of something that smells delicious. "You know what you've gotta do now, right?"

"What?" I ask, opening up my container to reveal ooey, gooey, cheesy yumminess. "*Ooh.*"

"That's the lobster one," she says happily, pointing at my food with her fork, and then she answers my other question. "You've gotta bring your new man to my party! My actual party, not just the times we're gonna celebrate me and my utter awesomeness."

New man? I don't think she's really understanding the nature of this relationship, but she's tipsy and it's her birthday and I don't want to pop her bubble at the moment.

"What are we doing for your actual party?" I ask, and Ami grins. "What? I've been sort of caught up in my own drama. I've missed the details. Sorry."

"It's okay, she's not grinning about that. She looks like that because she's got some news of her own," Maggie whispers my way, even though Ami can totally hear her. As she opens her own container, she prompts, "Ames is thinking a swanky but cheap get together at… drumroll, please."

Ami does her own drumroll, kicking her feet on the floor in a way that's absolutely going to irritate our downstairs neighbor, before she squeals, "Los Ingobernables!"

It's my turn to choke on my drink, and I cough repeatedly. "You think you can have something cheap at Los Ingobernables?" I ask. "That's one of the hottest restaurants in the city!"

"And I just happen to have a favor I can call in with the sous chef," Ami says mysteriously. Seeing my look, she shakes her head. "No, I didn't fuck him. I only assisted in helping him do something, so he's paying me back with helping with the party. Private room, fully catered, chef's menu."

My jaw drops, and I'm already looking forward to it.

"That's going to be amazing," I reply. "What else do you have planned for the month? It's kinda impossible to top that."

"I'll figure it out," she answers with a shrug. "Even if everything else is just 'twenty day celebration till Los Ingobernables', 'fifteen days', 'ten days', and so on and so forth, it'll be fun."

Suddenly, I'm excited for Ami's birthday month celebrations.

Laughing, I lift my glass, and we toast. "Thirty days and counting!" Ami cheers, starting her own countdown.

It's hours later when I finally wander off to bed after Maggie and I tuck a tipsy but happy Ami into a taxi. "You know," Maggie says as she brushes her teeth, "I think we're going to be okay."

I meet her eyes in the mirror. "I hope so."

As I lie down, curling up under my blanket, I sort of feel okay too. Or maybe even better than okay.

In one day, I've got a good job that's got a promising future.

I've got good friends.

And maybe, just maybe, I've got a man, too.

Could I have stumbled into having it all, the whole enchilada? Or is it the wine still talking?

CHAPTER 16

DYLAN

S o while your idea has merit, I'm going to need a little time to evaluate all sides of the situation, I type, pausing before deleting half the sentence and sitting back in my chair as I pinch the bridge of my nose. Turning down an offer is often hard, especially one of this magnitude and potential. Turning down an offer from a friend is even harder.

When Austin approached me about a potential deal he's trying to line up, I was intrigued. The car and truck market is at a point now where outside forces, both cultural and economic, are dictating changes. The traditional automotive manufacturers are going to have to adapt or they'll find themselves on the scrap heap of history. But Austin has an angle on another plan, merging the cutting-edge flexibility of a startup with the major automakers' distribution network.

If it works, he's poised to be the driving force of the biggest change to the American car scene in decades. And while he's got the money to push this through on his own, he's trying to diversify his investors to maximize his profits and his potential.

So he reached out to me, because he knows that I've got my fingers on the pulse of more cash flow than he does and that I've got other investments that could be beneficial to the project.

But what he's asking…

I'm excited to see your project come to fruition, I rewrite in the bland, clipped tones of business speak, *and I wish you the best. The possibilities on what can happen in this project are more than needed for the market. But right now, I'm going to have to pass on getting involved personally. Please keep me apprised, and if the opportunity presents itself in the future, we can talk.*

-Dylan

I hit *Send*, firing off the email to Austin. I know it's passing up on an opportunity, and some people would say I'm losing out. But one of the things I've learned in my time in business is that while the old adage of 'you win some, you lose some' might be true, a lot of losses can be chalked up to spreading yourself too thinly. So if I'm not able to stay on top and see where and when to make adjustments to the projects under the firm's umbrella, then a small issue can become a full-blown problem before I can react.

And I've already got expansion plans in place for the firm, loading up my plate as it is. The Dexstrom deal was signed, sealed, and legally delivered today to the appropriate government authorities. The Miller mining deal is waiting for a final vote at the university board level to rename their mineralogy department in his honor in order to give me two major footholds in the technology world.

All in all, I'm pleased with our current situation. Let Austin become the innovator of transportation. And when he *needs* more cash flow, I'll be here and hopefully in a position to push him further.

My computer chimes, and I see that it's five minutes to six. Raven is going to walk through that door any moment now. A hum of satisfaction runs through me. Each day has been better than the last, easier and more manageable to balance work with play as well. I fucking love what we have.

She's been nothing short of amazing, logging significant profits each day with her investments. In just this week, she's already made her entire base salary in profit for the firm.

She hasn't been perfect, of course. Nobody, not even me, is. Three of her trades lost money, but in those losses, she learned, and more importantly, she showed good instincts. She didn't hang onto her pride. She dumped the investment before a small dip turned into a nosedive, and in doing so, she kept her portfolio in the green for the day. I don't often feel pride in a new hire, but she feels like more than that.

I knew I was right about her. All those fuckers missed out.

Five days in the office, five days of profits. More importantly, five days of learning, of showing me that she knows exactly what she's talking about while still being hungry to understand more.

And so far, four days of coming to my office at six o'clock, with one to go, sitting under my learning tree while being unafraid to share her own thoughts and opinions. She challenges me, but respectfully. The pluckiness that she showed me before our date at the Faulkner event is still there. She stands up for herself while still acknowledging my superiority in matters of business.

And of course, each of these sessions has led to sex. Intense, fantastic, body wracking sex. She's fucking addicting.

The moment she's gone, I feel the loss of not having her in my bed.

She wants to keep it business and leave separately. As much as I respect the terms of the verbal contract, I'm certain there will be flexibility.

At least I'm hopeful there will be, given what this weekend is.

Tomorrow is the anniversary of my heart being turned to dust and my world being poisoned forever. The day I learned what betrayal truly meant, and that I was never going to marry.

As my thumb taps on the table, I remember that day like it was just yesterday. Not years ago. The anger brewing inside is at odds with the hope I felt.

I fucking loved Olivia. I know I did. And it was a mistake… every fucking second, every thought, every moment I spent with her.

Running up the stairs, I'm almost giddy because I've done it. Finally, I found the perfect wedding ring. Well, perhaps 'found' isn't accurate because I've devoted dozens of hours and hundreds of thousands of dollars to develop them, to create the works of art that I've got in my pocket. They're custom made, gorgeous, and one of a kind, like she is.

I reach Olivia's door, and my thumb's poised to hit her doorbell buzzer when I hear a thump against her door. Quickly, there's another, larger thump, and thinking something's wrong, I'm about to lower my shoulder and go barging through when I hear... a giggle? Carefully, I press my ear against the wood, the thick material making an excellent sound transmitter.

"You're so naughty," she says, clearly in pleasure. She's close, obviously just on the other side of the door, so her voice is easy to understand. "I never thought a boy from a good family like yours could be so bad."

My heart clenches in my chest, and I'm about to punch the door and scare the shit out of her and whoever it is in there with her when I hear, "You know you like it."

The voice freezes me. Evan? But...

"We shouldn't keep doing this," Olivia says before moaning. I know that sound. She always makes that sound when her nipples are being played with. My heart sinks and my body freezes. *Evan and Olivia...*

"You know it makes you wet just thinking about it, us sneaking around, him not having a clue," Evan says. "Isn't that right?"

"Yes. But—"

"But it would hurt our little Pip's feelings?" Evan says teasingly. My teeth set on edge at the mocking, dismissive nickname he knows I hate. He's often joked that I resemble the famous Dickens character, including the fact that I gave my heart away to a 'cold but beautiful bitch who'll never, ever be able to be trusted.'

Apparently, he was right, as their sounds quickly become the sound of one thing, and as she moans his name, I turn and walk away... leaving the rings in their bag on her apartment doorknob.

It wasn't anger. The betrayal did something much worse to me. My friend, one of my best friends and the woman I loved. Fucking hell.

The memory sears through me, making my teeth clench. He was my friend, but he betrayed me. It wasn't until later that I found out just how much he was stabbing me in the back in the business world as well. Deals that could have lifted me out of the grind even faster, that could have made me his equal, were silently sabotaged.

We had it out on that.

"You betrayed me," I hiss as Evan and I sit in the lounge, the curving booth and the round table between us preventing me from reaching out and choking the life out of him. That was my idea, not his. I'm not going to go to jail for murder because of this asshole. I just need some questions answered. "Why?"

He scoffs, ignoring my question. "You should be thanking me," he says, looking out over the bar and virtually dismissing me.

I lean forward and hiss, "For fucking my fiancée?"

He cuts cold eyes my way. "You should be thanking me for showing you exactly who and what she is before you wasted any more of your time on a meaningless fuck."

I change my mind. A life sentence would worth it to feel his heart stop in my bare hand. As though he can sense that I'm on the edge, considering jumping off, his eyes flare with excitement. He wants me to attack him and is virtually salivating for it to happen.

That alone is enough to give me pause. If he wants me to act on my rage, it's definitely not the right play. I'll never give him anything he wants again.

Seeing me tamp my emotions down, getting them under control, he smirks. "If you must know, she was all too keen to suck my dick. Bit of a family perk, you know."

He wears his last name like a protective cape. One day, I'll catch him without it and destroy him. Unfortunately, that day is not today.

I throw my vodka back in one swallow, needing the numbness. It's the last time I'll ever touch this particular drink, since he was the one who suggested that 'real players' drink vodka. From today onward, I'm going to be a whiskey man, or maybe rum.

Evan chuckles and sips his vodka soda before slamming his glass to the table. "Fine, you want the whole thing? First off, I don't owe a street hustler like you a fucking thing. And that's what you are, Sharpe. Sure, you're making some money. Enough to lift you up a few tax brackets above the poverty line. And someday, you'll find some bovine-faced bitch who'll marry you. She'll pop out a few kids, grow a fat ass, and you'll get to play with her flabby tits once a week if you're lucky. Or hell, maybe you'll be the even stupider type and keep chasing the dragon until you find yourself a plastic surgery-loving gold digger who'll drain your dick and your bank account dry. But in the meantime, you'll make money. Maybe even a decent amount. You might even be able to retire someday to some little retirement community in some dusty ass state, where you'll be able to eat your chocolate pudding and slowly piss yourself while watching *The Price Is Right*. But the truth is, Sharpe, you could make a billion dollars… and you'll still be chasing me, and people like me. So whatever I do, I don't owe you an explanation. I owe you nothing because you are nothing in this world."

"I'm going to ruin you," I vow. "Not today, but one day."

Evan chuckles, not considering me a threat for even a moment. "Face it, you're trash, man. Get out of my game."

The words haunted me, but in some ways, I have to thank Evan Faulkner. I thought I was driven before his betrayal. But he pushed me further. He 'Sharpe'ned me, if I'm allowed to have a few bad puns about the most searing trauma of my life. Trauma, but from that trauma came growth.

Without his stabbing me in the back, I would not be in the position I am today. Without the cold-hearted lessons he taught me, I never would have been able to become the powerful man I am today. Even if I haven't adopted his methods, he opened my eyes to what the rest of the Financial District was like.

Not that I could ever forgive the bastard. The one thing I truly, truly regret in my life is not wrapping my fingers around that son of a bitch's neck when I had the opportunity.

But perhaps I've gotten my revenge even more sublimely. He stole my fiancée from me, leaving her just a few weeks after I called off the wedding. Now, I have the woman he was too stupid to hang on to, and I'm not just richer than him, but I'm also on the trembling cusp of dethroning his entire family from their perch. The best part? Raven's going to help me.

He tried to destroy me. It's taken some time, but soon, I'll be the one pissing on the ashes of the Faulkner empire.

There's a knock on my door, and I glance up to see Raven enter my office.

She's wearing the same green blouse and black skirt combination that she wore to our interview, and I'm struck by how much has changed since then. Though some things haven't changed a bit, like the fact that I'm stiffening in my slacks from the mere sight of her.

"Mr. Sharpe."

"Miss Hill," I reply, and she smiles, that beautiful smile that frames her sensuous mouth and teases me by its very presence. I go to sleep at night remembering the sensation of those velvety lips pressed against me, or wrapped around my cock like she was yesterday. "Tonight, I wanted—"

"Wait, Dylan," she says, and I pause, lifting an eyebrow. She steps closer, and I can see in her eyes what she wants to say even before she says it. But I hold back, maintaining control. "I can't."

"You can," I reply with a frown, not quite adding, 'You will. Now get on your knees.'

I'm still giving her the choice, after all. It was one of the lessons that Evan taught me. I can't force loyalty. I can't force desire. That's not the sort of man I am. So I won't order her, even if the sentiment has merit in the right circumstances.

Raven shakes her head, almost as if she's reading my mind, and her lips twitch. "Not that, Dylan. I'm not saying no to you. You're… never mind."

"No, what is it?" I ask, and she blushes. I get up, going around my desk to lift her chin and look into her eyes. "Tell me, darling. What were you going to say?"

"I was going to tell you," she says as her blush deepens and her breath quickens, "I was going to say that you're cute when you're disappointed, but then I didn't want you to think I was being stupid or trying to demean you."

I sit back on the edge of my desk, stunned into silence by her gushing admission. "I'm cute?" An eyebrow cocks at her statement.

Raven nods, biting her lip. She looks unsure whether she should open up to me like this. It's touching that she's so courageous as to do so, and a reminder that while I'm letting her see parts of me the rest of the world doesn't, it's clear I'm still walled off and intimidating in a lot of ways. But she's going to keep trying. "Very. But as much as I would love to show you, I can't. I'm sorry, but I have to leave tonight. My mother texted earlier, and she's on the train down right now. Surprise!" she says brightly, but then her face falls. "I wanted to say goodbye before I left."

Relief strikes through me, making me sigh softly. It's an unfamiliar feeling, but at the same time, welcome. Reaching up, I stroke her cheek. "I understand. So, what are the two Hill women planning?"

Selfishly, I'd hoped to see Raven tomorrow night as well. She would be a much-welcomed distraction from the ghosts of my past that will come haunting in the late-night hours of the ugly anniversary. But I'm not entirely without a heart. Raven speaks fondly of her family, so of course, I'd want her to spend time with her mother.

She laughs. "I have no idea since I didn't know she was coming. I just hope Maggie doesn't mind another person in our tiny apartment."

She's joking, but I've been to her and Maggie's apartment, and from the doorway, I think I saw more than eighty percent of the space. Raven has teasingly said her bedroom is the width of her spread arms, and I'm not entirely sure she's exaggerating.

I reach across my desk, picking up my phone. "I'm booking your mother a room. I'd go with five-star, but I suspect she'd have too many questions if I did."

Raven looks shocked and reaches for my wrist. "Dylan, you shouldn't—"

"I should, and I am," I reply simply, pulling my phone out of her reach and holding it over my head like we're playing keep away. She wants to call me cute? She should see how she looks right now, reaching for my phone, her breasts thrust outward against my chest, her eyes huge and gorgeous. She's more than cute. She's hot as hell. "Seriously, Raven. I've seen enough of your apartment to know that there's no way that anyone's mother should be staying there for a visit to the city. Now, as for your explaining that to your mother, just tell her that you got a signing bonus with the firm and decided to treat her to a nice weekend. Or tell her the truth. She won't be coming around the office, I assume?"

She huffs a half laugh softly and pauses, meeting my eyes. "No, she won't. I promise. Are you sure about this?"

"Staying until Monday?" I question, and she smiles while nodding. "Yes."

I nod, quickly booking a place and slipping my phone into my pocket.

"You really didn't have to do that," she says before getting on her tiptoes to kiss my cheek. It's unexpected, and so is the feeling in my chest.

I pull Raven close, not wanting distance between us. "If you haven't figured it out after this week, Raven, you're mine. And I take care of what's mine."

For me, it's as big a declaration as I'll ever make and a leap into dangerous waters. As though she can sense the magnitude of my words, she looks up at me, her green eyes filled with tenderness.

I kiss her, not needing her to say anything. Not yet, not if she's not there. I am, and that's enough. She leans into me, and I pull her even closer, still wishing we had time for more but making do with imprinting myself along her body as I memorize the feel of her to get me through the lonely weekend.

Finally, when we both need to breathe, I pull back, brushing her lip with my thumb to get a smidge of lipstick that's worn off. She smiles. "Thank you."

I nod, studying her face and seeing something there that I never thought I'd see in a woman's face again. I see someone I can believe in, someone I can trust. "I'll forward you the reservation. It'll be in your name."

"Yes, sir," she says, her brow arching teasingly, and in my pants, my cock twitches.

"Be very careful, Raven," I whisper in her ear. "Words have meanings, and words have consequences."

"I know," she replies. "I'm looking forward to Monday. See you then… sir."

She leaves, and I go back to my desk, slumping into my chair. Maybe it's only been four days, but I've come to look forward to Raven's daily visits to my office and I'm struck with a profound sense of disappointment at the quickness of our time today.

I want more of her. Although I'm very aware that I need to be careful of my next steps with my little darling.

Not having her tonight leaves me feeling almost empty, and making the reservation for Raven's mother is a hollow victory at best. I do make one adjustment, though, upgrading the room to a full suite, hoping they'll both enjoy it for a bit of mother-daughter bonding.

Still, after texting the hotel and reservation code to Raven, I'm left with little to do. The work week is done, and I have no big urge to spend the weekend researching. And the concept of relieving the churning pressure in my balls with simple masturbation feels like a cheap substitute for having Raven pinned beneath me.

But there's one activity I haven't done in a couple of months that could kill two birds with one stone. I quickly dial again, and the voice on the other end of the line sounds surprised when it picks up. "Dylan? What's up, man? Emergency?"

I chuckle, leaning back in my chair. "Why would I need an emergency in order to give you a call, Austin?"

"Considering you just sent me an email turning down my offer, and you almost never call me when you just want to hang out," he reminds me, "I figured you had an emergency. No?"

"No, no emergency," I reply, drumming my fingers on the desk. "I just wanted to get in touch with you before you made any concrete weekend plans. Wanted to see if you'd like to get a game together tomorrow night?"

At one point or another, we always get together for a casual night of cards. We might go weeks or sometimes months, but men with money will always find a stupid way to lose it, especially if it involves a bit of alcohol, shit-talking, and fun. Sometimes, I even come out a winner, either in funds or information. This weekend, I'll take distraction as the biggest win.

Austin hums thoughtfully, and I can almost hear his mind working as he puts the date together with what he knows of my past. "Yeah, man. I can do that. How many do you want involved?" Austin asks. "Are you inviting others?"

"I was thinking Ollie. I owe him one," I admit. "Although

he's not exactly a short-term notice type of guy. Do you have any ideas?"

"What about Noah?" Austin asks, referring to a newer friend of his that I've only met once before in passing. "I think you two would get along well."

"Sure, why not?" I reply. "I'll poke around a bit more if Ollie says he's busy, but I'll get a fourth. Maybe a fifth if I can."

"Oh, I'll bring the fifth," Austin jokes. "I've got a fifth of whiskey I've wanted you to try for a couple of months, anyway."

"Deal. Say, six o'clock at my place, then?"

"I'll be there, buddy. And if you're not going to invest in my project, I'll just have to take you to the cleaners and get the money that way."

"Talking shit already, are we?" I taunt, grinning a little. "If I remember right, last time we played, I walked out ten thousand dollars richer."

"Ten thousand? Big deal. Pocket change."

"Pocket change now," I remind him, and on the other end of the line, he hums. Deep inside, Austin's still the hustler he was years ago. In all the best ways. "I know you don't forget."

"And I know you won't," Austin replies. "See you Saturday."

As I hang up, I'm all too aware that even with plans made, I feel a loss at not having Raven to myself.

CHAPTER 17

RAVEN

"I feel so… fancy," Mom says, giddy, as she steps out of her room and double checks the door. Tucking her keycard into her purse, she looks up and down the heavily carpeted hallway, almost swooning at the luxury surrounding her. "How did you make this happen, sweetheart?"

We've been over this, both last night when I met her at the train and detoured us to the hotel, where I helped her get checked in, and again, this morning over our room service breakfast. But she's not letting it go that easily.

"I told you," I reply, my heart swelling in my chest at seeing my mom's happiness. "My new job gave me a bonus."

"A bonus?" Mom asks, and I nod. "Already?"

I should've known the little white lie wouldn't be enough to satisfy her curiosity. I hate to let it snowball, but I can't exactly go back now and tell her my new boss paid for the room. That'd be even worse. "When you make the company six figures in profit in the first week you're there, they're grateful," I reply, thankful that's the truth, at least. We turn and start down the hallway toward the elevator. "The timing was perfect. I got the bonus, and then you texted me. Seemed sort of karmic to use some of it on treating you. I'm sorry Dad couldn't make it."

"Well, you know your father," Mom says as we reach the elevator and she pushes the down button. "He's not exactly Mr. Spontaneity, so he was all too willing to stay home with Mark."

I have to agree. I love my Dad, and he taught me a lot about hard work and preparation, qualities I've put into my work. But he's about as predictable as the sunrise and sunset. So, an unplanned trip down to the city, even to see me? Well, that just doesn't fit in his schedule for life. And with him and my brother at home, they're probably ordering take-out, holing up in their respective rooms, and nerding out in their own ways—Dad, with bowling on TV, and Mark, with his computers.

But Mom loves the opportunity to get out and experience life in the city. She's wearing one of her best dresses, there's a smile on her lipstick-pink lips, and she has a sparkle in her eyes. She's ready to tackle the evening and whatever may come.

I'm more than grateful for my mom and for the fact that we're able to spend some girl time together.

The elevator comes, and we step inside. "Mom?" She looks over at me, and I feel a little choked up, how much I've missed her hitting me unexpectedly. "I just wanted to say thanks for coming,"

I tell her honestly. "I know you've been worried about me."

Mom chuckles and takes my hand. "You're always going to be my little girl, sweetheart, so I'm always going to worry about you. That doesn't mean I don't have faith in you, but even when you get enough money to buy whatever you want, I'll worry."

"So this'll never end?" I tease, hoping it doesn't.

"Well, if you ever want to buy your parents a motorhome for our retirement, I wouldn't say boo."

I laugh. "Tell you what. If I can ever afford it, and Dad agrees to actually use it and not just let it sit in the driveway, we'll talk."

The elevator dings again, and we come out into the lobby of the Hotel London. Why London? I have no clue. But the hotel's nice, and the room is definitely bigger than my apartment.

Dylan went above and beyond, and silently, I thank him. Some people might think he's sugar daddying me, but I know the truth of Dylan. He did it because that's who he is. He'd do the same for his few friends as well. If anything, he's been too generous with me, because if the Hotel London is three-star, I'll eat a big ol' bowl of lima beans. Frozen.

I just wish I knew what caused such a big heart to become walled off and so hard to most of the world. Even as I waited for Mom to finish getting ready for dinner tonight, my thoughts turn to him. I miss him, and seeing the joy he's brought to my mother, even without her knowledge, is something I want to return to him as soon as I can.

But tonight is about Mom, and as the elevator doors open and we cross the lobby, I get to give her a little of her own medicine.

"Surprise!" the two women say in unison.

"Maggie! Melinda! What are you doing here?" Mom says, looking from them to me and then greeting them each with a hug.

Melinda answers quickest. "Raven told Maggie you were coming down as a surprise, so we did a little sneaky girls' trip planning too. I hope it's okay we invited ourselves to your dinner, Dianne?" She gives Mom a warm look, truly okay if Mom says she'd rather it be just the two of us.

But Mom loves Maggie, treating her like a second daughter, and Melinda is basically her partner in crime, if the crime is shopping a little too often and having a Cosmo or two too many. Melinda is more a Nordstrom's and Barney's type, and Mom is strictly TJMaxx, but somehow, they get along well with the common denominator of their daughters being friends.

"Of course you're welcome. The more, the merrier," Mom tells them. "I'm excited to see you too."

"Have you had fun?" Maggie asks Mom.

Mom sighs in bliss. "Oh, my goodness, yes. We had room service and went to the park this morning. Then, this afternoon, Raven took me to get this massage where you're floating in water. What was that called again?"

"Watsu massage," I reply, exchanging looks with Maggie, who gives me a little smile. She spotted me that one, giving me a coupon she'd gotten from the last time she went to her favorite salon. "And you had fun, admit it." Mom had serious doubts about that, saying it was going to feel like a weird swimming lesson, but afterward, she'd been wigglier than a bowl full of Jell-O.

"I did," she agrees with a laugh.

"Good. I would love to hear more about it over dinner," Melinda says, reminding us that we should go if we want to make our reservations.

We're going to a steakhouse in the theater district I know Mom will enjoy. It's likely she'll try to pay, especially when she thinks I paid for the hotel, but I don't want her to do that. I'd love to be able to treat her to a nice meal while she's in town. Unfortunately, I haven't actually received my first paycheck yet, so Maggie offered to spot me and I promised to pay her back as soon as I get paid. In the end, Melinda will probably snatch the check and it will be a moot point, but I'm glad to have a plan in place regardless since my funds are running lower than they ever have before.

We take a taxi to the restaurant, and Mom and Melinda chat the whole way, rehashing the latest season of a *Housewives* show they both watch before switching gears to swap dessert recipes. I can't help but crack up a bit as Melinda calls one of Mom's classic poke cakes a 'brilliant idea'. Delicious? Yes, absolutely. Brilliant? I'm not sure about that, but Mom's beaming so I'm not gonna pop her bubble.

"Do you all come here a lot?" Mom asks as she sits down at our table.

"I think I've been here with John before," Melinda says, mentioning Maggie's dad, who stayed home to give us a 'girls' night on the town'. She looks around and confides, "Probably for some boring business meeting he had. These days, I don't have to go to many of those dreadful things. Times change, and meetings are in coffee shops and tea houses more often than over white tablecloths." She looks pleased at that, then laughs as she shares a story. "Oh, my goodness, he went to a meeting the other day, and they gave him boba tea!" she tells us. "He said that when he took a drink, he thought he'd swallowed a crown and nearly choked himself trying to get it back up, only for it to pop in his mouth. Suffice it to say, he was not a fan."

She and mom laugh in full agreement with Mr. Levine's assessment while Maggie and I share a look because we like boba tea.

A waitress comes over, taking our drink orders and telling us the evening's specials, and when she gives us a moment with the menu, as I expected, Melinda tells us, "Dinner's on me this evening, ladies. No arguments, it's my pleasure."

Maggie doesn't say a word, knowing it's futile, and I stay quiet, grateful for the gift. But Mom, who grew up with a lot of pride in self-sufficiency because of Gramma's financial situation, opens her mouth, but then closes it and nods. "Okay. But you will be getting on my jelly and cookie list."

"Jelly and cookie list?" Melinda repeats, and Maggie grins. "You know about this, Maggie?"

"You're in for a treat," Maggie says. "Mama Hill makes the most amazing plum and apricot jellies that she sends to Raven, and the Christmas cookies? They're worth the New Year's Resolution, I promise you."

"We keep saying that we're going to share them out with Ami, but other than her snagging a few if she comes over around the time the box arrives, we demolish the whole thing," I admit, and Mom preens a little. "I hope that I can get that good someday."

"First, you've got to have a kitchen capable of real cooking," Mom points out, and Maggie and I laugh. "Raven, seriously. I've seen college dorm rooms with better kitchens than what you have. How you cook anything in that apartment is beyond me."

"It does take a special kind of organization," Melinda says with a fond smile. "Dianne, I remember my first big city kitchen, too. It was a single eye hotplate that plugged into the wall, and a microwave. Trust me, I got very good at one skillet meals. And microwave noodles."

"Let's order before my appetite disappears," Maggie says, catching the waitress's eye. "Raven keeps making these chili lime shrimp Cup Noodles that smell like death."

"Hey!" I argue. "Those are delicious."

Maggie eyes me comically.

The waitress returns, setting our drinks down, and we place our orders, keeping it relatively simple with a mix of beef wellington, pork chops, and two different chicken dishes. Apparently, we're sampling the menu tonight.

Maggie holds her glass up, clearing her throat. "To good moms, better daughters, great surprises, and new jobs!"

We clink our glasses together, toasting the evening and thankful we get to spend it together.

"Yes, tell me about your new job, Raven," Melinda says excitedly.

I give them a general rundown, keeping some of the not-so-appropriate bits to myself and focusing on the investing. "I'm learning a lot and enjoying every minute of it," I say, and Maggie nearly chokes on her wine. She's got to stop doing that, I think, flashing her a warning smile. She arches a brow as if to say, 'really?'

"I'll be honest, I don't quite understand all the details of what you're doing," Mom says. "But I'm proud of you." I swear, tears are springing up in the corners of her eyes. "When you were so driven by that little investment game back in school, I thought it was cute. You'd talk in all these acronyms I didn't understand. But it was interesting to you, and that's all that mattered. I certainly didn't think it'd become this. Now I see I was wrong."

"These kids will grow up and surprise you, won't they?" Melinda tells mom, agreeing with her sentiment. "Maggie used to wrap up in curtains and say she was a bride, then it became a model, and finally, she started cutting my good sheets up and hand-stitching them into dresses and blouses. I nearly came unglued the first time I found strips of my favorite Sir La Table tablecloth strewn about the floor."

Mom gasps. "The first time?"

Melinda pins her with a look. "It happened so many times, I finally had to lock the linen closet and get her a line of credit at the fabric store. Sounds ridiculous, but I think that saved me thousands of dollars over the years. And now she's on the marketing side of fashion. I never would've expected that, but I'm sure Raven's glad Maggie's not swiping the bathroom towels to use as 'accessories' these days."

I grin behind my glass, glad that Maggie's getting a bit of a smackdown instead of me this time.

"What about your son, Mark, right?" Melinda asks Mom.

She waves her hand. "Oh, you should see that boy. He's a foot taller than me. And you'd be shocked at how much time he spends in the garage, all sorts of little wires and doodads organized at his workstation in little boxes. Sometimes, it seems that he's just swapping parts around from one box to another, and sometimes, he's bent over a circuit board with his soldering gun for hours. I don't get it, but he's enjoying it. He's even getting an organization started, getting some of his classmates and friends to go out looking for these broken computers for him to fix and give away to families in need."

"Sounds like there will be a lot of families who are going to owe Mark a big thanks when it's all said and done," Melinda says. "Just think, all the students who'll have the tools to follow their dreams."

"Yeah, we're all pretty great," Maggie says and the moms give her a double dose of Mom-glare. She flinches dramatically. "What? You were singing our praises a minute ago, and now I'm supposed to be all humble and modest?"

"Alright, missy. If we're done talking about both of your meteoric rise to success in your fields, how about you spill the beans on the dating scene in the city?"

Maggie pales. "Spill the beans? Nobody says that anymore, Mom." Melinda's gaze holds steady, and Maggie tries another track. "The dating scene? Why? Are you leaving Dad?" Melinda and John Levine are solid as can be, and Maggie's completely kidding. With a desperate side of deflection.

"Ooh, yes. Do tell," Mom says eagerly, turning her attention to me. "Maggie told me about Evan last we talked... Do you want to talk about it?"

"Thanks for this," I deadpan, promising Maggie with my eyes that I will absolutely take the last cup of coffee and not start a fresh pot next week as payback for her getting both mothers on our cases.

"Nothing really to tell right now," I answer.

Of course, she doesn't have any big news on the dating front. I do, but I'm not sharing that with Mom. In some ways, I'd like to. I think she'd be horrified that Dylan is my boss, but I think she'd actually like Dylan himself if she got to know him the way I do. But the risks outweigh the rewards of spilling, so I stay tight-lipped about it for now.

"I'm keeping my focus on work," I tell Mom, which is basically the truth. Or close to it. I mean, Dylan is kinda part of work... *except when he's not.*

Thankfully, our food comes a few minutes later and we get lost in talking about how delicious it is, trying each other's entrees. Mom in particular never sniffs around my social life again during dinner, and after the meal is done, we step out into the chilly night air.

"I'm heading home tonight, so I'd best be going," Melinda says, giving us each a hug. "It was so good to see you, and thanks again for letting me invade your mother-daughter dinner," she tells Mom.

"Anytime," Mom says. "Great to see you too." We watch as Melinda hails a taxi, climbs in, and disappears into the night. Mom turns to me. "My train leaves bright and early in the morning, so I'm probably going to crash, if that's okay?"

"Sure, Mom. I'll come back to the hotel with you," I offer, but she waves me off.

"No, you two go out and have fun. I know it's still early for you city folks." She winks as though she's in on our secret of being up-all-night party animals, which neither of us is.

But…

"If you're sure, Mom. I don't mind crashing into bed and taking you to the train station early in the morning," I try again, just so I can say I made a fair effort even though I'm hoping she doesn't want me to go with her.

"You're gonna make me say it, aren't you, Raven?" She tilts her head, her lips pursed. I blink, not sure what she's talking about. She sighs. "There is a big, fluffy bed in that hotel room with my name on it. One I don't have to share, where I can't hear anyone snoring, and where I can sleep totally naked if I have a middle of the night hot flash and nobody will care. So leave me to it, sweetheart, and go have your fun."

My jaw drops open in surprise and then I laugh. "Well, okay, then. Good night, Mom. Call me when you get home tomorrow so I know you're safe."

She gives me a wry look. "That's my line. Except do not call me tonight when you get home. I will be blissfully sleeping." I hold up a hand, not wanting to hear any more about her nude sleeping plans, and she chuckles. "You just wait. One day, you'll know what I'm talking about. A big bed all to yourself is a gift and I'm not wasting it."

"I'm sure Dad would love to hear that," I deadpan, and Mom laughs.

"You think he doesn't know, and wouldn't do the same thing? I'm the one dealing with the hot flashes. He's the one dealing with me." With that, we say our goodbyes and I put Mom into a taxi headed for the hotel. She smiles, waving as they pull away.

"You coming home then, or…?" Maggie asks, raising a brow.

I twist my lips, thinking, and then sigh. "Yeah, I don't want to do the late night 'you up?' text thing, you know?" Honestly, I do want to do that. But I'm not sure I should.

She links her arm through mine. "Come on, let's spoil ourselves then and get a taxi too. My treat."

"You're the best," I say, laying my head on her shoulder. "This almost makes up for your getting our moms on our cases about our dating life."

Maggie huffs out a dry laugh. "Whatever, you love me."

I nod because she's right, I do love her. I especially love that she doesn't give me a single bit of shit as I pull out my phone the second we're sitting in the taxi and doesn't say a word as I text Dylan even though I literally just said I wasn't going to do that.

CHAPTER 18

DYLAN

Sometimes, I'm still a little shocked at how far I've come. I grew up not having a bed to myself until I was in college, and the first pair of brand-new, off the rack jeans I ever owned came during my sophomore year. Until then, everything I owned was a hand me down or thrift store special.

There was a time when my apartment wasn't much bigger than your average fast food restaurant bathroom, and I could cook dinner without getting out of bed. Heat was a luxury, and in the summer, I cooled myself off as I slept by using a single electric fan, smog or air quality be damned.

Now, my pantry's bigger than that first apartment, and I sit in the 'games room' of my eight thousand square feet, two-floor penthouse. With a touch of a button, I can make this entire place any temperature I want, including the floor. And if I feel like it, at a moment's notice, I can hop on a private plane and go anywhere in the world in less time than it used to take me to get across town.

And that's only some of the many things that have changed in my life.

The list could stretch from my balcony all the way down to the street, most likely. But it can all be encapsulated by the fact that I can look at a thousand dollars sitting on the table in between me and the four other men who are joining me tonight and not even blink as Austin takes another small stack of chips and pushes it into the middle. As he said when we talked about setting tonight up, a thousand dollars is pocket change to us. Currently, we're playing hold 'em, and it's Austin's bet. "Raise five hundred."

"Check, check, check, raise," Teddy, who's the dealer this round, complains. "Every fucking hand, he's the same way. Check his way through unless he has to see someone else's bet, and only then raise. Never fold, never call. You would think he's got ice in his veins."

"Maybe I do, Teddy," Austin says casually, leaning back in his chair. Teddy's grumbling is more than likely an act, but Austin's not going to get baited into revealing his strategy. "But it'll cost you five hundred to find out."

Teddy, who's a mutual acquaintance but not quite a friend to Austin and me, peeks at his cards again and sighs. "Not this time," he says, tossing his cards toward the muck. "Claire would kill me if I did."

We all laugh. Teddy is fairly recently married, and his being here tonight is a bit of a surprise considering his first child is on the way in a couple of months. But I suspect that while he loves his wife, Claire, more than life itself, they both needed a few hours to themselves. I'm actually jealous of Teddy in some ways. He wasn't stabbed in the back by someone he loves and has achieved it all—wife, baby, generational wealth, and most importantly, he seems truly happy.

"Speaking of Claire," Noah asks, "how's she doing?" He folded immediately after the flop and is more interested in conversation than the cards on the table.

"Round as a beach ball and never more beautiful," Teddy sighs wistfully, his eyes going soft at the thought of her. "We've both decided that we're not going to hire an au pair. But that means I'll be picking up a second full-time job, gentlemen. Daddy."

"No finer job, in my opinion," Ollie, who's also joined us, says. "Enjoy it."

Teddy deals out the next card, which is no help to me, a three of diamonds. But it's my move, so I decide to imitate Austin. "Check."

"Ollie?"

Ollie peeks at his cards and slides a hundred into the pot. "I'm feeling good."

The bet goes to Austin, who doesn't even look at his cards. He never does. He's got them memorized. The man has exactly zero tells in his game, which in some ways, makes him easier to play.

Against Austin, you don't play the man. You play the math. Ollie's more complicated, as he'll act pleased or not pleased with his cards. But how he acts and how good his cards actually are aren't always the same. You have to play the man and the cards with him.

"Just to change it up for Teddy, I'll call," Austin says, sliding the appropriate chips in. It's a bit of a surprise, but more about fucking with Teddy than changing his game strategy. It's just Austin being Austin. Turning to me, he looks at me with the emotionless, murderer's eyes that he can call on in a heartbeat whenever he wants. "Dylan?"

I knew what I was going to do even before Teddy laid out that three, but I still give an appropriate five-second pause before sliding my stack in. "A thousand."

"The raise is nine hundred," Teddy announces, and the table goes a little tense. For form's sake, we've limited raises to a thousand, mainly so nobody gets too stupid. Some of us are married, and while a thousand dollars might be simply pocket change to everyone here tonight, nobody wants to get real feelings involved. This is supposed to be a fun, relaxing night for all of us. Not blood sport.

"I think I'll have a drink instead," Ollie says, putting his cards down. "No offense, Dylan, but your bar is more fun than your poker table. And it has been much, much more friendly to me tonight."

"None taken," I assure Ollie as he gets up and goes over to the bar. "If I can make a recommendation, the DiBaldo saffron gin goes down very well. It's the golden bottle."

"Thank you," Ollie says, finding the bottle. He swirls it around, studying the contents before selecting an appropriate glass from the rack. "You know, I should be upset with you for snatching young Miss Hill from underneath me."

He says it conversationally, but there's a bigger question there. I went out of my way to bring Raven to the fundraiser, made a show of her on my arm, introduced her to Ollie as a prime prospect, and then hired her before he got back from his trip to Wyoming. It's bad form but was also a complete necessity, something he understands. Business is business, even between friends.

"Why do you think my bar is open for you?" I joke, and the guys laugh. And though Ollie smiles good-naturedly and was appreciative for the replacement prospects I sent his way, there's a shrewdness in his eye as he holds up his tumbler of golden liquor, toasting me. He's been in this game a long time and knows all the plays and players, and I'm not talking poker. I'm sure he's heard the rumor about Raven and me by now, and he probably received a call from Evan as well since Raven had an interview scheduled at Ollie's firm. His raised glass is a friendly warning as much as an appreciation for the drink.

I dip my chin in acknowledgement.

But even the mention of Raven reminds me that it's been too long since I've seen her. In truth, by the clock, it's been barely over twenty-four hours, but those hours have been hell. I ended up staying late at the office last night, forcing myself to work well into the evening, and then slept like hell.

Today has been worse. I 'celebrated' the shitty anniversary by starting with a punishing workout, getting out as much aggression as I could by beating on a heavy bag, imagining it was

Evan's face. Later, a soak in the hot tub, meditation in the sauna, and a cold shower did nothing to improve my mood.

This game has been a welcome distraction, though. And tomorrow, Raven's mother will return home. I should wait until Monday morning to see Raven again. That would be the reasonable thing to do, but honestly, I'm not sure my sanity can take not seeing her that long. My greedier nature hopes Mrs. Hill has had a lovely visit, takes a morning train, and then I can get Raven to my penthouse on Sunday for a private 'business' lesson.

Teddy lays down the last card, an ace of clubs. A little thrill goes through me, and I check, sending the onus to Austin, who also checks. It's a showdown, a test of wills and mathematics. The money isn't important.

"Okay, boys, show 'em," Teddy says, and I flip over my cards, the ace of hearts and the ace of spades. "Three aces."

Austin's brows slam down as his eyes fall to my cards. "Shit," he utters, turning his own hand. He's got a pocket pair of kings to go with the one from the flop. No wonder he's been cocky as fuck. He's known the whole game that his hand was a near-winner.

Until that ace in the river. Now, we both have a three of a kind, but mine's a higher rank.

I grin, victorious.

Everyone laughs, and as the chips get sorted out and Teddy feeds the cards into the machine to reshuffle them into the shoe, I go and get my own drink. Noah joins me.

"Thanks for the invite tonight," he says, looking over what's on offer and selecting a bottle of Neustra Soledad mezcal. "It's good to get to know everyone."

That's the other side of our poker game. Business is discussed here, connections made, and intel shared across the table.

I pluck my favorite tumbler off the shelf. "You're relatively new in town, right?"

"Just over a year," Noah answers, pouring his drink.

"Noah's mostly into real estate," Austin offers as he joins us and selects a bottle of his favorite, Japanese sake. "Although be careful, Dylan. I hear he's looking at getting into the restaurant game too."

"Oh, really?" I ask, and Noah nods. "Good luck. Truth is, I don't own Lionfish for the profits."

"Ah, your secret information source," Noah says, and I give him a sharp look. He shrugs, not meaning to offend. "Don't worry, Dylan, I think it's genius. I had a similar setup back home, with a club. Turned a good profit on the books, but the real value was in the club members."

"I'm sure you can find similar opportunities here in town," I note. Glancing over at the table, I quickly evaluate his stack of chips. "You play poker well. Either that, or you're incredibly lucky." His jaw ticks at the insult of his success tonight coming from luck rather than skill.

"I do okay. Though not half as good as the robot here," Noah says, nudging Austin with an elbow. "On a serious note, though, I would appreciate if you gentlemen know a good chef looking for an opportunity."

"I'll keep my ears open," Austin promises, and I know he

will. If anything, he'll have that 'solid' that Noah might eventually repay him, and it won't cost him anything to do it. "What about you, Dylan?"

"I can, but I'm not much into that side of the restaurant scene," I admit. "I leave the running of Lionfish in the hands of those who actually give a damn about the restaurant business. On the other hand, real estate is something I do know a bit about. How's that going for you here?"

This is the turnabout. He asks about my restaurant as a means to an end for himself, and I flip it back, asking about the real estate he specializes in to see if there might be information or opportunity I'm unaware of. It's how the game is played. We're all sifting through the polite conversations for tiny nuggets of intel that might prove valuable in the right circumstances.

"Excellent," he says, sighing in delight as he takes a sip of his mezcal. "But I suspect you know that already," he teases. "You own this building, yes?"

I'm not surprised he knows that. He's new to town, I'm a major player, and he was invited here tonight. If he hadn't done his homework on me, *that* would surprise me.

I nod. "Bought it five years ago," I say, thinking back. "Took over the penthouse three years ago."

Though he looks around as if seeing the room he's been in all night for the first time, he's likely doing some quick mental math about its value then and current worth, and putting that information up against what he knows of the city's real estate market. "It's lovely. Probably your housekeeper's worst nightmare with the black marble, though." His grin is bright as he gestures to the shiny surfaces in the kitchen, which all gleam with zero fingerprints.

I chuckle. "Honestly, I have no idea because I rarely go in there except to pull something out of the fridge. I can't tell you the last time I touched anything else in the kitchen. Meghan would probably chop my fingers off," I tell them, imagining my house manager finding me putting dirty fingerprints all over what's essentially her space since she's the one who cooks, cleans, and uses the area. I rarely ever see her, and that's one of the reasons I hired her. She's quick, efficient, and I don't have to lift a finger.

"Remember your roots," Austin jokes, and we all laugh good-naturedly. At this level, we all have a 'Meghan' who helps us. Ollie certainly doesn't clean his own toilet, and while Teddy says he'll be changing diapers when the baby comes, he's not whipping up family meals every night. Our time is better spent elsewhere.

But Austin's right, the boy I was would never have thought about leaving any sort of kitchen mess for hired help to clean up. Hell, the student I was would save money by patching my clothes and sewing up the holes on my undershirts or workout shirts instead of buying new ones. Even after I started making money, I kept up the practice until I realized that it was costing me more in lost money-making time to patch my old stuff than it would to simply have it mended or replaced for me.

I've come a long way since those days, but I still remember them.

"Don't worry, I still keep a few mementos of the past around,"

I tell Austin. He gives me a look of sadness, all too aware that I'm not talking about old T-shirts or childhood toys. The most important things I carry with me from those days are scars that can't be seen.

But tonight's game with friends, both new and old, has done a good job of keeping me from picking at them.

"Dylan, your deal," Teddy calls out, and we rejoin him at the table.

I'm dealing out cards when Teddy suddenly jerks, grabbing his phone from his pocket. "Sorry, might be Claire," he explains.

We don't have a no-phone rule. None of us can afford to be offline for long because even if the markets are closed, there are hundreds of other things that might happen which would send us immediately to the closest computer to buy, sell, or research something. Even during a night out.

He talks for a moment, promising to come home with chocolate cake, something that Claire urgently needs, apparently, and then hangs up. "Sorry," he says, but the smile on his face says he didn't mind the quick check-in with his wife.

"That's nothing to apologize for," Ollie says. "Money is good, but family? That's important."

"I don't know, Ollie," Austin says. He's as much an avowed bachelor as I am, and a man who's also seen his fair share of pain. He's never shared with me all the details, but I've seen that familiar haunted look in his eyes that sometimes reflects in my own. "Family love doesn't pay the bills."

"Bills?" Ollie echoes, shaking his head and tutting Austin

gently. "Austin, each of us in this room has more than enough money to never have to work a day in our lives again if we want. I could liquidate my assets right now and put them in a general, low-interest money market account, and my family wouldn't have to work for generations. I am literally rich enough to buy an entire country. Maybe not a big one, but still, an entire country. And each of you is close to the same. Am I right?" He doesn't wait for our agreement, knowing the answer. "But I'd trade it all, every last penny, if the choice was that or my family. They're irreplaceable."

Everyone is reflecting on what Ollie just said when Teddy speaks up again, his voice almost contemplative. "'There comes a time, thief, when the jewels cease to sparkle, when the gold loses its luster, when the throne room becomes a prison, and all that is left is a father's love for his child.'"

"What's that from?" I ask, unsuccessfully trying to place what is obviously a verbatim quote, and Teddy chuckles.

"*Conan the Barbarian*. Pretty good film. But that's stuck with me ever since Claire became pregnant."

Before we can give him too much shit about becoming sappy as hell, Ollie interjects. "I hope and pray that each of you gentlemen understands that someday. Truly."

It's kind of hard to argue against that degree of genuine sentimentality, and we fall quiet. Our game's temporarily forgotten, and I think about how much has changed. It used to be that I would never have thought like this. It wasn't even an option. I was going to take over the world. He who gets to the top first, while amassing the biggest pile of money, wins. That was it, the entirety of the game plan. But now…

Do I need the whole world?

What would Raven think of my home? Or of my friends, even?

What would she think of an oversized television, premium leather couch, or custom-made bed with Egyptian cotton sheets?

Would she see the sacrifices I've made to obtain all of this? Or would she see it the same way Austin jokes about my aircraft carrier model, a shallow, if not futile, attempt to make up for a hard childhood?

Would she be impressed by the trappings of wealth I've surrounded myself with as a shield to protect myself from my past? Or not give a damn as long as she got me in the deal?

And isn't that the biggest question of all? Am I enough, or am I simply a means to an end for her?

I don't know.

I don't think she's using me. She's too naïve, too innocent in her goals for that, but the damage done to my heart doesn't let outsiders in easily. I might have feelings for Raven, ones that go well beyond my desire for her body and appreciation of her mind, but only time will tell what it means. I don't know what I want from her, but I know I want more of her. I'm not exactly sure what all I'm willing to give in return, though.

We play a few more hands, but my mood has shifted. I want to see Raven. Fuck, I feel like I *need* to see her, if for no other reason than to confirm that she's still mine.

It's wishful thinking, well beneath my analytical mind, but

the foolish desire is there nonetheless, flitting about inside my warped heart.

It's nearly an hour later when my phone vibrates in my pocket. "Just a minute, gentlemen," I say, standing up and picking up my glass. "I need a refresher. Anyone else?"

I go over to my bar and open up my phone.

There's a message from Raven. *Thank you for this weekend. Mom loved the hotel.*

I'm glad. Are you staying with her tonight?

I need to know where she is, not because I have any claim on her, but so my mind will rest easier as I try to sleep later. It will be a futile attempt, but at least this will be one less concern on my heavy mind.

No, she's leaving early in the morning and wanted a good night's sleep. I'm at home.

My heartbeat skips and flips in a noticeable way. She is available. I could go to her, or have her brought here.

Come over. I'll send a car.

Dylan...

I swallow and type three words that show more weakness than I'd prefer to reveal. *I need you. Apparently, you have me addicted.*

I need her tonight more than ever. I need the distraction her body offers, the pinpoint focus her smile provides, the relief from the painful past that only she can bring.

I wait, watching for her answer, and when it comes and she's agreed to come over, I can't stop the unbidden smile that stretches my mouth. *Sending a car now.*

I slip my phone back into my pocket and glance up to find everyone's eyes on me, apparently watching the entirety of my text exchange with Raven play out on my face.

"I know what that grin means," Austin says.

"I'm sorry to say, that's the game," I announce. "Thank you all for coming over, but I've got something that needs my attention tonight."

Teddy grumbles. He's down about two thousand dollars, while Noah looks curious. Austin raises a brow at my wording, "More like *someone* needs your attention." He doesn't sound upset. If anything, he's amused at my quick turn of mood.

Austin's clarification gets Ollie moving quickly. "In that case, I believe we can cash out and be out of here in ten minutes, don't you, gentlemen?"

Austin starts counting his chips. He's willing to make a guess, if anything. "We can pick this up another night."

"That works for me," I tell them and glance at the clock, eager for them to get out so I can have Raven all to myself.

CHAPTER 19

RAVEN

My heart's in my throat as the elevator climbs up the shaft. The doorman in the lobby said nothing, not even raising a brow as he scanned the panel for me and sent me on my way.

I'm still not sure if I'm doing the right thing, neither by running over here like I'm at Dylan's beck and call, nor in what I chose to wear while doing it. But Maggie supported me when I told her my idea, helping me pick out an outfit. She even helped me knot the trench coat I borrowed from her closet, the remnant of an old Halloween costume of hers where she dressed as Carmen Sandiego. She's 'released me into the wilds', as she called it when the car Dylan sent showed up.

The elevator slows, and the door dings before opening, revealing a short, almost perfunctory hallway in front of a set of ornate, all-black double doors. Stepping forward, I clear my throat, swallowing my fear as the elevator closes behind me.

Am I doing the right thing? Is this reckless? Am I going to regret it?

I don't know, but I'm doing what every fiber of my body tells me I have to do. That I *want* to. That I want *him*. All night, during dinner, I felt like I was in the wrong place, that where I needed to be was in his arms.

Lifting a trembling fist, I go to knock on the door, but before I can, the doors swing open on silent hinges, revealing the foyer inside. He's standing there, just on the edge of where the foyer becomes what looks like a short set of steps to an elevated living room, and the rest of the penthouse suite stretching out beyond.

Of course he'd live in the penthouse. But he looks like he's exactly where he should be. I know that wasn't always the case. I learned that from my research about how he became a self-made man, and Dylan's alluded to rougher days in his past. But you'd never know it now. He's perfectly at home surrounded by opulence. It suits him.

He looks powerful and knee-quakingly handsome. He's dressed like he just got done at the office, his black suit pants tailored to his body, his shirt unbuttoned a few buttons to reveal his smooth, powerful chest, his sleeves rolled up, showing off the corded muscles of his forearms.

Holy hell. This man is bad for me in ways that feel too damn good.

"Mr. Sharpe," I rasp, my legs quaking. We're not at work, and there's no one who might overhear us, but I use the professional name intentionally, nearly purring it. "I missed you today."

"I missed you too, Miss Hill." There's a hint of tease to his voice as he plays along with me, but mostly, what I hear is the barely disguised need in his words. It sends a shiver down my spine.

"What have you been up to?" I ask casually. As if this could be an everyday occurrence as I walk deeper into his suite and look around while he closes the door behind me.

"Killing time until I could fuck you again."

I gasp, turning to meet his gaze. Hypnotized, I stand tall while his eyes grace over my body—my breasts, my hips, my exposed legs, and back up to my face. "What are you wearing?"

"This?" I say, reaching for the trench coat's belt and undoing it. The coat falls open, revealing the lacy, red see-thru lingerie and thigh-high stockings I'm wearing underneath. As soon as I saw them in my dresser drawer, I knew they were all I wanted to wear. They're the sexiest set I own. I look him in the eye, steeling my voice. "Or this?" I say, drawing my fingertip down the line of my cleavage.

"Fuck, Raven." He barely breathes the words as his bottom lip drops down. "I need you."

He steps forward, taking my hand and kissing my knuckles, his eyes burning with desire. I definitely chose the right outfit, and given the way Dylan's looking at me, I made the correct choice in coming, too. His reaction, both to my body and my presence, is everything I hoped it would be.

"Then take me," I say with soft smile.

He leads me through the living room and to the sweeping, curving stairs. All around me, I can sense wealth and luxury, but my eyes never leave Dylan as he guides me up the wide, shallow steps to the second floor, and then down a short hallway to an enormous bedroom that's dominated by a massive king bed. Stopping at the foot of the bed, Dylan looks me up and down. "You're beautiful, Darling," he says, brushing a lock of my hair back over my shoulder.

"I need you too," I tell him.

Dylan's hand travels to my shoulder where he presses down, and I sink to my knees and reach for his belt. My mouth goes dry as I undo his belt and ease his zipper down, freeing the length of his thick cock. Looking up, I see that he dips his chin in permission, and I lean forward, licking him from root all the way to his tip, tasting his warm skin and coating him with my saliva, before worshiping Dylan's cock with soft butterfly kisses around his head.

Dylan touches my jaw, and I open my mouth, staying very still as he takes my head in his hands and slowly feeds me his cock. Velvety steel fills my mouth, stretching my lips and pushing over my tongue. Reaching up, I roll his sac in my hand, weighing his balls and devoting everything to his pleasure as he invades my mouth, holding there for a moment before pulling back.

"I want you to touch yourself while I fuck these pretty lips of yours," he says, his voice tight and hard. "When I come, you're not going to swallow a single drop until I say so. Do you understand?"

"Mmm-hmm," I moan around his cock, and Dylan jerks forward, touching the back of my throat with his crown.

"Do it, Raven. Touch yourself. Obey me." There's a darkness to him now, and I welcome it, wanting all of him—the powerful, domineering devil he thinks he is. And while I know he can be that, he's also watchful and careful with me, pushing at my limits but respecting them. It makes me want to go further, just to prove to us both that I can.

I want to please him in all things. Personal and professional. And right now, sexual.

A warm tingle goes through me, and I do as ordered, reaching down between my legs to stroke my clit through my panties. I time my fingers with his thrusts, rubbing back and forth until I'm hot and wet and my clit is swollen and pressed electrically against the thin fabric.

Pulling my panties aside, I slide two fingers deep inside me, moaning around Dylan's cock as he fucks my throat. My cheeks hollow out, my tongue working for one purpose and one purpose only, to please him. I run it everywhere, up the underside of his shaft, around the flared ridge of his head, even into his slit when he pulls back far enough.

All I want to do is make him feel good, to please him and hear him moan my name.

"That's it… that's it… good girl," Dylan says as he speeds up. I open as wide as I can, letting him take me, my fingers squelching in the quiet bedroom. "So fucking good…." He pauses at the back of my throat, testing my gag reflex. "So fucking beautiful…" He does it again, and I whimper. "So fucking mine." He stays there this time, giving me shallow thrusts as he holds himself right at the edge of what I can take.

I am his. I realize it, and I know that he's claimed my body in a way no man ever has before. I've never given in like this to any man, but with him, I want to do it all.

My pussy's in need, my thumb rubbing my clit to bring myself to the trembling edge. I'm helpless, the back of my head gripped in Dylan's powerful hands as I try to get us both to the edge together. I want to come with him. I'm desperate to do so, moaning to draw him up higher and desperately strumming my clit. He can feel how desperate I am, and the bastard chuckles.

"You want me to come quickly, don't you?" he asks.

I whimper, looking up at him with tears pricking at the corners of my eyes. I nod, keeping him sucked into my mouth.

"You want my cum?" My brows furrow, the sense of deprivation overwhelming me—not of air, but of him. I want it, I want him, all of him.

He watches me closely. "Are you gonna take my cum like a good girl?"

I cry out, painfully on the cusp of coming without him as my pussy clenches. His answering grin is wicked. He knows exactly what he's doing to me, driving me mad, making me crazed, but only for him.

He pulls back until just the head of his cock's trapped between my lips as he uses two fingers to quickly pump his shaft. Groaning, he throws his head back as he starts coming, his sweet and salty seed coating my tongue and filling my mouth. At the same time, I stroke my clit again, moaning as I tip over the edge myself, coming around my fingers as he fills my mouth.

I want to swallow, I want to open my mouth and cry out, but Dylan told me not to spill a single drop. So I obey, my hips shaking and my thighs quivering until the wave passes and he's spent. Pulling back, he smiles, tilting my chin up to look at him. "Open. Show me how good you are."

I do, letting him see, and he pulls me to my feet, commanding me to swallow. Dylan lifts me, his hands digging into my ass as he turns and carries me to the bed, my arms around his neck as he kisses my neck and then my lips.

"You're such a good little cocksucker," Dylan praises me as he sets me on the bed. "My sweet Darling, my Raven." Every word that falls off his tongue hits a new part of my brain, making all of me come alive in different ways until I feel like there's an electrical surge jolting though my body. "Lie back, and hold your ankles for me."

Dylan guides me to the bed's surface. He slides my panties up my legs and off before I grab my ankles as he commanded.

He leans in and gives me a kiss before running a hand down my stocking-covered leg. "These fucking destroy me," he hisses in the sexiest groan I've ever heard. "I want you to wear them every fucking day. At the office, when we go out, wherever. You wear stockings so I know this pussy is right there, ready for me to have it." His gaze lingers between my legs, one hand still working his shaft.

"Fucking hell, Raven," he groans and then stands up, shrugging off his shirt and dropping his pants the rest of the way down his legs. I've never seen him totally nude before. We've always had some type of clothing on, but seeing him like this takes my breath away. He's formed perfectly, flesh that's been sculpted by the hands of an artist, it feels like, and my pussy clenches with need as he kneels on the edge of the bed, his wolfish grin promising me total release.

He's tasted me before, but this time, I have a close-up view as Dylan drags his tongue between my pussy lips and then up to kiss my lips quickly, slipping his tongue into my mouth. "Taste yourself," he orders, and I kiss him back hungrily, sucking the tip of his tongue and getting my own sweet flavor in return.

Dylan's eyes light up and flash with a primal hunger, and he goes back down between my legs. All the while, my heart races and my body hears.

He starts with wide, flat licks. He savors every inch of me, even licking a bit lower, playfully teasing me. I've never done anal, but if Dylan wanted it, I would try it.

He can have anything he wants, I realize. I've been so torn, asking myself if this is wise, worrying about what other people would think if they knew, and losing sleep over what Dylan feels about me when the truth is… none of it matters. I'm his. He's said 'mine', and my hopeful heart has believed him, giving itself over fully to him.

My mind races with thoughts I shouldn't be having.

The joy of what I'm feeling works through me almost as

quickly as the pleasure Dylan's masterfully forcing onto my body.

He goes back to my folds, snaking his tongue deep inside me, devouring my pussy before sucking on my lips until my eyes roll back and the back of my head digs into the mattress.

"Oh, my God," I cry out, and he stops.

"No, my name only. Say my name," he growls, looking up my body to pin me in his gaze.

"Yes, sir. Dylan, sir," I tease breathily. I know what hearing me say that does to him, and I throw it back at him intentionally, wanting to push him the way he did me.

He smiles, his eyes flashing devilishly, and I wonder if I'm ready for whatever he's going to do next.

He moves back to my pussy, his tongue circling around my core until he finds my clit with the tip of his tongue. Looking into my face, he watches my reaction as he tortures me, not with pain but pleasure. He pushes two fingers inside me, adding to the wondrous torment, and my entire soul writhes with need. It feels like it's the entire world, pulsating and quivering under his complete control.

It's all I've ever wanted, all I ever need, and more. As Dylan's tongue moves faster and faster, his fingers working that spot inside me, I'm left panting, drawing in breath almost to immediately exhale, my body burning with desire for him.

As I fist the sheets and my back bows, I barely hear Dylan.

"Come for me, my darling Raven. Give me what's mine," he orders before fastening his mouth around my clit and sucking sharply. My body falls apart, unlocked by his claim and his command to release fully. I cry out loudly, writhing as an intense, sweeping orgasm cascades through my body.

Dylan stays there, watching me toss my head from side to side, letting me ride every bit of my pleasure before he kisses his way up my body, trailing up my stomach until he reaches my bra. He unclips it, letting it fall aside to suckle on my right nipple.

Letting go of my ankles, I run my hands through his hair, arching my back to give him more and wrapping my legs around his waist. My stockinged legs slide against his lean midsection but still keep me open and available to him.

Dylan releases my nipple to kiss up to my lips, which he captures once more as his hard cock presses against my warmth. He pins my wrists above my head and slides all the way into me until I can take no more and whimper in fullness.

He breaks our kiss to ask, "Who do you belong to, Darling?"

"You," I respond, and I'm rewarded with a deep, quick thrust that makes the world spin.

"Say it."

"I belong to you," I affirm, and he rewards me with another thrust. "Fuck… please, Dylan, I'm yours."

"Only mine," he murmurs as he fucks me ruthlessly, taking me like he owns me.

There's a fresh desperation to his words, like he thinks I'm going to leave him. But I'm realizing there is no leaving Dylan Sharpe. Ever. I am ruined for anyone else. I'm his, and his alone.

My heart thumps in a way that slows time.

"What are you?" he asks, and I look into his eyes to see what he wants me to say.

I know, but I don't give it to him. Not yet.

"I'm your newest associate," I reply, squeezing my pussy around his cock with a teasing smile. "I'm the best talent you've ever hired." My lips are swollen and my breath is still coming in pants, but I tease him. He groans as though my disobedience is turning him on. I drop my voice, whispering hotly, "I'm also your sweet, dirty, naughty slut who spends every minute she's not making you money thinking about one thing and one thing only. Fucking you senseless."

I expect him to unleash on me, the power of the filthy words driving him wild.

"You make me so fucking happy," Dylan says, kissing me hard and thrusting deep inside me.

I gasp, at both the sweetness of what he just shared and the feeling of him filling and stretching me to the brink of near pain until it mixes with the divine pleasure.

The sensation of his fucking me with powerful strokes erases all thoughts from my mind. I hold onto him, crying out my pleasure.

There's no need for words. They're not intense enough as Dylan's hips rise and fall, his cock hammering into my eager, willing body. We say all we need to in our touch, in the way his chest presses against mine and his hands tighten on my crossed wrists. I say it in the way my legs lock around his waist, my stockinged thighs squeezing him, urging him to fuck me harder, deeper, longer.

Time evaporates, replaced with lust. Thoughts melt, replaced with feeling. And as my third release builds into a tremendous tidal wave of bliss, the only things left are Dylan and the desire to be like this with him... forever.

He groans his release, and I'm there with him, our bodies thrumming with the shattering of our coming together. I hold him there, both of us frozen until we collapse, Dylan falling to the side and rolling with me to avoid hurting me.

I notice... and in that moment, I become his all the more. I don't know when I fell, exactly, but I'm in love with him. As my heart settles, I know I have fallen for him.

Lying in his arms, my pulse still rushes through my veins, the sweat cooling on my skin as we come down from what just happened.

"Are you okay?" Dylan asks me, and I nod, kissing his chest and unable to admit aloud the thought I just had.

We lie like that, both lost in our thoughts. Tonight was big, probably the biggest leap forward we've had, and I think we both need some time to sit with that. Or at least I do, because now that I'm not chasing an orgasm, I can feel that something major has shifted.

"I should go home," I whisper, not wanting to but knowing it's probably the right thing to do.

"Stay," he counters.

I try to imagine what that looks like and gasp. "I am not doing the walk of shame tomorrow morning in a cheap red trench coat. My neighbors would never look at me the same way again."

He shrugs, unconcerned. "I can have clothes sent up for you."

I push up to stare at him in shock. That thought would never occur to me. Just 'have clothes sent'? Who does that?

Dylan Sharpe does.

I laugh. "No, I don't want you to do that," I confess. "I kind of like the idea of a naughty rendezvous in a skimpy outfit and sneaking out before the sun rises. It's a bit wild for me, like a scene from a cheesy movie."

He looks up at me, laughter teasing across his twitching lips. "Don't ruin it for me. I'll look better tonight than I will in the morning."

At that, he does laugh. "Okay, if you want to go, I understand. I think I might actually get some sleep tonight, which I didn't think I'd be able to do."

"Why?" I ask.

A shadow passes through his eyes and he shakes his head. "It doesn't matter because you've worn me out." He looks at me in wonder, like he's not quite sure how I did that. "Let me show you to the bathroom so you can clean up."

The bed groans as he helps me from the bed, leading me to a private bathroom that's as luxurious as I expected it to be, with a huge shower the size of my bedroom, a long double vanity I give a side eye to, wondering which sink he uses, and a tub I could nearly swim in. He gives me privacy, and I clean up quickly.

Back in the bedroom, he holds out a long-sleeve T-shirt. "Does it ruin it if you wear my shirt under the trench coat? It's chilly outside."

I smirk, letting him pull the shirt over my head and settle it down my thighs. Every time his skin brushes mine, something races through me. He's gotten dressed too, in a similar T-shirt and a pair of sweatpants. I look between us, taking a mental snapshot of the moment.

My heart does that thing again, and I wish it wouldn't.

He leads me back downstairs, out the front door, and to the elevator. As we descend, he reaches into his pocket and pulls out a small tag that looks a lot like an AirTag. "Here. For your keychain."

"What is it?" I ask, and he points to the sensor panel on the elevator. "Really?"

"It won't open my front door, so you can't sneak in to surprise me in the shower," he jokes, tilting his head as if considering the merits of that idea, and I laugh softly. It's not a front door key, but it's a big deal, especially to a man like him who has to protect himself from virtually everyone and everything.

We get to the lobby, where I find a taxi waiting for me.

"Thank you for seeing me on such short notice, Mr. Sharpe," I say in my most professional voice, teasing him with a tilt of my head.

"Anytime, Miss Hill. I'll see you Monday, then?" he says. He doesn't feign appropriateness. His voice promises he's going to see all of me on Monday, and I climb into the taxi, not knowing how I fell for him but afraid of what happens if it's entirely one-sided.

CHAPTER 20

RAVEN

Stretching my arms over my head, I feel my back crackle in three places as both shoulder blades and my left elbow let go of tension I've been holding inside for three hours. It's been a week since Mom's visit, and if she could see me now, she really wouldn't understand why I love what I do. But I absolutely do love it.

The markets were hectic this morning, with the news that a European billionaire got caught with a couple of bedmates, neither of which was her husband, causing a ripple effect on everything her company has a foothold in.

It's amazing how ridiculous traders can be, as the arrangement has clearly been going on for at least a couple of weeks, if not months or years. And this particular billionaire isn't even involved in the day-to-day operations of her family's corporation, an entity that's been steadily profitable for the past sixty years.

And yet, where and how this woman gets her personal itches scratched has certain people ready to declare that a five-generations-old conglomerate is going to go belly up.

But I was able to jump in, grabbing three hundred shares of the stock for my own portfolio on the dip and another five thousand for my professional account before watching in anticipation for the bounce, which came in mere hours when the family put out an official press release addressing the rumors. I submitted the sale on my professional account first, and then, mere moments later, on my personal account, losing only a quarter point in the difference. In both portfolios, I made a tidy profit, so I'm calling this morning a resounding win.

There's a knock on my cubicle wall, and I look over to see Hector Williams, one of my new co-workers, sticking his head around the corner. "Hey, Heck. How was your morning? You rake it in with the European market?"

"Not too shabby," Hector says, tossing his trademark locked hair from side to side. I'm actually not sure he's able to talk without his head moving. "I'm getting the numbers down for tonight's get-together. You're coming, right?"

"Where is it again?" I ask.

"McGinty's," he answers, then gives me the breakdown that I already read in the company email. "We all get together at the end of every month, usually on a Friday like today. This will be a bigger one than most, because we'll be welcoming the new hires, like you, Shanna, and Mitchell. Boss Man will come by and press palms, rally the troops, and then we're free to celebrate our wins and losses as we see fit."

"That sounds like code for hazing," I tease with a pointed look, and he shakes his head with a laugh. I didn't think that was the case, but still, it's good to confirm I'm not walking into a trap. Wait… "Who's pressing palms?"

"Boss Man. Mr. Sharpe. Just for a minute, though," he says, holding his hands up like people usually run away from the terrifying Dylan Sharpe. Luckily, Hector doesn't know that I'm the type that runs to him, literally at the drop of a text. "Six thirty? I'll put you down?" he asks, pointing at his phone where it seems he's keeping a running tally of attendees.

I nod. "Wouldn't miss it."

As Hector walks off and I hear him knocking on the next cubicle, I reach for my phone.

I hear you're making an appearance at McGinty's tonight.

Dylan's busy so I don't expect him to answer right away, but within minutes, I see the three dots and then his reply.

Monthly tradition, though I hate that it takes priority over our after hours work.

Honestly, I'm a bit disappointed to miss them too.

But getting together with the people from work is important. Especially with the rumors. I feel like I'm finding my place here and getting to know everyone, so being invited to go out with them is a must-do, even if it's still a bit of a work function, not a friendly outing. I was initially worried the news of mine and Dylan's behavior at the fundraiser would've preemptively poisoned people against me, but for the most part, it seems people at this level don't know about it. Or they simply don't care. Whatever the case, I'm thankful for it because I think I could really be good friends with some of my coworkers, and tonight is another step in the right direction.

Me too. I was excited to tell you about my morning.

Our after-work meetings always end in toe-curling orgasms, but they start with Dylan and me talking through my investments. He says I'm doing an even better job than he'd hoped, but he's also guiding me as I learn more. I thought my success this morning would be worth a 'great work', at least, or an orgasmic bonus at most, so I'm disappointed to not get to share it with him.

European markets?

Yes! It was amazing!

He goes quiet for a moment, and I think he's gotten caught up in something else, but then he says, *Checked your numbers. Great work, Raven.*

There it is—the warm, bubbly feeling in my chest when he praises me like that. I can't help the smile that slips onto my lips.

Thank you. See you tonight.

I do a happy spin in my chair before grabbing my lunch from my locker. I go back to my desk to eat while I see what else is happening on the markets this afternoon. And before I know it, the bells are ringing across the globe to close out another day. I do some recording and analysis of my various portfolios and wrap up.

Before long, thoughts about the day get tucked away as I step into McGinty's, heels clicking on the concrete sidewalk, then dulled on the wooden floor. It's an institution in the Financial District, an authentic Irish pub that traces its roots all the way to 1847, when Sheamus McGinty brought his family to the USA from County Cork.

I've been here before more than once. It's a pub that's garnered a reputation similar to Lionfish, just the junior league version. It's the place where young, hungry up and comers in the Financial District share a pint after a day's hard work.

It's also got a reputation of being a bit of a frat house, and as I join the sea of dark suits and the waves of faint cologne hit me in the nose, I'm reminded of the last few times I've been here.

Tonight, there's an actual band on the stage, playing traditional Irish music, and I give them a glance before scanning for people I know. Thankfully, I see Hector waving at me from across the room and head that way.

"Raven!" he calls, greeting me loudly. He's gathered by the long, black oak bar, his coat already ditched somewhere and his sleeves rolled up his forearms, which highlights his Rolex watch. "Glad you could make it. First one's on the company! Guinness?"

It's not one of my favorites, but it seems to be apropos, so I nod and a moment later, the bartender hands me a pint.

"Cheers," I reply, clinking mugs with him. Three other people around us hold their glasses up too, smiling and clinking with us. I'm not sure if they even work at Sharpe or are maybe just financial district types out for a nightcap after work.

Hector takes a sip, bobbing his head to the music. "You don't look like the Irish music type."

"I used to work here, back in college," Hector says, grinning at my surprise. "I know, I know. It's the locs, right?"

"Something like that," I admit, and he laughs.

"You'll see when I get up there and start belting out some Dropkick Murphys!" he vows, his voice rising as he completes his statement. It's greeted by a roar of approval, and behind the bar, a staff member rolls her eyes. "Worker's Song, Worker's Song!" he chants, and a few take up the rally with him.

"Worker's Song?" I ask when he quiets, and he nods. "Sorry, I'm unfamiliar with it."

"Best 'fuck the rich' song recorded in the past twenty years," Hector says quite seriously. "Pretty awesome bagpipes, too."

I nod, deciding to take his word on that because my musical tastes run a little more popstar and a bit less... bagpipe.

More people arrive, and the party really begins, though no one gets too wild. It's more of a 'who do you work for' and 'how'd you do in the markets today' than 'let's get as shit-faced as fast as possible' vibe.

Right at six forty-five, the doors open and Dylan arrives. A cheer goes up from everyone, and Dylan looks around, nodding and smiling.

He looks... divine. Handsome as always, but more rugged in some ways. His sleeves are rolled up, highlighting his strong forearms and masculine hands. He's removed his tie and undone a couple of buttons at his throat, and his eyes are bright and happy.

In that realization, I remember what he said... *You make me happy.*

It takes all my strength not to run over to greet him, which would be disastrous, so thankfully, I manage to keep my butt on my barstool. I run my fingers up and down the cold glass of ale.

"I see we haven't forgotten how to have a little bit of fun in this company," Dylan says to more cheers. He raises his hand, and everyone quiets. "But seriously, this month's traditionally been a good one for us, but it's been even better than usual... because of you." He looks across the gathered group who're hanging on his every word. "We've got our new hires here, so let's make them feel welcome. You've all been great mentors to them, which I appreciate. Keep up the good work there." A few people fist bump one another, like they've got their 'teamwork makes the dream work' on lockdown. "To the new hires, continue to learn from your colleagues. They've been where you are. They've built the house you work in today. So lift a glass, not to me, but to those who've come before, to those who come after, and to yourselves. Cheers!"

"Cheers!" the group replies in unison.

I lift my glass, toasting with the person I'm next to, Shanna. She's also young, and though she's been with the company for about six months, she was only recently officially hired on. Previously, she was an intern with the firm her senior year of college, and she impressed enough to be offered a job in the payroll department upon graduation.

"Cheers, Shanna," I reply, clinking glasses with her and taking a drink of my beer. "Welcome to Sharpe," I tell her, teasing since we're both new hires.

"You too," she answers with a laugh before she floats away to continue a conversation with a guy who I think works in HR. Or maybe he's an analyst? I'm not sure.

I continue to mingle, meeting new people and chatting with the ones I already know, and out of the corner of my eye, I notice Dylan making the rounds too. He stops by each group for just a minute, and I can tell he's being as political as he is sincere. It's not that he doesn't want to give time to the people here, but he knows this isn't quite his place. So he checks in, smiles, and moves on.

I'm over by the pub's long 'slingers' table, watching a couple of the team play the shuffleboard-like bar game, when I feel him coming up behind me, and I turn around. "Mr. Sharpe."

"Miss Hill," he says, and once again, I feel that tingle of desire that permeates every instance Dylan and I are together. "Enjoying yourself, I hope?"

"I am. Thank you," I say politely with what I hope is a warm smile, not an 'I've seen you naked' grin. "The European markets were quite the roller coaster today."

He licks his lips and smirks. "They were. I saw you made significant margins this morning. How was the afternoon?"

"Not as good," I admit, seeming disappointed in that. "But tomorrow's a new day, right?"

"That it is."

To anyone around us, it hopefully seems like perfectly pleasant, professional small talk. Nothing untoward happening here, certainly nothing rumor-worthy.

I feel eyes landing on us, then quickly looking away, and I arch a brow, reminding Dylan that we're keeping us a secret, so we can't blow it by making eyes at each other while we fake banal chatter.

Because despite my even tone, I can't help the stars in my eyes when I look at him. He's strong, powerful, and sexy, and there's a part of me that wants to say 'fuck this place and fuck the rumors' and climb into his car so we can go back to his place.

"Well, I'll see you later," he says, nodding goodbye and moving to the next group of people.

I watch him go, and I don't even realize I didn't say goodbye until it's too late.

Wait, does he mean later like later tonight, like he's inviting me over? Or did he simply mean later like sometime in the future? Or was it just a polite phrasing of goodbye?

I don't know, and I can't exactly ask with everyone around.

I make my way across the pub, where Shanna's standing by the bar, getting another drink. "Hey."

"Hey!" she says, sounding slightly tipsy already. "What's up, girlfriend?"

"Just having another," I reply after ordering another beer, and Shanna grins.

"Me too!" She makes it sound like we've got something major in common, not just something as expected as getting a drink in a bar.

"How many is this for you?" I ask, a little concerned. I don't know her well enough to gauge her tolerance, and she seems happy-tipsy, not over-served, but I still watch out for others.

"So far?" she asks, looking up. "Uh, Jason bought me one, Liam bought me one, Danny bought me one... ah... oh, and Eric bought me this one."

"Buying beers for you?" I ask worriedly, and she nods, grinning. "Is that, you know... all good?"

"It's no biggie," Shanna assures me. "They're just trying to hook up, and I'm the one getting the drinks from the bartender, so I know it's safe." She wiggles her fingers in a flirty wave, and I follow her gaze across the room to where the guys she's talking about are looking this way and returning her wave, encouraging her to come back to the table.

Her eyes clear a bit and she leans in, divulging in crisp, enunciated speech, "Besides, they talk more when they think I'm drunk. You can learn a lot."

When she pulls back, her glassy eyes are back and her smile is a bit knowing. Ooh, she's a smart one. I like her even more.

"Besides, it's not like we're a hookup den. But a little flirting to get through the long days at the office? No harm, no foul, you know?" she teases.

I shake my head. "Uh, sure?"

She's stepping into dangerous territory... dangerous for me. And I want to back away from it entirely.

Shanna tilts her head, considering me. "Oh, I thought you

were the one getting 'Sharped'? My bad, sorry." She takes her drink from the bartender, completely oblivious that she just upended my entire life. "Excuse me, better get back to the boys," she says, sashaying toward the table across the room.

She knows.

I look around, seeing the smiling, laughing faces of my coworkers.

They all know.

I'm fucking the boss. I'm fucking Dylan. I'm getting 'Sharped'. I didn't even know that was a thing, but it rolled off Shanna's tongue like it's something she's said before, so it must be.

They probably think that's how I got my position, which is exactly what I didn't want to happen. I thought I was being so sly, that we were being so careful that nobody would notice. Yet apparently, it's taken less than a month for me to be labeled as Dylan's personal plaything.

They probably knew all along, those rumors they never mentioned getting to them even before we met. Every interaction where I thought I was making a friend at work comes back to me rapid-fire. They were probably cozying up to me in the hopes of garnering favor with Dylan. I thought I was getting further and further away from the consequences of that night at the fundraiser, but the truth is, it's been following me like a shadow cloud just outside my field of view.

The realization makes my stomach churn.

I have to get out of here.

I flag down the bartender, hoping to tell him I don't need that beer after all, but he sets it down in front of me right as Hector stops at the bar. "Here, this one's on me," I tell him, pushing it his way. "I'm heading home."

"Oh! Thanks, but you're gonna miss my much-anticipated return to the stage," he teases with a grin.

"Next time," I promise, knowing there won't be a next time.

I weave through the crowd toward the door, feeling alone in the sea of people. People I thought were becoming my friends.

That's fine, I tell myself. I have friends—Maggie and Ami— and they're great. In fact, they're probably sitting at home on the couch right now, eating whatever Ami pulled the birthday card on to talk Maggie into ordering. I can go home and join them, knowing they care about me and don't give a shit about who I'm sleeping with as long as I'm happy.

And I have Dylan, who would spread me out on his desk, his bed, or any damn place and remind me that I'm beautiful, desirable, and his at a moment's notice.

In the big scheme of things, the fact that my co-workers know isn't all that catastrophic. But outside, as the night air blows through my already cold body, it feels like a big deal. A big, ugly, cringey deal that's going to ruin my reputation again right as I thought I was rebuilding it.

CHAPTER 21

DYLAN

"Tamara," I muse as she sits across from me at my desk, "have you heard anything about the Faulkners?"

"You mean like have there been any declarations of blood vendettas or swearing that you're going to have your head mounted on a flagpole outside the Faulkner Building?" she asks wryly, her eyes never lifting from the tablet in her lap. When I don't answer, she glances up. "Nothing more than usual. Why do you ask?"

"Oh, just… curious," I reply, and Tamara slides her glasses down her nose to peer at me pointedly. "What?" I ask.

"Mr. Sharpe, you have me in this position because I do good work," she says, which is an understatement. Tamara's worth twice the money I pay her, and she's already compensated at a rate higher than anyone else in an equivalent position in the Financial District. I know this because she knows this, and whenever she's come to me with a request for a pay raise, I sign off on it without question.

"You do good work. I would agree."

"I'm able to do that because you keep me in the loop on things," Tamara continues, "and in the years we've been working together, you've rarely kept me out of the loop without good reason."

"That you know of," I counter.

Tamara snorts. "Mr. Sharpe, there's three kinds of secrets in this company. There's secrets that you and I keep. There's secrets I keep. And there are secrets you think you keep. And when you've 'kept' information from me…" She pauses, doing tiny air quotes around 'kept' to let me know that it's in appearance only. "I've trusted your decision making. I understand why you've done it, usually for my own plausible deniability."

"I'm not going to hang you out to dry," I point out.

"But you don't need to hang out there alone, either," she says, her tone lowering. "Look, Mr. Sharpe. Truth is, I haven't heard anything through my network about you, at least in the past few weeks."

"The past few weeks?" I ask, and she nods. "Before that?"

"Mr. Sharpe, it's not my place to say, but your hiring of Miss Hill so soon after the charity event? With what I heard?" She tilts her head, giving me what I suspect is akin to her Disappointed Mother look. It's weak at best, given her daughter is a good kid who needs little correction.

"I see," I say flatly, warning her.

Tamara likely thinks I have a blind spot where Raven is

concerned and that the rumors she heard are the only reason I hired Raven. If that's the case, she's dead wrong. She may even wonder if, like many other men in positions of power, I'm getting played by a younger, pretty woman who sees me as a shortcut to Easy Street. She'd be wrong there too.

Tamara can read my face, and she rushes to reassure me that my concerns are unwarranted. "You have never, and I truly mean never, given me reason to question one of your business decisions," she says. "You might have had ulterior reasons for hiring Miss Hill. But I've heard the talk around the office about her being some sort of investment phenom, and I've seen her work and how she works with people in the office. She seems to be a good fit here. The research she was assigned..."

I nod, and she continues, "Her report hit my inbox this morning. In my opinion, it was excellent. In two and a half days, she produced work that we expect a freshman hire to take a week or more to complete. I've only known a handful of people who can produce quality work as quickly, and I'm sitting in the room with one of them."

"Why, thank you." I keep my tone tamed, although her decision to question Miss Hill's presence has me on edge.

Tamara and I have a professionally interwoven relationship based on keeping the firm afloat and steering toward the best heading. We don't often give each other compliments or atta-boys. Neither of us is accustomed to them or comfortable with it. But I do appreciate it this time... so long as it's followed by leaving Raven alone.

"Word is, she's making you money nearly hand over fist, putting pressure on more senior investors to improve their margins," Tamara says. "Her resume had no fluff, her references are impressive, and she seems to have found a place without ruffling too many feathers, which is a delicate balance with finance types."

I chuckle, acknowledging that 'finance bro' is a stereotype for a reason. We're not all ambitious, greedy, numbers types with egos the size of a BMW, but it's also, sadly, not too far off.

"So, do you think I should give her more responsibilities?" I ask. "If she's this good."

Tamara sits back, tapping the edge of her tablet as she thinks. "My father," she says, "is a baseball fan. Loves the game, loves the complexities of it. He gets into the layers of management, the farm system teams have, the stats, all of it. He would talk your ear off if you'd give him half a chance, but what I remember most was his uncanny ability to tell when a pitcher had been brought up from the minors too quickly. He didn't even need to look at the game. He'd tell me beforehand. 'Kid's gonna have a rough day' or 'he needs more seasoning.' Like a pitcher was a steak or something. I didn't understand then, but I do now."

"You think Raven needs more seasoning," I note, and Tamara shrugs. "Meaning?"

"Meaning that if you just want someone who's going to make you a ton of money, I'd say step things up," Tamara explains. "Use her talents to pad your bottom line as aggressively as possible before someone else snatches her away."

I frown at that, thinking no one is taking Raven anywhere, much less away from me or my firm. Tamara smiles as though I've let her into my thoughts unwittingly.

"However, if you want what I suspect you do, you may want to make sure Miss Hill has time to learn, grow, and truly be prepared for what's ahead… when and if things change."

"And what do you suspect I want?" I can barely get the question out before another comes, "and exactly what do you think is going to change?"

"That, Mr. Sharpe, is something I can't answer for you," Tamara says as she closes the cover over her tablet and stands up. "I'll get these reports ready for you by tomorrow morning. If that'll be all?"

I nod, and Tamara leaves. Rather than giving me answers, she's left me with a mind filled with questions.

What is it I want from Raven Hill?

After this weekend, an explanation, perhaps.

I'd spoken to her at McGinty's on Friday, keeping things surface-level and then moving away to speak with another group. Later, when I scanned the bar, I discovered she'd left without a word. I was worried until Hector had climbed on the stage for a bit of impromptu karaoke, dedicating his song to the company newcomers and mentioning that Raven had headed home early and would miss his much-anticipated return to the spotlight. I'd been disappointed because while we hadn't had plans, exactly, I'd hoped to see her after the get-together. Not a text. Not a word from her. It was unexpected.

And then, the last two days were essentially hell. I didn't hear from her at all apart from one-word answers and '*I can't. I'm busy*', and I had been on the edge of showing up at her apartment.

She's felt *off*. Like something happened, although I can't imagine what.

The only thing that stopped me was the recognition that my control where she is concerned is no longer slipping. Any semblance of control has slipped completely out of my reach, and that is unfamiliar territory.

So, I waited, using the weekend to turn her behavior, and my own, over and over again in my mind, all the while, wondering why I was concerned with her when she didn't appear to be interested. My thumb rubs against the pad of my pointer as I remind myself. It's business. And I'm Dylan Sharpe. I don't chase anyone. Although, for an answer… I'll allow it.

Glancing at the clock, I see that I only have a little longer to wait until I get my answer. Because right at six, I hear her high heels and their muffled click on the floor of the carpet of my outer office.

At this point, I know exactly what Raven's footsteps sound like. The rhythm, the weight, the way her right leg hits the floor just a little bit harder than her left, and how my cock's already stiffening in my pants as she opens the door to my office and stands there, looking at me.

"Mr. Sharpe."

There's no reply from me. I simply get up out of my chair and cross the room, stalking toward her like I'm starved. She retreats, looking at me with her beautiful eyes, half shock and half... desire.

She's missed my touch as much as I've missed hers, which tempers my approach the slightest bit. "Where were you this weekend?"

"I... I..." Her eyes widen, her breath coming in short pants.

I was wrong. I don't want answers or an explanation. I want to punish her for ruining my weekend, for taking control of my mind and distracting me. I was worried about her, desperate for her while she was out doing God knows what with God knows who, and I was a mess, thinking of nothing but her.

The fuck did this woman do to me?

I close the door, turning the lock manually. I push Raven up against the wall, roughly lifting her chin with my thumb running along her lower lip. Her eyes flare. "I'm sorry."

I cut off her words with a hard kiss, my lips bruising against hers as I claim her. As she kisses me back, her hands grip my jacket and she pulls me closer.

"Uh-uh, Darling," I growl, pressing her harder against the wall. "You aren't in charge this time."

She nods, gasping when I nip at her neck and then breathily moaning, "Yes!"

"Good girl," I whisper, and she shivers. "Are you my good girl?"

I'm too far gone to build her up to the depravity running through my body, demanding to be unleashed on Raven.

"I... I am," she rasps, crying out as I pull her skirt up and unceremoniously cup her mound. "Oh, fuck, Dylan."

"You're going to be," I tell her, stroking her through her panties and feeling her arousal begin to coat the fabric. "I'm going to punish you for leaving me wanting this weekend." I swat her clit with my fingers. "For not speaking with me all damn weekend." Another swat, and she swallows, fighting for air. She shudders, her legs trying to give out, but I hold her in place, pinned to the wall with my other hand wrapped around her hip.

She tries to speak, but I don't want to hear it. Not now. Maybe later after I've had my fill of her, marked her, and made her understand that this can't happen again. What she does to me... how she makes me question things... I can listen. But now...

"I'm going to fuck you hard, Darling, and you're going to take every bit of it the way a good slut does. Understood?" I stroke up the indented slit of her satin panties, finding her already-swollen clit and circling it until her fabric's soaked and her hips buck against my thumb.

"Oh, God, Dylan," she pants. "I... I'm sorry. I'm sorry."

"Not as sorry as you'll be in a few seconds," I promise her before I kiss her again, strumming three fingers against her clit. She cries out, pushed to her edge too quickly. She writhes against my hand, finding her release. She's fucking gorgeous, the flush of red that moves from her chest to her cheeks and the lust that shines back in her eyes. I swallow her cries, gripping her throat ever so slightly to muffle her, and it stretches the wave out, another round of spasms racking through her.

She looks up at me with hazy eyes, her mouth dropped open as she starts to smile like she thinks that's it. A dark chuckle passes over my lips, landing on the sensitive outer shell of her ear. "We're not done. We've barely started."

I step back, pushing her to her knees and wrapping a fistful of her hair in my right hand. "Now," I command, "open your mouth like a good girl. We're going to do something... intense."

She licks her lips, obeying even as she asks, "What?"

"You are mine, Miss Hill, so I'm going to have all of you," I whisper. "Including that sweet, perfect ass of yours. It's mine." She whimpers at my feet, and the small shred of decency remaining in my soul pauses. "Have you ever...?"

She shakes her head, but she stares up at me with desire. "I've had toys there."

My cock jumps at the idea of Raven with a plug in her ass. I bet that's a beautiful sight to see. "And did you come from them, Darling?" I demand. "Did you like it?"

"The first time... no," she confides. "But when I figured out what to do..."

Her voice fades, and I pause, lifting her chin to look me in the eye. "I know what to do," I promise her. "And if you can't, you tell me."

Still, her hands tremble when she pulls my cock out, and I seize them, shaking my head. "Your hands are for your beautiful tits and for rubbing your pussy," I command her. "Twist them, tweak them, make yourself come as you swallow every inch of me."

"Yes, sir." Her eyes flash, letting me know that while I'm in control here, it's because she's allowing it. She knows exactly how to punish me too.

She wiggles her skirt even higher, to where it's no more than fabric gathered at her waist, and then undoes the pretty purple blouse she's wearing, taking her time as she frees the gorgeous curves of her breasts from the prison of her lacy bra. All the while, heat races through my veins. Fuck, I need her. The dim light of the city behind us curves around her face and her breasts. Just the sight of them makes my dick twitch. Her eyes go to my cock as she smiles softly, pleased with the unconscious reaction she brought forth in me. She leans forward with her tongue out and takes in just the tip.

Fuck me. I plant a palm on the wall to brace myself and close my eyes, stifling a groan.

Her tongue is wicked, circling the head of my cock, tasting me hungrily, and coating me. I watch, entranced by the way she works me while simultaneously toying with her nipples. *Such a good multi-tasker*, I think, wondering what else she can do.

Fresh precum is already leaking from my cock as she sucks, and I push more into her warm mouth, watching as inch after inch disappears between her plump, sexy red lips.

"That's it, take it all," I murmur as her cheeks hollow. Fucking gorgeous, the sight of her on her knees. She's so tight, her lips a ring around my shaft as she takes more and more. I reach the back of her throat, but she doesn't stop, sucking me in until her nose is buried against my body and her eyes brim with tears. She tries to pull back reflexively but forces herself to choke on my cock.

"Relax, breathe through your nose." I can feel the moment

she relaxes, getting much-needed oxygen, and I smile, proud of her. "Good girl."

I pull back, letting her breathe freely, and she gasps as she looks up at me. Lower, I can see her hips bucking as she cups her pussy again, tugging her panties to the side. "Dylan... please..."

"Finger fuck yourself," I command. "In time with my cock in your mouth."

She rushes to comply, slipping two fingers inside her as I take her mouth again, this time not letting go of my control. As good as her mouth is, I resist the urge to let her bring me to the point of orgasm and instead punish her, thrusting in and out of her vacuumed lips and hollowed cheeks.

The vibration of her strangled cry as she rubs her clit has me on edge, but the thought of what's to come still holds me back. Instead, I tighten my grip in her hair, pumping in and out of her mouth until tears roll down her beautiful cheeks, leaving streaks of mascara behind and making her a mess.

Her tenuous grip on the edge slips away and she comes again, her body trembling and her moan muffled from my cock. The vibrations of it and the sheer sight of her are nearly my undoing. I pull out and I bend down, growling in her ear. "Does my good girl need more?" An answering shudder runs through her as she stares up at me with wide, wanting eyes.

I scoop her up, carrying her over to my couch and laying her on the leather surface. "Remember," I tell her as I push her skirt up higher and pull her panties down and off her long legs, "Tell me if it's too much."

"Mmmhmm," she vows in a hesitant murmur. Her body still trembles from her orgasm, and I don't wait for the pleasure to settle.

Reaching up, I pull down my tie, loosening it before I rip it off and then unbutton my shirt before giving up and just shoving it out of the way to return my efforts to Raven. I push her back more and more until the sexy, obscene sight of her wet, gleaming pussy is fully exposed for my hungry eyes. I lean down, licking a sweeping, swerving line from her clit to the pucker of her ass, and she clenches.

I swallow, forcing myself to slow down because what's about to happen is momentous and maybe even more than she can handle.

I go back to my desk and open a locked drawer. I put a supply of condoms and lube there for us, although we don't use lubricant very often. When I return, I kneel between her outstretched legs, kissing the insides of her thighs. The silk of her stockings rasps against my five o'clock shadow, only disappearing when I reach the even softer skin of her body.

Even as mad as I've been, the sight of Raven's face, her gorgeous green eyes wide and her pussy clenching above the pink curve of her ass, is heart stopping. Gently, I lean in, kissing her pussy lips softly before gathering a tongue full of her honey to savor her flavor.

She's intoxicating. She's addicting. She might be my ultimate ruin, but in this moment, I don't care. I'm hers, and I'm going to make sure she knows that she is mine. Which means she can't disappear on me for days on end. I won't allow it. I can't withstand it.

Every swipe of my tongue is bliss for the both of us, Raven's stomach clenching every time I dance over her clit and my cock leaking steadily as I devour her. But eventually, I go even lower, my breath tickling her back entrance. Holding her cheeks apart with my thumbs, I reach out with my tongue and press against her ass… testing her reaction.

Raven sighs in pleasure, her hips squirming, not to get away, but for more. She attempts to grip the sofa and slips, repositioning herself and breathing heavily. Her chest rises and falls as she settles in and rocks herself against me.

"That's it," I reply, gripping her ass cheeks sharply as I pull her open even more so I can lick her again. She whimpers, a flush coming to her cheeks as I start lathering and pressing on her asshole with my tongue. Her pussy is wet with her arousal, her breath catching again and again as I find the pressure, the wetness, and the stroke that makes her relax, to give in to my touch fully.

Uncapping the lube and squirting a dollop onto my fingers, I pull back, replacing my tongue with the lubricant. Pressing in slowly with a single finger, I talk her through the initial shock. "Breathe now… just breathe… there you go, Darling…"

My finger slips into Raven's ass, and she moans, her eyes opening wide as I gently massage and stretch her. "Oh, fuck, that's good."

"Stroke your clit. I'm adding more," I warn her, and she rushes to stroke her clit as I press in with another finger. It's harder this time, but easier than I feared. In moments, I'm finger fucking her delectable ass with two fingers as she rubs her clit, her eyes rolling in their sockets as the twin sensations course through her body. I can feel her ring clamping and relaxing around my fingers, wanting more, and I withdraw, looking into her eyes. "Are you ready?"

"Yes, Dylan," she promises me, and I skin myself, covering the condom in a generous amount of lube before pressing against her. She bites her lip, holding back a groan as I press harder, the head of my cock stretching her even more than my fingers. Raven responds by stroking her clit even harder, whimpering softly as I push past her resistance. With an inaudible *Pop* that shakes us both, I enter her, and we pause, our eyes locked.

"Holy fuck," she whispers, letting her head fall forward and her lips making a perfect 'O' as I rock in slightly.

Her reaction is adorably sexy, and I have to restrain myself from giving her too much, too soon. This will take time, both of us needing to ease into it.

Hell, I can barely breathe as my pulse races.

"God, you feel so fucking good, so tight," I tell her, holding still. Reaching up, I stroke her nipples, and she relaxes as her body adjusts.

I pull out slowly and press in faster, pacing myself and reaching in front of her to play with her clit myself. I need her to fucking love this. To love everything I give her.

An asymmetrical grin pulls at my lips as I remember, I'm her first. No man has ever fucked her like this.

"That's my good girl," I murmur by her ear and then kiss the crook of her neck, giving her more and more, faster and harder with every passing thrust. "Come on me, Darling. Come with my cock in your ass." It's an open-ended order. I want her to come as many times as possible. Punishment by pleasure might be my new corporate motto, but only for her. Only for Raven.

I put my hand around her neck. I don't squeeze, but I do hold her down as I thoroughly, deeply ass fuck Raven, thrusting in and out hard enough to make my sofa shake and the frame groan in time with my hips.

"That's it, take it like a good girl," I grunt as her ring tightens perfectly around my shaft. Another small orgasm runs through her, and I'm on the edge, but I hold back by sheer force of will.

"Please, Dylan, I need it," she pleads, and I speed up, my hips slapping against her spread open, violated ass. As she starts quivering, I give myself over to the flood rising within me.

My climax hits hard, making the whole world go silent and fall into a blur. And then she comes.

Raven tosses her head from side to side, her mouth wide open as she scrabbles to grab something. She finds the edge of the couch and grips it with one hand, her other going to cover her own mouth to muffle her cries of ecstasy.

Panting, spent, I slowly let her down onto the cushion as her high eases and we both catch our breaths. I run my fingertips down her throat, then lower, circle one nipple and then the other, and trace down her belly to right above her clit. She moans, unable to take more, but that's not what this is. I simply need to touch her, feel her, to have her at my mercy.

There were times this weekend when I thought I'd built this thing between us up in my head. It's stupid, I know, but there's a scar deep inside me that started whispering in my head late at night when I was wondering where Raven was and why she wasn't right there with me.

"Where were you?" I ask again, the vehemence fucked out of the words, exposing the hurt lurking behind them.

"Home, just home all weekend. Working on the side project and hanging with Maggie and Ami."

Staring at her, I search her eyes for any sign of dishonesty, any shred of deception. I wish I didn't feel this way, this fucking insecurity. Hiding her and keeping her a secret doesn't help. I don't fucking like it.

"I missed you too," she adds in my silence, and then my beautiful Raven smiles before letting her head fall back.

I believe her. She's too vulnerable at this moment, her defenses down after what we just did. Plus, I don't think Raven has the deep ugliness it'd take to lie to me.

I've been wrong about that before... and I haven't forgotten.

I move to get up, and she squirms before settling uncomfortably on the couch while I go over to my washroom to get a warm cloth to clean us up. Gently, I clean her ass before getting rid of it and the condom. When I come back, she's adjusted her skirt, pulling it back down before putting her breasts back into the cups of her bra and buttoning up.

Her chest still rises and falls like she's catching her breath, and her eyes close as she hums softly. Fucking beautiful. Raven

Hill is so damn beautiful.

I do the same as her, zipping up my slacks and rebuttoning my shirt. It feels like putting up walls between us. Maybe I should've asked these questions while I had her beneath me?

"Why?"

"What?" she asks innocently, but her eyes flash and I know she knows what I mean.

"This weekend was different. What happened?" I press.

She starts to shake her head, and I stop her. "Just tell me, Raven. I don't have time for games."

Tears appear at the corners of her eyes, and I fear the worst. She's figured out that I'm a bastard whose only real value is in his bank account, so she's leaving me. It's not the most rational reaction, but it's also not illogical considering it's mostly true.

"At the bar on Friday," she starts, and my stomach drops. I was right. Something happened. I'm silent as she continues, "I was having a great time. I felt like everything I dreamed of was finally right in the palms of my hands. The job, the guy, the friends, the future... all of it." She holds her hands in front of her symbolically, staring at their emptiness but obviously seeing much more.

I can hear it coming. "But?"

"But then, I was talking to Shanna and she said..." She takes a steadying breath, "That she thought I was the girl getting 'Sharped.'" My brow furrows in confusion because I don't know what the hell that means, and she huffs in exasperation. "Don't you see? They all know. I thought I'd gotten away from the rumors after the fundraiser when no one here mentioned them. I thought the friendships I was building were real. But they're talking about us, about me. They might not know for sure, but they suspect. And I don't want to be Dylan Sharpe's ladder-climbing slut."

Anger grows in my chest at her calling herself that because it is nothing like when we say it while fucking. She's insulting herself, and I won't stand for anyone putting her down, not even Raven herself.

She holds up a hand, telling me that's not the point with a roll of her eyes. "I told you before we started this. I want to earn my way through my business skills. I don't want people thinking I did it through my oral skills."

"You're better than that. You know it and I know it, so don't reduce everything you've accomplished down to that."

"What about everyone else?" she asks, fire in her eyes as she throws an arm toward the door, indicating the rest of the company. Or maybe the whole fucking Financial District.

"One, who the fuck cares what they think," I snap, not giving two shits what my employees or anyone else think of my personal life. "Two, Tamara says they're calling you some sort of investment phenom."

She pales, the compliment not even landing in her hyperfocus on what I said first. "I care," she cries, clutching her chest. "I fucking care."

I freeze. All weekend, I've been in my own head, torturing myself with thoughts of how Raven is leaving me.

The truth is… her hesitation is not with me, but with herself. She's young and hungry, the same way I once was, and feels the need to prove herself, something I can understand more than most. Honestly, it's something I appreciate about her. She doesn't want an easy way up or a shortcut.

But where does that leave us?

Because this is happening. I can't let her go. I won't wait for her to make a name for herself and then come back to me. I'm too selfish for that. But she needs to do things her way or she won't have faith in herself the way I have faith in her.

She looks up at me with wide tear-brimmed eyes. "I care," she says again in a harsh whisper.

I gather her into my arms, cradling her head against my chest. "I'm sorry. We'll figure it out. I don't know what we're going to do, but we'll figure it out."

"I'm sorry too. I was miserable all weekend without you, so I poured everything I had into that report."

I huff out a humorless laugh. "I haven't read it yet, but I hear it's some of the best work Tamara's seen, other than my own, of course."

Raven sniffles, looking up at me hopefully. "Really?"

I press a kiss to her forehead. "Really, Miss Hill. Good work."

CHAPTER 22

RAVEN

"Oh, yes, it's ladies' night, and I'm feeling right, oh, yes, it's ladies' night!" Ami sings as we get out of our Uber. Up front, the driver, a middle-aged guy with a bald spot, does his best to not roll his eyes as Ami grooves her way toward the door of the club with some sort of bouncing booty move that makes her look like she's already had too much.

"Sorry," I tell him as I type in his tip on my phone. "It's her birthday. Well, kinda."

"That won't even be the weirdest thing I see this hour," the driver says, sounding exhausted even though it's only nine o'clock on Thursday. I chuckle, and he adds, "You should see what it's like come prom season. I legitimately keep a squirt gun in the passenger seat next to me just to hose down the horn dogs. I'm not cleaning up bodily fluids." He shudders, and I can only imagine what he sees on his nightly rounds. "Have fun, stay safe, and good luck with that one." He lifts his chin toward Ami, who has paused in the middle of the sidewalk for a shoulder shimmy.

"You too," I tell him, thinking he needs the luck more than I do. Ami's ready for a fun evening, but there definitely won't be body fluids involved. For us, at least. The driver? No telling.

As the driver pulls away, I follow Ami, joining her and Maggie at the club's door. It's glossy black, surrounded by hot pink and neon lights, and guarded by a doorman with pumped-up pecs, shoulders, and biceps that strain his extra-large shirt.

"Hey, big man. I know what I want for my birthday," Ami teases, flirting hard as she boldly looks him up and down. "Are you performing tonight?" I don't think she's seriously coming on to the doorman, but she is excited for a bit of wild, silly fun for tonight's birthday festivities.

He laughs good-naturedly. "Sorry, Miss. I'm strictly security, here to keep the handsy ones away from the goods." He lifts a brow, already pinning Ami as one of his problems tonight.

She pops out her bottom lip in a melodramatic pout. "Too bad, so sad."

Maggie and I lock eyes, silently laughing at her theatrics as the doorman checks our IDs and lets us inside.

The Starlight Revue is, technically at least, a stage show, with multiple acts. On the advertising, it's described as a 'two-hour dinner show with live entertainment.' Which could mean just about anything from Broadway musical theater to a magician to a singing revival. Of course, none of those also promise sexy dancing, acrobatics, and nearly nude performers the way this show does.

Truth is, it's a strip club. A very fancy, polished up one with better lighting, but ultimately, it's a strip club, right down to the pole in the middle of the central stage, the champagne that is going to be downed like water, and the already bumping, bass-heavy music that I can feel in my chest.

"Wooo!" Ami cheers, holding her arms up. She's already in rare form tonight. A few other women look our way, all of them smiling and some giving answering wooos of their own.

Oh, God, it's a wooo girl kinda night.

"This is going to be interesting," Maggie says as we're shown to our seats. "Medieval Times meets Magic Mike."

"I'm sure it's going to be a very thoughtful and insightful stage show," I deadpan back and then grin. "How many Tony Awards is it up for again?"

"Depends how many Tonys are in the cast," Ami replies, grinning. "Thanks for this, you two. I know it's a little different, but I didn't want to do the usual dinner and drinks or dancing. This sounded fun and different."

She's right. We aren't party animals by any stretch, but we've done our sampling of the dance clubs, karaoke bars, restaurants, and bars around the city. This is something we wouldn't normally do, and that's what makes it a perfect birthday month outing. Time to check off boxes and bucket lists.

"I'm sure it'll be awesome," I tell her honestly.

"I'm just glad we get you tonight," Maggie says. "I swear, we're gonna have to arrange a visitation schedule with your new man."

My eyes jump to her, but she's smiling, not mad at all. "I guess I have been a bit busy," I hedge.

Maggie and Ami gawk at me for a split second and then burst out in laughter. "Babe, you come home from work later and later every day, and last weekend, when you were home, I don't think you picked your head up from the computer for more than ten minutes total. I was throwing cheese cubes at you to make sure you ate something."

She's right. Last weekend, I don't think I slept more than a couple of hours each night. I poured myself into that report, which was totally worth it to hear Dylan say that it was good work. And I have been staying with Dylan longer in the evenings. Our Monday after-work meeting ran way late, and then Tuesday, we ended up at his penthouse. Last night, we went to dinner at a French restaurant with private tables where no one would see or care who I am and who he is.

"Sorry?" I offer, not really sorry but feeling like I should say it, anyway.

Maggie scoffs. "I'm not giving you a hard time. Get your shit rocked and get that bag. I'm just happy you're here."

That's a far cry from where we started when she was all 'just once' and 'be careful' about this deal with Dylan, and I look at her in surprise, not sure what's changed. Well, I mean I know what's changed for me... a whole hell of a lot. But for her?

She tilts her head, reading my mind. "You're happy. That's all I care about. Besides, I relinquished all responsibility, so you are not my circus and not my monkey. Especially tonight when I think I'm gonna have to play ringmaster on this one and whip her into shape, *Fifty Shades* style." Maggie grins, pointing at Ami, who has lost track of our conversation and is dancing in her seat to the music while her eyes scan the stage in obvious anticipation for the show to start.

"Thanks," I tell Maggie, and then we both switch off the gushy stuff, focusing on the fun we're gonna have tonight in honor of Ami's birthday, which is still officially more than a week away.

The lights dim and the show starts with a bang, literally, as pyrotechnics pop and flash on stage. The entire crowd becomes instant wooo girls, including me and Maggie, with hoots and hollers sounding out from every corner of the room.

The first number is a choreographed dance introduction to each performer as they come out to the center of the stage one-by-one. They're handsome, I'll give them that. And the Starlight Revue definitely knows how to cater to almost every taste. Thirty men in all, each unique in their own way even though they're currently wearing similar costumes of gray athletic pants and muscle tees that make them look like the world's sexiest sport team.

I find myself thinking about Dylan… and wondering what he would think of this. I certainly didn't tell him the girls were dragging me out to a show and don't-tell night.

After the introduction song, the guys take turns with various themed routines, from cowboys who do some interesting things with their lassos, to a firefighter who gyrates and strips down to a jock strap that barely conceals his cock, and even a military themed performance where several guys do all sorts of acrobatics on an oversized pull-up bar jungle gym.

It's all in good fun, and Ami especially seems to be enjoying herself, crunching on her chips and salsa and catcalling to her favorite performers, which is the point of the evening.

The next act starts and a tall, sandy-blonde, sharp-jawed Adonis with steely blue eyes struts out in black slacks, a white dress shirt, and a power tie. He stalks over to the desk and chair that's been set up in the middle of the stage, grabbing the chair and spinning it on one leg, his pecs flexed beneath the thin material of his shirt.

Ami fans herself. "Jeezus, is that what your office is like, Raven?"

I snort, shaking my head. "Definitely not." I get why she'd ask. The guy on stage has the whole powerful boss vibe going on, and though he's sexy, he's nothing compared to Dylan's charisma and magnetism.

A few seconds into Adonis's routine, he leaps off the stage and into the crowd. Women go insane, screaming and reaching for him, and he smiles as he dances through the tables. Ami sits up taller, straining to see him, and then suddenly, he's right in front of our table.

He folds at the waist, holding his hand out to me like he's asking me to dance. But I shake my head wildly. "No, no, no, no," I mumble, having no intention of going on stage. For *so* many reasons. Yeah, one is Dylan, and I wouldn't disrespect him by dancing with a half-naked guy. But also, two, I am not a dancer. I mean, I have rhythm and can do a little wiggle when the time's right and the alcohol's been flowing, but that's on a crowded dance floor, not a stage, in front of people.

"C'mon, I don't bite… often," he purrs.

I shake my head some more and then push Ami his way, shouting, "It's her birthday!"

He takes the hint and holds his hand out to Ami instead, and she promptly grabs it. "Happy birthday to me!" she squeals, letting him pull her to her feet.

And thank God I volunteered Ami as tribute because Adonis squats down, wraps his arms around her thighs, and picks her clean up off the floor, carrying her back to the stage. She ends up sitting in the chair, looking giddy as can be about whatever's about to happen.

"I don't think you'll have to get her a birthday present now," Maggie shouts, and we lock eyes, laughing.

Adonis gyrates around Ami, sitting in her lap, and ultimately, leaning the chair back to the floor and climbing over her. Ami's hands are pressed to the floor, which he seems to have instructed her to do, and he runs his nose up her body from her belly button, over her cleavage, to her ear. He grips her hip, and she wraps her legs around him, an active participant in the show at this point.

"I don't think I'll ever have to buy her a birthday present again," I correct when Adonis does some fancy move that scoots the chair from beneath them while he flips them over. In a blink, Adonis' back is on the floor, his legs bent, and Ami is sitting on his hips like he's a mechanical bull. When he starts body rolling, holding her firmly in place against him, I send up another silent prayer of thanks that it's her and not me. The music reaches a crescendo, and Adonis bucks his hips rapid-fire, bouncing Ami roughly while she shouts.

And then the stage goes black.

"Holy fuck," Maggie says. "I think I would've embarrassed myself, coming right then and there." I stare at her wide-eyed.

"Think Ami's gonna kill me?" I ask, suddenly not so sure. That was… a lot.

The next act starts seamlessly, Ami and Adonis nowhere to be seen. But within minutes, Ami returns to the table, pink-cheeked and smiling. "Oh, my God, girls. That was so much fun!"

"Did you seriously just have fake sex on stage?" Maggie hisses, her eyes wide.

Ami draws a checkmark in the air. "Off the bucket list," she jokes. "Did it look okay?" Her eyes cut from Maggie to me and back again. We must look as confused as we feel because she clarifies, "He whispered in my ear asking if I was okay with putting on a good show, and I told him to bring it. He was great, telling me to make my O face and throw my head back, but he nearly bounced me off him. I was afraid I was gonna die on a strip club stage."

She doesn't sound sad about that possibility. In fact, she sounds like it would've been a great way to go and a funny story to tell at her funeral, and we can't help but laugh, reassuring that nobody could tell and it looked sexy as hell.

After a laugh escapes me, I shake my head, telling Ami, "I could not have done that in front of all of these people. I would've panicked and totally frozen." I pull a horrified face, freezing in place, and they laugh.

Ami shrugs like it was no big deal. "I don't care what any of these people think. I don't know them, they don't know me, and I don't live my life for people who don't feed me, fuck me, or finance me." She ticks the options off on her fingers. "And even then, my opinion's the only one that really matters."

I grin, glad she wasn't bothered by the public display, but then her words echo through my mind. I sit with them as the night goes on.

Am I putting too much weight in what other people think? People at work, especially?

I think back to when I freaked out at McGinty's about what Shanna said, and I have to admit, she didn't sound upset or judgmental about it. It was me. I was the one judging myself.

Maybe I should take a lesson from Ami and not care what they might say about me. Dylan said the same thing, but that feels so scary and is easier said than done.

But it would definitely make things easier to quit sneaking around, hiding my feelings, and pretending I'm nothing more than a passing acquaintance with Dylan when I know him intimately, both physically and emotionally. Especially as the nights get longer between us and I find myself wanting more and more.

It's something to consider, but I don't think I'm going to figure it out with half-naked guys dancing in front me.

Before long, it's the last act, which literally includes a dance line of a dozen men with rather sizeable erections making them bounce up and down in time to a reworked version of *Back Dat Azz Up*.

It's worthy of a standing ovation from the crowd, and afterward, Ami's ecstatic. "Thank you, thank you, thank you!" she says, hugging us both outside. She's only slightly tipsy, which I'm glad for. "That was so much fun!"

"It was," I agree as we wait for our Uber to arrive.

We talk through the various acts, dissecting and discussing our favorite performers and performances, until we drop Ami off with hugs and 'Happy Birthday' cheers. Maggie and I ride the rest of the way home with smiles on our faces.

It really was a good night. As I glance at Maggie, I remind myself of how grateful I am to have such good friends.

At home, Maggie goes straight to bed, and I get ready for bed, but I feel too amped up to sleep. Instead, I go back to the living room and sit down on the couch. I stare at the television, considering Netflix for a minute, but that's not what I want.

I want Dylan. I grab my phone, dialing quickly before I second guess myself.

"Hello?"

I smile just from hearing his voice and press my phone tighter to my ear. "Mr. Sharpe."

On the other end of the line, I can hear him shift around, and he clears his voice. "Miss Hill. I thought you were celebrating your friend's birthday... again."

"I did. We just dropped her off at her place, and now I'm at home."

"I see," Dylan says. "And why are you calling me at twelve thirty?"

I swallow, my nipples rock hard underneath my sleep shirt in a way that didn't happen the entire show I was just at, and the warm, pulsing desire between my legs is only for him. "I need you. I need to... I need you."

On the other end of the line, I hear a rustle, and Dylan comes back on the line. "On one condition."

"What?" I ask, wondering if he wants me to come to his apartment. It's late, but I would. I need him that badly.

"Turn on your video. Show me what I'm missing..."

The promise of what will happen tomorrow at work has a fresh wave of heat coursing through my pussy, and I turn my video chat on. A moment later, Dylan appears, his bare chest making my pulse thrum in my veins as he looks back at me. "Hello, Darling."

"Hello," I whisper. "I... this seems like I'm saying this all the time with you. But I've never done this before."

On his end, Dylan chuckles. I think he's lying in bed, or maybe he's on his own couch. It's a little too dark to tell, and I may be tipsier than I thought I was. "Me either. But there's a first time for everything."

"So, what are we supposed to do?" I ask, and Dylan's smile says his mind's already coming up with a lot of very naughty ideas. As I shift on the sofa, I realize just how turned on I am.

"Bring the phone down, and pull your shift down so I can see your chest," he says. "Every day, I see you in your work clothes, and I can trace the curve of your breasts through your blouse, and it makes me look forward to our after hours."

I smile and bring my phone down, showing the curve of my breasts through the thin cotton of my sleep shirt. "Is this what you see that gets you hard?" I ask, playfully stroking the underside of my left breast. The sensation makes me shiver, and I inhale deeply. "I love when you play with them."

"I know you do," Dylan says, sounding cocky. "What else do you like?" he asks and readjusts.

"I like… I like when you kiss me," I reply, bringing my hand up and teasing my nipple, gasping softly. "I like when you kiss me on the side of the neck… like right beneath my ear, and make me feel…" I trail off, not sure how to describe it.

"How do I make you feel?" Dylan asks, his voice thick.

I should say sexy or needy or on fire, because he does make me feel all those things. But that's not what comes out. "You make me feel wanted and… special," I admit, my thighs rubbing together as Dylan looks at me with hunger written on his face.

"You are special, Raven," Dylan says, licking his lips unconsciously. "You know I want you more than anything," he confides in me and then tells me to touch myself and to be a good girl for him.

"Show me too," I whisper, and Dylan smirks. I moan, and Dylan inhales sharply, bringing his phone down so I can watch as he strokes himself. His camera switches, and then I'm looking at his pants as he pushes them down, and then I see him. It's amazing, and strange at the same time, seeing him like this. I've had his cock everywhere, but seeing him like a voyeur as he wraps his fingers around the thick shaft and squeezes, making a gleaming drop of precum leak out, has me hotter than I ever thought it could. "Fuck me."

"That's what we're going to do," he says, his voice rough. "Put your camera up so I can see that pretty pussy. I want to watch you touch yourself."

Maneuvering, I push my sleep shorts down and adjust my phone so that he can see my fingers running down my belly and to the edge of my pussy, the lips already parted and wet for him.

"So fucking pretty," he praises as he starts pumping his cock in and out of his fist. "I love watching my cock disappear between those tight lips of yours, holding you still and pumping in and out of you…"

His words trail off, but I don't care. I'm entranced by the sight of his cock, his hand stroking up and down his shaft, his thumb gathering up a bit of precum before smearing it around his head. I moan, touching myself and wishing it were him. I use my other hand to rub my clit. It's not as smooth, but I'm too far and don't need much to get there.

We go quiet. I can hear his breathing pick up. He moans my name while watching me. I can see that he's holding back for me, waiting for me to shatter.

"Together?" I pant.

He grunts as if it's hurting him to be this on edge. "Come for me, Darling."

I gasp as the waves hit me, pulling me under. I force my

eyes to stay open, locked on my phone so I don't miss a thing as Dylan moans my name and comes undone.

"Holy... fuck," I rasp, panting.

Dylan chuckles, but he looks as spent than I do.

"Feel better, Darling?" His voice rumbles in his chest sexily.

I nod happily. "Yeah," I say with a smile. "And I have to get up early in the morning for work. My boss is kind of a stickler for the rules." I arch a brow, teasing him.

"I know the type," he deadpans, and I laugh. "Get some sleep. I'll see you tomorrow."

"Goodnight, Mr. Sharpe."

"Goodnight, Miss Hill."

CHAPTER 23

RAVEN

One of the largest adjustments I had to make when I moved from upstate to the city was shopping.

Back home, I did it like most people think of when they think of weekly shopping. I'd get in my car (or most likely, rode shotgun in my mother's SUV while Mom drove), and go down to the local shopping center. There, we'd go into the supermarket, pushing the cart up and down each aisle, picking up what we needed for a family of four for the week, and maybe at the same time, stop at the nearby Target for some fun retail therapy. We'd load it all up in the back of the car and drive home.

Shopping in the city is nothing like that. But I've adapted to city shopping, which means stopping by your local bodega or corner grocer on a daily or every other day basis, usually to grab the stuff you need to finish out your plans for the night. You can also, in some neighborhoods, find vegetable stands or meat shops, although that really varies depending on the economic status of the neighborhood you live in.

Then, when you need to, you go to a larger supermarket that might be a subway ride away in order to pick up the stuff that your local store doesn't have. In my case, my local markets don't have a lot of the spices I like, and the laundry soap choices all leave my skin drier than the Mojave desert.

So I take the subway out here, three stops, to the biggest shopping center near the Financial District, where I go up and down the aisles, plucking the things I can't get from my local market while keeping in mind that I'll have to carry them home.

It's a lot nicer doing this now than it was just a few months ago. I've got money in my bank account now, and as I pass a display of aloe vera and fruit juice drinks imported from Korea, I pause and grab two. That way, Maggie can try them too. Unneeded luxuries wouldn't have been possible not too long ago.

And then Dylan Sharpe came into my life. Just the thought of him forces me to smile.

After fitting my shopping into the big backpack I keep for these trips, I stop at Goldman's Cafe for a bit of personal indulgence. It's my reward to myself for battling the gauntlet that is the supermarket, and I've earned it.

I've just sat down with my slice and mug of cocoa when, out of the corner of my eye, I see someone stop beside my table and hear a throat clear. I glance up to find Evan looking down at me. He's dressed casually today, or at least what passes for casual for Evan Faulkner.

My hands go numb and my heart stops. *What the ever loving fuck?*

I don't say anything. Not a muscle on my face twitches as I stare at him blankly. His eyes flash as if he were expecting more from me, though I can't imagine what. Does he think I want to see him? Did he think I'd cause a scene this time?

"Can I have a seat?" he asks once the silence stretches uncomfortably. "I need your help."

"My help?" I echo, unsure whether I want to laugh or to throw my cocoa in his face. In the end, he doesn't wait for me to answer, but rather, sits on his own accord. Irritated, I arch a brow that he pretends not to notice. "If you need help, go to Elise. And how the fuck did you know I'd be here?"

"Elise can't. Not with this. But you can," he says flatly. "As for how I knew you'd be here… Jeremy Willoughby spotted you shopping and texted me. I know this is always your next stop. Still buying that hypoallergenic laundry detergent, huh?"

He chuckles like he's fondly remembering the time I freaked out because he used more than half a bottle of my preferred detergent to wash a single pair of underwear and one T-shirt. He hadn't understood how to do laundry in the first place but was 'trying' for me because I told him it was shocking that he didn't even know basic, functional life skills. Of course, I also never mentioned his lack of skills again either, so it all came out in Evan's favor, the way it always does.

"Of course. And why would Jeremy message you?"

Evan sits back, relaxing like we're two old friends catching up. "Because he knows that I want to talk to you." He flashes a too-perfect smile, his eyes searching my face for something. "I haven't come by your apartment because that crazy redhead you live with would probably try to castrate me if I did."

"She's got a good head on her shoulders." I point at my cheesecake. "You've got until I finish this to say what you need to say and get the fuck out, or else I start screaming. Go."

I pick up my fork, and Evan leans forward. "Come on, Raven. I get being pissed at me, even though…" He snaps before catching himself. I can virtually see him putting his charming façade back in place, using smoke and mirrors to hide the ugliness inside. More evenly, he says, "Look, the only reason Sharpe's with you is because he's trying to get back at me."

He watches me closely, like he's waiting for my heart to break at this totally earth-shattering news.

"You mean for fucking his fiancée?" I ask as I slide my fork through the cheesecake. "Yeah, he told me about Olivia. Apparently, you were fucking her behind his back. We've sort of bonded over that shared trauma."

"Bonded?"

"Yes. Bonded," I repeat, not giving him any more.

Scooping up my first bite of cheesecake, I tuck it in my mouth, luxuriating in the silky-smooth, sweet texture. "If that's it, you can go."

God, it feels good to be the one to dismiss him for a change. Unfortunately, it doesn't work.

"No," Evan says. "My God, don't you see he's doing the same thing to you that he did to her?"

"He's not doing anything to me," I say, then smirk, "well, not anything I don't enjoy." Is it petty to throw that in his face? Yep. Do I give a fuck? Nope. Not a one.

Evan frowns, not liking that one bit. "Or that he's made you think you like," he corrects. "Dylan's a control freak. He's mentally abusive. The man's a fucking monster, Raven. And while I should have said something to you earlier about Elise, I never—"

"Don't go there, Evan. You've got absolutely no ground to stand on."

Evan holds up a hand, begging off. "You're right. But what I never did to you is what he did to Olivia. Dylan Sharpe blackmailed her. Why do you think she left town? Sure as hell wasn't because she and I weren't happy."

That makes my fork pause, but I resume eating quickly. "Don't believe a word you say, Evan."

Do I think Dylan has the capacity to blackmail? Yes, absolutely. Mentally, emotionally, morally? All yes. To get ahead professionally, I think he'd do just about anything, especially back when he was coming up. He's told me how hard it was to fight his way through, clawing and scrabbling for every lead. Do I think he would now? No. He wouldn't let it come to that. He's too smart, too calculating, and he sees the moves to make long before others do.

Now whether I think, even a long time ago, Dylan would've done anything to hurt Olivia is an entirely different question. He told me how much he loved her, how it gutted him to discover her and Evan, of all people, hooking up, and how he blamed

Evan for taking everything from him. So no, I don't think he would blackmail Olivia.

Evan, maybe, but not Olivia. Maybe…

"Look, you think I want to fucking be here?" Evan growls, pushing my hand to the table so I'll stop eating and focus on him. "I don't want to be here any more than you want me here. But Olivia's not the only person Dylan Sharpe has shit on. That fucker's got info on me, too. And he's vindictive as can be. So I'm in a hard spot, and since you wouldn't have shit if it wasn't for me, I'm hoping you might find a shred of decency and help me."

The anger and intensity in his voice give me a moment of pause. I don't think I've ever seen him like this. *Desperation looks good on him*, I think with a tiny hint of sick satisfaction. "You do realize the size of the grain of salt I would need to take anything you say seriously, right?"

Evan scoffs. "You don't believe me? Ask him. He's a shit liar," Evan says. "It's how I took him in poker all the time. He can't fucking bluff. Dylan's barely able to hold his own in his little circle jerk of buddies playing together."

I know about Dylan's occasional card games. He told me about them after I first went to his apartment. But I didn't think Evan knew about them. What else does Evan know? "Still, you're out of your mind if you think I'm going to help you. Evan, your entire fucking world can burn down for all I care."

"Yeah? But here's the thing," Evan says, his eyes going shrewd. "If my world's going to burn, you want it to be because you caused it. Because you think I deserve it." He waits a second, like he thinks I might say 'oh, no, you don't deserve that,' so I pointedly lick my lips and then press them closed. He smirks like he finds it amusing. "You're still someone who believes in fairness and justice. That's why you want me hurt. Justice."

"Perhaps," I admit, knowing Evan's got me pegged to a T. Even in the backstabbing world of the Financial District, there are lines I won't cross.

"Justice is only justice if it's delivered at the hands of those who are worthy of dispensing it," Evan says. "Think that over. In the meantime, listen. All I want is an old email deleted. It's on Dylan's personal server and has some information in there he's lording over me. That's all I need."

"More dirty laundry?" I ask, and Evan shakes his head. "What is it?"

"Something that would make my family very… perturbed," Evan finally says.

I roll my eyes and stand up. "If they're not perturbed by you by now, I doubt anything short of—"

Evan reaches out, his hand quick as a snake, and grabs my wrist, cutting me off. "Look, he's blackmailing me," he hisses. "You want me to fucking burn? Fine. But at least let me fight from a fair standing against that asshole. That's all I'm saying."

I shake him off, jerking my hand free from him. "Don't you ever touch me again," I say loud enough to get attention. Last time Evan and I went face to face, I was worried about causing a scene, but I'm taking a page out of Ami's book. Who cares what anyone else in Goldman's thinks? "Because I swear to God, the next time your hand touches mine, I'll leave with your fucking eyeballs in my purse."

Ironically, it's Evan who cares about the growing scene.

He lowers his voice so that it's just between us, his eyes cutting left and right. "November sixth, eight years ago," Evan says. "An email from me to him. I sent it at two fifty-three in the afternoon. Subject line is *SUSHI DINNER AT KAZOKU'S*. Just delete it, then you can go on and try to destroy me, Raven."

Grabbing my bag, I turn and leave Goldman's pissed beyond thinking straight. But as I descend into the subway, I can't shut up the little voice in my gut that says there's a chance that Evan might be telling the truth. Or that, at the very least, I want to know what the hell is in that email.

What could Dylan have over Evan?

Dylan, by his own admission, hates Evan with an acidic vehemence that matches only mine. It's a hatred beyond the professional, into the personal.

Someone who hates that much… might just cross a line in order to enact his revenge.

When Evan leaves and the threat of having to listen to his voice and remember the time we spent together is gone, I can't stop wondering what the hell would be in that email? What does Dylan have that has Evan scared that much?

And did he really blackmail Olivia and force her out of the city? Questions pile up, and I don't like a single one of them.

CHAPTER 24

DYLAN

I strip off my shirt, just about ready to step into the shower for a well-deserved soak after a day where I accomplished more than I'd planned. I had to be out of the office for most of it, which means I've missed Raven all day.

Damned City Hall.

A meeting with the mayor and influential members of the city council ran longer than I expected. Two investments I'm making in town were being held up for purely political reasons, and negotiations on the required offset to clear the path took longer than I expected. But it was a productive day, all in all.

In the end, I gained approval for a five hundred million-dollar acquisition with the financially acceptable investment of only fifty million dollars. The offset? My agreement to renovate and expand half a dozen youth parks in disadvantaged neighborhoods in the city, something I would've happily done regardless of their rubber stamp on my proposal. I already give over a million dollars a year to programs there. I do it quietly, not trying to make a splash and gain attention for it, but those at the mayor's level know where their funds come from.

As the steam fills the room, I rub the back of my neck, replaying the conversations. It took a lot of dancing around the solution, but in the end, I was able to walk out with what I wanted. A rare use of a Monday afternoon and evening at home, where I'll be later joined by Raven for our usual nightly session. A grin pulls at my lips.

I'm eager to share the news with her. She'll understand more than most.

I drop my shirt to the floor, but before I can undo my pants, my phone's alarm goes off. My hand freezes, and I pull it out to see that the personal alarm I've got in my office has been triggered. It's not one that building security has, because anyone who's gotten that far clearly is someone who belongs in the building.

It's an inside threat.

But anyone who's breaking into my office is on a fool's errand. My desk contains nothing sensitive, and my computer has security that would make even professional hackers reconsider their options.

Who the fuck is in my office?

It only takes a glance at security outside the door a moment before to see. Raven.

My brow furrows, and a deep crease settles in my forehead. What the hell is she doing? She knows I'm not there. I wait a moment and then one more for her to remember my schedule and that I'm not there. But she doesn't leave.

It takes great effort to shut down every thought that comes to mind. I quickly change into some casual clothes, jeans and a T-shirt, before heading back to the office. The security staff give me a double-take. They've seen me after hours. It's just the clothes that seem out of place. I give them a wave and stride with purpose to the elevator.

Raven Hill. What are you doing? Anxiousness has my hands clamming up. I clench and unclench them, waiting for the floor to ping.

The office is dark, but it's the in-between time after everyone leaves for the day and before the cleaning crew makes their rounds. There shouldn't be anyone here. In fact, it's usually the precious pocket where Raven and I would be having our 'review' of the day.

That thought makes the blood in my veins run cold.

I walk silently, listening, and I don't hear anything. I wait a moment, waiting to hear the clacking of a keyboard or a drawer opening. Something, anything. But there's nothing.

I push my door open, hoping not to startle her but to see what the hell she's doing. She shouldn't be in my office and she damn well knows it.

What the hell is she thinking?

As I turn the lights on, she looks up, and I can see that her eyes appear haunted, like she's being torn apart by something.

"You know we were meeting at my place later, so what are you doing?" I ask quietly, shutting the door behind me.

A million thoughts bombard me at once. Betrayal, confusion, denial, and even a tiny bit of hope that I'm wrong because I trust her that much despite the current scene before me.

"I always come here after work. My feet just kinda brought me upstairs," she says, her voice monotone. She blinks, and a silent tear rolls down her cheek.

My heart races. She's lying. What the hell is going on?

"What's wrong?" I cross the room slowly, my footsteps on the soft carpet louder than they should be. Coming around my desk, I perch on the edge just to her side and force myself to assume a position of relaxation, crossing one ankle over the other and clasping my hands in my lap so I don't touch her. Not until I know what the fuck is going on.

Because something sure as hell is happening right now.

You don't know what it is, I try to remind myself, but the acid in my stomach is rising. Although I've been in this situation before.

She looks up at me, her eyes glassy, and for a moment, I think she's going to lie again. It takes everything in me to sit still and wait. To have patience.

Then she does it.

Raven looks up at me and swallows thickly. "I went grocery shopping this weekend. Afterward, I always go to Goldman's Café for cheesecake. I had just sat down when..."

She pauses, her chin dropping, but I can tell that her eyes

go distant, like she's reliving the moment she's telling me about. "When what?" I ask gently.

She drags her eyes back to mine and says three words I never expected to hear from her. "Evan sat down." She swallows thickly, and anger simmers inside me.

My fists clench on the edge of my desk, and I can feel the material creak underneath my grip. "What did he have to say?"

I imagine the worst—that she's going back to him. I imagine the best—that she ripped him to shreds right there in the café.

"He told me that you have an email, one that you've been using to blackmail him," Raven says. "He says you did the same thing to Olivia."

"And you believed him?" I ask and then correct myself. "You believe him?"

"Yes and no," she says with a shrug as if that answer doesn't stab me directly in the heart. "I don't think you would blackmail your ex. What you feel for her is too deep still." Her voice cracks. "When you told me about her, it was pain and hurt in your voice, not hate. Evan? Yeah, I think you would." Her eyes meet mine, and her lips tilt up ever so slightly at the corners. "But I don't think I care. I think I'd blackmail him too if I had anything on him that mattered." She licks her lips, like the ugly truth of the admission is bitter-tasting.

"You wouldn't," I say with certainty. "You think you could, imagine you'd get satisfaction from it, but when push came to shove, you wouldn't do it."

Her smile falls because she knows I'm right. She's strong,

capable, and brilliant, but she's not cold-hearted enough to do what she's imagining. That's why fucking with Evan in the first place was my idea, not hers.

"Would you? *Did* you? Have you ever blackmailed anyone?" she asks.

She knows better than to think I would back away from the option if the situation called for it.

But she needs all the information for us to move forward on level ground, so I add, "I've never outright blackmailed someone the way you mean, like a movie villain demanding money and threatening exposure, but if a tidbit of information is useful, letting me apply pressure to accomplish a goal, then yeah, I would... I have... and I'll do it again." I pin her with a gaze, making sure she hears that truth.

"You didn't blackmail him, then?" she questions.

"No," I answer honestly.

"So Evan's full of shit," she states with a scoff. "I knew it."

"Yet, here you are," I remind her.

She sighs, looking around my office before her eyes land heavily on my computer, making me wonder exactly what Evan told her.

"I thought being here would help me find clarity to figure out Evan's play, because I knew he was up to something, so I've been sitting here, trying to work it out in my mind and examine it from every angle. And I knew you'd come, so I was waiting on you."

I raise a brow, frowning. "You could've called me. We could've talked at my place tonight."

Her smile is wry. "I didn't want to warn you, and I was afraid I'd get distracted if I showed up at your house tonight. And…"

"And what?" I question as I watch her pick at a nonexistent thread on her blouse.

"I want you to show me," she says tightly before swallowing and then looking up at me.

"Show you what?"

She can barely look me in the eyes.

"What did Evan tell you, exactly?"

"He said you were mentally abusive to Olivia, which ran her to his arms for some sort of sanctuary, and in your fury, you blackmailed her, forcing her to flee the city. And then you're lording some email over him, which I'm supposed to delete."

That motherfucker! I jump from the desk, unable to stay seated and attempt to control my rising anger. He's a fucking prick through and through.

Raven flinches at my sudden movement and volume, but there is no fear in her eyes. She's looking back at me boldly. She says, "I want to see the email," and it's nearly my undoing.

"You don't believe that, do you?" I demand, feeling sick to my stomach. "That I'm abusive and she ran to him because of me?"

She shakes her head. "Of course not. But after Evan and Elise, I'm a 'trust, but verify' girl, especially on matters of the heart, and I… I am in deep with you, and I…."

She clears her throat but doesn't finish.

"You what?" I push, feeling a touch of hope from the way she's talking. "You what?"

"I just want to see the email, Dylan."

My pulse rages, and I stare at her, vulnerable, and I know it's an ultimatum.

What she's saying sounds reasonable, but what she's asking is too much. She wants me to rip through scars that I've long buried and hold my heart up to the light of her judgment, trusting that she won't see the worst of me and simply walk away, leaving me in shambles.

It's then I notice the tear stains on the sleeve of her blouse and the way she can barely look at me.

"Is there something else I don't know?" I ask her.

She shakes her head no.

"All of this because of Evan?" I press, and her eyes whip up to mine. Red-rimmed.

"I just want to make sure you're the person I think you are."

"Says the woman who broke into my office to give me an ultimatum," I counter in a low tone.

Her expression flinches, as if my words struck her.

A heavy sigh leaves me. "If there's no other choice…"

I have to pace, needing an outlet for the anger and fear coursing through me, so that I can force myself to go back to a time that I've blocked out for damn good reasons.

"When I found out," I tell her, "it tore me apart. I went to a very dark place for a long time, and I'll admit, I spent a lot of personal time and money digging into Olivia and Evan. I kept asking myself how I could've missed the signs. Signs that Olivia was unhappy, that Evan was a monster, that they were fucking right behind my back." I shake my head, remembering.

"What happened to Olivia?" Raven asks me. "Evan said she left town after you ruined her."

I bark out a laugh, which sounds more bitter than I would have thought considering how old the wound is. "Honestly, I don't know," I say. "When Olivia betrayed me, I had one last meeting with her in my apartment at the time. She tried to apologize, said it 'just happened', but I was cold and blunt, told her it didn't matter anymore. I gave her a file box with the things she'd been keeping at my place and took back my key. Other than that, I never kept up with her. I didn't even ask for the engagement ring back or the wedding rings I left on her doorknob. None of it meant anything anymore." It dawns on me as I tell her that the pain I prepared to feel isn't there. When I look back to Raven, though, staring at me like she's hoping I say all the right things to ease her worries, the agony I felt returns.

I offer more. "I imagine, Evan tossed her aside soon after. He didn't care about her. She was a means to an end, a way to hurt me." I release a shaky breath as I sit on the desk's edge again. "It worked. But it was a long time ago. Years at this point."

"Years ago or not, it's still working," she reminds me gently as she puts her hand on my thigh. "It's still hurting you or I wouldn't be sitting here as your means to an end to hurt him. That's what it is between us, remember?"

The similarity is painfully uncomfortable, but Raven and I have moved well beyond the revenge scenario we began with. What I feel for her has nothing to do with Evan. However, my desire for justice remains.

"Wherever Olivia is, it's her business and her life," I tell Raven succinctly, covering her hand with my own as if I can hold her here with me. "I'm not going to waste my time on her any longer. Evan's different. Hypocritical, I suppose."

"And what about Evan? The email with the blackmail?" she questions.

"What email?"

She rattles off a date and time.

"What are you talking about?" I ask her, and she looks at me like I'm lying to her. Not that prick Evan.

I swap places with her, and though it takes me a few minutes, going into my email and searching up the email Evan wanted deleted, I eventually pull it up on the middle one of my screens, letting Raven read it all. "This… this is nothing," Raven says, her brows knit together in confusion. "Why would he want me to do that? What does he have to gain from having me delete an email you probably haven't looked at in six years?"

"This is why," I reply, getting up and walking out of my office. Once I'm past the doorway's threshold, I hold my phone up so she can see it. "Do it. Delete the message."

Unsure, she sits back in my chair, her eyes bouncing from me to the screen as she moves the mouse. She clicks, and my phone buzzes. I walk up to my desk, showing her the notification I just received.

On my home screen is a security alert from my personal system… and a photo from my webcam, showing her looking at the monitor.

"How...?"

"He knew about the security systems I have in place," I explain, dismissing the alert. Immediately, the email reappears in my inbox, and I go back to her side. "No computer can delete any of my personal files without three layers of security. One, you've got to be logged onto my system, which requires a biometric password. Two, my phone has to be near the computer, or else the security system is triggered."

"What?" she says as she processes it all.

"If someone skips step two, you see what happens. My phone gets an alert, allowing me to confirm the deletion... or let the person who did it think it's been deleted until I dismiss the alert."

"That... but why would he tell me it was blackmail?"

"Evan knows, and he likely has it himself. My guess is he was trying to sabotage us. He knew if I saw that picture, I'd assume the worst of you. That you'd betrayed me like Olivia did."

"And then I went and did it. I came here to confront you."

"You didn't log in and try to delete it. And I know you know my login at this point." Her eyes meet mine, and she doesn't deny it.

"I thought about it... But I couldn't. I just wanted you to show me."

Raven's lip quivers, and I pull her into my arms.

"Dylan, I'm sorry. I knew he was up to something. I just... I needed to know what could be that bad and what you..."

"What I was capable of?" I finish for her, hating that he got to her and for a moment made her question who I am.

"I'm sorry." Her voice is tight as she looks me in the eye.

"Nothing to be sorry for, Darling," I whisper, holding her close. "We've both been fucked over, and I understand questioning things… especially when it's not supposed to be anything…" I can't finish the thought.

It was revenge. Then business.

"So, what now?" she asks, and I let go of her to hold her at arm's length, looking into her eyes. They're clear, focused… and sexy as fuck with the anger burning in their depths. She doesn't like that Evan tried to use her any more than I do.

Neither of us has said it aloud, though. The part that really matters. The thread that kept me hanging on tonight.

"Now, we have a choice to make." I force a smile, letting her know her feelings on the matter will be considered. "We can ignore what he tried to do and focus on us. You can be mine, I'll be yours, and this will simply be a failed attack on his part to break us apart."

"Or?" she hedges.

"Or we can make him pay like we intended when this whole thing started. We can destroy him once and for all."

I keep my face neutral while she mulls it over. I'd like to say that if she chooses option one, I'll go along with it, but the truth is, I'm not sure I can let go of the hatred I've felt toward Evan so easily. I would try for Raven, though, if it's truly what she wants.

"I feel like if we let this go, he'll only try again, and I don't want to live our lives constantly worried about what shit he's going to pull." She looks up at me and takes a steadying breath. "Dylan?"

"Yes, Darling?" I say, praying she's about to give the answer I'm hoping for.

"Destroy him."

"Fucking hell," I murmur.

"What?" she asks, truly not realizing.

"You're even sexier when you want to burn the world down," I tell her and steal her lips for a kiss before having her under me, moaning my name like she should have been doing an hour ago.

Chapter 25

Raven

I look over at Dylan nervously, still not sure if I made the right decision in inviting him to tonight's party. This is basically ripping him from the relative safety of his penthouse and throwing him in a pit with feral lions... or lionesses, I suppose, since I'm thinking specifically of Maggie and Ami.

My hands are clammy at the thought of Dylan seeing this side of my life, being a part of it and possibly us being... more. I try not to make it a big deal and I try not to overthink. But the fact that I pushed him like that, called his bluff and showed my ass and he still wants me... I don't deserve it, and my feelings for him have somehow grown even more. I feel like I'm perched on the edge and he alone has the power to push me over.

I love him.

It's so damn obvious to me. I love Dylan Sharpe. I know

we're different, though. Our lives are nothing alike.

"You're sure you're okay with this?" I ask him, pulling his attention away from the passing cars on the street outside. Thankfully, Vince, his driver, is too busy with the traffic as we head toward our destination because Dylan looks at me with amusement lighting his eyes because the PDA is a bit much. I lean into his side, and he wraps an arm around my shoulders. His touch and warmth are a soothing balm and reassure me.

He answers with a smirk on his face although his tone is deadpan. "It might be a bit... well, to steal one of Ami's words... wooo!" I can't help but laugh when his brows jump up his forehead at the odd sound coming from me. This man's heard me moan, cry, gasp, and more, but a 'wooo' is apparently the shocking oddity.

With his sleeves rolled up, his shirt unbuttoned, and a five o'clock shadow, he looks a touch more rugged today, and I freaking love this look on him. Laid back but handsome.

His answering smile is full of confidence when he leans back to look at me. "I'm excited to meet your friends and happy to do anything with you. Even if it involves 'woooing'." He says it flatly, like the concept of fun is foreign to him, but I know that's not true. He's absolutely fun, just in a very different way from Maggie and Ami.

I try to relax, warmed by his words and rarely seen dry sense of humor.

The night he found me in his office, I was scared and confused and not sure if I was making the biggest mistake of my life. I warred with myself on whether to just ignore it, like I did with my instincts when Evan cheated on me, or to get to the bottom of it. It very well could have ended my career, but when push came to shove, I needed to know that Dylan was the man I felt he was in my heart. Even if it meant costing me my job. Money comes and goes, but if I'm falling for a man, sleeping with him and giving him everything I have, I want to get to the bottom of every issue. I hadn't 'done' anything, but my struggle with reconciling what I knew of Dylan personally and who he was professionally with who he might've been years ago had me fighting a battle between my head and heart.

Our talk that night has led to so much more. It's like a boundary we didn't know existed has been lifted. No secrets, no hiding, just the two of us wanting each other and not giving a fuck about anything else.

I'm not sure what Dylan is doing to handle Evan, nor do I want to know. Whatever it is, I trust him to do it right, make it hurt Evan, and be technically legal while a bit morally gray, which I'm okay with. I appreciate that he's willing to do what I'm not, both because of my own character and my current position at the bottom of the power structure between the three of us. I feel like Dylan's my protective guard dog, one who's willing to bite back because he's been directly harmed by our attacker too.

As for us, we've been better than ever, taking the time to meet not only at his office, but to go to his place for more private, longer dates. And we don't only rip each other's clothes off. We talk, we share… we're something I never would've dreamed we'd become…

A couple.

It might not be splashed across the front page of the paper, and neither of us is making any public declarations, but for us, it's very real and very serious. Honestly, Dylan probably would stand up on the conference table at work and make an announcement if I was okay with it, but I'm trying to maintain some sense of discretion.

Which is why tonight's a big deal. This will be our first official, public outing as a couple, and I'm proud to be at Dylan's side as he meets my friends.

Vince stops the car at the curb, and there's a knock on the door a moment before it's opened by a man in black slacks, a black Polo, and black sunglasses even though it's well after dark. He holds his hand out, helping me from the car, and then Dylan joins me as the luxury car pulls away behind us.

In front of us is a wall of horizontal wide-plank wood paneling that's broken up by a pair of soaring double doors with black iron bar handles that are nearly as tall as I am. The sign above the awning reads *Los Ingobernables*.

Dylan holds the door open for me, and inside, I tell the hostess that we're here for the Ami Rossman birthday party. She leads us across the large space, expertly dodging white tablecloth-covered tables, a dance floor with only a few people on it at this early hour, and a bar surrounded by people. "Here's the rest of your group," she says as she opens a velvet rope to allow us access to the private VIP space, but Ami's already spotted us.

"Raven! You made it!" Ami squeals happily as she beelines directly for me. She wraps me in a tight hug, jerking me from side to side. "And you brought him! Bring it in, birthday girls get all the hugs." She holds her arms out wide.

Dylan glances at me, a little unsure and a bit amused at Ami's exuberance, but when I don't react, he gives Ami a polite hug that's over faster than a blink. "Nice to formally meet you, Ami. I've heard a lot about you. Most of it good," he jokes.

Ami beams and swats at him. "You don't want to know all the things I've heard about you. They are definitely not good." She laughs, certainly a drink or two in.

He chuckles while I glare at Ami, fighting back a grin. "Shut up!"

"What?" she says, feigning innocence. She spies a waiter passing by with a tray of golden-fried mini-muffin-looking hors d'oeuvres and points. "Those are little bites of heaven. I don't know what they are, but I've had like five of them already and I'm going for number six. Excuse me."

She chases after the waiter, her cream sundress fluttering behind her as she goes, and I'm pretty sure she actually grabs two or three of whatever the heavenly bites are.

Hand in hand, Dylan and I work our way around the room. His fingers intertwine with mine, and when he gives me a squeeze, I look up at him. I can't help all the emotions that flood through me. We say hi to Maggie, meet some of Ami's work friends, and I introduce Dylan to Ami's parents and then Maggie's parents and brother, Robert. He's charming in his own rough way, complimenting Melinda's dress and making business small talk with John before asking about Robert's schooling.

I've met Maggie's brother dozens of times over the years, and each time, he has a new obsession with a time period he's mid-deep dive into for his master's degree in history. I've heard lengthy lessons on everything from Queen Victoria to the Cold War. Based on the nearly full TED talk about the Korean War he's giving us tonight, that must be his latest. And though I lose interest quickly and resort to polite *Mmmhmms* while fighting with my eyelids, Dylan listens intently and asks thoughtful questions that Robert seems to appreciate until Maggie intervenes.

"Robbie, it's a party, not a lecture. Let them go," she teases in a way only a sibling can do.

Robert startles and then grins. "Sorry, I get a little lost in my work."

"I completely understand. I do the same thing," Dylan replies with an amicable smile of his own. "If you want to hear about mineralogy mining laws in Nevada, let me know. It's a recent project I've been learning a lot about."

Maggie pulls Robert away, and we continue our way around the room, mingling here, chatting there, and having a good time. We even confirm that those hors d'oeuvres Ami was obsessing over are indeed heavenly.

Everything feels so different than it did at the fundraiser, which was the last time we attended an event like this. We've come so far since then. Dylan is no longer cautious and closed-off, acting like everyone is either out to get him or a possible connection. He's friendly and open, laughing easily, telling funny stories, and impressing everyone with his knowledge of the city. I half wonder if he's always been that way and I just haven't been privy to that side of him or if now that we're together, something's changed for him like it has for me.

I'm always proud to be with him, but witnessing him relax feels like an important gift, like a trust he's giving not only to me but to my friends. They might not understand the unique treasure that he is, but I do.

As for me, I feel steady, settled into the moment with Dylan at my side. What's growing between us feels... real. And I couldn't be happier. But I'm always waiting for the other foot to drop. It's just too good. It's surreal. I got the dream job AND the dream man. I don't feel worthy of it, like this simply can't be real.

Eventually, Ami's mom, Jennifer, clinks a fork to a glass and invites us all to sit down at the long table off to the side of the room. We make our way over, and Dylan pulls out a chair for me, helping to push me in after I sit. He sits beside me, his arm naturally draping over the chair. He's claiming me. It might appear casual, but it's oh, so very bold, and I love it.

Dinner is delicious. It's a fusion menu, so there's a mix of spices and flavors I've never had together, but everything is really tasty.

"Here, try this," Dylan requests, holding up a forkful of his tilapia with chimichurri sauce. When I open my mouth, he feeds the bite to me, and I moan at how tender and tangy it is.

When I look back at the table, I find Ami and Maggie staring at me with stars in their eyes. "You two are so cute," Maggie teases and sways back and forth like a school girl, her short black dress swooshing around her thighs as she does, and I can't help but grin.

Ami nods. "My birthday wish is to have a man look at me like Dylan's looking at you."

Surprised, I cut my eyes to Dylan to see how he's looking at me, only to find it's the way he always does—with an intense blend of hunger and interest. Like I'm the only person in the room. Or at least the only one he cares about. Everyone else could disappear in a blink, and I'm not sure Dylan would notice or give a shit.

I lean forward, pressing a quick peck to his lips, needing to let him know that I see him too and appreciate him more than he could know. I lean back, smiling, only for him to catch my jaw in his palm and pull me back in for a longer kiss. It's still appropriate given our audience, but it makes me melt and wonder how soon Ami's gonna cut the cake so we can leave.

When Dylan releases me, I'm drunk on him, and he looks down at me, his eyes darkened. A single blink later, they brighten and he smiles, cockily knowing all too well where my thoughts have run.

"Birthday wish amendment," Ami says pointing her perfectly manicured finger. "That's what I want."

She gets her chance after dinner when the restaurant staff bring out a large cake covered in sparkling candles and we sing to her. Ami flashes me a wink, takes a big breath, and then blows the candles out. The smile on her face says her birthday celebration is turning out to be everything she wanted, and I'm so glad.

As it gets later, the party moves to the dance floor when a DJ takes over, promising to play a wide variety of songs and rhythms that'll have us dancing all night. To my utter shock, Dylan holds his hand out to me.

"Would you like to dance?"

I gawk at him. "You dance?"

I don't know why that surprises me so much, but it does. I wouldn't think he'd have the time or inclination to learn to dance. Heck, before this week, I wasn't even sure he knew how to let loose.

But I slip my hand into his, trusting that he can lead me… on the dance floor, in the bedroom, and honestly, anywhere.

I'm right. Dylan is a strong lead, and though I don't know how to salsa, I find myself doing it, or at least I think I am. I only manage to step on his foot once, and with every misstep, we both laugh. It's easy and light hearted, but the closeness of him and this moment lights my heart on fire. Whatever it is, I follow Dylan around the floor, knowing that at this point, I'd follow him into hell if he asked me to.

I'm not sure when it happened or if it was all once or in tiny percentage points, but I've fallen in love with Dylan Sharpe past the point of return. He holds my heart, and I trust him to treat it as the precious commodity that it is because he knows all too well how fragile it is since he watched as it was so-recently shattered.

But it's been repaired by my own hard work and Dylan's intensive care.

"Are you having fun?" I ask him, thinking that I know the answer but wanting to hear it from him.

He nods, his smile easier than I've ever seen it. "More than I would've thought."

"It's a pretty great party, right? Ami has been obsessively planning it for weeks."

He stops us on the dance floor, moving us out of the way so people can pass by as they continue their path around the wood floor.

"Your friends are lovely, this place is amazing, but the only reason I'm having fun is because of you, Darling."

Darling. My heart flutters.

He makes me beautiful. He makes me feel powerful. He makes me feel loved. He makes me feel like... his.

And I love it and him.

"Can we go home now? I'm ready to do a bit of celebrating of our own," I purr, letting the need I feel for him weave through the words.

"What did you have in mind?" he teases, his own desire becoming evident between us.

I glance down and then drag my gaze back to his eyes. "I was thinking I'd start by kissing and licking something or another..."

"Be careful or we won't make it home." His voice is nothing

more than a rumble.

A deliciously filthy thought pops to my mind, and I smile to myself. "You want me to be careful? Make me," I taunt, knowing my eyes are flashing with heat and happiness. I whirl in place to give him my back. "I'm going to go find Ami and tell her goodbye."

I feel like I got one over on him and am walking away the clear winner when I feel a short slap on my ass. I jerk my head, looking over my shoulder in shock to find Dylan staring at me. His face is charming, his handsome eyes narrowed with an arched brow. He's in boss mode, and I can't help the blush that heats my cheeks. "Make it quick, Miss Hill."

I trap my bottom lip between my lips to keep my smile from growing too wide and nod before answering, "Yes, Sir."

I'd love to say I came back with something witty or sexy. Instead, I virtually hop to do what he's commanded, nearly scurrying away to find my friend so I can enjoy the night with Dylan.

CHAPTER 26

DYLAN

"I have a request for you," I tell the middle-aged blonde woman sitting across from me. We're not at Lionfish. We're at one of the numerous coffee bars and shops that fill the Upper East Side, a virtual world away from the Financial District. That's on purpose, and my guest knows it.

Vanna Nicholson has been both the bane and the toast of the town for nearly thirty-five years. Originally one of the 'society girls', she was the previous generation's little hellraiser. Starting when she was only a teenager, she ran wild. Parties, scandals, and more were everyday life for Vanna Nicholson, all fueled by her family's billions.

She was the spoiled rich bitch plastered on every magazine two decades ago.

Guess that's what happens when you're the only daughter,

your parents are divorced, and your older brothers have clearly whipped out their dicks to mark the family business as their territory. A lesson to her parents—maybe a quarter-million dollars a month is a bit much for an allowance.

All of that came crashing down after nearly a decade. Her family's downfall dominated the pages for nearly a year, and afterward, Vanna found herself in a position she'd never dreamed. She needed a job. Thankfully, she had a gift for gab and lots of connections. She knew where the bodies were buried and which closets held which skeletons.

Hell, she'd helped put them there for so many influential men and women in this city. While her dirt may be scattered for all to see, she has the sordid details on everyone who is anyone in this city.

It's turned her into an institution in town, and for a quarter-century, she's been the society pages reporter, dishing out innuendo, scandal, and sometimes flat-out muck like it's candy from her pocket. And of course, dear readers have been eating it up, both in print and online, the entire time because the only thing people love more than money is gossip. Especially given money is of no concern for Vanna's targets.

"A request?" she lifts a perfectly plucked brow. "And what would that request be?" Vanna asks, stirring her skinny latte. Years of being a culture vulture have been oddly preserving on her. Her hair's still the same shade of blonde it was thirty years ago, her face shows almost no wrinkles, and her outfits have only gone from over labeled to quiet luxury.

It's only when you get to her eyes, her cold, icy, almost dead eyes, that you realize she's seen and heard about things that nobody should. She may fuel party rumors and spread gossip, but there's a darkness that's kept quiet. And some secrets are too dark even for the most endured.

"Evan Faulkner," I tell her. "I want him exposed and taken down. Permanently." My words are clearly spoken, although my voice is hushed and my tone far more casual than it should be. I clear my throat and roll up my sleeves while I hold her questioning gaze.

I've thought and strategized, turning over options and alternatives in my mind for days. Evan is likely doing the same, well aware that his attempt at coming between Raven and me has failed. If he'd let it go, it would be different. He doesn't know how to simply take the loss. There is something in the core of who he is who will keep at it until he's hurt Raven. I know he will. He knows her and knows how to get under her skin and into her head. I can't blame her for wanting answers from me. But I can put an end to the piece of shit whispering lies about me to her and about her to anyone in this city who will listen.

He'll readily see me coming, and I've had to come up with more diabolical, unpredictable methods to exact the revenge I need and Raven gave me permission to proceed with, like reaching out to Vanna. I could've done this long ago. She's been an option all along, but it's not until now, with Raven involved, that I'm willing to go to this drastic, and potentially public, length.

Vanna's fingers tighten on the ceramic handle of her latte,

and she leans forward, setting the cup down before it can spill. "The Faulkners? Oh, is that all?" She laughs lightly as though I'm joking, but when I don't join in, she sobers. "You're asking me to walk through a minefield, Dylan. Why now? That girl Olivia was years ago. I would think someone of your status would have let it go."

She knows all about Olivia and Evan... and me. She wrote the articles at the time, teasing that perhaps there was something even more unexpected between the three of us than the usual betrayal and cheating. It was scandalous, and fucking embarrassing, and added salt to the wound. Evan and I were such good friends, after all, and friends do share. She was shut down pretty quickly on that implication, and I suspect I have Evan, or his father, to thank for that because I certainly wasn't in the position to do anything about it at the time.

"As you know from personal experience, some wounds don't heal," I reply pointedly, and Vanna's mouth pinches. Her family was one of those families that had billions... until Jerome Faulkner decided that his ivory tower needed just a few more floors. He crushed the Nicholsons, using his own media connections to tear down the family name and devastate their business holdings until, in the ultimate display of humiliation, he bought out Vanna's father.

I'm hoping she has some grudges of her own to grind. I sold it to myself as 'the enemy of my enemy' when I started this thing with Raven, but perhaps it's morphing into 'victims of my victimizer', because Raven, I, and Vanna all share experience dealing with the pain of the Faulkners, ways and would love an opportunity to rise up against them.

"You have a point," Vanna concedes. "But if you know that much, then you also know why I'm cautious with the Faulkners."

"You have dirt on Evan and the rest of them, I'm sure," I say, leaning back in my seat and taking a glance around the bustling cafe. I don't recognize anyone, and no one seems to notice our conversation. "Their lawyers can only come after you for libel and defamation if what you print isn't true. And you and I both know that you can print all sorts of things about the Faulkners that are plenty true, and even more so destructive."

"You have *dirt* as well, certain information that would suit your cause," Vanna points out. "You could destroy him legally. You've had the means to do so for years but have held back." I start to say something, and she holds up her hand, quieting me. "I don't need to hear your excuses and reasons. I trust you've held your information for the right time, much the same way I do. But why should I put my head on the chopping block for something you're not willing to do yourself? At a time that serves you, not me?"

"Because the things I could prove would hurt others, people I do like and have some allegiance to." I adjust my collar as the back of my neck heats. She's correct in her assessment, but I don't want to burn the financial district to the ground, just one prick who deserves it more than others.

"Like your friends Ollie and Austin?" she guesses, poking around and hoping to strike informational pay dirt. "I hear you have a new fifth at your little poker games too. A newcomer, Noah? He's making quite the splash, buying up real estate to create an insta-empire." Her red lips curl with amusement before she takes a sip of her drink.

I can't fault her. It's what she does, and she's damn good at it. But I'm not selling out people I care about. Those I don't? Maybe.

I nod, giving her a calculating look. "I have met Noah," I say, not confirming where or when. "I wish him the best with his... what did you call it? Insta-empire." I also don't use my own language to describe Noah's business buying strategy, but rather echo hers, not agreeing or disagreeing with her.

It's a careful game we both play.

Vanna smiles serenely, as if something in my words answered a question for her, though I'm not sure how it could. She picks up her latte again after tapping her nails that match her lips perfectly on the cup, taking a polite sip as she looks over the rim of the cup at me. "How hospitable of you," Vanna says. I give her a dark look, ready to deal with the issue at hand. "I also hear you've taken a very personal interest in 'mentoring' one of your new, and rather beautiful, junior associates."

"That would be singular, perhaps." No doubt, she's aware, so I don't deny it. Certainly not now that we're public. But still, my throat is tight knowing all too well how reality can be twisted and so many don't bother with the truth.

"Perhaps there's been gossip that would bode well in the papers," she starts.

I growl and lean forward so she hears this loud and clear.

"Tread carefully, Vanna. Very carefully."

Rather than falling, her smile grows into something akin to eagerness and her eyes flare. She has no less than five follow-up questions she wants to ask, but my reaction is enough of an answer… for now. So she sets her latte down and gives a queenly nod. "I understand what you want, and I'll see what I can do."

"Thank you," I say, truly meaning it.

"Don't forget this is a tit-for-tat arrangement, though, Dylan. If I do this for you, I will expect something in return… at some point."

Her eyes narrow as she watches my reaction.

Don't I fucking know it. That's why I haven't been willing to cross this bridge until now when Raven was at risk. I offer a simple nod, not knowing exactly what the price will be. Whatever it is, to get Evan away from Raven, it will be worth it.

"Deal, then?" she asks.

I give her a terse nod, feeling like I've made a deal with the devil, but I would be willing to do so much worse for Raven. I would burn the entire world to the ground if she asked me to. Fuck, she wouldn't even have to ask. One bat of her lashes and I'd do it gratefully.

Still reeling from our discussion and plan, I go back to the office, where I immerse myself in work until the end of the day. Not a single task could hold my focus, but I made headway, at least. It's only five forty-five when my door opens and Raven comes almost bounding in, her face filled with excitement. "I did it!"

Tamara must've stepped away from her desk. Either that, or Raven blasted past her in joyful bliss.

With a cocked brow of interest, I push my keyboard aside, amused. "And what did you do, Miss Hill?"

My use of her name reminds her that it's still early, but she barely seems to register it. "Mr. Sharpe," she says most professionally, her eyes still alight. "I did it. My first seven-figure day."

My lips pull into an uncontainable smile. With the rumors and all, not a damn CEO in this city would claim they didn't want to fuck her too. Gorgeous, brilliant, and worth seven figures her first month... Let the gossip light the damn city on fire for all I care.

The average associate in my firm works two hundred and forty days a year, accounting for weekends, trading holidays, and time off. The max someone can work is about two hundred and fifty, give or take a leap year or strange Monday holiday here or there.

For someone below the level of a senior trader to make a million dollars in a week is an accomplishment. For a junior trader to do it in a day is something someone gets to hang their hat on for a long time. For someone who's technically a probationary associate? It's fucking unheard of.

Until Raven.

And hearing the happiness in Raven's voice, I can tell that not only is she excited, but she's expecting more days like this. It's only the beginning for her. She reminds me of how I was at the start of my career... addicted to that rush.

"I'm very proud of you," I tell her sincerely, getting up and coming around my desk.

Raven peeks behind her and closes the door, her simper turning needy. It's too early, too risky, but I can't help myself. I want to celebrate this momentous moment with her.

I close the distance in an instant, barely giving her time to shut the door, adrenaline racing though me mixed with my own desire. I wrap an arm around Raven's waist, cupping her jaw with my other hand, and take her mouth in a kiss. She gasps in surprise, cautious but also floating so high emotionally that she doesn't stop me when I use her open-mouthed reaction to slip my tongue in to tangle with hers.

"Mr. Sharpe, I just got a call from—"

It's Tamara, who started talking from my outer office as she opened my door, clearly in a hurry. She's frozen in my doorway, and Raven rips herself away from me, her expression one of both fear and shock. "Oh!"

"What is it, Tamara?" I question, swallowing thickly and correcting my tie.

Tamara clears her throat, and ever the utmost professional, she jumps straight to business. "Excuse me. Mr. Sharpe, Ms. Nicholson called, said she's, quote, working on it, end quote. I assume you know what that means."

"Yes, thank you, Tamara. Good night."

To her credit, she nods her head at both me and Raven. "Good night to the both of you."

Once she's gone and the door is shut, Raven turns wide, concerned eyes to me. "Oh, my God, everyone's going to know."

I arch a brow. "Everyone does know, remember? We talked

about this already," I remind her.

Raven breathes out her frustration, as if I don't get what she means. "It's different when there's a rumor going around that we're making out in your office."

I smile, reaching out to take her upper arms in my hands. Simply holding her seems to ease the concern etched into her forehead. I hold her gorgeous gaze. "Raven, Tamara is the last person you should worry about. She would never breathe a word about the things she sees, hears, and knows from being near my office." Raven pins me with a deadly look, and I rush to amend, "Professionally speaking, of course. And she's known about us for weeks now. She even gave me advice on going slow so you didn't burn out with your investments... or with me. Seems you're not the only one who thinks I'm 'a lot' to deal with."

I'm trying to make light of the situation so Raven doesn't panic and regress, not when we're doing so well. Because truly, nothing has changed. Tamara already knew about Raven and me, and I trust her implicitly.

Raven nibbles at her lip worriedly. "You didn't see how she was looking at me."

Tamara barely glanced Raven's way, and only to say goodbye. "She didn't look at you any sort of way."

It's the wrong thing to say. Fire rises in Raven's green eyes. "She might be fine with us, and might've known, but seeing it in stark, living proof in front of her very eyes is quite a different thing. And you didn't see how she looked at me," she repeats. "She had that mom look, like she's disappointed in me, like she thinks I'm sleeping my way to the top."

This again.

"Are you?" I ask, and Raven's brows furrow together sharply. "Didn't think so," I say quickly. "And you and I both know that. It was a surprise, it was shocking, but it's not a big deal unless we make it one."

She drops her chin, looking at the floor and thinking. I'm hoping she'll see reason because this truly isn't the issue she's making it out to be.

"I thought we were going public?" I ask her, and the look she gives me back isn't what I expected. My brow raises. "Aren't we?"

"Not at the office," she answers, and it takes me by surprise.

"Why not?" My voice is harder than it should be, but I'm on edge.

"I'm embarrassed," she says finally, her voice quiet.

"By what?" I ask, on edge. "Me?" My voice is harder than I mean it to be, but she's digging at those scars I thought I'd healed over. The scars that formed over stabbing words like 'you're not enough' and suggestions that I'm too-this or not-enough-that. They came from Olivia and Evan, but also much further back, to my childhood and my parents.

Raven's hitting on damage I want to leave in the past.

Her mouth opens and closes, but no sound comes out. She's as gobsmacked as I am… by both of our reactions.

"I don't want people to think–"

I cut her off, fully fucking uninterested in anyone else. Doesn't she realize how little their opinions mean? They don't know us. "If they want to judge, fucking let them."

"You may be okay with that... but I'm not," she answers back, exasperated.

"When will it end, Raven? At what point will you feel like you've made it on your own and be proud to stand at my side? After all, you just had a seven-figure day with zero input or assistance from me. Is that not a sign to you and everyone else that I have nothing to do with your success? That it's all you, all yours?" I swallow thickly. "Or will you forever be so worried about what everyone else thinks?" I wave a hand, gesturing to the world at large.

"Dylan, I—"

"I think you have some thinking to do, Darling. You seem to be under the incorrect assumption that there is a power imbalance between us in which you are the lesser party. To be clear, that only exists in your mind. To me, to everyone else, they can see that I'm so far gone for you that I would destroy the world for you. I would destroy myself for you."

I grit my teeth, the words spat out, wrenched from me without consideration, simply pouring forth from my soul with violent force. Raven looks like I've struck her. Honestly, my words probably did hit with painful impact, but it can't be helped. We have to move past this if we're ever going to move forward, and I want that with Raven.

I want her desperately. Loudly. Completely.

"I'm gonna go," Raven whispers, her eyes filling with tears.

Fuck.

"Raven, wait," I start and reach out to her, but it's too late.

"Don't come after me," she warns, and although I want to, chasing her down in the office is the last thing she wants. She doesn't want to go public.

She spins and virtually sprints from my office, leaving me standing here, lost to what just happened.

Fuck.

CHAPTER 27

RAVEN

I lasted all of an hour before I texted Dylan, and he told me his driver would come around to bring me to his apartment. Riding in the back, I twiddle my fingers, wondering how stupid I must look. "Vince?"

From up front, Vince's eyes cut to me. "Yes, Miss Hill?"

"Be honest with me. What do you think of Dylan and me?"

Vince clears his throat and then plays with the knot of his tie at the red light. I've barely spoken to him, apart from polite greetings and asking how his day is. He's a private man. But he's seen Dylan and me in the back of this car more than a dozen times now. And I know he's been Dylan's driver for years before me.

"What do you mean, Miss Hill?" he asks.

"Am I being foolish, sleeping with him and risking the entire firm finding out?"

Vince relaxes slightly, shaking his head and driving forward as the light turns green. "Miss Hill, I've been a driver for thirty years, starting with a taxi that I'd cruise around the Square at night, picking up tourists and barflies and more, taking them wherever they wanted. I've been a chauffeur, both rental and, for the past few years, on call for Mr. Sharpe. All that to say, there have been a fair number of people in my backseat, so I know what I'm talking about." He glances in the rearview mirror, making sure I understand he's an expert as far as he's concerned. "Mr. Sharpe barely smiled, barely spoke in this car unless it was a business call." He swallows and then tells me, "I used to tell my wife he needs a partner. Although I'd never tell him, and this stays between the two of us, right?" he asks, and his eyes search for mine in the rearview mirror.

"Of course," I answer him.

"You are a remarkable young woman, one who has made him a happy man for the first time in... well, as long as I've known him. And sometimes, we do things for people we care about that might seem stupid to people who don't understand the whole situation. Trust me. My wife could tell you stories."

I take a moment to embrace Vince's advice.

"It sounds like you think very highly of him," I answer, and I don't expect his response.

"I spent my twenty-fifth wedding anniversary in the Bahamas because of him," Vince explains, "and my son has a scholarship waiting for him that Mr. Sharpe doesn't know I know about. That's the sort of man he is." His eyes find mine in the rearview again. "He's a good man, and I think the two of you make for a beautiful couple. We're almost there."

Vince drops me off with a 'Good luck, Miss Hill', and I go upstairs on weak legs, where Dylan's waiting for me in his living room. Crossing the floor, I force myself to look him in the eyes, wanting to make him understand. "Dylan."

"Darling," he answers, his voice deep and the cadence doing something sinful to me.

We always start with a greeting, it seems, but hearing his name for me helps. I sit down on the couch, angled toward him but on another piece of furniture. My nerves flutter through me, and I can barely sit still.

"Would you like a drink?" he offers, but I look him in his eyes. The intensity that stares back begs me to simply let go. It promises that he'll catch me.

"No… let me just say it," I start and take in a deep breath.

He straightens, the cords in his neck tightening as he swallows. "Say whatever you'd like, and then I have something to say as well."

"Dylan, I'm sorry," I begin. "Today, I was embarrassed, but it wasn't you. It was me. I've spent so much of these past months either angry, or scared, or… well, lust-drunk. And when Tamara walked in, it felt like everything I'd been telling myself—that as long as no one saw, it didn't matter what the rumors were at work, not while I was doing so well on my own and they could surely see that—it all… disappeared in a blink, and I had to come to quick terms with being seen as the one thing I've fought against…"

I truly thought my biggest fear in all this was that I'd be seen as a gold-digging climber who is using Dylan, but when I dug a little deeper, there was an even uglier truth.

I swallow thickly and say, "I'm not good enough for any of this. I'm faking it in so many ways, acting like I have a clue when sometimes, I don't know what I'm doing. That's why I've been worried about everyone else. At some point, they'll figure out that I'm an imposter pretending to be confident. Because the truth is, I wasn't good enough to get an internship on my own—Evan had to help me—then I couldn't get a job on my own. You took pity on me. I wasn't good enough to keep Evan from straying…" Dylan growls at that one, but I don't let it stop me. My emotions get the best of me as every insecurity heats my body. "And now, I'm not good enough for a man like you."

"I'm the one not good enough for you," he corrects harshly. "But I'm trying to be. So fucking hard. I'm working my ass off to override a lifetime of hustle, of grabbing what I want with both hands and stubbornly refusing to let go, because I want you to choose me, not be forced to stay with me because you have no other option."

I stare at him, his words sinking in along with my own confession.

"You're not allowed to say you're not good enough. I get to decide that, and you are everything to me," he confesses, and my entire world slows. The walls are closing in. "I get to love who I want to love, Darling. So don't you dare think you're not good enough for me when I want you so desperately."

I blink, awestruck. "We sound like a pair of woe-is-me shitshows," I say, hiding my feelings behind sarcasm.

Dylan inclines his head. "Perhaps. Or like two people willing to grow and change and improve, for us and for another who's worth the growing pains. As long as you want me, I want you," he says.

"I do want you," I say earnestly. "I choose you, over and over, Dylan."

He exhales heavily, a small shudder working through him as the words settle into his body, heart, and soul.

"Good. That's the only thing that matters. It doesn't matter what anyone else thinks. I mean it, Raven," he stresses.

"What did you want to say?" I dare to ask him, not wanting to think about the office and exhausted from my own back and forth and racing thoughts.

He takes a moment, locking eyes with me and searching for something before he starts. "I need to ask you, Raven. What is it you want out of this? Out of your life?"

"I want it all," I tell him evenly. "I want to be respected for my accomplishments on their own, to be with you, to have you wrapped around my finger even as I'm helpless under your command." I offer him a small smile with that, and he huffs a laugh, breaking the tension that had gathered. My heart beats harder as I confess, "I want to be your partner, your darling, your confidant. I want everything. I want to be yours."

Dylan dips his chin just a fraction of an inch, nodding along with me. "I understand," he says quietly, "because I want everything you just listed."

"I want to be loved," I tell him, my heart going wild at daring to use such a word. But I have to say it aloud.

Dylan stiffens at the loaded word, and fear trickles through me, so I try to take it back, swallow it down until he's ready to hear it. "I… look, if I was too quick to say it, I'm sorry, I just—"

I get to my feet, regretting laying it all out there, but Dylan leaps up with me, pulling me in close. "Stay," he whispers in my ear. "Don't go. I want that too."

His words unlock me, and I melt against him, turning my head to kiss his lips tenderly. "Really?" I ask, knowing it makes me sound weak and needy but not caring this time. In this, I need as much as Dylan can give.

"Really."

It's enough. We both have trauma, the damage of betrayal ruining our faith in ourselves as much as in others. Our hearts are fragile little things despite our posturing to the contrary, so for now, for us… it's enough.

"Will you make love to me?" I ask, and he takes my hand, pressing a kiss to the back of it.

He gives me a slow smile before answering, "I would *love* to."

With my hand in his and lust coming over me like a haze, he leads me through his home, past all the open space and refined luxury of his things, but none of that even comes into our view. My entire world is Dylan, and he feels the same way.

We come into his bedroom, right up to the massive bed, and Dylan stops us. Kneeling, he reaches for my left foot, and I lift it silently, knowing what he wants. I have to lean on his shoulders as he takes off my high heel and runs his hand up my calf, his eyes drinking me in. "So fucking sexy," he says as he lowers my foot and switches legs. "So damn tempting."

Staying on his knees, he kisses my thighs through the form hugging dress I wore to work and never changed out of, nuzzling his nose against the gap between my thighs. "I want to worship you," he says, running his hands up the backs of my thighs and cupping my ass. "You are my every dream, my every fantasy."

Kissing up my body, Dylan gets to his feet, holding me in his arms as he backs me up to the bed's edge. Laying me down on the soft surface, he stands up, looming over me. He looks powerful and dominant, but there's a warmth in his eyes that makes me squirm. I'm not used to a man ever looking at me this way.

But Dylan does.

He looks at me like I'm his beginning and his end, and everything in between. It's a heady sensation, to hold the heart of a man like Dylan. It's a heavy responsibility too, one I won't take lightly.

Reaching up, he unbuttons his shirt, each inch of his body revealing itself to me and making me even more turned on. When he takes off his belt, I push myself back on the bed, scooting my dress up and pulling the clingy, stretchy fabric up and over my head to reveal that, though I'm wearing a bra, I don't have on panties.

Dylan's gaze is predatory. "Did you go to work with nothing

covering this pretty pussy? I could've accessed you like this all day."

Undoing my bra and tossing it away, I explain, "It ruined the line of the dress."

"If I'd known, I would've ruined your dress," he growls.

I can't help but smile, even though my entire body is on fire with desire.

I can only watch with heated anticipation as he undoes his pants and pushes them down, revealing himself in all his naked glory.

He climbs on the bed, gathers me in his arms, and kisses me again, the heady sensation of our bodies pressed tight together like this washing away any residual worries until it's only Dylan and me in this bed, no ghosts of the past remaining. The feeling of his skin on mine makes everything electric, and I'm hyperaware of every shift he makes as he kisses along my neck and across my collarbones, his left hand stroking my spine and down to gently cup my ass.

He thrusts into me deeply, taking his time and teasing me all the while. His masculine scent adds to the addiction that he is.

"Harder," I whimper, not wanting our lovemaking to be soft and sweet, but rather wanting him as he is, rough and leaving his mark on my body and my soul. In response, he squeezes, his fingers digging into my flesh and making me moan. I tip my nose against his, kissing his face and finding his lips as he rolls us until I'm on top of him, and Dylan smirks, seeming playful given everything we've just been through. "Why are you happy?" I ask.

"I'm the one on top."

"Mmm, but I know something, Darling," he says, and suddenly, his right hand lifts and smacks me sharply on my ass. "You like it when I do this. And now I've got two hands free."

I laugh, gasping as he spanks me again, and my hips roll in response. Between us, I can feel the long thickness of his cock teasing me. Every gentle rock hits my clit and sends a wave of pleasure through me.

I move up and down his cock, not fucking him yet, but mimicking the movement along his shaft.

Dylan pulls me down, kissing my lips and holding me close. I lift up, and when he lowers me back down, the moan that slips from my lips gets swallowed by Dylan as he fills me.

The sharp pain walks the line of pleasure, and my hips buck. Dylan's cock moves inside me, and I'm swept away. Looking into his eyes, I lift and fall on his cock, moaning and gasping as he adjusts to meet me. He stares into my eyes the whole time, watching me as I climb higher and higher. But what I see there isn't lust or mere desire. It's more, so much more, and as good as he feels inside me, his expression is what really sends me soaring. Finally, when I'm trembling on the edge, he reaches up and grabs my hips, pulling me down and impaling me on him, throwing me into bliss.

He's careful with me, but powerful and demanding as my orgasm rocks through me. He brings me down onto my knees, gets behind me, and fills me with one deep, hard thrust. "Who do you belong to?" he growls, thrusting into me again. I gasp, my pleasure climbing higher and higher. "Who do you belong to, Raven?"

"Y–You."

"Say," Dylan says, emphasizing each word with a stroke into my quivering, clenching pussy, "It. Say. Who. You. Belong. To."

"You!" I grunt, meeting his thrusts and pushing back into him. "I belong to you and only you!"

I try to meet him, but he's a man possessed, his hips hammering hard against my ass. This is what I want, what I need—to be entirely consumed by him. My palms give way, and I'm chest down on the bed, my ass up in the air as he fucks me mercilessly.

My knees start to slide on the bed cover, but Dylan doesn't let up. He savages me, groaning heavily into my ear until I'm lost in a sea of pleasure. I know I'm crying out. My throat burns as I scream his name over and over, begging him mindlessly to fuck me harder, to take me, to give me everything.

With a final hard thrust that pushes me flat onto the bed, we come together, Sending me into an oblivion of bliss. In the aftermath, he holds me, his strong arms around my body and his lips buried in the curve of my neck, kissing me softly and keeping me totally protected as we roll onto our sides.

"Good God, you know how to fuck," I murmur, and Dylan chuckles.

"Rest, Darling," he says, kissing the crook of my neck. I can feel him inside me still, but I'm too tired to worry about anything right now. "We've been through a lot tonight, but I'll take care of you."

I nod and yawn. He's right. I've lost the will to stay awake, and as sleep rushes up to me, I'm aware of only two things.

I am Dylan's.

He is mine.

Ding.

The sound drifts through the darkness of sleep, and I half turn over, my eyes still heavy with exhaustion. Sometime in the hours since I fell asleep, he's covered us both up and is pressed against my back, spooning me... or he was. Now my back is cold, and I rasp out, "Dylan?"

I feel him shift, and then the soft click-clack of something being put on the bedside table. He reaches up and tucks a lock of my hair behind my ear, making me smile softly. "It's okay," I hear him whisper, snuggling up behind me and wrapping his arms around my body again. Immediately, I feel safe and warm. "Nothing that can't wait until tomorrow."

"Oh," I murmur, realizing how late it is. I've never slept over, and if I want to get a decent taxi and some sleep... "I should go."

"Stay the night," Dylan whispers again, pulling me in closer. He kisses my neck, knowing how to make me melt. It takes me a moment of being held in his arms to realize he may want more.

I can't help but whimper in desire as he pulls me closer to him. "That's why you want me to stay."

He doesn't reply but keeps kissing my neck, and I press back against him. "Just promise me something."

He pauses, lifting his lips from my neck. "What is it?"

"You make good coffee?" I ask. "I'm going to need it to wake up tomorrow."

"I promise."

CHAPTER 28

RAVEN

MONEY... POWER... SEX?
Salacious details emerge on how certain young women are using more than their education to 'work' their way up the corporate ladder!

By: Vanna Nicholson

The intersection of power and sex has been the seed of scandal since the time Prince Paris of Troy happened to have seen a certain Spartan queen named Helen. Of course, in most semi-modern retellings, the young lad is struck by the pangs of love, but most of us know what really had Paris 'up' in arms.

At times, women have rebelled against this intersection of power and sex, usually in revolt against the pressures by some men who demanded that women earn their positions in the world on their *backs, or bent over the throne, or whatever the case may have been.*

We see you, hashtaggers!

But what if young women are using their feminine wiles to seduce their way up the corporate ladder? What if these young women, some of whom are doctors, some of whom are military leaders, and some of whom just happen to control the purse strings of your 401(k), aren't who they claim to be?

My hand trembles as I attempt to read the screen.

The story is lurid, heavy on the innuendo and suggestion and short on facts. It's typical trash journalism, the standard of the 'society' pages, whether they're in print or online. But when Maggie messaged me to read this, I knew she had a reason.

It takes me three minutes to find it. All the while, the nerves run through me and I feel sick to my stomach.

And then there's a certain 'Lady of Crows', shall we say, who's working for a rather Sharpe-edged boss, a boss who's been more than happy to indulge in all sorts of unprofessional acts with his latest physical distraction. Rumors are her beauty is truly her weapon, as she has a long history in the Financial District, having dated a scion of one of the FiDi's most powerful families for years before breaking up with him after she'd 'pumped' him for all the information and influence she could manage.

That was a lot of influence, and a lot of working after hours. Apparently, she was able to gyrate her way into introductions, influential internships, and after betraying her beau in order to score a high-paying position at his rival's firm, our raven-haired temptress may have even left with a bevy of corporate secrets that have already earned her a pretty penny in her new position. Well, new public position, at least. Her pubic position has, by all reports, remained the same.

My hand shakes, but I force myself to read the rest.

She slyly mentions Olivia too, somehow making her out to be both a whore and a victim, taken advantage of by Dylan before being sent on some sort of sexual spy infiltration mission to Evan, who isn't named.

With close to thirty-nine trillion dollars in various retirement accounts, and millions upon millions of Americans depending on investments in the Financial District, it's only a matter of time before one of these seductive sirens costs clients millions.

They may already have.

Rage coursing through me, I slam my phone down on my desk and storm my way towards Dylan's office. Along the way, I can see the glances from some of the other people. Shanna looks hurt, of all things, as if I somehow betrayed her.

Hey, weren't you the one asking if I got Sharped at the fucking party? I want to yell at her, but I've got another target on my mind as I storm into Dylan's office, where he's on the phone.

"Look, Bob, I'm not taking no for an answer!" Dylan says heatedly. His suit is crisp, his jaw cleanly shaven, but the bags under his eyes are heavy like he didn't sleep at all last night. "I don't care. I want you to have a plan on how to strike back and contain this. And I want Vanna's head on a goddamn platter… nix that, I'll handle her my damn self." Looking up, he finally realizes I'm standing across from him and clears his throat. "Look, just get it fucking done. I want to see a preliminary plan by noon. No, I'll call you."

Dylan hangs up and takes a deep breath as I slowly take the seat across from him. "So, I take it that you read it."

"Every fucking word," I manage, noticing for the first time the old-fashioned newspaper on his desk. I snag it off the desk, and he makes no attempt to stop me. Tears prick my eyes, but I'm more angry than anything. The print version is even worse, taking up an entire page complete with pictures. The largest? Me, with a tiny, tiny little black bar over my eyes. I even know the picture. It's me coming out of the Faulkner building, my dress not quite right and… "That's photoshopped."

"Clearly," Dylan says. "Look, we're going to handle this. Vanna said she was going to go after Evan, not us."

"What?" I exclaim, confused as hell. "You know her?"

"I spoke to her last week," he tells me, his expression hardened. I was stomping up here to get on the same page as Dylan, confident that we would handle this together. But…

"This isn't Evan's doing?" I ask, blinking away the shock. *He knows her? He spoke to her? To someone who could write this trash?*

I thought it was Evan. It's the only thing that made sense when I saw the article. It's exactly the sort of twisted thinking he's capable of, but what Dylan's said changes everything. "You did this?"

He shakes his head, pinning me with a furious glare. "Of course not, not this. I put Vanna on the opposite track... destroying Evan, like *we* agreed on." The reminder is sharp, and I flinch. I knew whatever Dylan did would be ugly, which is why I didn't want to know about it, but this? I don't know what I expected, but it wasn't revenge by gossip monger. "She has more reasons than us to hate the Faulkners, and I trusted her motivation for that."

"You trusted her?" I question sarcastically, and my tone is full of the shock and rage I feel.

He tilts his head, looking at me wryly. "I leveraged her," he corrects. "It's what I do."

Throwing my arms wide, I huff, "That backfired, didn't it?"

I'm panicking. My heart races faster and faster, thumping against my ribs. I can't get enough oxygen, and there are black speckles at the edges of my vision. The reality is that my reputation isn't worth a damn. All I will ever be known for is the fact that I slept with Dylan. I think I'm going to pass out...

Dylan is up and around his desk in a single second. At first, I pull away, but he presses. "Raven," he says, "please don't do this."

I wait a moment, and when he tries again, I lean into him. He's all I have. He wraps me in my arms. Gratefully, I sag into him, the top of my head going to his chest as I stare at our shoes. "What are we going to do?" I whisper, fighting back every racing thought.

I feel him press a firm kiss to my head, and then he lifts my chin, bringing my eyes to his. He looks murderous, but when he peers at me, it softens into something else entirely. The fury is still there, right beneath the surface, but he's controlling it… for now. He kisses my lips, a gentle promise in the movement of his mouth on mine.

His phone dings on his desk.

And then it dings again.

And again.

This is it, our new reality. People are coming after him, after me, after us.

"Enough!" I growl, pushing him away. For a second, he tries to cling to me, and I realize he's trying to escape this fucked up mess just as much as I am.

But I break free and grab his phone from his desk. My first instinct is to chunk it to the floor, stomp on it, and release the war cry that's churning in my soul. Instead, I hand it to Dylan, slamming it into his palm.

"Fix this. I don't know how, but please, fix this. Do whatever you have to do so that you're okay," I plead.

He looks at me in surprise. "You mean so that you're okay. Your name, or close enough to it, is the one splashed all over that article that everyone's reading and talking about."

I shake my head. "No, I don't care what people think about me at this point, because losing everything I've worked for in one fell swoop is nothing compared to what could happen if your investors think you've been played by some 'sexual siren' looking for a sugar daddy who pays with insider information.

The consequences of that could be catastrophic, Dylan."

Because that's the worst part of this. He's right that the article is about me, which is infuriating and makes me feel nakedly vulnerable even though it's all lies, but at its foundation, the article is about Dylan and how he's been so easily duped by a pretty face and some pussy.

And that could bring Dylan's entire empire to the ground.

I refuse to be the bringer of his ruin. I will not be his destruction.

Because I love him. I love him too much, but I don't know what to do.

So if I have to sacrifice myself to save him, then so be it.

"A sugar daddy?" he repeats what I said with disbelief. "Raven, no one thinks that," he says, but I pin him with a knowing look. That's a lie and we both know it. There are plenty who will think exactly that based on one little gossip column and my sudden switch from Evan's side to his. "Fuck!" he hisses, admitting that I'm right.

"I'm going to go home for the day, I think. If you need me, call, but otherwise, I understand that you have to do what's needed to save yourself and what you've worked so hard for."

Before he can argue, I lift to my toes, pressing a quick kiss to his cheek, and then I leave before he can stop me. Tamara side eyes me as I pass, her glasses magnifying the sadness I see in her gaze.

"Tamara!" Dylan shouts, and she jumps, getting up to rush into his office.

As I head downstairs, hurrying to grab my bag from my locker, sadness and anger war for top billing.

I hold it all in, saving it for the moment I can collapse in a fit of tears in private.

CHAPTER 29

DYLAN

"You look like a man out for blood," Austin says as he comes over with a tumbler of scotch. I take it, and he sits down in his chair, swirling his own tumbler around. "Tell me what all happened."

"You read the story, I assume," I start, and Austin nods. "What did you think?"

"That was the worst gossip line of shit I've read in years," Austin says. "I thought Vanna was better than that. Have you reached out to her?"

"She's not answering my calls."

"Ah," Austin says, reaching into his pocket and pulling out his phone. "Give me thirty seconds."

It actually takes him less than that, as he sets his phone down on his thigh in speaker mode and Vanna's voice comes out. "Austin?"

"I've got you on speaker, Vanna. There is an interested party listening in, one whom you owe an explanation to," Austin says. "Please don't tell me that you think you've outgrown your limits? That's going to seriously piss me off if you have." There's a threat laced through his words, a warning to Vanna in his dark tone that she should take seriously.

"No! No, God, no!" Vanna says, her voice tight with fear. "Austin, I'm not answering the phone from your... friend because I've got people paying very close attention to me. They're tracking who I'm talking to now."

"Hard position for a gossip columnist," Austin says. "So, can you speak freely?"

"I can speak. They're not tracking this program," Vanna says. "You're the only one who calls me on it."

I glance from the phone to Austin, finding him looking at me with a small smirk on his lips. He lifts his finger to his lips, silently telling me 'shh', and I realize Vanna, in her distraction and upset, has accidentally revealed one of her sources... Austin.

I'm surprised, but also not. Austin using any and all tools available to him, including information and information-collectors like Vanna, is right up his alley.

"End-to-end encryption's useful that way," Austin replies, giving me a pointed look. "You should look into using it with all your contacts."

Message received, Austin.

"I just might. So, you want to know about the article?"

"I would," Austin says. "So does my friend. He's highly

pissed off."

"Join the club," Vanna spits out. "I'm about ready to tell my editor he can stuff his contract up his ass, since they can't hold their non-compete clause over me any longer." She exhales loudly, her voice the slightest bit more controlled as she bitterly adds, "Potentially. My lawyer's telling me to wait on that last bit."

"What did your lawyer do?" Austin questions, and I hold my breath as if that would allow me to listen more intently.

"I wrote the article, just as your... friend stated," Vanna says. "It was fire and brimstone type of stuff. I had it all backed up, the data, the evidence of embezzlement and fraud from what they did to my family, all of it on a flash drive that I gave to my lawyer for safekeeping. Four thousand words, a bit long, but goddamn, it felt good to actually be writing something deeper than who's been fucking whom. And to get it out. To finally put the truth out there, threats from those pricks be damned. I turned it in to my editor, who read it and said it was good. Then three hours later, I'm getting called to the floor by him, telling me to rewrite it. I refused."

"Someone got to him," Austin guesses. Given how jaded Austin can be, he doesn't seem surprised by that in the slightest.

I actually am, though. Vanna's editor is a bastion of traditional journalism, having published articles on everything from war, to business, to exposés on the business of war. His reaction as compared to the article on the Faulkners seems out of proportion.

"Put it this way," Vanna says. "I'll give you three guesses as to who owns the bank that holds my editor's mortgage, and the

346 WINTERS & LANDISH

first two don't count."

I take a deep breath, pinching my nose. The fucking Faulkners. They have their damn hands in everything.

"So if you refused, how did it get rewritten?" Austin asks, holding up a hand, telling me to let him handle this. He knows what I need to know and how to get it. "It was your byline."

"You think I write that level of drivel? Lady of Crows? Sharpe-edged? Fuck me, I was cringing as I read that the first time for myself. If I had to guess, probably Evan's assistant or Bronson's wrote it. Though either of them could've written it themselves." Vanna hums as she considers that. "I'd put my money on Evan. It's too personal for anyone else." She mutters a curse I can't make out under her breath, then says, "My rep's going to need some serious rehab after this debacle."

"Can you prove this?" I ask.

Like a cockroach living through a nuclear attack, Vanna is a survivor. And though I don't think she would play me, there's an outside chance she decided to back the Faulkners and is the one who wrote the article, published it, and is lying directly to me now.

"If you want, I'll email you my original story," Vanna offers. "Anonymous drop box, of course. I've sent it to a few concerned parties already, just so you're aware. This shit may be out in public, but the truth is whispered in private. I do have lawyers involved as well. They put my name on something I didn't write or approve. There is a potential copyright issue."

"Who was concerned?" Austin presses, and Vanna tsks. "A number of people who doubted the story and have certain matters with Evan. "The water always finds its level and the truth comes to the surface. This isn't the first time there's been an obvious smear where Evan's been protected. It's good, I think, to let the real article circulate in private circles."

"Yes," I agree.

Austin tells Vanna to be careful, to let him know if he can be of service, and then hangs up.

A few minutes later, Austin pulls up the file, and I give it a read. Even skimming the first few paragraphs, it's a completely different story. "Those motherfuckers."

"You were blindsided," Austin says. "That's not like you. Normally, you know that sort of weakness."

"I…."

I can't argue that fact because he's right. I should've known about the editor if I was putting Vanna into play.

I'm too close to the problem, too desperate to see the angles clearly. But Austin's not.

"What now? What would you do if you were in my shoes?" I ask him, and Austin lifts an eyebrow. "You only look at me like that when you've got something to say that I won't like."

"You're right, but you also know the truth," Austin says. "Do nothing. This is lukewarm, grade-school shit at best, and by next quarter, everyone's going to forget about it. Evan takes the win this time, but the battle isn't over… unless you want it to be over."

"If her lawyers—"

"He said nothing that you could sue him over," Austin advises me. "Maybe Olivia and Raven have a case, but that'd just drag them into the public eye, put names to innuendo. It'd be a disaster for them. Especially Raven. The stories about her were some of the nastiest. And the cost of it? Astronomical, and for what? You can only sue for money lost and it's not like you're going to fire Raven over this." He pauses.

I sit back, shaking my head. "Would you be able to let something like this ride, knowing that it's hurt someone you care about and could hurt your own bottom line financially?"

Austin's answer is clear as he looks me dead in my eyes. He would destroy anyone and anything that threatened him. It's a reason worth lighting the world on fire to him. But that doesn't mean it has to be for me. We are different people, different men, with very different styles despite our friendship.

"That's a decision you're going to have to make for yourself," Austin says. "What does Raven think?"

I can feel a small smile play on my lips. Amid all this ugliness, she is the most beautiful thing in my life, by far. "She said to do whatever I need to do, making it sound like that included leaving her to repair my reputation."

Her willingness to sacrifice herself for me meant more than she will ever know, but there is no way I would or could do that. I would give up everything I own before I gave Raven up. She's all I need now.

"I don't think it will take much to repair this," Austin says, interrupting my thoughts. "Gossip interests those of small minds, but your investors act based on bottom lines, and there, where it matters, you make them money. If anything, many of them will relate to fucking an intern or having a scandalous affair with a junior exec." He waves a hand dismissively.

I growl, "That's not what this is."

His smile is easy, showing no reaction to my snappishness other than to put both of his palms up. "I know that, and you know that. I simply said they will relate your relationship with Raven to something all too familiar in our world and not jump to overreaction."

My ire settles… slightly.

He takes a sip of his scotch, then stares into the amber liquid as if it's a crystal ball. "You could go to the governor's Young Leaders ball. You do qualify, you know."

"And how would that help?"

"Simple appearances," Austin says. "Evan and his family think that they've embarrassed you. Embarrassed her. And that you'll go scurrying back to the hole they think you belong in. Well, throw it right back by acting like the article meant nothing and Evan's beneath you. Because the truth is, he is. You go, you drop some gratuitously obscene donation for the governor's reelection campaign, and walk out of there with the prettiest girl, the biggest dick, and the fastest growing bank account. Any chatter volleyed about by gossip rags or concerns by investors would be assuaged by a showing of you and Raven as a united force, unswayed by the lesser." He pins me with a powerful glare as he says, "And then, you go on with your lives together, leaving Evan in your combined past."

It's so straightforward and obscene, a short huff of a laugh leaves me.

"Just ignore it?" I ask him with barely contained outrage.

"His time is coming, and when it does, he will suffer. It doesn't have to be at your hand for you to enjoy it. We know what he's done… and I know well that his time is coming." He looks me dead in the eyes, and I hear the unspoken. "Don't get mixed up in that."

With a deep inhale, I sit back in the chair, considering my options.

"How long will I have to wait?"

"Years." His answer is quick.

"Legal matters, then?" I ask, and Austin nods. The knowledge that he'll get his due is comforting, at the very least. "And what about Raven?"

"Have her on your arm. Kiss her like you're grateful to love her. And do it in front of everyone. She won't care about rumors if she knows you love her more than anything."

I nod, letting it all sink in slowly and ease the anger. *Go public.* We were going to do that, anyway. Might as well do it big.

This whole mess started with a fundraiser. Perhaps the way to end it is with one as well.

And Austin's right. After we handle this, ironically by not dealing with it head-on the way I'd first wanted to, Raven and I can have our ultimate vengeance by not letting Evan or the Faulkners cast any shadows on our future together. Perhaps, the best revenge truly is simply getting to love her.

CHAPTER 30

RAVEN

"Are you sure about this?" Maggie asks from the bathroom doorway. She's eating a bowl of cereal—Rice Krispies with a dash of salted caramel coffee creamer added to the milk—while she watches me get ready.

"No," I admit, meeting her eyes in the mirror. I lower my mascara wand so I don't poke my eye out and turn to face her fully. "But Dylan said this is a way for me to save face, for him to put on a show of power, and for us to move on… together. So, even though I'm nervous as all hell, this is what I'm doing." I wave the mascara wand around, indicating that I'm getting ready for the governor's Young Leaders ball.

The truth is, when Dylan called, I was mostly expecting him to say we needed to play it cool for a while. In the insecure pit of my stomach, I thought maybe he'd say I needed to work somewhere else or not come into the office. I know how finicky the markets can be, and the smallest problem can have a ripple effect that reaches far and wide.

A scandal like this could be disastrous.

So when he told me the new plan was a very public display to hard launch our relationship, I was confused to say the least. But once he explained PR was on board and that he wanted it too, I couldn't say no. I shake out my hands and breathe deeply. Never in all of the racing thoughts did I think Dylan's plan would be to introduce me as his girlfriend to everyone. I thought it was all lost or at least barely being held by a thread, but if tonight goes as he said it will, it could be the start of a dream life I never even dared to dream.

That doesn't mean I don't have hornets buzzing around in my belly at the thought of walking into the ball, watching all eyes turn to us, and hearing the whispers work their way through the room.

That's her. The one in the article.

Poor idiot doesn't realize she's a gold digger.

And any other snide remark made under their breaths. But I'm trusting that with Dylan at my side, I can face anything. I'm going to do this… for him.

Taking in a deep breath, I remind myself not to fuck it up, and it feels like that same moment from months ago, when everything is riding on this one moment.

All the small moments play in my mind as I reapply another coat of blush I don't need.

From 'it's just business' to 'he's the love of my life'. Damn, that happened fast. But then again, Dylan is a power to be reckoned with, and it's no surprise he would take my life and my heart by storm.

"Okay, then," Maggie says, smiling at my action over fear approach. "Go with the red lips again. They make you look like you could suck Dylan's wallet—or his soul—out via his dick." I gape at her, and she shrugs, shoveling another bite of cereal into her mouth. She crunches as she says, "What? They're gonna be saying it. Might as well give them something to work with. And it's your color and it's sexy as fuck."

I laugh, shaking my head as I pick up a lip liner. One to go with my favorite red lipstick because she's right. I'm going in big, loud, confident, and bold. And red is a confident color.

"Want me to quiz you some more?" Maggie offers.

I've treated this ball like a work project, deep diving into my research on who will be there, what they do, and paying special attention to the governor's politics, like his targeted tax relief for the working class and his wife's pet projects, which literally includes pets. She's both a dog and cat lover, so I'm hopeful that's a good sign.

"I think I'm good, thank you, though. And thank you for studying with me the last couple of days." I cap the lipstick and turn to my friend to look her in the eyes. "I know it wasn't your idea of fun."

She shrugs. "No biggie. Just promise me that if anyone asks about the article, you'll shove a flute of champagne up their ass."

I laugh at the image that creates in my mind, cocking my head as though considering it. "Not sure I can do that, but I'll try."

"Alright, hair and makeup done. Next, get dressed." Maggie lets me by, and in my bedroom, I pick up the silver gown I bought for tonight. On Dylan's card, no less. He sent me to a fancy boutique, told me to buy whatever I wanted to feel beautiful and ready for war, and I'd known the instant I put this dress on that this was it.

I slip the dress up my body, sliding the thin straps over my shoulders, and then pull on my new red Louboutins. I might've been shopping with Dylan's money, but I tried to be reasonable, and the red heels will get infinitely more wear than the silver heeled sandals the salesperson suggested. Plus, they kinda reminded me that, like Dorothy, I'm no longer in 'Kansas' anymore, but rather, I'm in the big leagues.

I turn, facing the full-length mirror.

I look stunning and powerful, confident and beautiful. And when a smile tilts my lips… sexy.

It's perfect.

And just in time, because barely five minutes later, there's a knock on the door. I strut across the living room, opening the door to reveal Dylan in a crisply tailored tuxedo. Good God. He is the definition of perfection.

It's not the typical prom-slash-wedding number. The jacket is black, but so is his shirt and his long silk tie. He's quite literally the man in black, and with the dark look on his face, he seems ready for war too. I can't help how the butterflies act up when I see him. Or how my body heats. Or the tension that grows between us.

Even knowing why we're dressed to the nines and where we're going.

"Mr. Sharpe," I say, fighting off the urge to keep him here all to myself and be a no show tonight.

"Miss Hill, you look gorgeous," he replies. His eyes trace over me before returning to mine, and I can see that he's struggling with the same desires I am.

A smile pulls my lips up, and I have to admit to myself that I love it. That this man who gets to me in every single way is affected by me just the same. My heart pounds, and it only stops when we're interrupted.

Behind me, Maggie says, "You two are something else. Do you call each other Mr. Sharpe and Miss Hill while you're in bed too?" We laugh, but our eyes never leave each other.

"Shall we?" Dylan says after clearing his throat and holding his arm out.

We say goodbye to Maggie, whom I promise a full report to, and then take the jerking, terrifying elevator downstairs. Vince holds the car door open for me, inclining his head in silent appreciation for my appearance. I thank him with a smile as I climb in. Once we're settled, Vince heads off into the night.

"Nervous?" Dylan asks, his thumb drawing circles on the back of my hand. It's soothing, but I don't think anything will calm my nerves down. It feels like everything is riding on this moment. All eyes on us. Every word and subtle movement judged. And either we pass the test and the threat of devastation ceases to exist, or everything tumbles down and there will be hell to pay that could affect the entire company and Dylan's reputation.

I blink once, remembering his question. "I was, but I feel better now that I'm with you," I confess.

One side of his lips tilts up in a hint of a smile. It's just the tiniest bit, so slight I wonder if he even knows he's done it. "Me too."

The drive is short, both of us silent as we alternately look at each other and out the window. It's a comfortable silence, though, like we're both mentally reviewing our talking points for the evening.

When Vince stops in front of the International Hotel, I have a moment of panic. Dylan's quick with opening the door and helping me out, his hand in mine, but it's all too much. The lights are bright and the press is three deep as we step out onto the red carpet. There's more than politics here tonight. There's business, there's entertainment, there's everything the Faulkner event was trying to be, turned up to the max.

"There they are!" someone calls, and a machine gun burst of flashbulbs goes off.

I freeze for a split second, but Dylan squeezes my hand, and I turn my eyes to him rather than the crowd. He seems completely at ease, like the continuing flashes aren't even happening, and when he smiles at me, I relax enough that my legs move on their own accord even though I feel like I'm going to fall if he lets me go.

Sensing my returning comfort, he smirks and with a tug of my hand, spins me into his arms, kissing me. He even dips me back ever so slightly, and I lift a leg for balance, my red shoe peeking out at the hem of my gown. The press and the looky-loos react just as he anticipated. "Whooooooo!"

"Good work, Darling," Dylan whispers when our lips part and he lifts me back up.

We keep going, and I keep moving through the motions although it's all so surreal. We skip the press line as Dylan sees his friend Austin standing by the door, an amused look on his face. He offers his hand as we approach, and I shake his hand for the first time. "I hear you're partly responsible for this?" I joke lightheartedly, although it doesn't come out as confidently as I wish it did with all the nerves gathered.

"You're welcome," Austin replies, and I can't help but laugh at his deadpan delivery. "You're going to be the talk of the city tomorrow morning."

"What about the talk of the nation?" Dylan asks, wrapping his arm around my waist. Austin notes the move and laughs a little.

"Raven, I do hope you can keep your boy on a tight leash tonight. Don't let him do anything stupid." The advice is delivered with a friendly smile that Dylan returns.

Austin looks past us, his eyes going hard and cold in a blink. The change is uncanny, and it seems Dylan's right. Austin is a bit rough around the edges, but if he's earned Dylan's trust, then he has mine too. "If you'll excuse me, I see someone I need to speak with," Austin says, his voice clipped.

Austin goes inside, and I give Dylan a look. "He seems nice."

Dylan chuckles. "He would be offended to hear you say that, but he's a good guy, a good friend."

"I bet he'd say the same about you." I nudge him slightly, looking up at him through my thick lashes.

Dylan beams. It's a genuine smile, and it powers us through the night. The ball tonight is different from our first night together at the charity event, because I'm not trying to impress or curry favor with anyone here. And I've earned my seat in a number of ways. Maggie reminded me of how well I'm doing. She said that's what the industry should be talking about. Hell, the scandalous pairing might be a match made in the heavenly slit of their wallets. So that's what I keep in mind while we walk through the throngs of people.

And that's powerful. It's like everyone, from the local star quarterback to the governor's wife herself, is drawn to us.

"Don't you worry," the governor's wife says while we sip champagne together. Dylan's across the room, talking with Austin and the governor while supposedly getting appetizers.

"Worry about?" I echo, my smile falling ever so slightly. My stomach drops as she's the first to say anything aloud. I've been enjoying our polite conversation about a local street photographer who specializes in dog portraits, but this is it... the moment it goes off the rails and turns ugly, I think. She's going to tell me not to worry what everyone thinks or what the gossip rags say while simultaneously looking at me hungrily for any tidbit she can have.

I peer at her, all my hackles on high alert, but she smiles easily.

"My husband's going to try and rope Dylan into politics. He'd be good at it too, but I don't think Dylan's interested. He's always been so singularly focused on his business, although that attention seems to branching out in lovely ways." She gives me a look, but rather than judgment or snarkiness, she sounds… kind and genuine. "Congratulations to you two, by the way."

"Oh, uhm… thank you."

Reading my concern, she gently bumps my shoulder with hers. "What do they say about press? The only bad press is no press." She shakes her head, laughing lightly.

"I'm not so sure I agree?" I whisper, my heart pounding.

When she sees my nervousness, she adds, "If I believed a quarter of what's written about me, about my husband, or about us, I'd spend my days in a fetal position, bawling my eyes out. I'd like to think most people understand that. You just have to stand strong through the storm and show them who you are unapologetically and so loudly that they can't help but hear you, see you, know you."

"Wow. I didn't… uh… Thank you," I say with more certainty this time. "I really appreciate that."

She tilts her head gracefully, acknowledging my words. "Though my husband speaks fondly of Dylan, I don't know him all that well, but what I do know is that he hasn't taken his eyes off you the whole time he's been forcibly detained for a discussion he has no interest in." Her eyes sparkle as she cuts them across the room.

I follow her gaze and find Dylan smiling politely at the governor, who's talking passionately about something. But Dylan's eyes are on me. He lifts a brow in question, and I nod, offering a small smile and a wave, letting him know I'm okay.

Because I am… I'm okay. We're okay.

After that moment, the fear of someone saying anything is released. It's like I simply let it go. Instead, the night is filled with chatter and laughs, champagne glasses and cheers.

The night is seamless, and I can't believe it's over when Dylan wraps his arm around me and tells me it's time to go. It flew by. With the ball over and so many others leaving, we make our way down the way we came in, and once again, it feels surreal. Only this time, for a different reason.

As Dylan and I walk out, I can feel him silently gloating. "What is it?"

"You were amazing," he says, "and I couldn't be happier."

"Did you see the Faulkners there or something?" I ask, the nerves threatening to come back up again, and Dylan shrugs. Holding the door for me, we slide into the back seat of the car, and Vince closes it for us. "What's that mean?"

"It means I didn't notice or even think to look," Dylan says. "I only had eyes for you."

My first response is the warmth that flows through me, but the second is a sobering realization.

I realize that he's right. I didn't see Evan or any of his family there tonight, but I also wasn't even thinking of them. I was enjoying myself, meeting people in the industry, talking about the city, and grateful for being at Dylan's side, watching him have a good time.

Everything else seems insignificant outside of that.

I lean over, pressing a kiss to his cheek. "I saw that," I tell him with a pleased smile. "Did the governor try to talk you into joining him? His wife seemed to think he would."

Dylan huffs out a long-suffering sigh but seems more amused than annoyed. "Every time I see him, he does. I'm not opposed to being on the city council, but I don't know how I'd make time. Tamara would probably throw my schedule at me and tell me to figure it out myself." He laughs, and I do too, knowing that his assistant would do no such thing.

"As long as she pencils me in," I tease.

Dylan pulls me to his side, cupping my jaw. Right before he kisses me, he murmurs, "I don't know what I'd do without our standing six o'clock meetings every day."

And then his mouth is on mine, his lips moving lower, and nothing else in the world matters as the back of the car gets hotter and hotter.

CHAPTER 31

DYLAN

I'm sure Vince hurries as much as is humanly possible, but I'm not sure we're going to make it. I need to be inside Raven. Now.

Fuck, I've wanted her from the second that apartment door opened, and as the night went on, all I could wonder was what was hiding under that silver dress.

As I kiss her, I try to think of anything other than how her hands feel on me and how fucking hot those small moans are that she gives me when I break away for a moment of air.

I settle on the night. On the PR. On how fucking perfect it went.

She was magnificent tonight. There were curious glances and whispers, of course, but if she noticed, she didn't let it show. She was confident, beautiful, proud to be with me, and spoke eloquently to every person she interacted with. She has utterly bewitched me, but tonight, she cast a spell on the entire room. It was glorious, and I nearly had to pinch myself every time I remembered that she is mine.

She is mine. In every way.

Thankfully, Vince somehow cuts through the city traffic and gets us to my penthouse in record time. I don't wait for him to open the car door. There's no time for that. I throw it open, help Raven from the car, and virtually carry her toward my private elevator.

It takes twenty-three seconds to get to my floor at the top of the building, two seconds for the door to unlock, and one more to slam it shut behind us.

"Get that dress off or I'm going to tear it off," I warn her, my breath coming in pants that have nothing to do with my frantic need to get Raven alone and everything to do with my tenuous hold on my ever-present desire for this woman.

I yank at my tie, needing it gone so I can breathe. I toss it… somewhere… and start stripping. First, my jacket, which I drop to the floor, not caring about designer labels or expensive fabrics. Then, the buttons on my shirt.

Meanwhile, I keep an eye on Raven who, rather than do what I said, is watching me as heat fills her green eyes.

"Darling." My voice is a low rumble.

She spins, giving me her back as she struts her way to the living room. She's enjoying this, I realize, and I groan, my cock twitching behind my zipper.

"Aren't you going to offer me a drink, Mr. Sharpe?" she teases, licking her lips as though parched. "It's the polite thing to do when a guest comes over." She can't even pretend to not want the same thing as her chest rises and falls with her catching her breath.

"You're not a guest. And I know you're as much in need as I am."

Instead, she sinks to the couch, sitting down in the middle of the cushions. She crosses her legs at the knee and stretches her arms out along the back, the pose highlighting her tits, waist, and hips. But also... her smile.

"You look good on my couch," I tell her, coming closer. My shirt falls to the floor, and I undo my belt first, the metal clanging loudly in the quiet room and then, the leather swooshing through the belt loops.

There's a sparkle in her eyes as she glances at the belt in my hands, and her chest begins rising and falling faster. I fold it in half, letting the leather loop dangle at my side. "Something interesting, Darling?"

Her eyes lift to mine again. "Tonight was intoxicating. And for the first time, I felt like I belonged."

"You do belong," I assure her.

"I felt powerful." Her words are measured, as though she's tasting them as they pass over her lips. "Next to you... all of them knowing that I'm with you," she adds.

My grin is evil. "You are powerful. And beautiful... and sexy... and brilliant." I step closer to her with every word, my eyes locked on her, and she watches my approach, not moving so much as a muscle.

"Take your pants off, Dylan."

It's an order. There's no mistaking the commanding tone, and I arch a brow, considering her. She doesn't blink, but her gaze drops to my dick before returning to mine, testing me, testing herself... her power.

A grin slips across my face. I make a silent plea that she'll spread her legs and tell me what to do next.

Okay, I can play along with this. She has handed me power over her body countless times, and perhaps a bit of turnabout is fair play. Raven wants to experience her power? She can do that with me.

I drop the belt to the table, undoing my slacks and toeing off my shoes. When my pants fall to the ground, Raven purrs, "Good boy." I can't help but to smirk. I have never been called that. "Those too." She motions, and the blush rises to her cheeks.

I want to tell her she's doing well, but I bite my tongue, letting her have her fun for the moment.

I'm not shy, especially when Raven sounds so eager to see me. I slip my thumbs into my waistband and push the fabric down my legs, freeing myself. I'm rock-hard, standing up against my belly, and I instinctively grip myself, giving my length a tight stroke. "Like what you see?"

Raven uncrosses and recrosses her legs the other way, clenching her thighs. She's as turned on as I am.

I stroke myself once and then move even closer. I want to tell her to open her mouth. I want her hands on me, her body on mine so she can feel what she does to me.

I grit my teeth, not doing any of those things by the barest grip on my control. Precum leaks from the tip of my cock as I stroke myself again, waiting for her to act on the hunger in her eyes. Leaning forward, she keeps her gaze locked with mine until the tip of her finger rests on the head of my cock and she moans.

She licks the salty fluid from her finger delicately. "Mmm," she moans, and another drop slides down my shaft. Her smile is beautifully wicked.

She uncrosses her legs once more, standing this time, but rather than coming to me, she slips the straps of her dress from her shoulders. A quick zip at her side and a small swaying wiggle, and the dress falls to her feet, much the same way I want to.

She's gorgeous. She's sexy. She's mine.

Her breasts are free already, having been supported by some invisible magic of the dress, and her nipples are hardened nubs begging for my mouth. Her panties consist of a scrap of flesh-colored silk, which she slips off easily, and she doesn't have on stockings this time, so she's finally nude before me.

"Raven," I groan.

She shudders but stays steadfast in her mission of driving me to madness. "Lie down on the couch," she purrs, adding, "Sir," when my bottom lip drops.

Nodding with a smirk, I make quick work of stretching out along the length of the couch and reach out for her, intending to guide her to my cock.

But she doesn't do that. She moves up by my head, shocking me. "I'm going to sit on your face like it's my throne, and you're going to lick my pussy until I tell you to stop."

"Yes, Ma'am," I say, wanting it to sound teasing, but it comes out as a strangled plea. Fuck. This woman does something to me. I am weak for her.

Raven throws a leg over me, kneeling on the couch with her knees at my sides and her feet near my shoulders. Her position pins my arms, making them useless to touch her but also making me unable to touch myself. Her pussy hovers just above my mouth. I can smell her arousal. Fuck, I can nearly taste it in the air between us. And her pretty pussy lips are glossy with it.

She teases me, lowering herself by millimeters while my tongue waits for her, desperately flicking at nothingness so that as soon as she's close enough, I can touch her.

Finally, she lowers herself to my mouth, and I lick her, grateful for a taste of her heaven and moaning at the deliciousness. I lick her as if my life depends on it because she is my life. After so many times, I know what she enjoys most, and I nibble along her lips, press soft kisses over her clit, and finally, fuck her with my stiffened tongue.

When I do something she particularly likes, she rewards me with a stroke of her soft hand and teasing fingers along my shaft. But it's always just one touch, enough to drive me wild but not to get me to the edge, though I can feel the wetness of my precum puddling on my stomach.

She rides my face, her arousal covering my mouth as her body trembles. I can feel her climbing, getting closer and closer to coming, and I double my efforts, needing to suffocate in her, wanting to drown in her. Suddenly, she pitches forward, her breath whispering over my sensitive cock as she cries out, coming hard. And screaming my name. My name.

When the shudders subside the slightest bit, I use the opportunity of her momentary blissful distraction to free my arms. I grip her hips, pulling her to my mouth even tighter.

"Dylan," she gasps.

"Mine," I growl against her, flicking my tongue over her clit again. She's barely come down and she can go again. I've done it to her before—one good orgasm turning into a second earth-shattering one if I work her back up quickly enough.

Her moan turns into a grunt as her hips buck, not pushing me away but chasing my tongue for more. I pull away for a split second to keep myself from coming.

I'm about to. From licking her, having her on my face, and her infrequent, glancing touches, I'm about to come. And she knows it. This is the power she has over me.

She wraps her finger and thumb around me again, squeezing tightly, and I hiss.

My toes are curled, digging into the leather, my abs are clenched, and my balls are pulled up tight to my body in preparation for the one thing I'm not ready to do. I need more of her.

I need her to come. Now. Because I can't hold back. I can't.

I suck her clit into my mouth and push two fingers inside her, thankful to have my hands free now. I hit the spot that I know triggers her nearly instantly, and I don't let up. She squirms, overwhelmed with the onslaught, and I keep torturing her with pleasure.

Her breath catches, her body goes tight, and then she detonates. Her hips drop another inch as her knees give way, her pussy presses to my mouth, and her cries echo through the room. Through it all, I somehow manage not to come yet.

But she doesn't say anything. She doesn't beg me to fuck her like I need her to do, so I keep going until she breathlessly pulls herself away. "Stop, stop, stop…" she gasps out between heavy pants.

I help her sit up and then stand on trembling legs. "Now what?" I demand, needing my next instruction like I need air. It had better fucking be to slam my cock into her pussy or her mouth, or I might die.

"Fuck me, Dylan. Please… fuck me."

As she says it, she throws her leg back over me, mounting me this time with her pussy centered over my cock. She slides down my length, impaling herself on me and gasping as I stretch her.

"*Fuck*," I groan at the feeling of her hot, velvety walls gripping me so tightly.

I hold her hips and buck up into her for a few strokes while she gets her bearings, but then she pushes on my chest. "Let me ride you. I'm in charge, remember?"

She's going to kill me. Can you die from unreleased pleasure? I'm about to find out because she lifts and lowers herself onto my cock slowly, grinding at my base before starting her next stroke.

Her tits bounce in front of me, and her ass claps down onto my thighs loudly with every stroke.

My body is on fire for this woman, especially when she pins

me with sex-crazed eyes and demands, "Whose are you?"

"Yours," I answer, forcing the word through gritted teeth. "I'm yours, Darling."

"Say my name." Her head falls back, her hair falling down her back in a sheet, and her nails dig into my chest, likely leaving half-moon shapes on my skin, and I arch into it, welcoming her mark.

I reach up, gripping the back of her head and forcing her gaze back to me. Looking deep into her eyes, I answer, "Raven, I'm yours. And you are mine." I add on the part I need her to know, to feel down to her soul. Her lashes flutter as her eyes try to roll back in her head. She's close again, so fucking close to coming on my cock this time.

Unbidden, I say, "I love you."

Her movements go jerky as she loses the rhythm. Her eyes pop open, pinning me for a split second as she realizes what I've said, and then she falls off the edge into bliss.

Her body quakes over me as she collapses down to kiss me desperately. Amid the kisses, she gasps, "I love you too."

At her words, my cock gives one last twitch before I explode, my orgasm rocking through me.

My vision blacks out for a moment, and the only sound I hear is Raven crying out her own release, but as the orgasms fade away, we return, panting and spent. Raven collapses onto me, boneless, and I wrap my arms around her, smoothing her hair back from her face as we rearrange ourselves to lie together on the couch.

She nuzzles into my chest, placing a tender kiss there. She's quiet for a moment, and I can nearly hear her thoughts running through her mind.

Wanting to reassure her that I absolutely meant every word of what I said in the heat of the moment, I say, "You should move in."

She raises up, her eyes wide as she stares at me like I suggested moving to Mars, not my penthouse. I smile back, encouraging her to say yes, and she tilts her head. "Well, you do have a bedroom the size of my entire apartment, a bathtub I could swim in, and that coffee maker... ugh, to die for." With that, she lies back down, snuggling into me like she's weighing her options.

I laugh lightly. "The coffee maker? That's the perk of living here? Not the twenty-four, seven dick on demand?"

I feel her nod against my chest as she agrees, "It is a very nice dick."

"Nice?" I bite out, teasing her. "I'll show you nice." She laughs, wiggling wildly as I smack her ass, the sound echoing loudly. I don't know how I have any energy left in me after tonight, let alone the last forty-eight hours. But this is right. Everything about her is right. She is my one and only. I think I knew that the moment I met her. I just wasn't ready to admit that I needed her.

Her finger traces shapes on my chest, and more seriously, she says, "We're moving fast."

"When you know, you know," I argue. "Think of it, we can wake up every morning, fuck in our bed, go to work together, make tons of money, fuck on my desk, come home, eat dinner, and fuck anywhere we damn well please."

"Interesting counterproposal," she says. I can hear the smirk in her tone. She sighs. "You're gonna think this is stupid, but I'm kinda old-fashioned. I don't think I can live with someone until marriage is on the table."

My heart stops in my chest. I'm not getting married. Ever.

I drew that line, not in the sand, but in concrete the day I heard Olivia and Evan fucking behind my back. Yes, Raven is different. We are different. But marriage is... marriage.

"I'm not rushing that," Raven says, sensing my shift in mood. "If it's too fast to move in, it's definitely too fast for marriage. But that's how..."

She keeps talking, but my mind has been ripped to the past, filled with memories. Not of Olivia or Evan, but of Raven. Her smiles, her strength, her poise in the face of adversity, her intelligence, her willingness to sacrifice herself for me, her love. And in the same flashes of memory, I see my own growth, the way she's cracked through the stone walls around my heart and I've let her in, giving her the deep, dark, ugly parts and trusting that she won't run from them or from me. She makes me a better man, and she is a better woman than Olivia could've ever been.

Because she's my Raven. There is no other. There could never be anyone like her. She was meant to be mine, and I was meant to be hers. I want her here. No, I need her here. If marrying her is what she wants, I'll do it. Because what I want is her.

"Marry me."

"What?" she exclaims, lifting up once again. Her green eyes are wide and wild, but there's the tiniest glimmer of hope hiding deep there. I can see it, can feel her excitement even as she doesn't fully risk believing me.

"Raven, I love you," I start and then freeze. I chuckle at myself. "I'm not sure what I'm going to say since I didn't plan this. That's very unlike me, so I'm gonna speak from the heart."

She nods, tears threatening to spill.

"I love you. I didn't mean to fall for you. It was supposed to be business, nothing more, but it could never be just business with you. You intrigued me that first day, you impressed me at the fundraiser, you amaze me with how your mind works at the office, and you challenge me to see every day, not as a competition for who has the most money and power, but as a gift. You have healed scars on my heart and in my soul that I thought I would carry until the day I died as a lonely, old, bitter bastard. And you ask for nothing in return. You want to make your own way, stand on your own merits, of which there are many, and be seen as the beautiful, strong woman you have always been and will always be. I don't want to get in the way of that. I want to stand by your side and witness you conquer the world, loving you every step of the way. I want you beside me. I want the world to know you're mine. Marriage makes sense. So, Raven Hill, will you marry me?"

Tears started tracking down her face right about the time I repeated, 'I love you', and they're flowing freely now.

"It's too fast, and…"

My heart stutters to a stop as I consider that she might say no, or at least no for right now. She continues as panic runs through me, "And I don't care what anyone thinks. I care about you, I care about us, and this" —she points at herself and then places her hand on my chest, where my heart has started beating again— "feels special. You are everything to me, Dylan, and I would do anything to protect you, to make you feel cherished, and to love you. So yes. Yes, I'll marry you."

Thank fuck. The moment she says yes, I can breathe again.

She falls into me, kissing me hard in her excitement. I wrap my arms around her, holding her tightly. We simply exist in the magic of the moment, the two of us promising to become one.

"Oh, my God," Raven says, pulling back. "We have to do this again."

"What?" I laugh, not understanding the sudden horror on her face.

"I cannot tell my mom and dad… or Maggie… oh, my God, Maggie… that I got engaged while naked on a couch after screwing like that," she explains, her smile only growing as she paints the picture of us as we currently still are.

I shrug. "Thought you didn't care what anyone thinks," I remind her.

She glares at me, or tries to, anyway, but the laughter's winning. "I didn't mean my mom!"

"Okay," I say, shifting her so that she's lying on top of me once again, "I'll propose every day, buy you as many rings as you want, and marry you as many times as you need, as long as you, Raven Hill, marry me, Dylan Sharpe. And be my forever."

EPILOGUE

RAVEN

"See you for lunch?" Dylan asks me as we pause at my office door. "I'm thinking... Thai?"

"Thai it is," I reply, giving him a kiss on the cheek. "Go kick some ass, Mr. Sharpe."

"You too... Mrs. Sharpe," he says in that 'boss' tone that he knows makes my panties damp even after months of being married. Just hearing that I'm Mrs. Raven Sharpe makes my heart speed up a little bit, and having my husband in the same office with me?

It's all my dreams come true.

Going into my cubicle, I have to grin. When the news spread that Dylan and I were engaged, in other words about five minutes after I walked into the office with him the Monday after the governor's event while wearing my new ring, people were

376 WINTERS & LANDISH

wondering how long it was going to be before I was going to get moved into one of the senior executive offices.

Months later, here I am, in the same cubicle I've had the entire time. That's the way I like it, though, because I'm still learning and I don't want preferential treatment. I'll earn my way. I know damn well that I will, and my husband will respect that. Dylan and I made it very clear to everyone, in a company-wide meeting done right in the middle of the floor, that while we were going to be a couple and the rumor mongers could fuck off, I'm going to earn my way up the ladder in the firm.

The only change? I've picked up a habit from Dylan of reading the morning paper before I start trading. In fact, as I check my clock, I see I've still got some time before the morning markets open, so I decide to take a quick look.

And right there, on top of the business page, I see something that makes me smile ironically.

The Faulkner family fall from grace following investigation by SEC
By: Vanna Nicholson

"Guess you didn't forget that little slight, did you?" I murmur as I give the article a quick read.

As it turns out, Vanna was telling the truth. Evan was the one who wrote the scathing article about me and joyfully applied the pressure to the editor to print his version of events. I guess he thought Vanna was another person he could squash beneath his thumb. Her revenge wasn't a tit-for-tat gossip situation, though. She went more scorched earth, took her proof of every dirty deed straight to the feds, and now, the Faulkners are weeks into an SEC investigation that will be their ultimate downfall. It's not the first time he's done something untoward, and apparently, a number of accusations, some with proof and some without, have been made.

Word is, the Faulkner patriarchy is furious that Evan's dick-measuring contest and poor behavior is the downfall of them all, and they've threatened to cut him off from the offshore accounts the SEC can't touch. If that happens, he'll have to get an actual job on his own merits. As if he has any.

Oh, I can only wish Karma would be that good.

Vanna was clearly happy to write about the latest update to the investigation, sparing no punches in her description of the Faulkners, with phrases such as, *The once untouchable family, now reduced to being fading bit players in the Financial District's power structure, has yet to make public comment about the latest embarrassment.*

"Note to self," I comment as I turn the page. "Vanna Nicholson's not someone you want to piss off. Fuck around and find out at your own risk."

The rest of the business news is relatively mundane, but there is one part that catches my attention. It's half-buried in the morning roundup section, a sort of bullet-point story that covers events in the Financial District in quick fashion, with a bit of gossip speculation thrown in. Not something I put too much stock in after what happened to Dylan and me, but still, it makes me smile.

The Financial District's reigning power couple, Dylan and Raven

Sharpe, once again made social waves with their appearance at last night's basketball game. Sitting courtside, the Sharpes cheered on our local heroes while being seen chatting it up with both the mayor and the city's most influential celebs. Could the Sharpes be looking at expanding their empire beyond the Financial District? Mayor Sharpe has a pretty good sound to it.

The last line makes me laugh because I know that's not on Dylan's plan anytime soon. But maybe one day. Closing the paper, I jump onto the computer, getting into the market. I use the combination of guts, research, and feel that I've developed over the past year to guide my account.

My account. It feels amazing, thinking about the amount of money at my fingertips. I've still got my personal account. Dylan and I love seeing it grow too, but helping the firm's clients grow is even more important to me. I was just recently given control of an entire school district's retirement fund, and while it's a small district, it's important to me. People's lives, their futures are in my hands, and that means a lot to me.

I'm so into my work that I barely notice the knock on my door, and Dylan comes in. "Mrs. Sharpe."

I look up from my research, smiling as I do. "Mr. Sharpe. How goes the dragon slaying this morning?"

"More than well," he says, coming around to rub my shoulders. "Did you read the paper?"

"I did. What did you think of the Mayor Sharpe comment?"

Dylan chuckles and kisses the top of my head. "I think the

governor is putting that in their ear as another way to pressure me."

He might be right. We've had dinner with the governor and his wife several times now, and with his term limit coming up, he's looking for a protégé to mentor into the office.

"And while he may have plans for me, I'm not interested. I've got three things that I love. The market, you… and family." Dylan runs his hand down, resting it on my belly, which isn't growing yet, but will be soon. "Expansion's a good thing."

I place my hand over his, thinking of the day when we'll soon be able to sit like this and feel a little Sharpe kicking back. "A very good thing. When are we going to announce it?"

He turns around, perching on the edge of my desk, his lips twisted up uncertainly.

"What's wrong?" I ask him.

His cheeks go a shade pinker. "I already told a few people. I couldn't help it. I'm too excited." We agreed to wait until I was through my first trimester, but that's been harder than expected. For both of us, apparently.

I laugh, shaking my head. "Who?"

"Tamara, of course, because of my schedule." He ticks off on his fingers, making me wonder just how many people he's told. "Juliana, because I asked her to look into our health plan and see if it was the best we can get, and Austin because… well, he's my friend."

I press my lips together, trying not to laugh at how cute he looks right now. Plus, I already told people too. "Mom and Dad know, Maggie and Ami know, and I talked to Tamara too,"

I confess.

"What?" he says, his eyes wide. "Did you tell Tamara before or after I did? She didn't say anything."

Of course, Tamara didn't say anything. If I tell her something in confidence, she won't repeat it. The same holds true for Dylan. Tamara's a lockbox, which is a great thing to have in an assistant.

"You should give her a raise," I suggest. "Especially since it sounds like we're about to be the office scandal again."

"Some things never change, Darling. Nor do I want them to." He takes my hand, pressing a kiss to the back, and then asks, "Ready for lunch?"

"Yes, I have a company I want to show you. They might be looking for an investor." I grab the file, putting it in my bag to bring with us. Because while we're married and madly in love, in some ways, it's still just business.

About the Authors

Thank you so much for reading our co-written novel. We hope you loved reading it as much as we loved writing it!

For more information on the books we have published, bonus scenes and more visit our websites.

More by Willow Winters
www.willowwinterswrites.com/books

More by Lauren Landish
www.laurenlandish.com

This is the Discreet Edition so no-one knows what you are reading.

You can find each edition at

www.willowwinterswrites.com/books

Made in the USA
Columbia, SC
29 December 2024

50852075R00233